ODIN'S CHILD

Brinnlanda
Ende
Ulvheim
Vestvarjin
Varjin
Eiksbana
Frossabu
Gardfjella
Vestynnsjo
Elvesoa
Foggard
Kolskaug
Blindbol
Brekka
Trygge
Beott
Kleiva
Kleiv
Hjalt
Innbrott
Nådvellir
Eldein
Himlifall
Småle
Seule
Gåltnes
Saurpassa
Karpe
Mara

Ym

the eleven kingdoms of Ym
after 773

Bik
Eise
Kobb
Skodd
Losna
Blossa
Madrul
Elare
Osmanadas
Falla
Meldun

EISVALDR

Gretel Saule in the
service of the Seer 983

THE RAVEN RINGS

SIRI PETTERSEN

ODIN'S CHILD

Translated by Siân Mackie
and Paul Russell Garrett

a work of fiction. Names, characters, places, and incidents
m the author's imagination or are used fictitiously.

W1-Media, Inc.
Arctis USA
Stamford, CT, USA

Odinsbarn first published in Norway by Gyldendal, 2013
First hardcover English edition published by W1-Media Inc. /
Arctis Books USA 2020

Visit our website at www.arctis-books.com
Author website at www.siripettersen.com

1 3 5 7 9 8 6 4 2

The Library of Congress Control Number:
2021934317

ISBN 978-1-64690-801-1
eBook ISBN 978-1-64690-600-0
Translation by Siân Mackie and Paul Russell Garrett

Jacket design by Siri Pettersen
Printed in Germany, European Union

To Mom, for life.
To Dad, for death.
To Kim, for everything in between.

And to you. The one who was always reading books no one had heard of. The weirdo at the back of the classroom. The one who grew up in a dark basement, your fate determined by a roll of the dice. The one who still dresses up. The one who never really fit in, and who often felt like you were in the wrong place at the wrong time. This book is for you.

PROLOGUE

Thorrald barged inside but couldn't get the door to shut behind him. The driving snow was forcing its way in faster than he was able to kick it away. He clasped the bundle in his arms and charged at the door like a bull. In the end, he managed to draw the bolt. Home. Safe now.

He looked through the peephatch. No one could see in from outside. Especially not in weather like this. Still. He put the bundle down on the table and closed the shutter.

You can bar the doors and windows all you like. Nothing can stop Kolkagga.

Crones' talk! What would Kolkagga want with him? He'd done nothing wrong! Though the moment the thought struck him, his entire life flashed before his eyes. The drugs he sold outside the guildhall. Opa to people who smoked themselves to death.

He shook his head. If the black shadows came for him, it wouldn't be because he sold harmless herbs out of a cabin at the ends of the earth. If they came for him, it would be because of *her*.

Thorrald stared at the bundle on the table. A malformed creature. It wasn't crying. Maybe it was already dead. That would make everything simpler. He shuddered. The bearskin around his shoulders was so thick that he almost filled the room where he stood, but it was no help against the cold from within. He fumbled with the lacing. His fingers, frozen to the bone, refused to obey. He blew on the embers in the hearth. Turned his hands over the heat. The frost melted from the fur and sputtered in the fire.

That cursed Olve had been waving his sword in a drunken stupor. What had he been looking for? Was it this abomination? What else could it be? It didn't matter anyway. Olve hadn't seen the child. It was safe.

Safe?! Are you out of your mind? You have your own life to live!

Not a life worth singing about, sure enough, but that didn't mean it was fit for a child. At least not a child like this. He had to act fast.

Thorrald drew his knife and stared down at the creature. She was asleep. His fist was bigger than her face. He raised the blade. The child opened her eyes. They were green. Fearless. Thorrald howled and slammed the knife into the table next to her. "Blindcraft! That's what you are! Deadborn!"

He grabbed his ale tankard and downed the tepid dregs. Then he unwrapped the child from the blanket as if she were a present. She lay there waving her fists.

Old crones' tales forced their way into his mind. Cock and bull stories he knew he should ignore. All the same … He pressed his thumb against the blade of the knife until a drop of blood trickled out. He let it drip down into the child's mouth. Nothing. He cursed his own stupidity. What had he expected? Fangs?

The blind don't exist!

Thorrald rested his arms on the table and snarled, "What in Slokna are you, then? You're not a ghost. And you're not one of the blind. Are you just deformed?" He flipped her onto her stomach and ran a finger down her spine, stopping at the base where her tail should have been. Seer knows he wasn't one to listen to crones' talk, but the child was living proof. She was not a child of Ym.

Rot. That's what you are.

He stared at his fists, as though they ought to have rotted already. "I can't have you here. Nobody would want you!" He picked her up and held her out in front of him. She was only a few days old. She had soft downy hair on her head that shone the color of copper in the light of the fire.

"I should kill you. That's what I should do. Save my own skin." But he knew he wouldn't be able to. He'd known that the moment he dug her out of the snow by the stone circle. "You'll never thank me for this, girl. It'll mean a miserable life on the road for you. And you'd find better company than me under the tables at the tavern."

The girl smiled. A toothless grin. He put her down again. He knew what he had to do. It felt worse than killing her, but he had no choice. He couldn't be seen with a tailless girl. He stared at the splash of ale that was left in the tankard. Then he pulled down the case of dreamwort from the shelf. Strong enough to kill such a tiny bundle. He had to be careful. Thorrald sprinkled a pinch of the powder into the tankard and swirled it until it stopped foaming.

"Do you realize how much this costs, girl?" He dipped a cloth into the tankard and held it to her mouth. She accepted it like a mother's teat. Then he waited till her eyes started to droop shut. He pulled the knife out of the table. It left a pale gash in the timber.

Thorrald dug the tip of the blade into the child's back. She let out a scream. He curled his hand over her mouth. Her sobs cut into him as surely as he was cutting into her skin. Blood ran onto the blanket, and he was relieved that she could bleed. But what had he expected? Was he being hysterical?

Thorrald didn't stop carving until the child had a hollow at the base of her spine, with furrows that looked like they'd been left by claws. "If anyone asks, a wolf got your tail. Do you hear me? A wolf!"

Her eyes shut. She'd stopped crying sooner than he'd expected. Suddenly he was afraid he had given her too much dreamwort. He held his ear to her chest. Checked she was breathing properly. Not that he knew what properly was for such a creature.

Cursed child. You're going to be the death of me.

Thorrald left her lying on the table. He wrapped the fur tighter around himself and went back out into the storm. Like a frightened old woman, seeing shadows between the frozen spruce trees where there were none. Nobody was there. No Kolkagga. No sudden death waiting for him around the corner. Not yet.

The only thing he could see was Ulvheim. For the very last time. He pulled the shovel out of the snow and started to clear a path to the wagon.

RIME RETURNS

The half-rotten spruce lay across the Alldjup like a bridge. Its bark had cracked into great sheets, its trunk growing increasingly bare as the years passed. It was about twenty paces over to the other side. A shortcut for brave squirrels. No place for people.

Hirka steeled herself and took another step out. The trunk groaned beneath her. She doubted it had ever had to contend with this much weight before, and the suspicious stench of decay didn't do much to allay her fears. She found herself thinking kind thoughts about the tree, as if that would prevent it from snapping in two and sending her tumbling into the gaping wound in the landscape, from breaking her on the rocks in the Stryfe, which babbled indifferently below.

I am not afraid.

She looked up. Vetle was sitting farther along the trunk, whimpering like a dog. He was fifteen winters old, the same age as Hirka, but although his body continued to grow, his mind remained that of a child's. Vetle trusted people too much, even though he was afraid of everything else. So how in Slokna's name had the other boys coaxed him out here?

Miserable worms! May the blind take them all!

The boys responsible were sitting safely at the edge of the forest. Hirka could feel their eyes boring into her back, desperate to see her fall. She didn't intend to give them that pleasure. But she *did* plan to have bruised knuckles once she'd gotten them both out of this mess. Kolgrim wouldn't be able to eat anything but soup until autumn. She clenched her fists. Her hands were clammy.

Vetle had started to rock dangerously between sobs. Hirka took a couple of determined steps toward him. A knot in the trunk splintered under her foot and she started. Her arms started to windmill as if of their own volition, helping her regain her balance before she'd even quite realized she'd lost it. Her heart was in her mouth. Her knees shook.

"Feeling a bit wobbly, tailless?"

Predictably, Kolgrim's shout was followed by a chorus of guffaws. The echo bounced between the rock walls of the Alldjup. *Tailless! Tailless! Tailless!*

Hirka drew herself up to her full height. She wouldn't let them get to her. Not now.

Vetle was terrified. He sat bawling in a clump of spindly branches that had long since shed their needles. He had buried his face in his arm, as if not seeing the danger would make it go away. He clutched a small wooden horse in his fist.

"Vetle, it's me, Hirka. Can you look at me?"

He stopped crying and peered over his elbow. A smile spread across his ruddy face, and Hirka realized her mistake. Vetle jumped to his feet and charged toward her with his arms flung wide.

"Vetle! Wait!"

But it was too late. He threw himself at her and she lost her footing. She twisted around as she fell and threw her arms around the trunk. Vetle landed heavily on her back, knocking the air out of her lungs.

The wooden horse dug into her cheek. The tree gave a series of ominous cracks.

Crows alighted from the treetops, shrieking as they disappeared into the forest. Scattered shouts revealed that Kolgrim and his cronies were making a run for it. Everything and everyone fled the scene as if Slokna already had them in its grasp.

"You're a coward, Kolgrim!" Hirka shouted as she clung to the tree. "A dead coward!" she added, hoping for the opportunity to make good on her threat.

The trunk started to sag and Hirka's stomach dropped. The top had broken away and the branches were scraping down the rock wall on the far side. The angle was becoming increasingly precarious.

So, what's it gonna be? Live or die?

"Run, Vetle! Now!"

As if by some miracle, Vetle recognized the urgency in her voice and scrambled forward. His knee sank mercilessly between her shoulder blades, but he managed to clamber over her and bound up the trunk.

Hirka clung on. She squeezed her eyes shut and waited for the inevitable plunge. She heard roots being torn from the earth, snapping like bowstrings. Moss and stones rained down on her.

Then, quite suddenly, everything was still.

She opened her eyes. Only one at first, to check whether there was any point opening the other. The roots had held. She was hanging against the rock face. She heard Vetle cry out from above.

"Jomar!"

The wooden horse sailed past her into the gorge. It ended its days with a hollow splash in the Stryfe. But Vetle was safe. He had made it up over the edge. *Thank the Seer,* Hirka thought in a rare moment of faith.

Carefully, she looked up. The roots hung like a gaping troll's mouth not far above her. They were impassable. Blood oozed from the palm of her hand down her forearm. She needed to act quickly—before the pain caught up with her.

She pulled out her pocketknife, plunged it into the tree, and pulled herself up until she reached the roots. Dry earth trickled over her face. She shook her head and tried to blink it away. She huffed out a laugh.

At least things can't get any worse.

She wrapped her thighs around the trunk and sheathed her knife. Then she reached up and fumbled at the roots. She needed to find a handhold. Something she could use to pull herself up and over.

Then a strong hand gripped hers.

"One point to me if I pull you up?"

Hirka almost let go. Was she dreaming? That voice … she knew that voice! Or had she hit her head?

One point to me? It couldn't be anyone else.

Rime's back!

True, she hadn't heard his voice for three summers, and it was deeper than she remembered, but it was definitely him. No doubt about it. Hirka hesitated before answering. Maybe she was imagining things. It would be just like her, if what people said were true. But people said a lot of things about her.

What in Slokna was he doing here?

Rime's hand was warm and firm around hers. To her disgust, she realized that she'd already transferred a lot of her weight to him.

"Well?" a cool voice prompted from the edge.

"I don't need help!" she said.

"So you still think you can fly? Or do you have some other strategy for getting past these?"

She heard him kick the roots just before more earth dropped down into her face. She turned away and spat. He thought he'd won, the spoiled rat. Here she was, risking her life to save Vetle, only for him to come swaggering in to win points in a desperate situation. It was inconceivably childish. What a nerve! But he remembered …

Hirka bit her lower lip to conceal a smile, even though no one could see her face. Her shoulders were screaming. She hated to admit it, but there was no way she was getting up without help.

"I'd have been fine if you hadn't distracted me. You can have half a point."

He laughed. A deep, husky laugh that triggered an avalanche of memories from a time when everything was simpler. A lump formed unbidden in her throat.

"You always try to change the rules. One whole point or nothing," Rime said.

"Fine." She had to force the words out. "One point to you if you pull me up."

The sentence was barely out of her mouth before she was torn away from the tree trunk. For a moment, she dangled helplessly over the edge of the gorge, and then she was lifted to safety. Rime let go of her and she took a few shaky steps to make sure her legs still worked. It went better than expected.

Vetle was slumped like a sack of potatoes on the ground, plucking absently at a tear in his sleeve. Rime stood before her as if he'd never left.

"Where does it hurt?" he asked.

He was the same as ever. Always seeking out the weak spots. Like a predator asserting its superior strength, its ability to endure what others couldn't.

"I'm fine," she said, hiding her hand behind her back. It probably looked like carrion.

Rime helped Vetle to his feet. The boy sniffed, his tail hanging limply. Hirka watched from the corner of her eye as Rime's hands explored Vetle's neck and joints, checking for injuries.

His hair was longer than she remembered, but no less blindingly white. It came down to his shoulder blades and was tied with strips of leather. Shorter hairs had come loose to frame his face, which was narrower than before. Markedly so. But there was something else … something she couldn't put her finger on. Something about the way he moved now.

And he was armed.

Her eyes fell to two swords in black scabbards. They were narrow and attached to a wide belt around his waist. He was dressed like a warrior, in a light shirt with slits on both sides and a high collar. Wide leather straps crossed his chest. He glowed like a snow cat against the dark backdrop of the forest.

Hirka looked away. Rime was an idiot. Why come here dressed like that? The money those clothes cost probably could have fed half of Elveroa for a whole winter.

When he turned to look at her, she noticed the embroidery on the left-hand side of his chest. The Raven. Its famous wings spread wide. The mark of the Council. The mark of the Seer.

Panic gripped her, cutting deep like claws.

The Seer ... the Rite!

Her blood turned cold as she realized why he'd returned.

No! It's too early! It's still summer!

His pale gray eyes met hers. She lifted her chin and held his gaze. She refused to let him see her panic. He cocked his head and appraised her with amused curiosity, as if she were an animal he hadn't seen before.

"Didn't you used to have red hair?" he asked.

Hirka raised a hand to her hair, dislodging a fair amount of sand. She tried to brush it away, but her fingers just got caught in the tangle of red. Rime's eyes sparkled like ice. She remembered that teasing look of his all too well. It was out of place with the uniform he wore, but it only lasted a moment before he looked away. He had remembered who he was.

Rime meant danger. She could feel it in every nerve in her body. She'd thought she recognized him, but this wasn't the boy she remembered. Not her childhood rival. Not her friend. He was the son of a powerful family. He was Rime An-Elderin. He was bound to the Council by blood.

It just hadn't mattered before.

"I won't be here long. I'm going to Mannfalla with Ilume," he said, as if reminding her of the distance between them.

Hirka crossed her arms. "Normal people call their grandmothers *Grandmother*. I would, if I had one." It wasn't the best gibe, but she couldn't think of anything else. Her brain had turned to mush.

"Not if she were Ilume."

Hirka looked down.

Rime took two steps closer. His clothes smelled of sage oil. Behind him, Vetle craned his neck to peer down into the abyss that had swallowed his wooden horse.

"They've still got a lot to do before the Rite. It's your year too, isn't it?" Rime asked.

Hirka nodded lamely. Time had caught up with her. She felt a stab of nausea. The others in Elveroa who were turning fifteen this year had been counting the days. Making clothes for the occasion. Commissioning tail rings made of gold and silver. Planning the journey everyone had to make at least once in their life. Hirka was no exception. The difference was that she'd have given everything she owned to avoid it.

Rime reached for her hip. She jumped back, fumbling for her knife, but it wasn't there anymore. It flashed in Rime's hand. Hirka swallowed and backed away from it. For a moment she thought he'd seen through her and planned to kill her then and there, just to save the Council the trouble. Instead, he walked over to the tree roots.

"I'll take Vetle home," he said, cutting the few roots that were still holding on. The tree crashed down into the Alldjup. All that remained was the scar in the earth and a cloud of dust that glittered in the spray from the Stryfe. The Alldjup seemed much wider now that the two rock faces were exposed on both sides.

"Get your father to look at your hand," Rime said.

She snorted. "I've been patching people up since I was seven!"

He came closer. She fought the urge to back away. He was almost a head taller than she was. Leather creaked as he leaned toward her and pressed her knife back into its scabbard.

"Jomar," she heard Vetle whimper. She understood how he felt. He could get a new toy, but it wouldn't even matter if it were made of pure gold. Jomar was gone.

Hirka turned and started walking. She felt as if she were walking away from something important, but she didn't look back.

THE RED WAGON

Hirka started running as soon as she was sure Rime could no longer see her. She left the woods behind her and followed the ridge to the sea, where she would have less chance of running into people. By the time she caught the smell of seaweed on the wind, she could see the cabin. It was situated high up, pressed against the cliff as though it had been driven from the village and crawled there to lick its wounds.

The Hovel, people called it. The Council guardsmen had caught up with an outlaw there years ago and set fire to the place. But the cabin wouldn't burn. It still stood there, staring obstinately out to sea, its eastern end charred black. One of Glimmeråsen's tenant farmers had once ventured up to make off with the shutters, but then, scared witless, he had dropped them on his feet and broken two toes. And that had been that. No one had been there since.

That is until Hirka and Father had made it their home. Father didn't listen to old crones' tales. All the same, Hirka felt uneasy whenever she saw the cabin. She certainly wasn't scared, and she felt at home there, but she always got a feeling something bad was going to happen when it came into view. Something she had to hurry to prevent.

The path crunched under her feet. It was covered with the scree that the cliffs shook off every time there was a storm.

Rime was back. *Rime An-Elderin.*

The name should have been light on her tongue, but it felt like a rock. Like the scales that Seik used—everyone knew his weights were too heavy, but never when the guardsmen came to inspect them. The merchant had two sets, it was said.

The same went for Rime. He had two names. He had left Elveroa with the short, light version she had called him since she was nine, and now he had returned with the long, heavy version. The one that had taken him back to the family home within the Seer's white walls in Mannfalla, a world away from here.

Sylja of Glimmeråsen could go on about Mannfalla's streets of gold until the cows came home, but after having lived the better part of her life in a red wagon along roadsides, Hirka was content simply to have somewhere she could call home. Somewhere she could say she came from. What more could you ask for?

She stopped in front of the door to the cabin. The basket! She'd forgotten the basket. The plants she'd spent all day gathering. She'd left them at the Alldjup. Hirka cursed to herself. She couldn't leave them there. Tomorrow was Midsummer. The woods would be trampled by superstitious villagers going out to pick herbs that would help them dream of suitors, herbs she could have sold at market had she not been so forgetful.

Hirka turned to head back, but then she heard a sound. Sporadic scraping against the walls from somewhere inside. Then it went quiet. She froze on the doorstep.

They were here. The Council had come to take her away.

Pull yourself together! You are of no importance to the Council.

Hirka opened the door. The room was empty. Emptier than normal. There was vengethorn hanging from the roof, but all the dried herbs were gone. Two of the walls were lined with boxes, jars, and pots of all sorts and sizes, but the bottom shelves were empty. Just the faint outlines of books remained, etched in a thin layer of soot from the hearth. One of the chests, which also served as a bench, was open. It was packed haphazardly, as though Father had just swept everything off the shelves and into the chest. Tea, elderberries, redroot, salves, and tonics. Amulets and Seer trinkets—the things they sold every single day. An unease grew inside her.

Hirka picked up a familiar grooved wooden box and turned it in her hand. Aged draggan tea from Himlifall, where the Might was strong. If a cup of that didn't make you feel better, you probably already had one foot in Slokna.

The scraping sound returned. Hirka returned the wooden box to the shelf where it belonged and went outside. She followed the sound around the corner of the house on the seaward side and was careful only to step where there was grass, so no one could hear her footsteps. She looked around the corner, and her unease turned into such heavy certainty that it sunk to her feet.

Father was sitting in his wheeled chair, scraping red paint off the old wagon using a rusty spade she'd never seen before. He must have borrowed it. The only shiny bit was the freshly sharpened edge. It screeched angrily against the wood as Father pushed it upward. The wagon shed sun-bleached flakes, which settled around his feet like autumn leaves.

The back of Father's shirt was dark with sweat, and the veins in his arms were bulging. Father was strong, and because he always cut the sleeves off his shirts, his muscles were there for everyone to see. Hirka could remember a time when he wore his sleeves like everyone else, but that was many years ago.

"Going somewhere?" she asked, realizing she'd folded her arms across her chest in an effort to look tougher.

Father stopped and flashed her a guilty look. But he quickly recovered. He was a man of Ulvheim, after all. He thrust the spade at the ground. It fell over in the low grass. Not even Father could make a spade stand on rocky ground. He rubbed his close-shaven head with his hand, making a rasping sound.

"The raven has come," he said.

Hirka knew it. She'd known it the moment she saw Rime. The raven had come. Eisvaldr had set the days for the Rite.

How much time do I have?

Father bent over and picked up the spade. He continued scraping off the paint.

"So, have you made any progress?" he asked.

Hirka clenched her jaw. Of course she hadn't. And that was the reason they had to leave. "Are you going somewhere?" she asked again.

Father grabbed the wheels and swung the chair around so that he was facing her. He lifted himself up until he was practically hanging over the chair, with his arms supporting his entire weight.

Hirka took a step back. It wasn't fair. She knew what he wanted from her, it just wasn't in her power to give it to him. And why should she? There were a lot of other things she could do! Should she be judged on the one thing she couldn't do?

"So I can't bind. So what? It must have happened before. Surely I'm not the only one?"

Her question was left hanging in the air unanswered. He knew she couldn't bind. He'd always known that. Why should it matter today?

The Rite. Everything was about the damned Rite.

The cold numbness returned. Her heart beat quicker.

"It *must* have happened before!" she repeated. "I can't possibly be the only one in the entire world? In all eleven kingdoms?"

Father looked at her. His deep-set eyes were as shattered as his legs. So that was it, was it? She was broken. Unable to bind the Might. Cheated out of something that everyone else had. Mightless. And tailless.

Kolgrim's shout echoed in her head.

Tailless ...

Hirka turned and stormed away from the cabin, ignoring Father's shouts. At the end of the mountain ledge, she climbed up the tallest of the three birches, as high as she could before the branches grew too weak. She sat facing the trunk and wrapped her arms around it. Her hand stung. It was bleeding again. She'd forgotten about that.

Rime is back.

Suddenly Hirka was embarrassed. She was a hopeless child. Climbing a tree wouldn't solve anything. That wasn't the sort of thing grown-ups did. Normal people. She was the reason that they weren't normal, that they had lived on the road, that they never mixed with people, other than to help them when they got sick. It was her fault, because she wasn't what she was supposed to be.

Hirka hugged the tree even tighter.

She had saved Vetle. Surely that had to count for something?

No, Vetle had managed on his own. Unlike her. She'd needed Rime's help. But she'd dared to try! She dared to do many things. She'd swum in the Stryfe early in Helfmana, before all the ice had melted. She'd dived off the rocks at Svartskaret while everyone else stood gaping. Hirka wasn't afraid of anything. So why was she afraid of the Rite?

Because Father is.

Father was afraid. So afraid that he wanted to leave Elveroa. Get out the old wagon and live on the road. Sell miracle cures to anyone they happened upon. Make soup from the same bones, day in, day out. A life that was impossible now that he could no longer walk, but he wanted to do it all the same. Run away. Why? What was the worst the Council could do to a girl who couldn't bind?

She didn't want to think about it. She started to count the leaves on the birch tree. When she reached six hundred and fifty-two leaves, she thought she heard Father shouting. She didn't reply. He didn't shout again.

THE RAVENER

Rime kept an eye on Vetle as they walked the path to the ravenry. The boy was dramatizing random fragments of what had happened at the Alldjup without stopping to come up for air. Now and then he became so excited that he choked on his words and had to start again. Every time he tripped over a tree root, Rime had to grab hold of him and steer him back onto the path.

The heath was deep green and bathed in sunlight. The bountiful summer had made the birds drowsy and subdued. This wasn't a day for impossible conversations. But that was precisely what awaited him. Rime found himself starting to walk slower.

It was liberating to walk like this, together with someone who never pretended to be anyone but himself. Vetle was Vetle, regardless of who he was talking to. He didn't have any hidden agenda. Greed would never have any place in his eyes. He made Rime forget who he was, which was a rare pleasure.

People in Elveroa more or less treated Vetle as if he were a farm cat. He could come and go as he pleased. Charmed housewives gave him honey bread and ruffled his golden curls. But no one expected him to sit still like all the others while the augur delivered the message at the Seer's hall. The boy was beautiful, a blessing from the Seer that often spared him from people's fears and superstitions, the doubt that came with everything out of the ordinary. Time wasn't the same for Vetle as it was for others. He was only ever concerned by what was happening in the moment. In the here and now. Understandably enough, Hirka was today's focus.

The girl hadn't lost any of her mettle in the last three years, Rime had to give her that. She still acted before thinking. Vetle extolled her as a goddess from Brinnlanda. Rime reflexively pressed his hands together in the sign of the Seer. In Mannfalla, the old gods and goddesses had long since departed this life.

Rime and Vetle crossed a mossy field in the shadow of huge oak trees. Vetle took off toward the house, which blended in with the forest on the other side of the plain. It looked like a small tower of vertical logs propped up against the huge trees. But these trees also served another purpose. They were supporting pillars in a latticework of branches extending halfway around the plain.

At first glance, there was nothing unusual about them, particularly now in late summer, when the foliage was dense and green. But then you heard the chattering of the ravens and realized you were looking at a large, circular enclosure.

The ravenry.

There were several ravenries back in Eisvaldr, and the Council never sent letters by other means. Ramoja alone was responsible for the most important correspondence to and from Elveroa. Normal letters were sent by cart here, like in Mannfalla, but when they needed to be sent overnight, and in secret, nothing could beat the ravens. They were dark messengers. The Council's wings. Sacred bearers of news and of orders concerning matters of life and death. Much of Mannfalla's unrivaled power was the result of its network of ravens that never rested.

Rime could hear the ravens whispering about a stranger approaching. He was being watched. He was being weighed up. When he was recognized as a son of the Seer, the ravens settled down.

Rime stopped. The silence smacked of anticipation. Of hunger. Of a beggar's greed. Dark shadows shifted impatiently between the branches. He started walking again and the cawing resumed, now more aggrieved.

A throaty voice joined the fray.

"They said a friend was coming, but I'm still not sure I believe my eyes."

Ramoja emerged from the ravenry. Her hips swayed from side to side as only hips from Bokesj could. Jet-black hair had been gathered into a thick ponytail from which tight braids sprouted like a crow's tail. He could tell she had lost weight despite her billowing trousers. They were secured around her ankles by strings of gleaming beads that rattled as she walked. Just like the ones the dancers in Mannfalla wore. After years in Elveroa, Ramoja still clung to her status as an outsider.

Vetle ran toward her. "Mama! We fell into the Alldjup!" he told her proudly.

Ramoja calmly set down a blood-splattered iron bucket on the moss and put a hand on the boy's shoulder. She held him at arm's length as she looked him over to check he was still intact. She turned to Rime again. He searched for signs of worry in her eyes, but there were none.

They were a remarkable sight, the ravener and her son—him almost fully grown, as fair as she was dark. The boy started to explain, and Rime interjected to ward off the horror story he'd heard several times on the way over. He told Ramoja what had happened. She took the news in stride. She didn't scold the boy. Vetle had always been allowed to go where he wanted, despite the obvious dangers.

"No one fell. That's the main thing," Rime said, even though Ramoja didn't look like she needed reassuring.

"All of us fall sooner or later," she replied.

She picked up the bucket again and came toward him with her free hand raised, as if to pat him on the cheek. But she didn't. Her hand dropped to her side again. Ramoja had been like a mother to him for as long as he could remember. Now she saw something in him she didn't want to touch. The same thing that had made Hirka turn and leave. It was as if they knew. As if everything he'd seen and done in the last three years was written on his face. In his eyes.

Ramoja adjusted her grip on the bucket, the handle creaking. There was a smell of raw meat. "I haven't seen you since ..."

"Since the Rite." Rime fought down a pang of regret.

She looked at him. Dark eyes in a dark face. They flickered between warm and cold, brimming with things she wanted to say, but all that came out was a low confirmation. "Since the Rite."

Ramoja shook off old memories and ushered both Rime and Vetle into the house. She set the bucket down on the floor and hung a pot of water over the smoldering hearth. Rime looked around. It was just as cramped as he remembered. A curtain fashioned from fishnet created another small space at the back of the room, where sunlight streamed in through a hatch that allowed the ravens to come and go. There was a ladder up to the second floor, where Rime knew vast quantities of paper were stacked in small pigeonholes, sorted by size and weight. Down on the first floor, the closest corner was full of shelves dedicated to an abundance of small sleeves made of various materials: leather, wood, and ivory. Some of them were strewn across a narrow desk made of green glass. A raven was in the process of sorting them with its beak—one by one—onto the correct shelf. Its talons clacked against the glass as it shuffled to and fro.

The bird turned to Rime as he sat down at the table by the window. It had sensed him before seeing him. It flapped its wings, hopping over to Rime's table and coming toward him. It stopped by his arm, which was resting on the table, and cocked its head. It was a large raven with a narrow face. Its feathers shone purple and blue in the light. Soft, downy black feathers surrounded the base of its beak. Rime could see small scratches in it from a lifetime of use. It blinked.

Rime wanted to give the raven what it was after, but he couldn't use the Might here. As if realizing it was out of luck, it started tugging at Rime's sleeve with its beak.

"Arnaka!"

Ramoja scooped up the creature in both hands as if it were a common chicken and threw it up toward the hatch in the ceiling. It flew away with only a few indignant caws.

"She's not usually any trouble." Ramoja handed him a bowl of tea and sat across from him. Then she went on. "It hardly came as a surprise."

It took Rime a moment to realize she was still talking about the Rite. About the confirmation that the Might was strong in him. As it had been in his mother. As it still was in Ilume. As it was in all twelve Council families who had been interpreting the word of the Seer for generations.

Ramoja kept her eyes fixed on him. She reminded him a lot of his grandmother in that respect. But these eyes were the polar opposite of Ilume's. These listened. These were a mother's eyes.

Ramoja had left a prestigious position as ravener in Mannfalla to accompany Rime's grandmother to Elveroa in service of the Council. And Rime knew why. It was difficult to look at Ramoja without thinking about it, even though he wasn't supposed to know about it. But even before he was ten winters old, the pile of things he wasn't supposed to know had been taller than the bell tower in Mannfalla.

Rime drank. The heat washed through his mouth.

"There's more of her in your lines every time I see you," Ramoja said.

"We're all getting older," he replied, unable to think of anything else to say. He didn't know what his mother looked like, having no point of reference other than the woven image of her hanging in the winter garden at home in Eisvaldr. A woman with narrow hands reaching up toward the pine cones in a knotty old tree that still stood in the garden that bore her name. Rime hadn't been more than six when his parents had lost their lives to the snow.

"*Older?* You're eighteen," Ramoja laughed and crossed her legs, making the golden beads on her hems rattle.

Her expression suddenly turned grave again. Rime steeled himself for what he knew had to be coming.

"What are you doing, Rime?"

"What do you mean?" He was buying time. He knew exactly what she meant.

"They say you're training to be a guardsman. A protector."

Rime nodded and looked for somewhere he could rest his gaze. Two rabbit carcasses lay on a worktop by the hearth. Probably for the ravens—they often ate better than people. Vetle wandered aimlessly behind the fishnet as if searching for something without knowing quite what.

Ramoja caught Rime's eye again. "Have you spoken to her since you got back?"

"She's in Ravnhov until this evening. I'll talk to her then."

She shook her head. "Rime An-Elderin, Ilume's only grandchild, born and raised in Eisvaldr—and you refuse your seat on the Council?"

"I'm not refusing anything." He knew it sounded hollow. It was impossible to explain such a decision as anything other than refusal. But the truth was worse.

"Is this really what you want?" The doubt in Ramoja's voice wasn't unjustified. She leaned forward with her hands on the table. Her bracelets jingled.

"I just want to serve," he heard himself tell her.

Ramoja leaned back again. "Well, it's hard to deny the need for protectors."

It was true, but her support made Rime cringe inside. He longed to tell her the truth. To stop hiding behind all the masks. To Ramoja, he was a weak son of a strong family. To his grandmother, he was a traitor. Only the Council knew the true path he had chosen. He couldn't share it with anyone else.

"Did you know that augurs in Mannfalla are already protesting?" she asked.

"The Seer's eyes are always protesting. It'll pass. They'll have forgotten all about it by next month."

"Forgotten?" Ramoja scoffed. "The first time there won't be an An-Elderin on the Council since the Twelve? Rime An-Elderin, the child spared by the Seer? The boy they were naming Seer's halls after, even before he was born?"

Her words made the corners of his mouth twitch. He fought a primitive urge to bare his teeth. It was more difficult than usual. Perhaps because it would soon be over. He would no longer be required to perpetuate his own legend. All that remained was the confrontation with Ilume.

Ramoja was still searching for the answer in his eyes. He let her look. She would never find it.

"Have you sworn the Oath, Rime?"

He nodded and watched pain ripple across her features. So she had also thought he would change his mind.

"You think I'm betraying my mother's memory," he said.

"No, no!"

Ramoja's eyes widened and her veil of composure slipped for a moment. Few other than him would have noticed. He had grown up with untruths and learned to see through them. She was telling the truth.

"You have to follow your own heart, Rime. Not the dead's. No one can take that from you, not even ..."

"No. Not even her." He smiled. That was always everyone's first thought. What would Ilume say? How would the matriarch of the An-Elderin family take the news of her grandson choosing the path of a warrior, not the obvious path to one of the twelve chairs that ruled the world, and which always had?

Ramoja shook her head. Not even she could imagine what awaited Rime.

"I'd always hoped—thought ..."

The final word came fast, to cover up the slip, but it was too late. Ramoja had hoped he would follow in Ilume's footsteps. Rime was surprised. He would never have believed that she, of all people, would cling to tradition. She had plenty of reasons not to. It made her loyalty to Ilume and the Council all the more touching.

Ramoja got up, and then Rime heard one of the ravens come in through the hatch behind the curtain. She pulled the fishnet to one side and ushered Vetle out. The raven perched on her hand without being commanded to. It knew the drill. She untied a sleeve attached to the inside of its leg.

Rime noticed that the mark of the Council had been burned into the ivory sleeve. He had grown up under that mark. The mark of the Seer. The black raven everyone had thought he would also bear on his forehead.

Ramoja took the letter out of the sleeve and checked the seal, making sure it was intact. The letter was for Ilume's eyes only. She put it back in the sleeve and put it in her pocket.

"There was a raven yesterday as well. About the Rite. I hear it's early this year?" She looked at him as if he might be able to explain.

"Yes," he said simply. There was no point talking about Council business as if he knew nothing about it. At least he was no longer destined to become one of them.

"People will think the rumors are true," Ramoja said. "But you know how tongues start wagging in the run-up to the Rite. There's always at least one sighting at this time of year." She chuckled, but her smile didn't reach her eyes, which were fixed on Rime as if seeking a reaction to what she was saying. Just like everyone else, she assumed he knew more than most about what the Council was up to. To be fair, he generally did.

"The Council should be glad people have such vivid imaginations," he said. "What would the point of the Rite be if it weren't for the blind?"

Ramoja gave him a crooked smile.

"It's Vetle's year too, isn't it?" Rime looked at the boy, who had settled on the bench with his head against the wall. His eyes opened when he heard his name, but then closed again straightaway.

Ramoja gathered the empty bowls and turned away. "Yes," she replied.

Rime got up too. He knew Ramoja rarely traveled to Mannfalla, only when she had no other choice. She was so averse to it that she was staying in Elveroa even though Ilume was moving back to the capital. It seemed his visit was over, but that didn't stop him from laying a hand on her shoulder. He was unlikely to ever see her again. He might glimpse her in the crowd during the Rite if he was able to be there, but he had come to say goodbye. She just couldn't know that.

Ramoja turned to face him again with an apologetic smile. "I haven't got used to the idea of being here without you."

Rime smiled. "I haven't been here in three years."

But he knew what she meant. Ramoja was part of the An-Elderin family. Ramoja had lost her best friend when his mother died. Rime knew she had never entirely gotten over it. There was nothing he could say to make her feel better.

"We should never have come here in the first place," he said. "It was a fool's errand." He was surprised by his own honesty. Perhaps it was because they were going their separate ways. Perhaps it was the freedom of knowing he would never follow in his grandmother's footsteps. He wasn't sure. But he pressed on. "The Council stationed Ilume here for years because it's the closest they can get to Ravnhov.

That's no secret. But how many Seer's halls have they managed to open in Ravnhov?"

Ramoja gave him a guarded smile. They both knew the answer to that. None. Ravnhov was strong. An old chiefdom and the thorn in the Council's side. Ravnhov was the only place in the world Mannfalla would never convert, even though the cities were only a few days' journey from each other. But between them lay Blindból, the dark heart of Ym, the impenetrable mountains everyone feared and took pains to avoid. So while other kingdoms had bowed to the will of the Council, one after the other, Ravnhov had retained its independence. They had paid their debts and were getting stronger every day.

"We're leaving a couple days before the others," Ramoja said. "Nora's going to watch the ravens while I'm gone. She's ready for the responsibility."

Rime nodded. To think the blacksmith's daughter was old enough to apprentice in a ravenry. He remembered her as being a terrified child who refused to join in with any of their antics. Antics like climbing the western face of Vargtind …

Rime could remember sitting at the summit, convinced he was the only person who would manage to scale the vertical mountainside. That was until Hirka had heaved herself over the edge, her knees scraped to ribbons. She had plopped herself down a short distance from him, nonchalantly, as if nothing out of the ordinary was happening. She had tried not to smile, but he could see she wanted to. The girl had been like nectar. The only child in Elveroa who never yielded to him or used his title. She was like Vetle, in a way—always exactly herself. It didn't matter who Rime was. She used to challenge him and tell him to go to Slokna—an outburst that would have cost her dearly had anyone overheard. Rime had seen people killed for a lot less.

But it didn't matter now. He was no longer a pawn in the Council's game. He had found his place. He was already dead.

ODIN'S CHILD

Hirka sat in the birch tree with her cheek resting against the bark. Her body felt like a sack of firewood. She stayed there as the sun went down and the colors faded. The turfed roofs of Elveroa merged into the surrounding landscape. Hirka had lived in many places, but never for as long as she had lived here.

The village lay at the bottom of a valley that opened to the sea. One of the old gods had tried to crush the first travelers with an enormous thumb, but they were northern folk, and they had refused to be broken. They had settled in the resulting depression in the landscape, exposed to the sea but protected by blue cliffs and lush forests that stretched as far as the eye could see, east toward Gardfjella. Some distance off, the Alldjup ended as a fissure in the cliff face. The Stryfe thundered tirelessly onward, flowing down into the valley and wending its way to the sea. Farms sprawled across the hillside up to the cliffs, surrounded by fields. They were concentrated on the far side of the valley, where there was sun all day.

Magnificently situated on that hillside was Glimmeråsen, Sylja's farm. It was bigger than any other farm in the area. The family at Glimmeråsen had spent an inconceivable amount of coin preparing Sylja for the Rite. It was all the girl could talk about. Dresses, jewelry, gold tail rings, perfume. A new carriage with shiny blue varnish—it even had doors! Nothing would be left to chance when

Glimmeråsen's only daughter was coming of age and receiving the Seer's protection against the blind.

Hirka felt her chest tighten. Looking forward to the Rite had to be a wonderful feeling—imagine it was her? Imagine she was like Sylja, like all the others, with butterflies in her stomach. Dreaming of visiting Mannfalla, of seeing Eisvaldr—the home of the Seer—said to be a city in its own right, and the legendary Rite Hall, the music and the dancers and the Council and …

Rime.

Why had he even come back? Ilume An-Elderin was a *madra*, a family matriarch on the Council, one of the twelve. She was fully capable of traveling on her own—that was all she ever did. Surrounded by guardsmen on all sides, as if anyone would have dared to attack. And even if an entire pack of highwaymen were to make the mistake of doing that, Hirka would still put her money on Ilume.

Rime hadn't needed to come. He hadn't needed to strut around bearing the mark of the Council on his chest, as if she didn't already know that he belonged to a different world than hers. As if she didn't know his name.

Rime appeared in her mind's eye. Dressed as a warrior. Probably one last hurrah before he had to don the tunic for good. Everyone who was selected during the Rite and schooled in Eisvaldr wore the tunic of the learned, until they had chosen their place—or their place had chosen them, as it were. Until they had sworn the Oath. The Council schools produced the world's most learned people in every art, from warriors to chroniclers. But what many people dreamed of was becoming an augur: one of the Seer's eyes. One learned in His word. All who sat on the Council had been augurs, and Rime was Ilume An-Elderin's only grandchild. Destined for a seat on the Council. A seat many would be prepared to kill for.

Hirka had never understood why, and never would. No song of Mannfalla or Eisvaldr made the thought of traveling there more enticing. Sylja could keep her daydreams of being chosen for the schools to herself. Fraternizing with Council folk? Drinking wine from crystal? Hirka snorted. She would gladly have sacrificed everything to get out of the wretched Rite.

I'm not afraid.

What was the worst that could happen? Maybe *nothing* would happen. Maybe she would never even make it as far as the Rite. Not even enter Mannfalla. Maybe they'd see her for what she was as soon as she reached the city gates, and bar her from entering. Or maybe the entire city would be able to tell that she couldn't bind, and then they'd stone her. People mean danger, Father always said. Maybe they'd have her dragged through the city streets by horses until she was unrecognizable. Imprisoned. Tortured, or put on display for all to see. Or burned alive!

Hirka heard a creak below her and gave a start. She caught a glimpse of Father through the foliage. She had been so caught up in her nightmare that she hadn't heard him approach. The creaking of wheels had intermingled with imagined sounds of swords clanging amid a screaming throng of people. She pretended not to see him. If she made eye contact, he would win, and they would end up on the road again. The trick was not to look. She could wait. Up here she was nothing but a leaf in the wind.

The powerful blow of an axe broke the silence.

The tree trunk shook against her body, and she nearly fell. She clung on and stared down in disbelief. Father raised the axe to strike once more. Was this really happening? He took another swing, and the tree shook again. His upper body strength was unbelievable. He could pick up Hirka and Sylja at the same time as though they were kindling. Three able-bodied men couldn't measure up to him. After just four swings, she heard the trunk give way. Just like in the All-djup. It was a bad day to be a tree.

Hirka leaped up on the branch and prepared to jump. She swayed with the tree for a brief moment before it crashed to the ground. She flung herself to the side for all she was worth and hit the grass at a roll. The tree with over ten thousand leaves struck the ground behind her. Hirka swiftly rose to her feet and spat out a blade of grass.

Father watched her. He didn't look happy. But not furious either. More as though he was wondering if he would ever figure her out.

Hirka crossed her arms and looked away. "I was about to head back anyway."

"Come," Father replied. He rested the axe on his lap and started to wheel toward the cabin. "There's something I have to tell you."

He struggled to get the wheeled chair inside. Hirka didn't help him. She'd learned it was best not to. The wheels got caught on a swollen board in the doorway that didn't normally cause him any problems, but on this occasion his movements were too sudden. He was tugging too hard on the wheels. Was too tense.

With one final push, he made it inside, and Hirka followed him. The cabin seemed smaller than normal. The air was thick and smoky from the smoldering hearth. It took some getting used to when you had spent the whole day outside.

Hirka sat down and by force of habit started to sweep dried leaves and remains of ground herbs off the table. She caught the sweet smell of opa, but said nothing. At least he had removed any visible traces of it. The Council's healers guild imposed strict rules for handling and trading the plant. Father had always sold it under the table, and Hirka had always passively indicated her opposition. But opa was far from the only risky plant they dealt in. That was another reason they'd spent so much time on the move. A traveling peddler and his daughter.

And now he wants to leave again.

Father rolled the chair up to the table and slid a bowl of fish soup toward Hirka. It was lukewarm, but she was so hungry that it tasted like a gift from the Seer. She ate greedily with one hand, while Father cleaned her wounded hand with a cloth. She wasn't going to tell him that she had run into Rime. Father had made it abundantly clear that she wasn't to trust men. But he had no problems with Vetle. She could tell him about Vetle if he asked what she had been doing. But he didn't ask.

"I found you," he muttered, without looking at her.

"I wasn't trying to hide, if that's what you think," she replied.

"That's not what I'm talking about."

Father rubbed some salve onto her hand. It stung. He turned away and rolled over to the hearth. He sat there, blocking the fire like a solar eclipse.

"I didn't *have* you, I *found* you. It's not difficult to grasp, girl."

His words stung like ants. They warned of danger, even though she didn't understand them. Or didn't want to understand. His voice sounded like distant thunder. Stormy words, with nowhere to seek shelter.

"This was years ago. You were a baby. I hadn't yet left Ulvheim. Did well for myself there. Bought and sold with little risk. The Council's dominion has always been weaker farther north. They didn't even have a healers guild. Wise women drew out illness, teeth, and babies without giving the Council a second thought."

Hirka heard longing in his voice. As though he were talking about a dream world.

"But they had a man in Ulvheim. A binder, it was said, but Olve couldn't have bound a fly to the ground. Any abilities he might once have had, he'd drunk away by the time I met him. He used opa. I knew he was the Council's ears in Ulvheim, not that he heard much, and he knew what I got up to. Neither of us had any reason to complain. It was early in Ylirmana, just after the polar night had set in. The days were short. It was bitterly cold. The kind of cold you only get in Ulvheim."

Father leaned a little closer to the hearth.

"Olve was good and drunk when he arrived. It was late, and I told him to go home. I lied, said I had nothing for him. He used too much as it was. But he just needed a ride. He could barely walk and was waving a bottle around, but he was deadly serious, saying that he had to get to the stone circle in Sigdskau. By order of the Council. The entire trip the snow was drifting down, and he was going on about all the senseless errands the Council sent him out on."

Father was mimicking the gravelly voice Olve must have had.

"And he wasn't the only one, he told me. Every stone circle in each of the eleven kingdoms was being checked that night, provided the ravens made it through the storm. And why?"

Hirka wasn't sure she wanted to know, so she continued to push her spoon around in the fish soup without saying anything.

"Because a stone whisperer had felt some change in the flow of the Might. Gone on about the old stone doors being open again. About something passing through."

Hirka felt the hairs stand up on her arms. It was said the blind had passed through the stones, and that they could return through the stones too. That was what the Rite was for: to protect people.

But that was just what people said. Nobody had ever seen the blind. Not for hundreds of years. They no longer existed. If they ever had in the first place.

"Olve said he wasn't a superstitious old crone. He wasn't afraid of the dark. I asked why he couldn't take the wagon and go on his own then, but he had no response to that, the lily-livered milksop. When we arrived at the circle, he staggered between the stones in the dead of night, blind drunk, with his sword in hand. A ghost of a man, on the lookout for monsters he had orders to kill. He fought off the shadows bravely, till he slumped against a rock and started to snore."

Here it comes, Hirka thought. She'd caught wind of something she knew she didn't want to hear. Like an animal. The air grew closer in the cabin, the world pressing in on her almost unbearably.

Father began to speak slower. As though he wasn't sure that he wanted to go on.

"I don't know what made me decide to have a look around. A gut feeling, I suppose. The Council had sent people out in foul weather to check Seer-knows-what, and Olve wasn't up to the task. So I plowed my way through the snow, around the stones. Just to see. Just to make sure.

"And then I found you.

"You were no more than a few days old. Someone had wrapped you in a blanket that blended in with the snow. You would have been easy to miss. A pale face barely the size of my fist in an ocean of frost. The snow was falling on you, but you weren't crying. You were just looking up with wonder in your big green eyes."

Hirka swallowed a limp piece of fish that threatened to come up again. She willed her body to move, but she felt paralyzed. She wasn't sure what she was hearing. Father wasn't ... Father?

But he just kept talking. Maybe he'd forgotten that she was sitting there.

"There isn't a man in Ym who would abandon an infant to a drunken fool like Olve. So I dragged him into the wagon and put you on my lap. Both of you slept the entire way back. I drove Olve home, back to his mistress. You stayed with me. I lay awake all night, with you in one hand and my sword in the other. I saw Kolkagga in every corner. Heard them in the howling of the wolves. And in the branches scraping against the wall. Jon at the tavern, he used to say Ulvheim's so cold that Kolkagga would turn back halfway. But I don't know. You never know when it comes to the Seer's dark shadows."

Father suddenly turned to face her.

"You know I have little time for gossip, girl. But what does that matter when the world is the way it is? I had no choice. If the Council had more drunkards on its payroll, the story about the stone circles and monsters could spread. People would be on guard. I couldn't raise a tailless girl!"

Hirka's hand jerked to the scar on her lower back like someone had branded her. Now he was way off the mark. She'd *had* a tail. She hadn't been born tailless! "The wolves ..." She swallowed. "You said the wolves took my tail."

"What in Slokna was I supposed to tell you?"

"But the scar ..." Hirka felt the lump in her throat grow until it hurt.

"*I* left the scar, girl!" Father shouted, as though it was her fault. "I carved bite marks into your back. It certainly wasn't easy. It had to look real. And you screamed. I had to hold my hand over your mouth or you'd have woken half the town." Father was dark red in the light from the hearth.

"Sorry ..." was all she could manage.

She saw his face crack, as though she had struck him.

"Do you understand now, girl? Do you understand why we need to leave?"

Hirka couldn't look at him. She lowered her gaze until it landed on the yellowed wolf fang resting on her chest. She'd worn it around her neck her entire life. A reminder. A reminder of something that had never happened. A false badge of honor, bought from a market stall for a copper piece.

Father must have realized what she wanted to ask, because he thundered on. "You entered the world tailless, in the stone circle near Ulvheim, and you can't bind. I don't know where you're from or what you are, but I don't care, we're leaving. If you're one of the tailless ... one of Odin's kin ..."

Hirka's heart clenched.

"If you're menskr, the Council will find out during the Rite. And then what will happen to you? You are my daughter. Nobody is going to succeed where Olve failed. I won't risk you."

Even though Father's voice was gentler now, Hirka could hear it wasn't up for discussion.

She forced out a laugh. She couldn't believe any of this. "Have you ever seen a child of Odin, Father? Have you ever heard of anyone, anywhere, who has seen one? We've traveled across all of Foggard, and never—"

"Never met anyone else tailless, who can't bind? Who's unearthed?"

Hirka closed her eyes as she tried to think back. "That enormous man in Frossabu, he only had a stump!"

"His old lady chopped it off. He'd been with a girl."

"The three girls at the market in Arfabu who had …"

"They were Silers from Urmunai. They swear off men and devote their lives to dance. It's their custom to bind their tail up along their backs."

"Olve! You just said Olve couldn't bind!" Hirka was desperate now.

"Of course he could bind. It's just he was no longer able to use it for anything anymore. Even though as a boy he was chosen during the Rite and studied in Eisvaldr for many years. Hirka …"

"I am not one of Odin's kin! I had a mother!"

Father shut his eyes. Hirka sensed where that was going to lead, but she didn't want to stop.

"I had a mother," she repeated. "Maiande."

"You remember her, do you?" Father's voice was different. Almost mocking. But his assumption was correct. Hirka didn't remember her. Only the few things Father had told her.

"Maiande was a girl in Ulvheim who I … knew for a while," he said. "She made soaps and knew to sell them to weak men at the taverns. They spent more on soaps than on ale. You'd have struggled to find cleaner drunkards."

Hirka felt his words pressing down on her like boulders. Each one heavier than the last. She was going to end up crushed to death. She managed to stand. For a moment she felt like a visitor. As though Father were a stranger. A stranger bearing false witness.

It was impossible to breathe. She had to force the words out. "People are born without arms and legs, strong and weak binders alike! We can't be certain—"

"No," he interrupted. "We can't be certain. Nothing is certain, but I won't risk meeting the Council and being the one who brought the rot to Ym."

Children of Odin. Menskr. Bringers of the rot.

"Crones' talk!" she shouted. The only words for *nonsense* she knew he'd understand.

Air. She needed air. Hirka opened the door and filled her lungs. It felt like she hadn't taken a breath in a long time. She could hear her father's voice behind her but didn't hear what he was saying. She just walked away. Things weren't the same anymore. He was stuck in his chair and couldn't stop her. She walked faster and faster. She jumped over the fallen birch tree and started to run.

She had no idea where she was going. All she knew was that she had to run. The evening was dark. There was nobody around. Nobody to see her. She was invisible. A ghost. A monster.

A child of Odin.

She no longer existed, so she ran. But within her something continued to live, something that noticed branches and leaves whipping against her face, and that she was nearing the Alldjup. Suddenly her foot caught, and she crashed to the ground.

She lay there gasping. The air felt dead. It wasn't supplying her with what she needed to breathe. She had to get up.

The ground under her hands was covered with moss. It smelled rotten. She was part of the earth. Larval. An insect that could crawl around and disappear inside the tiny holes in the moss. Forever. She let her gaze follow the forest floor until it disappeared over the dark edge of the Alldjup. The gorge that had nearly been the end of her only a few hours earlier.

Maybe that had been the point the entire time? Maybe that was the Seer's punishment for having cheated death?

Can the tailless die? Can I *die?*

Hirka pressed her eyes shut. She tried to block out everything Father had said, but it wouldn't stay away. *I didn't* have *you, I* found *you.*

She did her best to stifle a howl. When she opened her eyes, there were red teeth marks on her forearm. What had she expected? Had she thought that her skin would suddenly have turned to stone?

What did she know about the tailless?

That they don't exist ...

Children of Odin were a myth, like the blind. An old folk tale. She didn't believe in folk tales. Father was a fool!

But if the blind don't exist, then why do we have the Rite?

The Rite was supposed to protect everyone from the blind. So surely the blind must have existed at one time? Had she not personally placed coins over the eyes of newborns? Given them the blood to reassure their mothers? That's what was done. What had always been done. Surely not without reason? And if the blind existed, then maybe children of Odin did too?

Child of Odin. Menskr. Embling. The rot. That last one was the worst. The one that stung the most. She'd heard it before, outside the tavern. Kolgrim's father had accused Iron Jarke of cavorting with his girl. Iron Jarke had replied that he'd rather risk the rot. It had cost him two teeth.

Hirka drew her knees under her. So that's what she was. An insult. An atrocity. And everyone would be able to tell when the Rite came around. The pieces fell into place. *That* was why she'd never been able to bind. Why they'd lived along the roadside her entire life. Why Father had always kept them away from people. It wasn't just the illegal herbs. It was her. *People mean danger.*

Hirka shivered. She felt the cold traces of tears down her face.

If the Seer discovered during the Rite that she wasn't an ymling, the Council would punish her. Burn her! And what would happen to Father? Father, who had taken in the rot? Would they kill him?

No.

Nothing was going to happen to him. Nothing was going to happen to her either. Hirka wasn't an insect! She was an ymling. A strong girl who did what she had to. That's the way it had always been.

Hirka glimpsed a familiar outline against the moss. Her basket, right where she'd set it down when she went to save Vetle. *That* was who she really was. Brave. Strong. Unafraid. She was going to make it through the Rite like everyone else. And when it was over, she and Father would be left alone. Then they could live in Elveroa and never be afraid of anything again. The Rite would give her what she needed. A home. A place in the world.

That's how it was going to be. That's how it *had* to be.

Hirka felt an unexpected calm. She was tired. She heard the sound of wings flapping, and then a raven landed in front of her. It cocked its head and stared at her for a moment. Then it went over to her basket and started to peck at it with its powerful beak.

A raven. An image of the Seer. A sign of good fortune, everyone knew that, Hirka thought, before reminding herself that she didn't believe in signs. She and Father had given raven amulets to a lot of people seeking to ward off illness. Some died, some didn't.

She closed her eyes.

Alone in the woods, she dreamed that Father came. Walking on his own two feet, like before. His strong arms picked her up in the darkness and carried her home.

THE EMPTY CHAIR

What is a father?

A teacher? A rock? A guiding light? His entire life, Urd had listened to others describe his father as all these things. But to him, his father was nothing more than a bloodstained wooden bucket of red meat. His father—Spurn Vanfarinn—was dead.

The gravity of such a death—in such a family—had sent shock waves through the eleven kingdoms. Mannfalla was a city in mourning. The Council was shaken that it had lost one of the twelve. People were saying it couldn't have happened at a worse time.

Perfect.

Not only had Spurn Vanfarinn left behind significant wealth, he had left Insringin one councillor short. Urd was only interested in the latter. He stood tall, refusing to blink as sweat trickled down his forehead into his eyes. This was the most important day of his life. He was close. So close. This was his time. He was perfect. The perfect son. The perfect successor.

Ten of the eleven remaining members of Insringin stood before him, brought together to pay their respects. Mannfalla was laid out behind him. A silent sea of people subdued by heat and sorrow. The Ravenbearer was so close he could almost touch her. The drums that had followed the procession up to the plateau had settled into barely audible sighs. This was it.

The doors were flung open next to him, and a sea of ravens

turned day to night. They circled the cliffs, making surprisingly little noise. The Ravenbearer made the sign of the Seer and emptied the bucket onto the ground in front of her. She took a step back and let the ravens eat.

Spurn Vanfarinn was nothing more than bloody pieces. Tiny, tiny pieces, smaller than Urd could ever have dreamed. Faceless, boneless. Torn apart. No longer a great man. Never a great man. Urd suppressed a smile. At long last, the battle had been won. The silent war that had been waging ever since he was a child, ever since his father had snarled that Urd was no more fit to be a councillor than the whores by the river, that he would be the first break in their family's seven-hundred-year line of councillors.

The only downside of his father's death was that he couldn't bear witness to how wrong he had been. Unless the Might could convey this to him somewhere in eternity.

The chunks of his father became fewer and smaller. He was consumed, carried away on gleaming black wings, slowly but surely devoured. Along with his endless contempt for his eldest son. A contempt that had chased Urd toward the darkness before he was even old enough to take the Rite. Into a dismal game that had cost him almost everything. This was the first time it had borne fruit. Now, fifteen years later, he could open the stone way by himself. He finally had what he had been promised.

The same irritating question pushed its way to the forefront of his mind again. *Why now?* Why after all this time? Had something slipped through back then? Unseen? Blood that had matured in Ym?

Inconceivable. He, Urd, had become stronger. That was the only reason. All the same, it wouldn't hurt to keep his eyes peeled during the Rite. Even though no one would dare hide something like that from him. No one. Not even Him.

Urd shuddered and fought the urge to raise his hand to his throat. It was nothing. Nothing. Just the usual pain. The collar was secure, like always. No one could see anything. Oh, how he hated the constant fear that someone would see.

The drums became louder again. The ravens were called back. All that was left now was a red smear on the cliff's edge, overlaying the darker brown tones left by generations of councillors who had journeyed into eternity from here.

Urd prepared himself. It was up to the Council and the Seer to choose a successor to join Insringin. If he acted strategically now, that successor was likely to be him. Each and every one of the councillors would pass him and offer their condolences.

Tyrme Jekense was among the first to approach him. The Jekense family had little love for the Vanfarinns, but Urd thought he could at least cultivate their gratitude: Tyrme's brother owed his family a pretty sum.

Tyrme shook his hand and offered his condolences. Urd thanked him before leaning closer to the tall man and whispering: "And of course, all obligations toward my father died with him."

Tyrme looked surprised for a moment, but then gave his thanks and moved on.

It was difficult to predict how that would play out, but Urd had done what he could. The next councillor in line would be much easier.

Miane Fell had been on the Council with his father as long as Urd had been alive. They'd had a good relationship, and Urd thought he had seen a yearning in her eyes. He couldn't be sure, and the feeling hadn't been mutual, but he had to take the chance. Miane's eyes were puffy and shone with tears as she took Urd's hand. He felt more certain of himself already. He smiled at the elderly woman and whispered: "Father said his only regret in life was not being able to be with you."

Tears spilled from Miane's brown eyes. She stared at him in disbelief for a moment before squeezing her eyes shut and guiding his hand to her brow. Urd was convinced he could feel the mark on her forehead burning against the palm of his hand. He smiled. He was as good as in.

A PUZZLE

A raven sailed through the dark woods, only an arm's length from Rime. Its flapping wings were like a breath of air on his face, before it disappeared into the night. Rime made the sign of the Seer.

Then he noticed a figure lying on the ground ahead and stopped. He grabbed the hilt of his sword while scanning the woods. Was there anyone else there? The moon gave off only a weak silver glow. He sensed movement, wind toying with the branches. The sound of a night warbler reached him; a slow wail that went unanswered. Otherwise there was no sign of life. Rime was alone. Apart from the figure lying motionless in the moss.

He stepped closer. Skinny. Red hair. A grazed knee visible through torn trousers. Hirka.

With a twinge of anxiety, he crouched down and placed a hand on her back. She was breathing steadily. Furrows in the moss suggested that she had tripped and fallen. Her face was dirty and her woollen tunic tattered, but it had been that way for as long as he could remember. She appeared to be unscathed—apart from her hand, but he knew she'd injured that earlier in the day. Rime ran his thumb over the cut on her palm. The girl was impetuous. But with the heart of a wolf.

She had most likely saved Vetle's life. But why was she here now? Maybe the whole experience had shaken her more than she let on? And she'd come back here to confront her fear? That didn't add up. Rime looked around and spotted an overturned basket lying nearby.

She'd been running. From something or someone.

Did she know? Had she seen him?

No. Of course not. He was careful. He trained in the grassy hollow atop Vargtind, where the Might was strongest. Few could manage the trip, and in the unlikely event someone did come, he'd hear them long before they reached him. And they wouldn't understand what they were seeing anyway. A protector practicing combat techniques. A warrior. Swordsman. Nothing unusual. Obviously, the safest thing to do would be to keep a low profile while he was here, but he had commitments. He had to devote his time to getting stronger. To …

To avoiding Ilume.

Ilume had returned that evening, from what Rime expected was the last reasonably amiable handshake between Ravnhov and Mannfalla. Between north and south. He'd seen the carriages arrive, but he continued his training. He put off going home until the moon came up, until he was sure that his grandmother had turned in for the night. He knew this was weak. Shameful. The irony was laughable.

The night warbler wailed again. Rime had to get Hirka home. The night was getting cold. She was lying on her side, so it was easy to roll her over into his arms. He reached for her tail before he remembered that she had lost it as a child. That just made it easier. Her basket weighed next to nothing, and it hung lightly from his fingers. Hirka let out a kind of growl and her head slumped against his chest, but she didn't wake up.

Anyone else would have been surprised to find her out here, but not Rime. Hirka was three years younger than him, and he knew that she rarely needed an excuse to do her own thing, whether that was swimming up the Stryfe or jumping from roof to roof down by the quay. Rime smiled involuntarily. Hirka fascinated him. She had spent barely a winter in Elveroa when Rime arrived there with Ilume. He had just turned twelve, while Hirka was nine, and he had never met anyone like her. He had grown up in Mannfalla, the home of the Seer, under His wings. Rime had met other children, naturally. But they always came with their parents. So stiffly dressed they could hardly walk. Silent and wide-eyed they had stared at him—a boy no older than they were, sitting to attention between the Council guards, ready to lay his hand on anyone in need. As if anyone had ever benefited in any way from such a thing. Not even at the age of twelve had he bought into his own myth, but as long as others did, his fate was sealed, his duties inextricably linked to people's need to have blessings bestowed on them.

Coming to Elveroa had been the escape he had never thought possible. Somewhere small, far from the corridors of Eisvaldr. In Elveroa, the children got dirty. They played rough and they got into all kinds of scrapes. And nobody more than Hirka. Rime remembered the first time he had seen her. Kolgrim had been trying to put the new girl in her place, and she had responded by giving him a thorough hiding—a first for Kolgrim. She didn't even come up to his shoulders, but was she ever scrappy.

Shocked by their behavior, Rime had jumped in to separate them. Hirka's fist split his lower lip, and he experienced the taste of his own blood. Certainly not for the first time. His Council lineage meant that he knew the ways of the sword and was trained from the day he took his first step. But it was the first time any living creature outside the walls of Eisvaldr had laid a hand on him. He wiped off the blood and stared in turns at the red on his hand and the equally red hair of the girl who had hit him. She sent him a crooked smile and shrugged, as though he only had himself to blame.

Rime remembered looking around for fear of there being witnesses. If word of the incident reached Ilume, at best it would cost

Hirka her hand, at worst her life. In any case, he would never be allowed to see her again. That couldn't happen. So they made a pact, solemn and half-hostile—in a way only children can—and it stayed between the two of them.

That was the day the battle for points had begun. And since then it had nearly put an end to both of them on numerous occasions. They'd swum until they were on the verge of drowning, climbed until their fingers broke, jumped until they felt like their legs might shatter. Neither wanted to fall short of the other. So much passion, and so much pain. All for points. Worthless tallies to keep score in a never-ending duel. Through all that, Rime had never seen Hirka cry. But now dirt clung to her cheeks.

Rime carried Hirka's sleeping body in his arms noiselessly through the woods. It would have been the easiest thing in the world to wake her up, but he liked seeing her asleep. Her face was so open. Unmasked. He wanted this to last. Besides, he knew that she would be furious if she woke up and discovered that she had been carried like a child.

Rime smiled. He left the trees behind him and emerged on the crest of the hill above Elveroa. Soon he would leave this sleepy settlement for good. Fog inched through the berry bushes on the way down to the village. The only thing he could hear was the distant roar of the Stryfe. Had it always been so beautiful?

My path is chosen.

In her sleep, Hirka pulled herself closer to him. Rime spotted a shadow moving farther up the ridge and instinctively crouched down.

What was he thinking? He was in Elveroa, he had no enemies here, there was no danger. He straightened up again. The shadow became a broad-shouldered figure, on … wheels?

It was Thorrald, Hirka's father, in that strange contraption built from metal and cart wheels. A stroke of genius on the part of the blacksmith. A chair he could move around in, unaided. Indoors, at least. Outdoors was another story. He had made it a little way from the small cottage, but he was clearly having issues wheeling himself through the grass. Rime could see panic in his every movement.

Thorrald looked relieved when he spotted them. It only lasted a moment, then his eyes darkened. "Give her to me!" he growled, his powerful arms outstretched.

Rime was used to reading fear and desire in the eyes of others, but this was a different kind of fear. One he didn't recognize.

"She's asleep," he whispered. "I found her near the Alldjup."

He hadn't meant it as a question, but he realized it had sounded like one. Thorrald's gaze fell to Hirka and his shoulders sagged. He dragged his hand wearily over his face.

"She's … had a rough time of it."

Rime continued toward Thorrald's cabin without replying. He heard the creaking of the wheeled chair behind him. The night was cool. Neither of them said anything else. The notched outline of the cabin came into view on the mountain ledge. The Hovel. It had stood untouched for more than twenty years, ever since the Council guardsmen set fire to it and dragged off its lawless owner. The wind had saved the place, but since then nobody had braved living in it or tearing it down. Not when they all knew that the Seer had wanted it to be burned down. It was ridiculous. The Seer had plenty of things to concern Himself with, but building or tearing down houses was hardly one of them. Thorrald and Hirka had clearly understood that.

He bent down to step through the low door. Hirka's weight left a pleasant ache in his arms. The hearth was still aglow. *Is nobody sleeping tonight?*

The room was small, and almost too hot. The walls were covered with shelves bearing jars, boxes, and bottles of all shapes and sizes. Tea everywhere he looked. Dried herbs had been strung from the ceiling, and there was a smell of mint and exotic spices. A little too exotic, if the rumors were true. Rime had heard that Thorrald dealt in blacklisted plants, but he had never mentioned it to Ilume. That was probably just one more thing the Council wanted to control, though he doubted it would be important enough to matter to the Seer.

Thorrald directed Rime into an even smaller room with a beautiful wooden bed. Carved into the headboard was a flowery meadow, with the wings of a bird stretching from the middle out toward the sides. Thorrald was known for more than curative teas and good luck charms. He was also a talented woodcarver. It had cost him the use of his legs in the accident at Glimmeråsen.

Rime noticed that the corners of the bed were joined without nails so that it could be taken apart and put back together again. Maybe they needed to make space for other things sometimes? Rime envied them. Everything they owned within reach, in two small rooms. Loved ones never more than a few steps away. It was a world away from the An-Elderin family home in Mannfalla, where Rime was convinced there were rooms he still hadn't seen. He could scream at one end without being heard at the other. Not that he ever needed to scream—there was always someone at hand to ensure he had everything he needed.

Rime consoled himself with the knowledge that he had turned his back on that life, once and for all. Everything was different now. He hadn't slept in silk for three years and would never do so again. He was going to serve the Seer in his own way. He was finished with the Council. For good.

He put the basket on the floor and set Hirka down on the bed. He left it to her father to take off her shoes and tuck her in for the night. It was good to be able to move his arms again, but he wasn't tired. In recent years, he had carried far more and for far longer.

Rime felt like he was intruding on what seemed to have been

a difficult night for Thorrald and Hirka, so he headed toward the door.

"Are you back again, Són-Rime?" Thorrald asked from behind him.

The title settled like a weight on Rime's chest. *Són*. Blood of the Council. A small word that formed a chasm between him and everyone else.

He turned to face Thorrald again. "I remember you giving me eight stitches on my forearm when I was twelve. And you never said a word to Ilume. I was just Rime then, and I'm just Rime now. I'm not here to stay. I'm going back to Mannfalla with Ilume."

"Yes, of course, she's leaving us." Thorrald ran his hand over his stubbly head a couple of times.

"Most people at least try to sound disappointed," Rime said with a smile.

Thorrald grinned back and rested his arms on the table. They were strong enough to lift an ox. His forearm was inked with a small flower, no bigger than a knuckle. Time had faded the color, blurring the blue lines.

"Would you like a bite to eat? We've got halibut soup. It's simple, but fresh." Thorrald turned toward the hearth and scraped the bottom of the pot with the ladle. "It'll be hot in a moment." His voice betrayed the fact that he didn't actually want company.

"That's kind of you, Thorrald, but I have to get back," Rime replied, but he sat down all the same. Thorrald stared at him. Rime could see the same wariness in his eyes as in Hirka's. A new distance. They didn't know him anymore. He wasn't one of them.

"So what should we do then, Rime? We mere mortals? Prepare for war?" Thorrald leaned over the table. Rime scratched his nose to conceal a smile. Thorrald's cheeky question had lessened the distance between them, and he enjoyed the feeling.

"Ravnhov and Mannfalla are just banging their shields. They're always doing that," Rime said, knowing he sounded more sure of himself than he actually was.

"Banging their shields?"

"Nobody's going to die because of it, Thorrald."

"None of *you*, maybe." Thorrald leaned back in his chair. The divide between them had returned. Rime got up. He'd have given anything to stay for good. Talk about this and that. Get up the next morning and maybe go out to repair the charred roof, alongside this man. But this world didn't belong to Rime either.

Thorrald smiled uneasily. "Thanks for being there, Rime. For Hirka."

"She's always been there for me," Rime replied.

Thorrald's eyes widened to reveal both surprise and suspicion. He'd always kept to himself, and tried to keep Hirka to himself, like a treasure. He'd never known how much time his daughter used to spend with Rime, and perhaps it should have been left unsaid. But it didn't matter anymore. Those days were long gone.

Rime went out and shut the door behind him. His feet carried him toward the edge of the grassy ledge, where he stood in the dark, looking out over Elveroa. The past three years had taught him that nothing ever stayed the same. It was the Seer's first teaching. *Nothing is perfect. Nothing lasts forever.* All the same, Rime was sad about what he was putting behind him. He was abandoning more than the Council. More than the families in Mannfalla, and more than Ilume.

A raven croaked from the roof of the cabin. It sounded like the hoarse laugh of a sage. "What-did-I-say! What-did-I-say!" An old proverb from Blossa came to him: *No one knows what the raven says.* This was the second raven he'd seen tonight. Rime made the sign of the Seer once more. Even after a lifetime under His wings, Rime still couldn't interpret the ravens' words. Had he been able to, they might have given him some advice. For tomorrow he would stand face-to-face with Ilume An-Elderin, his mother's mother, one of the most powerful women in the world.

He took a deep breath, stepped over a felled birch tree, and headed down into the valley.

THE FIGHT

Hirka was awakened by the cries of seagulls from the shore. She went over to the window and opened the shutters. It was early. The boats had returned to the quay far below. The fishermen cleaned the catch as the hungry birds circled above them. The fish thrashed around in barrels, getting nowhere. Whitecaps rode distant waves, and only a couple silver-edged clouds revealed where the sun was hiding.

The wind nipped at the skin of her arms. At Glimmeråsen, they had windows made of stained glass. Hirka just had a hole in the wall, which was much better. From there, she could smell what the day would be like. And see things as they really were. Glass distorted everything. Like in a dream. She had dreamed during the night. About flying through the forest. About ravens. About … Rime?

Reality hit her in the face like the smell of rotten fish, turning her stomach. Father was her father, yet he wasn't. He'd found her when she was a baby, taken her home with him, like an unusual stone or a crow feather. She had been abandoned. Cast out. And she wasn't a child of Ym.

Hirka backed away from the window, clinging to the bedpost as if to the liberating nothingness she'd basked in before she was fully awake. But it was gone.

The last thing she remembered from the night before was falling asleep in the woods. Father must have asked Iron Jarke to help carry her home. Like a helpless child. Hirka looked down.

Her hand was wrapped in a white bandage, and her undershirt had twisted around her body while she slept. She looked like a wrung-out washrag. She needed to get outside, to feel the wind on her face.

She opened the door to the hearth room. It creaked, and Father jerked awake in his chair. He grabbed a mortar and started grinding chamomile as if he'd just nodded off. Hirka could tell he hadn't been to bed. The fire hadn't been put out. The embers were still glowing. The table was a mess of plants, boxes, jars, and salves. He'd been working all night.

"Was that everything you got?" he asked hoarsely, nodding in the direction of her basket, which was sitting on the table. It seemed he'd decided this was a normal day, just like any other. She didn't know what she'd been expecting. Certainly more than this. She could feel the weight of the things she wanted to say, but she couldn't remember any of them. She lifted her clothes down from the rafters, where they'd been hung to dry.

"I went almost all the way up to Gardakulp," she said, pulling her trousers on. The hole in the knee had gotten bigger but patching it would have to wait. "And I ran into Rime." She glanced at Father, giving him the chance to acknowledge that everything was different now, but he didn't even react.

"I found soldrop," she said when the silence became too oppressive.

"Good. Half the village will want it for the bonfire this evening. I'll give you some to take with you. Don't—"

"Hang around with people, and talk as little as possible," Hirka supplied. Their eyes met.

"Don't give anyone anything for a promise. Coin or nothing."

Hirka cut the corner off a piece of goat's cheese as Father went through her route. She knew who needed what, but she let him speak. If the weight of the basket was anything to go by, she would be visiting a lot of people. Chest salve for Ulla, enough for several months. Mint tea for Kvitstein. He had a huge oven and sold bread to the entire village from a sourdough thought to have been around since his great-grandfather's time. But the flour made it difficult for him to breathe. The mint helped a bit, and Hirka had enough in her basket to last him until the snow came.

Did Father think she was stupid? That she didn't know what was going on? These would be her final rounds in Elveroa, and he wasn't going to say anything about it. They were leaving again. How they'd manage that with Father in his wheeled chair was beyond her, but if he thought she was going to ask, he could think again. She shoved a boiled egg in her pocket, picked up the basket, and went out.

She took a detour around Glimmeråsen so she wouldn't have to talk to Sylja. She didn't particularly want to talk to anyone, but that would be impossible. The raven had come. People would be congregating around the Seer's hall.

The Stryfe meandered along the bottom of the valley as if it had all the time in the world. Hirka's feet carried her to its banks. She kneeled down and peered over the edge. Her own face peered back apprehensively. She couldn't see anything different. Her hair was just as red. Short in some places and long in others, with the same knotted braids. Was it obvious she wasn't like everyone else?

Ripples in the water pulled her face apart and put it back together again as if she were a ghost. A reflection that only half existed. And was it her, or was there something animalistic about the sharpness of her canines?

"Hirka!" Sylja's voice cut through the air like a scythe.

Hirka leaped to her feet.

"Where were you yesterday? You missed everything!" Sylja rolled her eyes and grabbed Hirka by the tunic. Hirka barely managed to scoop up her basket before she was dragged across the wooden bridge. Sylja's dress danced around her ankles. It was the color of the sea, with clovers around the neckline and along the edges. It was even prettier than her usual dresses, and this made Hirka fear the worst.

"The raven's come," she said, beaming. "I found out yesterday, but you weren't home. Come on! They're going to announce the days for the Rite!"

"Now? Today?" Hirka pretended she was surprised and made a half-hearted attempt to free herself from Sylja's grasp.

"Yes, now! Before the morning message. Honestly, Hirka, what would you do without me?"

Sylja pulled her mercilessly toward the square in front of the Seer's hall. So much for staying away from people.

Hirka swallowed. "I can't, Sylja, I have to—"

"And guess what." Sylja stopped halfway up the slope behind the tavern. She always stopped when she had something really dramatic to say, to ensure that everyone's attention was on her. The urge to gossip blazed in her eyes as she gripped both Hirka's arms. "You'll never guess who's here!"

Rime. Hirka bit her lip to stop from saying his name aloud.

"Rime! I swear, Hirka. Rime An-Elderin, none other. He's taking Ilume-madra back to Mannfalla before the Rite." Sylja widened her eyes. "Mannfalla, Hirka! It'll be our turn soon!"

Sylja started pulling her along again. The thought of the square full of people made Hirka feel ill. If it hadn't been for Sylja, she might have been able to stick to the shadows, but …

"Honestly, Hirka! I don't think you'd know what was going on anywhere if it weren't for me. Did you even hear that Audun Brinnvág broke his neck?"

"Who?"

"Brinnvág! The jarl of Skodd? He fell out a window when he was drunk, they say. But you know what?" Sylja leaned toward Hirka and whispered, "They swear they saw someone on the roof. A shadow!"

"Who swears?"

"People! The servants? It doesn't matter. He was a friend of Ravnhov. I think—" Sylja glanced around before continuing. "I think the shadows took him."

"The shadows," Hirka repeated dubiously.

"The warriors who are never seen and never die," Sylja whispered.

On a normal day, Hirka would have pointed out that someone *had* seen shadows on the roof, so clearly they weren't invisible. But Kolkagga? Warriors who never died? Everyone died. Them too, if they even existed.

But she couldn't bring herself to say anything. After all, she wasn't supposed to exist either. People like her had only existed in people's imaginations until yesterday.

The streets were packed with people. The low stone houses sat end to end on both sides of the road. Some of them doubled up as homes and market stalls. The road led onto a paved square in front of the Seer's hall. It was chaos. People were moving stalls and goods to make room for the announcement.

Sylja suddenly let go of Hirka's arm, a sure sign that the rest of Glimmeråsen wasn't far away. Sure enough, Sylja's parents were making their way across the square, sticking close to the entourage surrounding Ilume and Ramoja. Conversations trailed off into quiet whispers as they approached. Hirka's hands were sweating. She moved back through the crowd. It was easy enough, considering most people wanted to get farther forward.

People parted before Ilume as if an invisible plow were being pushed ahead of her. Her face glowed from within the hood of her pitch-black council robes, which were edged with gold. She seemed to glide across the ground. Three protectors walked behind her, with Sylja's mother, Kaisa, on her left. Ilume said nothing. Kaisa was doing most of the speaking, and she was wearing that smile that never seemed to reach her eyes. She clung to Ilume almost all the way up to the steps, catching people's eyes to make sure they had noticed her walking together with Ilume-madra. One of the Council's venerable matriarchs. One of the twelve members of Insringin. As close to the Seer as you could get.

Hirka felt hideously exposed. She tried to be as inconspicuous as possible. Sylja went to join her parents, and Hirka was relieved to see the back of her. Now she could make her escape.

There was only one problem. She was in the middle of the crowd, which had fallen completely silent. If she tried to leave now, people would notice.

Father always thought the worst of people, so she'd kept her distance, never understanding the danger. Today, she understood. Today, she knew what made her different. Why she needed to hide. But now she didn't have a choice. She would have to stay put for the duration of the announcement.

Hirka couldn't see over all the heads in front of her, but she knew what was happening. It was the same every year. She gazed longingly up at the turfed roof where she had lain the year before, watching the same ritual. Ilume stood in the middle of the steps, with Ramoja a short distance behind her, both of them surrounded by protectors. Ramoja lifted the raven that had come with the letter from Mannfalla. The letter was presented to Ilume as if she hadn't already seen it. She opened the small scroll and read from it.

This would be her last time making the announcement, Hirka suddenly realized. Ilume was leaving Elveroa, people said. Who would announce the dates for the Rite next year? Perhaps the augur from the Seer's hall? Or Ramoja?

Next year?

Hirka stiffened at the thought. She wouldn't be there next year either. She looked at the faces around her. They were all there to find out when the Rite would take place. If it was early in Tvimana, she had two moons left to live.

Ilume's voice carried across the entire square.

"The raven has come!"

"The raven has come!" people cheered around Hirka, raising their hands into the air. In previous years, she had smiled at the ceremonial rituals associated with the announcement. Today she had nothing to smile about. Ilume raised her hand, and everyone fell silent like obedient dogs.

"The seal belongs to the Council," she continued, assuring them that the words to follow could not have come from anyone else.

Let it be known.
The Seer shelters all those who come to Him.
Let it be known.
His hand protects against those who live in the darkness.

To Hirka, the words were mocking. *Shelter. Protection.* She would be denied those things because of who she was. She wouldn't be afforded the same protection as everyone else.

Ilume waited in silence as the crowd murmured and crossed the palms of their hands across their chests in the sign of the Raven. It was getting harder to breathe. Hirka tried to move back, but there were too many people around her.

"The raven has come," Ilume repeated. "The seal is the Council's. The dates for the Rite have been set."

Hirka's heart was pounding. This was it.

"In the year of the Seer 998, the Rite will take place in Heymana. On the eighteenth day for Elveroa and the surrounding villages. The Council's word is final."

Heymana? Heymana?! Hirka felt dizzy. That couldn't be right. Next month! They couldn't bring the Rite forward a whole month! She looked around in confusion and realized she wasn't alone. Mumbling turned to shouts. She wasn't the only one who was surprised. But the people around her had other reasons to be disgruntled.

One voice carried above the others. It sounded like Alder, a goat farmer from the north side. "That's mid-harvest! We can't just drop everything during Heymana!"

Ilume raised her hand and the clamor died down. "Would you care to submit a complaint to the Council?" Her voice was like frost on roses. Alder plucked at one of his suspenders without answering.

The announcement was complete. People started swarming toward the center of the square in the hope that the doors to the Seer's hall would open. Hirka ducked into a narrow street behind the leather goods stalls and slumped against a wall, half-hidden behind a pile of goat skins as people screeched about the unusual timing. The Rite was always in Tvimana. Always. Now she had even less time than she'd thought to figure out what to do.

A familiar laugh cut through her thoughts. She poked her head out and spotted Kolgrim and his cronies. Kolgrim, who could have cost both her and Vetle their lives at the gorge. What Kolgrim needed was a good thrashing.

He's not worth it, Hirka reminded herself. Just because he threw punches at the other kids when he felt like it didn't mean that Hirka should start a fight with him. She couldn't.

But a child of Odin could ...

Hirka straightened up. She could. A child of Embla. Mythical beasts with false tongues. Normal people had to behave, but she wasn't normal people anymore. She was the rot. Hirka bared her teeth in an involuntary grin.

She didn't stop to think it through. She put her basket down against the wall. Her feet carried her over to Kolgrim. He was sitting on the ground with the other kids from the north side, openly chewing red root. He saw her coming and stumbled to his feet. Hirka could see the panic in his eyes. He'd run when the tree had started to fall, and he clearly knew that had been wrong. But he was quick to settle his features, propping himself up against the wall as if he hadn't a care in the world.

Hirka pointed at him. "You could have killed Vetle!"

Her body tingled. An intoxicating mixture of dread and anticipation. At last, Hirka had found a deserving outlet for her anger and fear.

"What kind of coward picks on people who can't defend themselves?" she continued.

Kolgrim smiled derisively. "If I picked on people who couldn't defend themselves, I'd be picking on you, tailless." He snickered at his own joke, and his cronies quickly followed his lead.

He grabbed his tail and waved it in her face. "This is where a tail belongs, not in a wolf's belly!" The others burst out laughing as if they couldn't imagine a funnier barb.

If only he knew. What would he do if he found out that she'd never had a tail? That he was face-to-face with the rot? That a kiss could transform him into a rotting corpse as the others looked on? She smiled broadly as she imagined the expression of disbelief on his pale face as it collapsed in on itself.

Kolgrim clearly wasn't sure what to make of her reaction. She could almost smell the fear emanating from him. He glanced down at the others, who sat waiting to see what he would do. He tried another tack.

"Maybe people who can't defend themselves should stick together," he said, smirking again. "Isn't it about time you and witless got married?"

Iben, one of the lackeys, erupted into laughter. Now that Kolgrim had made good, the others were quick to join in.

Hirka took two steps closer to Kolgrim. "His name is Vetle!"

"Can you imagine?" Kolgrim continued, fueled by his friends' response. "Witless and tailless, together as one!"

Hirka gave him a lopsided smile. "Aw, are you proposing, Kolgrim?" She crossed her arms over her chest and waited for the insult to bore its way through his thick skull. Kolgrim's smirk faded slowly.

He lunged at her and they fell to the ground. Kolgrim's gang egged them on as they rolled around. He threw a punch at her face, but she blocked it, driving her elbow into his jaw. He let out a shriek. Desperate now, he felt around for something. Then he raised a fist that looked twice as big as it ought to.

He was holding a rock.

He's crazy!

Hirka tried to shove him off, but he was much bigger than her. The rock rushed toward her head. She heard a gasp from the gathering crowd, and then a shout from nearby. A rough voice, an unfamiliar word. Her body tingled. She squeezed her eyes shut. Then, an explosion.

But there was no pain. Nothing. She cracked her eyes open slightly. Kolgrim sat astride her with nothing but gravel in his fist. The rock had shattered. He looked confused for a moment before grinning at his friends as if he had supernatural strength. But that wasn't what had happened at all.

Hirka saw an opening while Kolgrim was busy gloating. She was getting ready to punch him in the stomach when he was suddenly torn away from her. Kolgrim thrashed in the air like a fish before landing heavily a short distance away.

Hirka peered up at Rime, outlined against the sun. She tried to get up but fell back again. Rime didn't notice—his eyes were fixed on Kolgrim.

"You'll never be a man if words are all it takes for you to lose your head, boy!"

Iben laughed reflexively, only stopping when Kolgrim glared at him. Hirka surveyed the crowd that had gathered. Everyone was watching Kolgrim and Rime. Only one person met her eyes.

Hlosnian. Old Hlosnian. The stone carver. Hirka knew him well. She had oil for him in her basket.

"Hirka!" Sylja gasped. Sylja's mother was there too, staring at Hirka and leaning back. It was as if she were trying to put as much space between them as possible without actually moving. Her long face became even longer as she raised her eyebrows. She sneered as if surveying spoiled meat.

Sylja gaped at Hirka, her eyes imploring, *What are you doing?!*

Hirka could feel her cheeks turning red. Rime was talking to Kolgrim. He had lowered his voice, but Hirka could see the tension in his jaw. She couldn't hear what Rime was saying, but Kolgrim backed away from him like a hissing cat, his eyes lingering on Rime's sword. Then he clambered to his feet and ran from the square, his friends following close behind.

"I must say!" Kaisa said, putting an arm around Sylja as if to protect her. "How blessed we are to have you here, Són-Rime!" The emphasis on his title was clear, but Rime didn't seem to have noticed. He came toward Hirka, who lowered her eyes to discover that the egg in her pocket had been crushed and smeared across her trousers. The crowd was a beast with a hundred eyes. Hungry, unfamiliar, dangerous.

Rime held out his hand. He stood over her, stronger and fitter than ever, offering a lifeline because he didn't know what she was.

"Are you all ri—"

"I had him!" she interrupted.

Everyone's jaws dropped. Of course. She'd forgotten who she was talking to. Again.

"You didn't need … you shouldn't have …" She scrambled into the alleyway, scooped up her basket, and ran away as fast as she could.

ILUME

Rime raised his hand to stop the guardsmen. He watched Hirka as she disappeared between the stalls. Trouble had a way of finding the girl. Yesterday she had been hanging over the Alldjup, and today she had barely avoided getting her head smashed to pieces. Had it not been for Hlosnian …

Rime looked for the stone whisperer, but he had left the crowd. He hoped, for Hlosnian's sake, that Ilume hadn't seen him use the Might that way. It might have saved Hirka, but good reasons went up in smoke when face-to-face with Ilume.

Rime felt the hairs on the back of his neck stand up. He turned around. Ilume stood at the top of the steps to the hall. Her gaze cut through the waiting crowd and locked on him. It was like she was trying to freeze him to death because he had come dressed as a guardsman. In the open, for every idiot to see.

Ilume broke eye contact, turned away, and disappeared into the Seer's hall through the gilded side entrance reserved for her and her servants. And for Rime. Everyone else had to wait outside. Rime took a deep breath. He was done waiting. He had to talk with Ilume, get it over with. He crossed the square in front of the Seer's hall. The crowd parted to let him through. Their eyes raked over his clothes. He could hear them whispering.

Rime sighed. Vanfarinn's death had weakened the Council. Ravnhov was sharpening its claws. The world was on the brink, but was that what people were whispering about? No. They were whispering about him. The heir apparent who'd become a warrior.

Rime entered the Seer's hall. He resisted the temptation to use the same doors as everyone else, going through the door that was intended for his family. Ilume didn't need any more fuel for the fire before this conversation. He shut the door behind him, and the whispering faded away. It was darker and cooler inside. The oil lamps in the ceiling flickered. He could hear Ramoja and Ilume talking in the assembly room. Ramoja sounded upset. Rime walked down the corridor until he could see them through the archways.

Ramoja held out a scroll to Ilume as the raven shifted uneasily on her shoulder. Rime assumed it was the announcement for the Rite that had just been read outside—but then he heard Ilume speak.

"I've given them my no. That's my vote."

"But he's already—"

"It will never happen. Pull yourself together, Ramoja!"

My vote …

They were talking about the empty chair. The Council was in a hurry to fill the place left by Vanfarinn. If they were in enough of a hurry, they might even consider his son, Urd. No wonder Ramoja was upset.

Rime stepped out of the shadows so they could see him. Their conversation ceased at once. Ramoja lowered her gaze.

"I'll wait outside," she said and walked quickly past Rime without meeting his eyes. Her jewelry jingled. The sound disappeared down the corridor and left an oppressive silence. He was alone with his grandmother.

She stood with her chin raised, looking down at him. Quite an achievement considering he was a head taller than her. But it wasn't her size that made Ilume the imposing figure she was.

The raven's enormous wings were spread behind her. The Seer's wings. They curled around the pulpit and formed a sacred space from which the augur could speak to the people. Every single feather had been brought to life by Hlosnian's hands, like brushstrokes in black stone. The beak was half-open as if frozen in a screech. The eyes were shiny and reflected Ilume. A stretched and distorted image that made her arms look longer than her body. She opened her mouth.

"You'd dine with rats if the opportunity presented itself."

She'd obviously seen him with Hirka and Kolgrim out on the square. He'd been friendly, like he was one of them. Forgotten who he was. An accusation that had followed him his entire life. Rime was about to defend himself, but he was interrupted by the augur, who came running in with his palms crossed in the sign of the Raven in front of his gray tunic. His fingers were trembling.

"Ilume-madra, people are waiting for the message to begin. What can I say to—"

"Out!"

Ilume didn't need to look at him. Her voice sent him scurrying back the way he'd come. Rime was tempted to follow him, but both he and Ilume had been waiting a long time for this moment. And she was the one to start.

"You can't even bring yourself to look in on me when you come home."

"You were in Ravnhov when I arrived."

His answer seemed to annoy her even more. Her meeting in Ravnhov clearly hadn't gone well. Not that he had expected it to.

"I was in Ravnhov, trying to keep the kingdoms together. For the Council's sake, and for yours."

Rime stifled a snort. Ilume turned her back on him.

"When you chose the sword after the Rite, I thought it was an act of childish rebellion, to defy me. I said nothing because I trusted your judgment. You are an An-Elderin! I expected you to make the right decision, just as soon as you'd had your bit of fun with those savages."

She spoke in her usual firm tone. Uncompromising. Hard as the stone floor she was standing on. Her hair hung in impeccable silver braids down her back. Only the color belied the fact that she had lived for almost a century. Even there she had an advantage over the people she wouldn't touch: she would live longer than all of them, and her years would leave fewer traces. That's how it was with powerful binders. That's how it would have been with him too. But Rime had freely given up all hope of growing old.

She turned to look at him again. "Your contempt for me knows no bounds. You're willing to renounce the Council, renounce the Seer, and abandon the people just to make a point?!"

He'd never seen her eyes so wild. She had reason to be angry, but he couldn't bring himself to swallow her lies.

"I'm not renouncing the Seer! I am renouncing the Council, to better serve Him. Better than I can do as a sleeping giant in Eisvaldr."

"How dare you?!" She took a step closer, but he didn't budge. "You dare to speak as though you know anything. A pup! A pathetic pup who wants to measure his strength against mine!"

The words bounced between the stone walls. A hollow echo, and for the first time Rime noticed the emptiness of the Seer's hall.

"It's not about you," he said. "It's got nothing to do with you."

Rime felt the liberating truth of his own words. He respected Ilume. She was the head of the family. But he had no love for the kingdoms' most powerful men and women, who had never done anything other than be born with the right name. He himself had been born with the best name imaginable, but his greatest deed had been to turn his back on his birthright.

They stared at each other.

Rime had already made his choice, and he knew that was what pained Ilume most. There was nothing she could do. He'd sworn the Oath. He had blood on his hands. She was powerless. That was new for her, and she didn't wear it well.

"You were to be the youngest," she said. "The youngest ever." Her voice lost some of its force. "You were to be the youngest and the strongest to take the chair in a thousand years."

"You'll have to find someone else."

"Someone else?! We have no one else! Should we let the other families eat us alive? Would you see our family history go up in smoke? Your roots? Thank the Seer my daughter can't see you from eternity!"

Her words spread like poison in his chest. "Then let the people you claim to serve choose their leaders for themselves!" he struck back.

Rime saw the blow coming but made no move to avoid it. He let her strike him. A stinging sensation spread across his cheek. Her eyes bore into him, but he felt nothing but calm. An inexplicable, deep calm.

"I-Ilume-madra," the augur stuttered from the shadows. He didn't dare step into the light coming through the windows. "They're—they're waiting. For the message ..."

Ilume answered him without breaking eye contact with Rime.

"Open the doors."

Not needing to be asked twice, the augur disappeared. The doors were opened, and Rime was annoyed by his sense of relief at not being alone with her any longer. People poured in and filled the benches behind them. Ilume sat on the chair nearest the pulpit, shielded by the wings of the Seer. Rime sat by her side.

He hated attending messages. The Seer was everything to him. All he had. But the messages were a nightmare. Always had been. Sitting motionless, facing everyone else, on show. You'd think it would get easier over the years, but Rime now realized that he'd never been supposed to get used to it. His purpose was completely different. His way of serving the Seer was different.

The augur began to speak. At the same time, Ilume hissed into

Rime's ear, "As a son of the people, you'll soon sink down to their level."

Rime steeled himself against her words.

"I've been invited to Glimmeråsen for dinner this evening," she went on. "It wouldn't be appropriate for me to go, as well they know. They're as insolent as they are power-hungry. But they could be of use. They can plead our case in the north when we've left Elveroa. It would be strategically unwise to turn them down, so you'll go on your own."

Rime stared reluctantly at the front row, where all of Glimmeråsen were sitting. Kaisa nodded and smiled at him. She jabbed her daughter Sylja with her elbow, who jolted in confusion until she realized Rime was looking at her. She gave him a playful smile, and he fought back a shudder.

He whispered to Ilume, "I think the Seer would understand if I didn't go."

"You're not going because the Seer told you to," Ilume hissed. "You're going because *I* told you to."

THE STONE WHISPERER

Hirka stopped to catch her breath at the top of the hill behind the tavern. Her cheeks burned, and there was no point pretending it was because she'd been running. Rime had been back two days. And for two days in a row she'd behaved like an idiot. He'd dragged her away from a fight as if she were a wild dog. And people had laughed. Not that that bothered her.

But they'd crowded around her. A square full of people, staring, as if she were a caged animal. Father would have ruptured something if he'd seen her. And she'd wasted valuable time. The message had started, which meant that now no one would be at home. She would have to wait to make her rounds with the basket.

Hlosnian. Hlosnian will be home by now. He never goes to the Seer's hall.

He'd done something in the square. Shattered the rock in Kolgrim's hand somehow to save her.

Hirka walked back down the hill, crossed the bridge over the Stryfe, and headed up toward Hlosnian's house on the north side. It was a crumbling stone building that had once been an inn. Though it had a lot of rooms, Hlosnian lived alone. If he hadn't made his home there, the building would have fallen into ruin a long time ago. It was as if it stood only because he willed it to.

Hirka followed the narrow trail through the high grass to his door. There was a rusted frame hanging from the corner, but the sign itself with the name of the inn was long gone. Hirka jumped as a raven took flight and disappeared behind the house. It had been sitting so still she'd thought it was a fixture. But a raven was always a good sign.

Unless you're me, that is.

The door was ajar, so she squeezed through. She was reluctant to open it farther just in case the house decided then and there that it was too much effort to remain standing and buried her alive. It was dark, but she'd always liked the dark. She could see everything, but no one could see her.

The windows had been boarded up, the lead glass long since sold to Glimmeråsen. She saw a counter. Two tables. No chairs.

"Hlosnian?"

No response.

Hirka heard a sawing sound and followed it into the next room. Sunlight fell to the floor from large, curved openings in the stone wall. Hlosnian's workshop. He was sitting in the middle of the room, as much outside as in, his body hunched over a stone figure he was shaping. He had his back to her, absorbed in his work.

The room had once been a stable. It was divided into stalls and smelled reassuringly of horse. A pair of dirty fingerless gloves hung from a nail in the wall. She knew he wore them in the winter.

Sculptures and stones were heaped in the corners. Masterpieces of all sizes stacked like firewood. Some were broken, some were still in the early stages. Suspended in stone, waiting to emerge. Everything she could see was covered in white dust.

Most of the sculptures were of trees. She was standing next to a white tree that came up to her chest. The branches looked so alive that she half expected them to move. She reached out to touch them. Carefully.

"You shouldn't be here."

Hirka snatched her arm back. Hlosnian was still sitting with his back to her. The stone dust danced in the shafts of sunlight and settled on his pale red tunic, the only touch of color in the room.

"I don't like going to the messages," she replied. She wasn't afraid of saying this to him since he never went either. She went over to him and he regarded her with one bushy eyebrow raised, as if he hadn't understood her response. His hair and beard were thick and gray with streaks of white, reminding her of the last snow on Gardfjella.

He turned back to his work. Hirka wanted to thank him for his help at the square, but she wasn't really sure what he'd done, if he'd done anything at all. She took a brown glass bottle out of her basket.

"I've brought your oil."

She put it on the bench.

"That's a lot," he said.

"Yes. It's … a gift."

"I see. Don't suppose you've brought the recipe as well?"

Hirka could feel herself blushing. She'd had that same thought. Father would say she was giving away his livelihood, but what else could they do? Walk away from the village and leave people in the lurch? The only other healer in the area was Ilume's, and they'd be leaving soon as well.

"You can make it yourself. It's really very easy. You just need almonds and oats and—"

"I don't have time to make it myself." Hlosnian met her gaze. He had deep creases in his forehead. His eyes were clear and blue. One of his eyelids drooped a bit more than the other. The kids in the village said one side of his face was asleep. Hirka thought it made him look kindly and mysterious.

He opened the bottle and rubbed a couple drops into his hands and up an arm covered in old scars. Hirka didn't know what had caused them, but she knew the oil helped him when the skin felt tight. The horse smell turned to almond as he massaged his arms.

"I don't have time, but I might have to find time, is that right?"

Hirka pretended not to hear the question. "You're very talented," she said, looking around. She picked up a spiral-shaped stone.

"I didn't make that. The Might made that. A long time ago. Before people, almost before the world came to be."

"Oh … you're still talented though."

He snorted in response.

"I've seen what we can make with our hands. I can't call this anything more than a pastime."

He wasn't just being modest. Hirka knew that Hlosnian had made an icon of the Seer for the Seer's hall that people traveled long distances to see, but he himself hadn't set foot there since it was finished. Ramoja said that was the curse of perfectionism.

"What have you seen, then?" she asked.

Hlosnian put down the stone figure. He stared absentmindedly into the dust.

"The tree. The Seer's tree. I saw it once, when I was a stone whisperer in Eisvaldr." Hirka wanted to ask what a stone whisperer actually did, but she didn't want to interrupt. Hlosnian had worked in Eisvaldr! The city at the end of the city. Home of the Seer.

And Rime.

The tree was the Seer's throne. A world tree, wrought of stone. Black and glistening, with branches that reached out and filled the room. An impossible piece of work. He had never seen anything more beautiful. Everything had changed that day. He didn't want to make anything other than that tree. But it was impossible. It had been shaped by old forces. By the Might as it once was. Before the war. Before people.

Hlosnian's eyes were veiled by a pain Hirka couldn't fathom. "What did you do?" she asked. "Did you stop working for the Council?"

"You never stop working for the Council," he replied. He looked at her. "You are what you are. And you are what you do. When the time comes, the best thing you can do is the right thing. The worst thing you can do is nothing."

Hirka looked down, embarrassed. What had she done? Gone after Kolgrim. Like a fool. Hlosnian was right. She was what she was, but she had a choice. She could choose to act differently, and she could choose not to leave.

Hlosnian watched her as he polished the small stone woman he had in his hand.

"Be care—" Hirka exclaimed, but it was too late. A crack appeared and the tail broke off the sculpture. The old man gave a laugh that belied his years.

"Now it's like you." He put the tailless figure in her basket along with the spiral-shaped stone. "Not to worry," he said. "I can always start again. These things happen when you don't pay attention to the stone. You need to listen to it. Always." Then he started mumbling, mostly to himself. "The question is how you could have known ..."

He got up and started rummaging in a drawer in his workbench. He found what he was looking for and handed Hirka a stone disc. Round and no larger than the palm of her hand. It was decorated with pale characters she didn't recognize. She wondered for a moment whether it was another gift, but then Hlosnian knocked her arm, making her drop it. It fell to the floor with a crash and broke into several pieces.

"Sorry! I didn't mean to ..."

But Hlosnian wasn't listening. He crouched down and studied the pieces, all while mumbling to himself. She suddenly felt like an interloper. He'd fallen into some kind of artistic reverie. A rough finger poked at the broken pieces.

"You're not supposed to be here," he said again.

Hirka gripped her basket and started backing cautiously out of the room. He was old. He didn't always know what he was saying anymore.

"I have to go," she said.

"I know," he replied, and he began to polish another stone.

INSRINGIN

Urd paced back and forth along the balcony. He looked up every time he reached the end but didn't cross the bridge leading to the Council Chamber under the dome. The bridge was suspended high above Eisvaldr, with ornately decorated archways that didn't hold his interest today. He simply paced. And waited. Waited, and choked back the bitterness of being forced to wait for a no. Ilume's no.

Luckily, Ilume wasn't the only member of the Council. The ten other councillors also had to cast their votes. Maybe they had *already* cast their votes. A dizzying thought. Urd realized that his fate might already have been decided. Either he was in or he wasn't. Once Ilume's vote arrived, he would know. If only that mangy bag of feathers would get here! How long could it possibly take a raven to make such a trip?!

He'd done another lap and reached the bridge again. He stopped for a moment. Narrow stone bridges connected many of Eisvaldr's towers, but this bridge, Asebriggi, was the oldest of them all. The carvings of ravens and serpents had been almost completely worn away by the elements. The corners were no longer sharp and probably hadn't been for hundreds of years. Round columns supported a vaulted roof, which was more worn on the western side, where the winds came from the mountains in Blindból.

On the other side of the bridge lay the Council Chamber, and there they sat deciding his future. While he was forced to wait out here like a dog!

Urd turned his back on the bridge and started to walk along the balcony again. It was the safest way to prevent his temper from getting the better of him. That couldn't happen now. Fortunately he was an extremely patient man. Probably the most patient man in all of Ym. He had waited a long time. He could wait a little longer. Soon, he would find out if it had been worth it.

Urd shivered. Not because of the wind, though it was howling between the columns, but because of the waiting.

His deceased father had said that a man should never risk more than he could stand to lose, and Urd felt in every inch of his body that he had risked far too much. Absolutely everything. And this was his only chance. If they said no to him today, it was a no for life.

"They say she's already on her way." Slabba's annoying voice interrupted Urd's chain of thought. He'd almost forgotten that the merchant was sitting there. Though *sitting* was the wrong word. In his shapeless embroidered green tunic, it was more like he was *spilling* across the glimmerstone bench.

"Who?"

"Ilume-madra." Slabba pulled out an already damp handkerchief and wiped the sweat off his fingers. Each was weighed down with gold and sparkling with gemstones. It made him look pathetic, like a wealthy old dowager. Urd turned away in disgust, but Slabba continued.

"They say she's cleared out her house and is only days from Mannfalla."

"Who says?"

"I have … contacts," Slabba said, trying to make it sound offhand.

Urd stifled a snort. *You. Contacts.*

Slabba didn't know more than most people, but he was fond of citing a wealth of sources of valuable information. He could be useful sometimes, but as far as Urd's ambitions were concerned, the merchant might as well be deaf and blind. A fat fly in the web, with delusions of being the spider.

Idiot.

"What do we do when she's back?" Slabba's throaty voice grew less assured. He was scared of Ilume. It was infuriating.

"I'll tell you what we do: we enjoy the moment. She's back! And *why* is she back, my friend?" Urd felt the last word stick in his throat, but he smiled for all he was worth. He leaned toward Slabba's face, as close as he could stomach, while Slabba's eyes darted back and forth in bewilderment. He didn't have a good answer. But Urd did.

"She's back because she failed. Ilume failed! After years working on Ravnhov, she's done nothing more than make them stronger. Has she opened any Seer's halls there? Has she gained any political ground? On the contrary! Ravnhov is stronger and more obstinate than ever!" Urd flung his arms out, enjoying his own words. He was rarely granted the privilege of being able to say precisely what he thought, even to Slabba.

Slabba began to wheeze with laughter, like bellows fit to burst, and Urd continued.

"What's more, she has succeeded in breaking down the only thing Mannfalla and Ravnhov have in common. The Rite! Because do you know what *my* contacts say?" Urd lowered his voice to a theatrical whisper, and Slabba's eyes grew greedy.

"They say several families in Ravnhov are planning to forgo the Rite this year. A clear display of animosity. A declaration of war!" Urd sneered.

"Yes, I've heard that too," Slabba said, clearly lying. But Urd wasn't finished.

"Ilume is weak. Her house is dying. Her grandchild is throwing his life away playing with swords. A guardsman! The boy could have her seat this very moment, and with the people's blessing! Can you imagine how that news must have broken her? And now she's returning to Mannfalla with her tail between her legs, having failed to bring Ravnhov into line. Slabba, I can promise you, Ilume has better things to do than put a spoke in our wheel."

Urd heard the sound of shoes clacking on stone. Brisk strides. A messenger rushed past them without paying them any heed. An ivory sleeve was just visible in his clenched fist. Urd didn't let it out of his sight until the runner disappeared across the bridge and inside the red dome.

The small tube contained Ilume's resounding no. He was sure of it. No, she didn't want him to take his father's place. No, she couldn't see that he belonged on the Council. No. No. No. But if he already had six votes, it wouldn't make a difference.

Urd felt himself getting dizzy. He grabbed his neck and turned away from Slabba. His throat was hurting again. He tasted blood and bent his head back to swallow it.

Think about something else.

Before him lay Eisvaldr in all its glory. A wealthy pocket within an even larger city—Mannfalla. White walls marked the dividing line between the home of the Seer and the rest of the city. Outside the walls was a different reality. From up here it looked clean and calm, but Urd knew that people were living miserably mediocre lives out there. They worked, sweat, ate, slept, and lay with one another. The streets stunk of horse manure, because out there, there was less concern about keeping things clean. Especially now, with the Rite approaching and everyone in the world arriving, some with children and animals in tow. The poorest areas of the city were enough to make you nauseous. The stench was one thing, the din was another. And this year it was worse than ever.

But Urd was high above them all. If the Seer had merely a fraction of his supposed power, He would have to hear this prayer. Urd realized that he had closed his eyes. He could hear Slabba talking behind him. Talking about the heat, even though the clouds above the city were heavy with rain. Talking as though Urd's life didn't depend on what was soon to come.

Heavy doors opened on the far side of the bridge. They were preposterously large compared with the figure who emerged: the Ravenbearer. Eir-madra. The woman who bore the Seer.

Now she stood alone, with no staff and no raven. The most powerful woman on the Council. The most powerful woman in Ym. The wind whipped at her pale robe. The mark of the raven on her forehead was so dark it was like a window into her mind. It was also embroidered over her left breast. Seer in mind, Seer in body.

"Urd Vanfarinn?" She said his name as though she didn't already know it was him.

"Yes." Urd felt the pain tear at his throat, but he managed to keep his voice steady. He'd had plenty of practice. She lowered her hood in a slow movement.

"Welcome to Insringin."

Urd felt a strange stinging in his eyes. It took him a moment to realize that tears had formed. Eir hadn't seen them. She'd already turned around and was on her way back into the Council Chamber. He heard Slabba's congratulations from somewhere behind him but couldn't distinguish one word from the next. Insignificant noise from an insignificant man in a different world entirely.

Urd set one foot in front of the other, taking his first step as a councillor, and at last, he crossed the bridge.

FORTUNE SEEKERS

The meat on his plate was cold. Every time Rime tried to take a bite, he had to stop before his fork reached his mouth, either to answer a question or just to smile politely at something someone had said. And they had plenty to say. But he supposed he hadn't really been invited to Glimmeråsen to eat.

Kaisa was reeling off truisms she thought he wanted to hear. Such as how outrageous it was that Ravnhov was sabotaging the unification of the eleven kingdoms. How ridiculous it was that the barbarians there were allowed to maintain an archaic chiefdom, remnants of a kingdom.

Rime had no trouble understanding Ravnhov's opposition. If the other parts of Ym were as strong as Ravnhov, they'd have been independent as well. Greed and fear were all that bound any of them to Mannfalla. But Rime said nothing. He was used to not taking things that had little to do with him personally. People just wanted to be closer to his name. Closer to the power in Mannfalla.

Sylja hadn't taken her eyes off him, unless it was to lower her gaze in a show of false modesty, or to engage in a silent dialogue with her mother. Rime glanced at Vidar, but Sylja's father was about as talkative as the paintings on the wall—a passive pawn in the evening's game, despite the fact the farm was his. Kaisa had married into a wealth that she now managed as if she'd been born for it. When Rime tried to ask Vidar about the farm, Kaisa broke in.

"Let's not bore Rime, Vidar. He has more on his mind than our insignificant problems." She smiled icily and handed her husband a linen napkin. His face was clean, but he wiped himself off nevertheless. He didn't speak another word.

"Tell us about Ilume-madra instead," Kaisa continued. "We're so sorry to hear that she has to leave Elveroa."

Rime was sure she was even sorrier that Ilume wasn't here this evening. He reassured Kaisa once more that Ilume would have liked to come but that it hadn't been possible. There was a brief pause while Kaisa clearly tried to work out what could be more important than visiting Glimmeråsen. Rime took the opportunity to have a bite of his veal. They'd spared no expense this evening.

The room bore witness to the family's fortune. The southern wall was covered by a long tapestry from Andrakar depicting the Seer with outspread wings. Many of the ornaments were somewhat out of place for a dining room. Rime suspected that Kaisa had filled the room with anything remotely valuable. What she hadn't found space for in the room, she'd hung around her and her daughter's necks.

Sylja gave him an expectant smile. Had she asked him a question?

"Sorry?" Rime asked, hoping it wasn't clear how badly he wanted to go home.

Kaisa laughed and rolled her eyes. "Oh dear, you really must forgive my daughter, Rime. She can be refreshingly direct."

"Mother! I just want to know how good my chances are!" Sylja pushed her plate away and leaned over her arm so that her breasts were pushed up. Rime needed no explanation. This was about the Rite. He'd been expecting the question. Everyone with children who turned fifteen this year had asked him exactly the same, despite him spending his days up on Vargtind, as far away from people as he could get. No matter how scarce he tried to make himself, they stopped him in the village square. Offered him gifts he politely declined. Asked him to touch them. Asked for the Seer's blessing. And all of them wanted the same thing: to know what they could do to improve their children's chance of being chosen to become a servant of the Council.

Rime couldn't blame them for asking. He was well aware that he had been born without many of the concerns that others struggled with. People in Foggard lived from hand to mouth. A life serving the Council had to seem like a life without care to them. Food, clothes, a roof over their heads. People in Eisvaldr were excused from everyday troubles so they could focus on what was important.

But the Rite was what it was. The Seer chose, they said, even though Rime knew that wasn't the whole truth. The Seer transcended everyday life. He didn't concern himself with practical things such as the Rite. Or other trivial matters. And that was the source of all Rime's ire, the reason for his choice. The Seer's elevated position was for inspiration, but it was also the reason corruption was able to permeate His halls. Friends gave positions to friends. Young hopefuls entered Eisvaldr's schools in exchange for coin. Rime neither could nor would help anyone into such a viper's nest.

He pushed his chair away from the table and stood up. "It's getting dark. I hope you'll excuse me. Thank you for your hospitality this evening."

Kaisa was instantly on her feet and moving toward him. She put a hand on his back and tried to usher him into an adjoining room. "My dear, you simply must stay for a slice of cake!" She had strong arms for someone so slight.

But Rime stood his ground. "I appreciate the offer, but my place forbids me."

Sylja got up. "Mother, he's a guardsman! They don't eat cake." She looked at him and he nodded in agreement.

Kaisa raised an eyebrow. "No cake?"

Rime smiled. "Regrettably not."

He nodded to Vidar, who opened his mouth to say something but ended up wiping his face with his napkin again. Rime headed for the door, painfully aware of the frantic whispering behind him. Then Sylja was suddenly at his side. She lifted her skirts slightly and slipped her shoes on.

"It's a lovely evening, Rime. I'll accompany you part of the way."

Outside, the air was cool and liberating. The valley dozed as the sun sank down behind the mountains. Sylja talked about Mannfalla and about how nice it must be to live where everything happened. She asked whether he was looking forward to getting back but didn't stop talking long enough to let him answer.

Glimmeråsen disappeared behind them. Sylja stumbled slightly and gripped his arm. She gave him an apologetic smile. "A rock." She didn't let go again. Her nails were painted red, as was the fashion in Mannfalla.

Daudtarn lay still and black, its surface like an eye in the forest. The cliffs rose up on the eastern bank, and Rime could hear the Stryfe babbling somewhere in the distance.

"The children say it's bottomless." Sylja stopped.

"Everywhere has a lake people say is bottomless," he replied.

"Imagine if I fell in!" She gripped his arm tighter, but she sounded more eager than afraid. "Imagine if I fell in before I'd truly lived."

Rime could feel his irritation growing. He'd had enough of this charade and very much felt it was time for him to take his leave.

"At least you're better off than most people," he said, trying to walk on.

Sylja snaked her way around him so that her face was inches from his own.

"Not like you, Rime." There was a hunger in her voice. "If I were able to live like you, I could make a difference."

Rime took a step back from her warm body.

"You can make a difference wherever you are, Sylja." He took a couple steps back, but she grabbed him.

"I just want to serve the Seer!" Her eyes darted around as if she were looking for a way into him.

He was running out of patience. It had been a long evening. "If He needs you, Sylja, He'll choose you during the Rite. You have nothing to fear." He started walking again.

"But I'm scared, Rime!"

He stopped. She smiled and came toward him again. "I'm scared I'll do something wrong. The Seer chose you, Rime. I know you can help me." He could feel her breath against his throat with every word she spoke. "If you help me, Rime …" She lifted his hand and pressed it to her chest. "I'd be so grateful, endlessly grateful. Always …"

She started moving his hand down toward her breast. Rime felt his body react and tore his hand away. He backed away and stared at the creature before him. "You're fifteen summers old! You haven't even been through the Rite, girl."

She laughed indulgently, like her mother had been doing all evening. "If you're scared of breaking me, you've nothing to fear, Rime An-Elderin. I may only be fifteen, but I'm not naive."

Rime felt dirty and used. All she wanted was to be chosen during the Rite. Was there no one who looked on him as a man? Just a man. Not a door to another world. Was there nothing pure and good, apart from the Seer?

"I know what you want, Rime. And I can give it to you. If you give me what I want …" She twisted a lock of hair around her finger.

"What? What is it you want?!" He took a step toward her. "To serve the Seer? Is that all you want?" He jabbed his finger at her, and she took a step back.

"You want to be a custodian? A stone whisperer? Do you want to be one of those people who spends their entire lives listening to stone? Listening for screams from Slokna? Cries from the blind?" He hardly recognized his own voice. An unfamiliar snarl.

"I've seen people with scars all over their bodies! I've seen grown men peel off their own skin to stave off the dreams. Is that what you want, girl? Or perhaps you want to be a warrior? Do you want to sit there, endlessly honing your sword while you wait for an order to attack friends and brothers in Ravnhov? Do you want to stab a man in the gut and feel the heat of his blood on your hands?"

Her bottom lip quivered. It was infuriating. After three years of training, was this all he was good for? Losing his self-control in front of a girl who didn't know better? Rime covered his face with his hand. He stood there for a moment listening to the river in the distance. When he looked up again, Sylja was standing there sniffling. He couldn't see any tears, so he started to walk away.

She shouted after him. "You can't just leave me here!"

He knew she meant more than just there next to Daudtarn. But it didn't matter. He would leave them all.

A SETBACK

The sun never came up. The clouds descended in the sky above Elveroa, and the air promised rain. Hirka tried to shake off the remnants of last night's quarrel with Father as she walked down the ridge toward the Stryfe.

After paying her visit to Hlosnian, she'd tried to make Father understand how the people of Elveroa depended on them. What would they do if the two of them moved? But Father had no sympathy for people who treated them like dogs right up to the moment they needed help with a rash on their knob or wanted to smoke themselves into oblivion on opa.

He'd said the same things in the past, but without sounding like he had given up. He'd laughed at how people avoided him until they had no other choice than to beg for his help. It hadn't mattered then. Maybe because they could always leave again? Maybe deep down he'd always hoped the next place would be better? Then they'd find somewhere that felt right for them?

Everything changed after the accident. Father was bound to his chair. But now he was planning to leave anyway. Because of what she was. A monster who had to be kept away from people.

Hirka had tried to find all the reasons to stay in Elveroa, without mentioning his wheeled chair. She'd claimed she could learn to bind, and Father had said that a stool had a better memory than her. He'd tried to teach her before, had she forgotten?

Hirka hadn't forgotten. She wanted to try again. For a moment Father had almost looked hopeful while she sat on the grass attempting to visualize the earth's life force, exactly the way he had told her to. Imagining the Might as its lifeblood, trying to draw it toward her.

But the earth wouldn't share its blood with her. Because she didn't belong here.

Still she had tried. Until her jaws practically locked, until she forgot to breathe. But to no avail. Father had begged her to be careful, as if she were an egg that might crack. She'd asked what it was supposed to feel like when you bound. And he'd replied: "Like you're no longer alone."

But she was alone. In every way. All she had was Father.

That was when she'd realized what she needed to do.

Father was not a strong binder. He was an ordinary man. There had never been blue blood in his veins. Hirka needed someone who was good at binding. Someone familiar with the Might. But most importantly, she needed someone who wasn't afraid to let her learn, even if it meant a few scrapes along the way. Someone who wouldn't treat her like she might break.

She needed Rime.

Hirka wasn't sure how best to explain it to him, so she settled on a white lie. She would tell Rime that she could bind—of course she could—just not very well. And that she was scared that it wouldn't be good enough for the Rite. It wouldn't be easy lying to him, but what else could she do?

She came to a stop. Spread out before her was the row of trees leading to Ilume's house. Hirka wasn't sure anyone in Elveroa had been inside the magnificent building. Even the servants had been brought from Eisvaldr.

What if his grandmother answered the door? Would Ilume realize that something was wrong? *Will she know what I am when she sees me?*

Hirka got annoyed with herself. She'd met Ilume lots of times. Why would she suddenly see something other than the same tailless girl?

I'm the only one who knows I'm different.

Hirka gritted her teeth and started walking again. She shrunk to insignificance between the old maple trees. The house grew in front of her, imposing and impregnable. The stone building appeared almost black in the wet weather. What would happen to the house now that Ilume was leaving? It was the only building in Elveroa with a tower. The round tower at the western end—the one with all the stained-glass windows—accounted for almost a third of its size.

Hirka had heard that the whole house would fit *inside* one of the rooms of the family home in Mannfalla. But Sylja had told her that, so there was no knowing how true it was.

Hirka walked past the stable and two enormous six-wheeled carriages with hide canopies. Both were partly loaded with boxes and sacks. They had already started the move. Outside the house were several trunks and large pieces of wooden furniture. Hirka jumped when she suddenly caught sight of herself. A mirror. She'd seen them before, but they'd been small. This mirror was taller than she was, and crystal clear. Hirka had never seen herself so distinctly. Her hair looked like a red haystack. Her clothes needed mending again. Her green woollen tunic was practically hanging by the threads. One of the knees of her trousers was worn thin. The other was torn. She looked like a small wood troll, opulently framed in flourishes of gold.

Hirka smiled at the contrast. The smile faded when she suddenly saw a figure in the mirror. Ilume An-Elderin was standing behind her. The black symbol on her forehead was like a third eye—the mark of the Seer, the Council's black raven—which immediately told the outside world exactly who they were looking at.

Startled, Hirka took a step back from the mirror. It was a misjudged instinct, because she backed into Ilume. She turned and tried to say sorry, but her throat was too dry. Hirka had to remind herself that she hadn't done anything wrong. She had nothing to hide.

I have everything to hide.

Ilume was barely a hand taller than her, but in a strange way she filled the entire courtyard. It was like the earth they were standing on and the old woman were the same age. Hirka had heard that powerful binders could become one with the earth. Become part of eternity. Maybe that was why it always went quiet just before Ilume arrived, like something else preceded her. Something you couldn't see.

Ilume's arms were folded across her chest. Her gray hair was brushed back and gathered beneath a tight hood, apart from two thin braids that hung from her temples and nearly to her waist. She had narrow, light gray eyes, a similar color to Rime's. But unlike the eyes of most older people, these were razor-sharp. Hirka could feel them in the pit of her stomach. Like Ilume could see right through her. Quietly searching, like an owl on the hunt.

Her tunic gleamed in the light, like fine paper, tapering in at the waist before dividing to reveal another layer of fabric beneath, woven with a different technique. Her tail came into view behind her, also different than most older people's. It hadn't become shaggy or lost its luster. The lower part was adorned with a sand-colored ribbon, tied in a herringbone pattern. The hair at its tip was still dark. It was oiled and neatly trimmed. Hirka grew extremely conscious of the fact that she didn't have a tail of her own. But like everyone else, Ilume knew the story about the wolves. Hopefully she no longer thought about Hirka's obvious imperfection. Not even now, face-to-face.

The Council and the rot.

Hirka looked up, trying to avoid staring at the black raven on her forehead, but it was impossible not to. It felt like the mark was looking right back at her. She couldn't help but feel like there were more than just the two of them present.

"Hirka," Ilume said, after what felt like an eternity. Judging by her voice, she was neither surprised to see her there nor curious about why.

Hirka swallowed her uncertainty and got straight to the point. "Ilume-madra." She bowed before continuing. "I'm looking for Rim … Són-Rime."

The old woman cocked her head, the way Rime often did, and looked her up and down. What was she thinking? Why wasn't she answering? Hirka closed her eyes for a moment so they wouldn't waver and reveal how nervous she was.

"Rime is out. He has much to prepare before our journey."

Hirka got the message behind her words.

He doesn't have time for me.

But he *had* to have time! Her future depended on him having time.

"Do you know where I can find him?"

What am I doing?! She's said what she has to say. Leave! Before it's too late.

Ilume's gaze grew sharper. Hirka felt her knees twitch, as though they were about to run away without her. She felt bare to the bone. But the old woman still looked unmoved. "He will be told you're looking for him."

Hirka dared not press her luck further. She thanked the older woman and left. Forcing herself to maintain a normal speed, she walked through the row of green trees. It felt like they were mocking her with their rustling leaves.

Stupid girl, what did you expect?

Hirka had been fobbed off. Very politely, but fobbed off nonetheless. Ilume had never appreciated Rime spending time with other children. Apparently, that hadn't changed. Hirka wasn't surprised. And she had no intention of taking the hint.

She paused by the Stryfe, looking at the village. Rime could be anywhere. Maybe he was at Ynna's having some clothes tailored for the journey? Or maybe he was overseeing the packing? Inspecting the carriage wheels? Mannfalla was days from Elveroa by carriage. If you had to prepare for such a long trip, where else might you go?

Where had he been since he came home? Her gaze followed the ridge until it reached the mountains. Then she smiled.

The peaks of Vargtind stretched up to the clouds, looming over Elveroa. It was a steep slope, but manageable, as long as your lungs held out. It was only the vertical western face that was virtually impossible to climb, though Hirka had managed it once. Today she contented herself with taking the path, which was hardly more than a faint line worn into the mountain.

Near the top, she carefully clambered over some vengethorn. If she cut herself on the jagged barbs, her body would be stinging for days. It was something she had experienced once, and once was enough. The bushes tore at her clothes. She searched in vain for thornless patches. The dry branches cracked beneath her, having spent the entire summer under the scorching sun. But she had reached the peak.

Hirka suddenly felt like she should announce herself. She looked up. Vargtind rose up like the jaws of a wolf against the colorless sky. Jagged and ferocious, it snarled at those who dared approach. But if you conquered the beast, you could rest in a lovely, grassy hollow, surrounded by sharp stone teeth. Hirka had spent many of her childhood hours here, wandering among the ruins of the old castle, on the hunt for forgotten stories and treasures. Old Annar claimed that Varg was the name of the man who had built the castle, and that was why it was called Vargtind. But no one knew for certain anymore.

Hirka clambered up over the final edge and eased herself down into the hollow.

And there was Rime. Standing right in front of her.

The pale sky was almost the same color as his hair and the tunic that stretched down to the middle of his thighs. The double sword belt made his waist look narrower and his shoulders broader. Hirka didn't need to look to know that there was a black raven embroidered just over his heart. Sweat glistened on his forehead.

Has he been running? Here?

He was standing with his arms crossed, as though watching an intruder. Hirka felt like she had lost a place that had always been hers. Now she had to explain why she was there.

"You weren't home."

His pales eyes sharpened. He had inherited a lot from Ilume.

"Someone told you I was *here*?" There was a note of surprise in his husky voice. She found herself longing to hear more.

"No, I …" She fought back the urge to lower her gaze. "I figured you might be here."

He coughed and looked at her skeptically. As though she were a child again, trying to talk her way out of something. Hirka pointed at the Alldjup.

"You were there when Vetle and I fell. Either you just happened to be walking by, or you must have seen us from somewhere."

He raised an eyebrow and she continued to fumble for words.

"But you didn't just happen to be walking by, because you'd seen that Kolgrim was the one who got Vetle to go out on that spruce." Hirka could feel herself getting nervous and spoke faster and faster. "So you must have been somewhere where you could see everything, but somewhere that still took a while to reach us."

In the past, she would have felt really smug about working it out. Why did she no longer feel the same? "I think," she concluded lamely.

Was that a smile? He turned away too quickly for her to tell. "What do you want?"

Hirka was gobsmacked. She hadn't expected that question. She had imagined a normal conversation. Nice to see you again, or something like that. Maybe talk about what he had been doing in the capital these past few years. And then—when the opportunity arose—she would ask him for help. But it hadn't gone that way. Neither Rime nor his grandmother wanted to talk with her. She couldn't blame them. They were important people, both of them. They had bigger fish to fry.

She didn't want to ask for his help. He didn't deserve any more points. She knew it was a childish thought, but it meant something to her. He'd always enjoyed showing her that she couldn't manage on her own, and she was loath to prove him right.

But he's my only chance.

"I wanted to ask you about the Rite." She stared at his broad back and hoped he would turn around again. He didn't.

Hirka felt cold inside. But she couldn't stop now. "I ... need to know the way things are."

"What things?"

How was she supposed to answer? What could she say? Hirka could feel her determination waning, and that was only after a couple of words. She needed help but couldn't say it. Of all the people in the world, she couldn't tell Rime. He was only a few steps away from her. But between them was a mountain she couldn't see any way over. He belonged to a different world. And their competition for points had built what now felt like a wall of pride. Even if she managed to get over these obstacles, what was she going to do next? Tell him she was a monster?

Her entire life had been about surviving, about getting by on her own everywhere they had lived. She didn't need help! She wasn't the sort of ymling to give up.

The sort of embling.

The problem was that she needed Rime to prove that to the rest of the world.

"I think I need … some advice on the Might. It's not long till the Rite now, and …"

"I know. We've got a lot to do before the Rite."

Hirka bit her lower lip. *Foolish girl, he doesn't have time for you.*

Why couldn't he just show her how to bind?! After all, he understood it better than most. It probably wouldn't take him more than a second.

"I don't think I have enough of a handle on the Might. I'm worried I won't be able to do enough. That—"

"Of course it'll be enough." He turned around, visibly irritated. "It isn't a competition. Everyone can do it. On the rare occasion the Might isn't strong enough in someone, they just come back the next year. A lot of people from Brekka are unearthed until they're ten, twelve years old." He looked at her. His lips were curled up like he was feeling nauseous. "Is that why you're here?"

Hirka felt panic spreading through her body. She took a step toward him.

"No! No, that's not it." But Rime walked across the grass, right past without looking at her.

"I just need a little help so—"

He spun around and cut her off. "So you can be chosen? Do you think you're the first one to ask?" His eyes were blazing. "Don't you think everyone has already asked me? Sylja won't *stop* asking!"

Sylja? Hirka searched for words but couldn't find any. Had Sylja asked for help to be chosen? Had she asked Rime to speak to Ilume? To put in a good word for her with the Seer? Why would she bother?

The Seer always chose them personally, usually opting for those with blue blood in their veins.

Rime didn't wait for her to answer. He started down the mountainside. Everything he thought of her was wrong, but she couldn't tell him the truth either.

Hirka could feel a scream brewing in her belly. "I don't want to be chosen! I just want to be able to bind!"

Rime's voice grew more and more distant as he walked away. "Oh, really. Everybody can do that. I've got better things to spend my time on."

Hirka turned and looked down the slope. "It's not like that," she whispered. He couldn't hear her. She couldn't even see him. She blinked feverishly, staring upward to hold back the tears. The same trick that had worked for fifteen years. The sky had grown darker. She heard a raven calling in the distance. Probably the same raven she'd seen earlier, and near the Alldjup. A magnificent, sacred bird beguiled by a single piece of cheese from an overturned basket.

It was going to rain. She'd failed. Hirka stood with her eyes shut and waited until she felt the first raindrops on her face.

SECRETS

"The library."

Eir had borne the raven as long as Urd could remember. She had to know Eisvaldr like the back of her hand, but all the same he could hear the awe in her voice.

"The library," he echoed through clenched teeth in an effort to conceal his impatience. This was it. This was everything he'd fought for. So of course it was the last thing the old bat showed him.

They'd been walking all afternoon, since the clock struck two. Through archives, gardens, historical museums, schools and halls, until his feet ached more than the fresh mark in his forehead. The raven. It burned like a third eye above the bridge of his nose. Sweet, sweet pain. He had the mark in his forehead. He was a councillor. *Urd-fadri.* He smiled.

Now, Eir led him across the shiny stone floor. Her footsteps echoed up through the space before fading. The library was in one of Eisvaldr's oldest towers. It was so large that it wasn't immediately apparent that the room was round. A column reaching into the sky. And wherever you looked there were books, scrolls, texts, papers … information. Shelf upon shelf. Box upon box. Small books and books so large that even two men working together would have struggled to open them. Books bound in woven silk, leather, wood. Books with covers made of solid gold and silver. Records of everything that had ever happened. Of everything that was happening, and probably even things that were yet to happen. The room smelled of leather. And power. This was how power was supposed to smell. Eternal. Immortal. Infinite.

Silent, gray-clad women and men, like wandering shadows, carried stacks of books, wrote, or tidied. They went up and down the book-lined staircases, of which there were four, one at each cardinal point. Countless dark ladders on rails served as shortcuts for the more experienced among them.

Urd watched a woman springing up several rungs at a time as her ladder sailed along the curved wall. When she reached the next floor, she grabbed another ladder and used her momentum and body weight to get that moving as well. In this way, she moved between floors with a speed and precision that could only have come from living her entire life in this tower. The occasional rumbling of the ladder rails interrupted the constant scratching of writing implements from hundreds of scribes.

Eir stopped and turned to face him. He stared at the Council robe she was wearing, several layers of different fabrics, all white and with the traditional tabard. The only break in all the white was the black trim along the seams at the front and on the hood, framing Eir's face.

For a moment, his jealousy left a familiar bitterness in his mouth, but then he remembered he was wearing the exact same robe. His father's. It was a good length on him, but a little too wide. It would have to be taken in at the sides, but the measurements had already been taken. By morning, the Seer's best seamstress would make it his and no one else's.

Eir stared at him with her owlish eyes. He still hadn't gotten used to them, even after spending the entire day with her. They made him feel itchy all over, just like Ilume's, and he knew he had to be careful about what he said. The two women were allies, thick as thieves. But they were like night and day to look at, even though they were both over three-quarters of a century old. Eir's eyes and face were round, and her skin was loose and brown, whereas Ilume's was smooth and pale. It was plain to see that Eir was from Blossa in the east, and her family was named for Kobb, a simple hunting community where people ate whale blubber and moved from place to place in tents. Urd didn't know why they hadn't adopted a name better suited to their standing hundreds of years ago. It had to be embarrassing for one of the world's most powerful women to have nomads in her family tree.

"If someone's written it down, it's here in the library," Eir said. "Here you can find everything we are, everything we do, and everything we've ever done. Every decision we've ever made has been written down. How every family has voted and how their predecessors voted. All the way back to the war with the blind. We have no secrets from one another."

Urd suppressed a snort. He had to give her credit for keeping a straight face.

"You're the youngest councillor in a very long time," she continued. "It has to have been four generations since we've had someone less than forty winters old." He was irritated by the absence of respect in her voice. She just stated it as a matter of fact. "And you came in with the narrowest margin I've seen in my lifetime. Your father was a great man. You have a lot to learn."

Urd felt his face fall, but he recovered quickly. She was testing him. She wanted to see how he would react. But still … he was a councillor. How dare she. He'd make her pay. One day, when she least expected it.

"I'm glad not everyone sees it that way," he replied as calmly as he could.

She continued as if he hadn't spoken. "I voted against you."

For a moment he admired her honesty, but then he remembered what she'd just said. That everyone's votes were recorded in this room. He'd have found out anyway, and she knew that.

"But here you are." She turned her back on him and continued through the library. "I hope I was wrong about you. Only time will tell."

They went up several floors, out onto a balcony, and crossed a bridge to the next tower. And the next. And the next. The sky was dark and forbidding. Rain was imminent, and it was cold that high up.

Eir opened a door into the next tower, and they entered a dark hall. Urd hid his astonishment at seeing several other councillors there. All of them had their hoods pulled forward over their heads, as if performing some sort of ritual. Urd felt his hand twitch, but he resisted the urge to raise it to his throat. The collar was in place. It always was. No one could see or know anything. He had to learn to relax. To have more confidence in himself. After all, he was the most powerful man in the world.

Eir ushered him toward a chair in the middle of the room. A disappointingly ordinary wooden chair with a spindly back. Something you might find in a servant's room.

"The Council protects the people from dangerous truths, Urd-fadri," Eir said. "Truths that would burn all bridges. And how you tackle these truths will determine whether you can live as one of us."

Urd sat down and looked up. A portcullis made of black fireglass hung above him. The points gleamed in the light from the oil lamps. He supposed if he said the wrong thing, they'd just drop it on him.

Or would they kill him anyway? Perhaps they knew everything.

No, of course not. They'd never have let him in.

"But I'm sure you have nothing to worry about," Eir said. "Only two people have ever fallen at this stage in proceedings. They lost their minds."

Urd didn't dignify her with a response.

The sky was black and dismal. Urd managed to stumble his way down the steps outside the tower, but then he had to stop and clutch at a balustrade like a drunkard. He leaned forward to quell the nausea, unsuccessfully. The rain poured down into the empty streets far below.

His clothes grew heavy as they took on water. The rain streamed from his hair down over his face. It plummeted from the sky and hit the balcony in a regular, merciless rhythm.

Urd squeezed his eyes shut to lock out the truths—and the lies—he had just heard. He was a strong man. He had grown up here, had seen and heard unbelievable things. He had no illusions about Insringin. He was also a practical man. He had a better understanding of the political game than most. He *was* the political game, for Seer's sake! But this …

He raised a hand to his throat. Tasted blood from a wound no one could see, and no one could heal. Ever. But that wouldn't stop him. Ordinary people let all sorts of things get in their way, but Urd wasn't an ordinary man. He was exceptional. Hadn't he got exactly where he wanted to be? Hadn't he succeeded in everything he'd done? Didn't everything he touch turn to gold? And now he was one of them. Urd had nothing to fear anymore.

The rain eased off slightly. Still a little unsteady on his feet, he continued down the steps. Somewhere in the mountains behind Eisvaldr, a raven cawed three times, as if in protest at the weather. The world was boundless and his for the taking. No one else's. This was going to be ridiculously easy. If only he'd known.

Father knew.

His father had lived with this knowledge since he had taken his seat on the Council at the age of fifty. All those years, and not a word. Urd pictured his bedridden father's face. Pale and sickly but still unwilling to let go. But he'd had to let go in the end. He'd drawn his final breath while staring at Urd. Not in fear, but in disgust.

But who had won? Who was the only one able to look back in disgust now? Spurn had possessed the knowledge, but he'd never used it for anything. He'd never pushed the limits. Weak. Fawning over a system older than time itself.

Urd crossed Seer's Square. With the Rite coming up, it was full of flowers and offerings from all over the world. Some people had written prayers on flags or ribbons, and others had engraved them in stone. Tokens of good luck. Prayers to the Seer from small people with even smaller problems. Illness, money, love …

Urd started to laugh. He pulled his hood up and went through the closest opening in the imposing wall for which Eisvaldr was named. A wall of white stone, built a thousand years ago as a safeguard against the blind. The Seer's best warriors had marched into Blindból to stop them, but the people were afraid. They built the wall after the warriors had gone. Shut out the first twelve. Sacrificed the bravest among them to save themselves. But the warriors had survived. Won. With the Seer's help, they had saved every man and woman, and they formed the first Council. Or so the story went.

The wall had been impenetrable when it was built. Nowadays it was riddled with archways, like a multilevel bridge from one end of Eisvaldr to the other. Nothing more than an impressive, symbolic partition separating Eisvaldr from the rest of Mannfalla. A gateway from the ordinary to the extraordinary. From poor to rich. From filthy to hallowed.

Urd pulled his cloak more tightly around him so he wouldn't be recognized by the guardsmen on the gate. Members of Insringin rarely left Eisvaldr unaccompanied. He hurried through the streets. The squalor worsened the farther east he went. He hid his face the few times he passed someone. He couldn't be seen where he was going. Not as Urd-fadri. Most of the people he encountered were drunks who had tucked themselves beneath whatever shelter they could find. Or people ranting in foreign languages. People who were here for the Rite but didn't have money for lodgings.

A young girl suddenly appeared out of the darkness, startling him. She stepped in front of him and looked him over with hungry eyes. "I have warmth to share, stranger," she said, bringing a dirty hand to his hood.

He twisted his head to the side and pushed her away. Bloody whores! They didn't know what was good for them. Could he be sure she hadn't seen his face? He'd have to worry about that later.

He pressed on through narrow alleyways until he found the place he was looking for. He opened the door and went down the stairs. Heat and sickly sweet smoke hit him like a wall. And music. Seductive rhythms from drums and harps. It was always packed here, but the rain had drawn in even more men than usual. It was the day of rest tomorrow, so people were huddled around tables drinking as they gawped with half-open mouths at two of the girls who were dancing on the stage. He didn't have to look at them to know that neither was Damayanti. Damayanti always danced alone.

Urd crossed the room without looking at anyone. He went up the stairs to the side of the stage and knocked on the red door on the second floor. He went in without waiting for a response.

Damayanti sat with her naked back to him. He met her eyes in the mirror. She gestured almost imperceptibly with her hand and the two girls attending her left the room through a rattling curtain of black beads.

Now Urd and Damayanti were alone. But the room still felt full. It was the smells that did it. Sweet, spicy. Almost nauseating. Some new, others so old they had probably settled in thick layers over the oil lamps.

Damayanti glued one last gemstone to her face. There were lots of them, in several colors. They framed her eyes, which were rimmed with kohl. She looked pleased with the result. Urd sat by the fire in a spacious chair, his fingers tented in front of him as if he had all the time in the world.

She got up and crossed the room, then slid herself down in front of him onto a bed swathed in velvet. She lay on her side with a round cushion under her arm. Jewels wound their way around her brown body like gleaming scales, sparkling when she moved. They licked their way down her throat, only just covering her nipples, filling her navel and winding around her hips, from which a sheer skirt hung. A shadowy triangle teased from behind the fiery yellow fabric.

Damayanti was probably the most beautiful woman he had ever met, but unfortunately, they were too alike. So much so that she also preferred women. But she knew he desired her. And she delighted in it. Every evening she danced with only one aim in mind: driving men wild. It wasn't difficult. She was a legend. People who could afford it came from all over the world to see her perform.

If they'd known where her talent came from, they'd have burned her instead. Urd was smarter than most people. He knew blind-craft when he saw it. Damayanti had no physical limitations. She only limited herself because she had to. A balancing act. Legendary talent, but not so much that it aroused suspicion.

But she could do other things as well. And Urd needed her, though he hated needing anyone. He'd needed her for years, but that would all change soon. Soon he would be his own master.

"Urd. How fares my soup-drinking friend?" she asked.

He started to lift his hand to his throat but caught himself. That was what she wanted. To see him react. But she wouldn't see his need. Not this time. Instead, he lowered his hood, exposed the mark in his forehead, and waited for a reaction.

She looked at the mark and laughed. A murmuring laugh that flowed like poison into his body. But he was pleased to see that her eyes flickered for a brief moment. She wasn't unafraid. She knew what power the mark gave him. Her life was in his hands. It was just unfortunate that the reverse also held true.

"A lesser man might think you were surprised," he said coolly.

"Of course not. I achieve my aims."

Urd clenched his jaw. Damayanti had a tendency to turn things on their head. And now she was taking the credit for his work. As if he wouldn't be where he was without her. *Whore. Dancing whore.*

She gazed at him as if she could hear what he was thinking. "A man of the Seer. What can I do for you, councillor? A membership of this fine establishment? Food and drink? Dancers?"

She was teasing him. She knew exactly what he wanted, but she was going to make him suffer for it. It was nothing more than a desperate attempt to preserve her dignity and authority. She was unnerved by the mark, Urd knew she was. Anyone would be. She was just damned good at hiding it.

"I don't have time for this," he said, dropping a stack of coins onto the table.

"Time has always been your greatest weakness, Urd."

She got up and unlocked a cupboard. She bent over, as if looking for something, giving him time to study her from behind, before coming back over and setting a small silver bottle down on the table. It was shaped like an ornate spearhead, and small enough that Urd could hide it in his hand. He leaned across the table, forcing himself to take his time. He put the bottle in the leather pouch and gave the empty bottle he'd brought with him back to Damayanti.

She left both the bottle and the money on the table and lay down again.

"Arrogance, as well. Time and arrogance. You should be more careful, Urd. No one doubles their capacity to bind the Might overnight. Only a fool would believe that possible. A cleverer man would investigate."

Urd felt his lips quiver. He reminded himself that every single word this snake formed was ripe with fear. Now that her position was threatened, she was doing her utmost to convince him that he needed her. That didn't stop him from feeling uneasy.

No one doubles their capacity to bind the Might overnight.

He had become stronger. He had broken down the wall between worlds. An ability thought to have died out long ago. But Damayanti was right. He had done it overnight. Why? And how could she know about it?

An old sense of unease reared its head. Was he not as strong as he thought? Had someone helped him? *Impossible!* Only the Voice could have helped, and the Voice knew nothing about what Urd had done. Unless …

Unless the child had survived all those years ago. What if she had? What if she had come *here*? It would be about time for her to go through the Rite. Fifteen winters, and open to the Might. A chill went down his spine as he imagined what that would mean. The rot in Ym. One of Odin's own running around the eleven kingdoms. A tailless aberration in the forests, or in a village somewhere. If she came to the Rite, it would be his downfall. She was the only connection between him and the blind. It would all be over. Absolutely all of it.

The very notion was absurd. That was some comfort. Firstly, the ritual hadn't worked. The child had never come through. She'd disappeared into the void. Swallowed by the raven rings. Consumed by stone. Secondly, even if she *had* come through, she would have surely died out there in the middle of winter. Newborn. Naked.

More naked than Damayanti. Urd watched her stomach muscles ripple. He could feel himself starting to sweat when suddenly the door opened. Urd was quick to pull his hood up. A man spoke, barely audible over the din from downstairs.

"You're up, Damayanti."

"I'll be right there," she said. The door closed and Urd stood.

"Heaven forbid I get in the way of your art," he said, hoping she would catch the sarcasm. He left her, closed the red door behind him, and squeezed his way through a throng of men toward the exit. No one looked at him. All of them were only interested in one thing.

Silence descended on the premises and a soft drumming started. *Damned Damayanti! Damned blindcraft!* His hand was on the door, but he couldn't bring himself to leave. His eyes, along with all the other eyes in the room, were drawn to the stage.

Damayanti stood on her toes with her arms intertwined above her head. Then she dropped as if her knees had broken. Men gasped. The drums stopped. Then they started up again. Slow and rhythmic, like a heartbeat. Damayanti lifted herself up from the floor in an impossible arch. It was as if she were hanging from an invisible rope through her navel. An otherworldly force pulled her up until she was standing again. The drums trembled. She lifted a leg and wrapped it around her neck, with no apparent difficulty. Her tail curved and lifted her skirt, tantalizing every single onlooker with what lay beneath.

Urd bared his teeth, flung open the door, and ran out into the street. He took a deep breath. It was still raining, but he'd gotten away. He wasn't like other men. He refused to let himself be molded like clay. He was stronger than them. Of course he was. He was Urd-fadri. Councillor.

He started walking up the street, on the darker side. He hadn't gone far when he spotted the girl he'd encountered earlier. He stopped a short distance away and she turned to look at him. She'd learned to notice men who hesitated.

She smiled and swayed her hips as she walked over to him. She wasn't ugly to look at. Younger than twenty with long, coppery hair. Her dress was worn and caked with mud where it brushed against the ground. But her neck was clean. Slender and unspoiled.

"You came back." She pressed her chest against him, but this time had the good sense not to touch his hood. He ran a finger from her chin down her throat. It was irresistibly bare, and it would be the first thing he would feel enveloping his hardness. Until she stopped breathing. Until she fell silent. She only had herself to blame. What else could he do? Hope she hadn't seen him? Wait for the rumors to spread along the river and up into Eisvaldr? No. If he'd learned anything this evening, it was that he was free to shape his own fate. A raven pendant hung between her breasts. A good luck charm. The Seer's protection. It was impossible not to laugh at the irony.

"Come with me," he whispered.

She smiled and followed him like a lamb.

A FAVOR

The rain had a muggy hold on Elveroa. The weather had put Father in a foul mood at breakfast, but Hirka didn't really mind whether it was wet or dry. She had things to do. A new plan. Not a particularly good one, but it was all she had.

She followed the path along the Alldjup while she tormented herself thinking about everything that had gone wrong the previous day. Rime standing, impregnable as an icon, before the dark cliffs of Vargtind. Her asking for his help.

Hirka squeezed the basket she was carrying even tighter, but it didn't drive away the memory of his frosty gaze. The sneer on his face when he'd thought she was trying to curry favor with him, trying to be chosen, like any other fortune seeker. She got a knot in her stomach just thinking about it. The rain pattered dully against her cloak and she pulled her hood tighter, so that it framed the narrow path between the trees.

Rime was a moron. Hadn't they known each other since she was nine? How many times had she helped him come up with foolproof explanations for the holes in his trousers, for all the scrapes on his elbows and knees? She'd felt bad for him, having to sneak out at night to do the things she did without even thinking. It hadn't made any difference to her that he had blue blood. His name and history meant nothing to her. She didn't give a hoot about his wealth—there was more of it than she could wrap her head round. If people wanted to fawn over Council people in the village, like they did at Glimmeråsen, that was their problem. Hirka had no interest in being bound to the corridors of Eisvaldr. Quite the opposite. And accusing her of trying to exploit him? Imbecile!

Hirka hurried her pace. The path dipped through a boggy patch and the ground squelched beneath her feet. She was going to have to clean her shoes when she got back home. They were wetter and dirtier than that pesky raven. Kuro, she'd started to call him. He flew from tree to tree, always just ahead of her on the path. He sought shelter under the treetops while he waited for her to catch up to him. A gleaming shadow. Always close at hand, but impossible to reach.

Hirka sighed. She couldn't blame Rime for suspecting her of ulterior motives, that was the worst part. She'd seen the way Kaisa from Glimmeråsen stuck to Ilume like salve. And Rime had told her Sylja had asked for help. What in Slokna could a girl who had everything want with Rime?

She heard Sylja's laugh like an echo in her thoughts. *Mannfalla, Hirka! Sparkling wines, silk dresses, and blue-blooded boys who want to dance the night away!* Hirka ground her teeth. She'd never seen Rime dance. Fortunately. Not that it would matter if she had. Why should it matter?

The pattering against her hood stopped. The rain had finally let up. The path opened onto a field, and she heard the sound of a hundred ravens in quiet conversation. Ramoja and Vetle's towering wooden house lay up ahead. Hirka brushed the raindrops off the hide covering the basket, which fortunately had survived the rain. She had a chance to make someone happy today. And if she was lucky, Ramoja would offer some help. Help that could get her through the Rite in one piece. Hirka was more nervous than she had imagined.

Between the trees she could see the latticework Father had helped with. The ravenry had taken three men an entire summer to build.

The ravens sat motionless, gleaming black like somber fruit in the trees. An optimistic finch started paying its tribute to the sun but was cut off by a gurgled "kraaa!" from one of the ravens. It didn't start up again.

Hirka reached the house and was about to knock when the door opened. Ramoja's face appeared, smiling broadly. "Time to eat. Come join us."

Ramoja came out carrying a bucket that smelled of blood. Hirka followed her into a small chamber that was isolated from the rest of the cage. The ravens knew what was coming. They started to fly back and forth in an attempt to get closer, but the bars prevented them from reaching Ramoja's bucket of red meat and leftovers.

Two ravens were sitting on their own on a log inside the antechamber, within reach. Damp and glistening from the rain. The light played across their feathers, gleaming blue and purple. Ramoja put the bucket on the floor and walked over to them. They leaned sideways out of habit so that she was better able to reach underneath them. With practiced movements, Ramoja loosened two letter sleeves. The ends were waxed to protect them from the elements. She put them in her pocket without opening them, whispering calming words to the ravens as she did so. Hirka tried to listen. The sounds were strange, lots of *r*'s and long *o*'s. She spoke to them like they were children, and that was exactly why Hirka was here. This was her plan, and she sensed the opportunity presenting itself.

Ramoja let the raven closest to her perch on her arm. There wasn't enough room for it to stretch its wings, but it tried to shake the rain off anyway. Its impressive beak opened in a silent yawn, as though it just wanted to demonstrate its power. To show off.

Hirka felt her skin prickle. If this perfect creature was a normal raven, what did the Seer look like? Was He bigger? Angrier? An image flashed in Hirka's mind of a chamber containing the men and women of the Council. She was on trial, staring at the black bird on the Ravenbearer's staff. The raven grew bigger and bigger. It beat its massive wings until they quickly filled the entire room, then opened its beak to screech at Hirka.

"He likes you today," Ramoja said.

Hirka gave a start and returned to the present. The raven shifted and looked on smugly with its beady eyes. This was the best chance she was going to get. It was now or never.

"How do you know? Do you understand everything he says?" Hirka asked, trying to make her voice sound as natural as possible.

"He understands more than me," Ramoja quipped, but Hirka didn't think it was a joke.

Ramoja opened the door separating the antechamber from the rest of the ravenry and spoke a couple of incomprehensible words. The two ravens took to the air and flew inside. The cawing from inside grew more agitated. Hirka tried to listen, hoping she might understand some of their language. But it meant nothing to her.

Ramoja picked up the bucket and entered the cage. The ravens stayed calm as she walked down the middle and poured the food in a trough. The birds sat in a row and ate. Hirka was surrounded by them. She smelled blood, dirt, and rain. She suddenly felt embarrassed. She had come to the ravenry out of pure desperation. As though the ravens or Ramoja would be able to tell her what to do. This morning it had seemed like her last resort. Now that she was here, it just seemed ridiculous.

She didn't have the gift of ravenspeak, and she didn't have a lifetime to learn it. Even if she did, it probably wouldn't have helped when she was face-to-face with the Seer. But she already *was* face-to-face with Him, in a way. The ravens were the Seer's children. The eyes of the world. Maybe they already knew who she was? Maybe they knew but chose to do nothing. And maybe that meant that it was okay?

Hirka clung to that thought. Surely the ravens would have attacked her like a slaughtered animal if they thought she was the rot and deserved to die?

"I've been meaning to thank you," Ramoja said.

"For what?" The bucket was empty and Hirka followed her out of the cage and toward Vetle, who came racing out of the house. He threw his arms around Hirka's neck and squeezed just hard enough that you knew something wasn't quite right with him. For the first time, Hirka was afraid of his unabashed intimacy. She wasn't the same person now that she had been the last time she saw Vetle. What if he got too close? What if he suddenly kissed her? Would he rot? A wave of sadness hit Hirka. The feeling of having opened a door she couldn't shut made her tremble.

Don't think about it.

"Vetle, I've got something for you," she said, and the boy let go of her. Hirka pulled back the cover from the basket and took out the stone figure that Hlosnian had given her.

"Jomar!" Vetle shouted and pressed it against his body.

"That's not Jomar," Hirka laughed. "Jomar was a horse. That's a woman."

Vetle didn't seem to care. He looked at his mother and gave her a big smile. "Jomar!"

Hirka pulled a linen bag out of her basket and handed it to Ramoja. "That's for you. Father got some cinnamon from the ship that arrived from Brekka the other day. The captain's private supply." She left out the fact that he'd likely traded it for opa.

Ramoja untied the ribbon and breathed in the smell of home. A contented smile spread across her face, and she went into the house for a moment. Hirka sat down on a wooden bench and watched Vetle playing with his new Jomar out in the field. His knees and elbows were soaked. The occasional sunbeam managed to break through the clouds, transforming Vetle's hair into gleaming gold. It only lasted for a moment, then everything was colorless again.

"You flew him up out of the Alldjup, I hear." Ramoja handed Hirka a small bun, but her eyes were fixed on Vetle.

Hirka felt her cheeks getting warm. "He pretty much got himself out of it," she replied, sipping her tea while searching for a way to tell Ramoja why she had come.

"I know what you did for him, Hirka. Rime told me what happened."

Rime's name blasted through Hirka like a cold wind. *He thinks I'm a fortune seeker.*

The tea suddenly tasted sweet and sickly. Hirka glanced at Ramoja. She was also one of the Council's servants. A ravener. But Ramoja wore no raven on her chest. And she didn't wear the Council's heavy robes. Ramoja wore green and brown, in thin, floaty fabrics. She wore bangles and jewelry that jingled when she moved. Her black hair hung in hundreds of small braids, secured with colored pearls. Ramoja was dark and bursting with color, warmth, and smells. She was different. But she was still far too close to the Council.

I shouldn't have come here.

Hirka got up, but she was immediately assailed by black wings and a loud cawing. A raven! She was being attacked! She waved her hands frantically for a moment before realizing the raven wasn't trying to hurt her. It wanted to sit on her shoulder. And this was no random raven. It was Kuro.

He'd never sat on her before. He was clumsy and heavy. She could feel his talons through her cloak, but she didn't dare move, not wanting to scare him off. Ramoja's dark eyes stared at her like she had just sprouted wings herself. Hirka felt the need to explain.

"He's been following me for a few days now. I gave him some cheese one day, up near the Alldjup, and ever since he's kept close. I call him Kuro."

Most of Ramoja's ravens seemed bigger and more distinguished than Kuro. Hirka's new friend had a couple of unruly feathers sticking up on his head, and he looked around like a curious child. Ramoja reached out and scratched the obliging raven under the beak.

"Occasionally young wild ravens hang around the ravenry looking for company. But they don't like people …"

"I'm people!" Hirka bit her lip.

Ramoja gave her a piercing look. "Yet he came to you?"

Hirka shrugged. She searched for something to say that would make her sound as normal as possible, but she couldn't think of anything.

"If you're going to have a raven," Ramoja said, "there are a few things you should know."

They sat down again, and the tips came thick and fast. The raven was wild and shouldn't sleep indoors, unless there was an open window and good ventilation. She shouldn't feed him after the snow had melted. Creamy cheese and honey bread were not appropriate food, and so on.

Hirka seized her opportunity. She hadn't even considered using Kuro as a pretense. "Can I talk to him?" she asked.

Ramoja looked at Hirka for a moment before answering. "The number of people who can really talk to ravens can be counted on one hand. There are plenty who claim to have mastered the art. But either way, they've all had to spend years in Ravnhov or at the Council's ravener schools. Many years."

Hirka hung her head. She was asking the impossible and asking about something she had no right to know. The best raveners didn't even need to send letters. They could tell the ravens what they wanted to say, and they passed it on when they found the recipient. You had to have a good handle on the Might to do that.

At the very least, you have to be able to bind.

Hirka's heart sank. Her visit was over.

Ramoja got up from the bench and went out into the field. She stared up at the sky, and after a while Hirka could see a black dot growing into a raven. It flew into the antechamber right behind them and had barely touched down before Ramoja was there to relieve it of its letter. Between the bars, Hirka could see the ravener staring at the small sleeve she had taken from the raven. She opened one end and unfurled a piece of paper, which she started to read.

Then she crumpled.

Hirka ran to her. Kuro alighted from her shoulder and disappeared. Ramoja had grabbed hold of the door and quickly recovered. She looked paler, and her eyes were darting around as though she didn't know where she was.

"What's wrong, Ramoja?" Hirka feared the worst. She put a hand on her shoulder and tried to make eye contact. Ramoja clenched her fist, the small letter crumpled inside.

"Are you okay, Ramoja?"

"Hirka ... Yes. Of course. Bad news, that's all. An old friend." The corner of her mouth curled to reveal her lie. Hirka managed to see the Council's mark on the pale sleeve before Ramoja slipped it into her pocket.

Vetle came running into the cage. "I'm hungry!" he shouted, oblivious to the tension.

Hirka put her hand on Vetle's stomach, like he was a child, even though he was almost as tall as her. "Food's almost ready. Why don't you run inside and rub your tummy to warm it up, hm?" Vetle laughed and ran back inside. Hirka directed her attention back at Ramoja, who had recovered her composure, but her pupils were still the size of pinpricks. She followed Hirka out of the cage and shut it.

"Hedra and Hreidr," she said. "Hedra and Hreidr. Here and home."

Hirka stood in the field, watching as Ramoja headed back toward the house. Had she lost her mind? Maybe she should get Father. Hirka had to remind herself that getting Father wasn't exactly as easy as it used to be. People came to him now.

The ravener stopped and turned to face Hirka. "He hasn't been trained, so he might never listen to you. But if he does, then you'll have to expect some confusion before he understands where home is." She paused, then added, "And Hirka? Let's keep this between the two of us." Ramoja walked inside and shut the door.

Hirka could feel her smile getting bigger and bigger. Ravenspeak! Ramoja had taught her ravenspeak! Two words. Hirka repeated the words in her head as she walked up the path. Kuro was flying high above the bushes, but he was still following her.

"Hedra!" Hirka shouted, then looked around nervously to see if anyone had heard her. But she was alone on the path. Kuro didn't come. He sat at the top of a spruce tree, craning his neck.

"Hedra!" she repeated, with no luck. She said the word several times, but Kuro wasn't impressed. She could have sworn he was laughing. Hirka's own smile faded. Ramoja had been right. It was going to take years. Kuro could maybe be a friend, but he couldn't help her with the Rite.

Nobody could.

THE LIE

Summer loosened its grip in the days that followed. The days grew cooler and the insects ceased their flurry of activity. Elveroa was inundated with sweet, ripe berries. The ships started coming in from Kleiv, and even all the way from Ko—the southernmost of the eleven kingdoms—brimming with dried fruit, spices, glass, and stoneware. Carts arrived with the year's second tea harvest from Andrakar.

Hirka wished they would stop. The passage of time was a constant reminder that the Rite was approaching, and she still wasn't able to bind or speak to ravens.

She took an exaggerated step over some vengethorn growing on the mountainside. The climb was no easier than last time, but she didn't have a choice. She knew Rime came here every single day, even if she couldn't understand why.

She found a good place to stop for a moment, envying Kuro as he soared effortlessly through the blue sky. If only she could fly wherever she wanted. Then there'd be no climbing, no rites, and no people to deal with. And no one who cared who she was. But Hirka was earthbound. She had no choice but to observe the laws of others. Laws that hadn't been written with people like her in mind.

The wind cooled the sweat on her brow. Not far now. As she approached the summit, she stomped a bit to announce her presence. Rime was annoyed enough as it was, no need to surprise him. But when she peered over the jagged edge, she saw that Rime looked anything but surprised. He was sitting cross-legged on a rock, looking right at her. She pulled herself up before she could think better of it and flopped down on the ground a short distance from him. She'd rehearsed this moment, but she didn't know where to begin. She was no fortune seeker, but she suddenly realized that announcing as much would be a stupid thing to say.

She watched as his chest slowly expanded, as if he were drawing breath to say something, or perhaps to shout.

"I don't feel a connection with the earth," she said before he could get out a word.

There. She'd said it, and she already regretted it. She looked away so she wouldn't have to see his incredulous reaction. What had she been thinking? Rime was as close to the Council as you could get! She might as well have told the Seer Himself.

He said nothing, so she glanced back his way. He got up and took a couple steps toward her, his eyes narrow with doubt. "Everyone can feel the earth," he said, his tone landing somewhere between question and statement.

"I'm not lying."

His face softened and he cocked his head like he always did when he couldn't quite figure her out. She crossed her arms and then quickly dropped them again, not wanting to appear defensive. She didn't want to seem like she had something to hide.

"I tried to tell you last time," she said, "but you wouldn't listen."

He smiled. A broad, familiar smile that made her entire world shift on its axis. Hirka could feel the truth of who she was bearing down on her like an avalanche. She was the only thing standing between that truth and Rime, and it would have been so nice to just let go. To tell him and let him do what he wanted with that knowledge. He came even closer. She took a step back and stumbled. He grabbed her before she fell.

"Try," he said.

Could he read her thoughts? "Try what?"

"To bind."

"I've tried more times than you have bones in your body. I can't bind."

"Are you—"

"I'm sure. I'm unearthed, Rime."

Rime took a couple steps back and studied her again. He uttered a brief "hmm," making her feel like one of the math problems Father had forced her to do when she was little. A solvable but not particularly interesting conundrum. Her hands were clammy. What if Rime could solve the math problem? What if he knew why she couldn't bind?

"What happens when you try?" He sounded genuinely interested, but she didn't have an answer for him.

"Nothing."

"So what is it you do, then?"

She shrugged.

"Do you try to reach out to it or to draw it toward you?"

What was he talking about? She didn't say anything, so he asked again.

"When you try to bind, Hirka. What do you do?"

"I … try to reach out to the earth."

He smiled again, like that explained everything. "It's better to draw the Might up toward *you*. Not the other way around. Sit." He sat down cross-legged on the ground and looked at her. Hirka followed his lead. He seemed almost eager now. "Don't force yourself on the Might. Let it fill you."

Hirka tried. At least, she pretended she was trying, because she had no idea what she was supposed to be doing. All she could feel was a rock digging into her bum, and the closeness of Rime. It was starting to dawn on her that even he couldn't help her. She was what she was. Maybe she was risking his life just by being here. How much contact was needed to spread the rot?

Crones' talk! That wasn't how it worked! She'd never seen anyone rot, and she'd been stitching people back together since she was a child. Touched open wounds. Held people crying in fear. Lifted newborn babies, still slick with blood.

But she'd never kissed anyone.

Rime leaned forward. "And now?"

Hirka pulled away from him. "Nothing."

"You're just not trying hard enough."

"I don't feel anything!" she yelled. "That's why I'm here!"

She stared at the ground. The wind whistled between mossy stones in the old castle ruins. She heard Rime get up. He crouched down in front of her. She could hear her heart pounding in her ears. Her unease threatened to turn to panic. She had to make sure he didn't find out. She wouldn't be able to look him in the eye if he did. She swallowed.

"I mean … I can feel the Might, but I can't reach it."

The lie left a bitter taste on her tongue, making it feel swollen, like it had been stung by a bee. Silence hung between them for a moment.

"I know it can be painful," he said. "Some people think binding should hurt. Is that why?"

"Yes," she said. What else could she say?

Rime got up again. Hirka looked up, squinting at his silhouette.

"The Might doesn't hurt."

Hirka flushed in embarrassment. She heard him walk away. His footsteps fading as he headed down the mountain. He'd tricked her. It wasn't fair! She tried to feel angry about it, but it was all too much effort. After all, she was the one who had lied. What was going to happen now? Would he work out what she was?

Fragments of an old folk song came back to her. About a girl who had taken an embling as a lover. The song had many verses in which the tailless creature begged her to sleep with him, but the girl said no every time. Until the final verse, when she gave in and said yes. She rotted in the forest like a tree stump. Hollow. Unrecognizable.

It's just a horrible song.

But nothing was *just* anything anymore. Hirka had seen enough sickness in her life that it was all too easy to imagine the rot. For the first time, she realized the enormity of what she was. What it took from her. Something she'd never had, but still it hurt. She brought her hand to her chest, felt the wolf tooth against her palm. A lie she'd grown up with. She let go.

Her fingers dug down into the earth. The earth that hated her. That shut her out. She tore up a fistful of topsoil and flung it at the castle wall.

"If you don't want me, I don't want you either! You hear me?!"

Kuro landed on the ground in front of her. He came closer and rested his beak on her thigh.

"Kooor," he said.

"Yeah, great. That solves all my problems," she replied sarcastically, plunging her fingers into the earth again.

"Kooor."

But she didn't know ravenspeak, so it didn't matter.

UNEARTHED

She's unearthed!

Rime hopped off the edge of the cliff and used the Might to ease himself down from the top of the mountain. He was now strong enough to manage a drop the height of five men, and he was getting better by the day. Enveloped by the Might, it was as though the ground was trying to repel him as he landed. Like the air was syrup. It had cost him several broken bones to get to this point. But he had to get better. He had to make his master proud. Svarteld was the most powerful binder Rime had met. He'd seen Svarteld cross a lake without getting his feet wet. He owed no debt to the ravens, as people used to say.

But the same couldn't be said for Hirka.

She'd lied to him. She was unearthed. He'd never heard anything like it. Children could be unearthed, and he'd heard that extremely old people could lose the Might. People who had lost their wits, maybe. But normal people …

Hirka had given Rime three years of freedom. Three years of breakneck challenges. Precious time for him. Games for her. She'd always been something of a puzzle to him, but this was something else entirely. Had they really never discussed binding in those three years?

No. Why would they have? Rime had grown up with the Might. It was the affliction that made him who he was. He realized now that she had avoided the topic as avidly as he had. Rime felt vaguely disappointed that he hadn't noticed that something was wrong earlier.

He'd always been alert to nuances. To pretense. A blessed child who uncovered truths in words exchanged between people in the corridors. Words that were never spoken. Looks. Quiet displays of power. The game that ruled an entire world. Books in the library he knew he wasn't allowed to read. His grandmother's mysterious scriptorium, letters sent by raven that could be read if you held them up to an oil lamp or a candle. He was too young to understand much of what he learned back then. Rime glanced back up at Vargtind. He might still be too young to understand a lot of it.

He took a detour around the village. The sun was low in the sky and the trees cast dark shadows across the road leading to the house. He was going to miss this house. Here he didn't get lost in the rooms. They were made for people, not for giants. He had been born and raised in the house in Mannfalla, but it had never been a home. The distance between the walls was just too vast. It was magnificent, and he could appreciate it for its beauty, for its history. But the house in Elveroa felt like a home.

There was only one other place in the world where he felt like that. There were no palaces there, just trees and open space among the mountains. No furniture, except for a few benches and cushions. And there—together with Svarteld and the others—he would remain, putting the rest of his life behind him.

Rime walked through the entrance. It was twilight. An oil lamp on the floor illuminated Oda, who was standing on a stool, dusting the paintings. Half of them were leaning up against the wall, wrapped in linen. Ready for the journey home. Oda bowed and smiled at him.

"Són-Rime. Out before the sun rises and back when it's set?"

Rime returned her smile and avoided commenting on her use of his title. Ilume left no doubt whatsoever as to how the servants should address him. He would just make life difficult for them if he objected.

"Is that bread I smell?" He realized he was hungry.

Oda started to climb down, but Rime stopped her.

"No, no. I'll get it myself," he said.

He walked down to the kitchen and ate a warm slice of bread while he thought about what he was going to say. He wanted to know why Hirka couldn't bind. He'd never heard or read of anyone who couldn't even feel the flow of energy in the earth. Of life. Through the ages, many artists had shouted about having lost the Might. It was said that Frang, the children's portrait artist from Ormanadas, had thrown himself from the wall in Eisvaldr more than two hundred years ago because the Might abandoned him. Rime didn't buy it. Artistic temperament. Drama. Too much wine, maybe. But mightless? No.

Rime let the Might fill his body for a moment, as though to make sure that he still could. The world had to seem so empty to someone who couldn't experience this feeling. So meaningless. A world without any life force. Without the Seer.

He washed the bread down with apple juice and went back up to the scriptorium. The room was bare now. Furniture and rugs were already on the way back to the family home in Mannfalla. Only the desk remained, a dark, oaken colossus, where Ilume sat bent over a letter.

Behind her, the sunlight pierced the image in the stained-glass window: a picture of the Seer flying above outstretched hands. Dappled brown light danced on Ilume's white robe, almost making it look dirty. But Rime knew that as soon as she stood, she would be clean again. That's how it was with Ilume, with the Council. They met, they decided people's fates on a daily basis, then washed their hands in the huge silver basins after every meeting. Always clean. Would she emerge from this clean as well?

Ilume's service in Elveroa had come to an abrupt end after six years of negotiations, or at least that's what the Council called them. Six years of trying to persuade Ravnhov to see sense. All these years in Elveroa, and now Ravnhov was banging its shields. Whispering about the blind and blaming the Council. The situation was fragile. So fragile Ilume had been summoned home.

Rime realized that Ilume's opponents would accuse her of having failed, because still Ravnhov was not a part of Mannfalla.

Rime took a step into the room. His grandmother looked up at him. He waited the brief moment he knew it would take her to accept a conversation. Ilume set her pen down in an ivory dish and sat up in the chair, folding her hands. Maybe this was going to be easier than he had thought. After the night at Glimmeråsen, Ilume's open hostility had given way to a frightening indifference. She was planning something.

Rime searched for the best way to introduce the topic. He knew Ilume loved to lecture him on who he was. That was the surest way to get an answer.

"How strong was my mother in the Might?"

"Not as strong as you."

Rime seized the thread. "How do you know how strong someone is?"

Ilume looked at him. "Those who want to know, know. You know."

"Is everyone born that way?"

"That way?"

He started to walk around in the room. He ran his hand along the shelves of the empty book cabinet that was going to remain here. It was free of dust. The words were gone. He tried to find his own words. Hirka had lied to him, but he knew something about her that presumably nobody else knew. Something he was certain he shouldn't expose.

"Is everyone able to feel the flow of the Might through the earth the same as everyone else, I mean. Is everyone the same?"

"Obviously not. Each family has their own share of the Might, some have more than others."

Rime was well aware of that, but he let her continue.

"You couldn't have become a servant of the Seer if you didn't have the blood for it, Rime."

"But who has the strongest blood?"

Ilume laughed. Rime eyed her wrinkles. They were almost never visible, only when she laughed. He wished she would laugh more often.

"If you asked Family Taid, they would reply, 'Us!' And if you asked Family Jakinnin, they would say exactly the same thing."

Rime was growing impatient. He wasn't getting anywhere. "Does anyone ever show up who is a lot stronger or … weaker … than others?"

Ilume's smile withered and she raised a thin eyebrow at him. "Have *you* met someone who is stronger than you?"

He hadn't, so it wasn't difficult to meet the gaze of the old woman. "No."

She held his gaze.

"Perhaps some of those chosen during the Rite will be," he tried.

Ilume sighed and laid her hands on the armrests. "The Rite is not what it once was. Few have the same connection with the earth that everyone used to. The Might is thinning. Ebb and flow will soon be the same. Trickling brooks that dry up over the years." Ilume spoke almost gently, gazing out the window. "Who knows how eternal the Might is? Who knows if it has always been there or simply runs through us in order to dissipate? Is it precious and rare, or eternal in abundance? Have we drunk too much, or will there always be something left in the glass? Should we choose incorrectly, we deprive the world." She looked back at Rime.

"But someone must lead us forward," she said, and her gentleness was gone.

Rime felt an unease in his body. "Is the Seer punishing us?"

"We're punishing ourselves." Ilume looked out at the empty room. Her eyelids grew heavy. Outside, the last light faded. The colors died and his grandmother's silhouette was swathed by the twilight.

"Grandmother?"

Ilume rose suddenly and rolled up her papers. "You can only call me that when you show some remorse. When you understand your place, and pull the knife out of my back. *Then* you can call me family. Do you feel remorse?"

"Of course not. I'm serving the Seer."

Rime wasn't going to get a straight answer out of her. As Ilume said, he was no longer family. The Council and the fate of the people were not his concern. Ilume was welcome to her secrets. Rime had no desire to know.

But when you were as close to the Council as he had been his entire life, it was frustrating to see them fumbling in the dark. He knew that he shouldn't say it, but he said it anyway. "We all do our part. I fight for the Seer. And I'll do what I can if we're threatened."

Ilume stopped rustling her papers and silence seized the room. She looked like she was going to say something, but then changed her mind. Instead, she continued, "If we're ever threatened, that is your job. To serve blindly. Without knowing or questioning."

Rime caught her almost inaudible stress on the final word. He nodded and left the room. She had nearly allowed herself to be tricked into asking how he could know that Ym was threatened.

Rime suddenly felt old. Only a few years ago he would have been beside himself with satisfaction at being able to surprise Ilume An-Elderin. He was eighteen winters. She was three-quarters of a century, and she was a member of Insringin, the Council's inner circle, and he had gotten her to share information involuntarily. But tonight that just made him uneasy.

He went to sit down in the library, but there were no chairs to sit on. Or books to read. Empty rooms. There was a knock downstairs, and he heard Oda open the door. Ramoja's voice. And Vetle's. He heard them come up the stairs and saw her hurry past the door to the library with Vetle in tow.

"Ramoja?"

She poked her head in. Her cheeks were red. "Rime. Can you . . . ?" She lightly nudged Vetle toward him.

"Of course."

He waved Vetle over and Ramoja went in to see Ilume. Obviously, there was an urgent matter. Everything was urgent at the moment. And when something was urgent, you could count on Ilume. Ramoja had counted on Ilume ever since Rime's mother had died.

Vetle sat down on the floor and Rime sat down with him. The boy was playing with a stone figure. A girl. She was beautifully detailed, but the tail was broken off. Rime thought of Hirka and smiled. *Hirka Has-No-Tail*, as Kolgrim used to call her.

Hirka Has-No-Tail, who couldn't bind.

Rime felt the hairs on his arms stand on end.

THE CONFESSION

Hirka couldn't bring herself to move. Rime had left Vargtind ages ago, but she could still hear his voice.

The Might doesn't hurt.

Rime An-Elderin, Són-Rime. Direct descendent of the twelve. He might have been working it out at that very moment.

Kuro hopped to and fro, trying to get her attention, but he soon got bored and flew off. Darkness descended on Vargtind. The sun had set. She was getting cold.

Hirka got up and walked over to the edge of the ruins encircling the flat hilltop. Some of the stones were several times taller than she was. They thrust themselves skyward as if they thought they might be able to tear a hole in the heavens. The wind whipped at her, trying to lure her over the edge. But Hirka wasn't afraid of the edge. Or heights. She was dizzy, but for a different reason.

She was dizzy because she knew she was all alone.

A child of Odin, from a different world, who couldn't bind. Father couldn't help her anymore. He had kept her safe for as long as he could.

And now she had driven away the only person who might have been able to help her. Hirka wrapped her arms around herself. She should have brought her cloak. Father was right. Sometimes she couldn't see farther than the end of her nose. She had to learn to think ahead. But there was only one thing in her future.

The Rite.

For a while, she'd even had herself convinced. Convinced she could learn, be like everyone else and go through the Rite unnoticed. She'd been wrong. Father had known all along that would never happen. They had to leave, and there was nothing Hirka could do. They were destined to live a life without rest, traveling from place to place.

Hirka felt a longing she hadn't expected. They'd lived that way most of her childhood. It wasn't that bad, was it? Living like the ravens in the forest. Like a wild animal, with only itself to rely on. It could be a good life.

But it wasn't fair. She was tired of hiding. Of always moving on to the next place. Of never having anyone besides Father. There had to be another way.

Hirka started down the mountainside. The sky was a deep blue and the stars were already out. She saw light out of the corner of her eye. The torches were lit down by the quay. She could see people carrying boxes to and fro. Another merchant ship with goods from Kleiv, or perhaps from Kaupe. Hirka walked through Elveroa and down toward the quay. The stalls that were usually so busy were closed for the night. The counters had been folded up and the goods locked in. Hirka could hear voices on the quayside, and so she stopped; an instinct as old as she was. Why did she feel the need to avoid people? And the more there were, the worse it was. As if something horrific might happen if they saw her. What did she think they'd do? See her for what she was and burn her alive?

She walked on. The ship rocked in its mooring as if sleeping through the loading and unloading. Several men climbed the masts, lashing the sails into place. Strong men carried sacks and wooden chests past Hirka and into the storehouse she'd once fallen through the roof of. She made sure to keep out of the way.

People crowded together on the pretense of helping out, but

most of them were only really interested in gossip and news. Sylja's mother stood talking to one of the men. She was counting out silver pieces for him, but she didn't look happy. She never did when she was parting with money.

"Hirka!" Sylja hissed nearby. "Over here!" Sylja grabbed her and pulled her behind the closest storehouse.

"What are you d—"

"Shh!" Sylja peered around the corner before throwing herself back against the wall again. "Mother will never let me stay if she sees you!" Sylja looked at her and unleashed the smile that made all of Elveroa think she was marvelous. "Orm's here!"

Hirka couldn't help but smile back. "Wine Orm? Are you sure?"

"Yes!"

Sylja looked around the corner again before turning back with a satisfied grin. Her mother was gone. They left their hiding place and walked past the torches. Hirka felt the warmth creep back into her body. A couple of men asked why they weren't in bed, following the question up with self-congratulatory guffaws. One of them shouted something about the length of his tail. Sylja stared at him, pretending to be shocked.

"That's not what I've heard," Hirka replied without looking at them.

Hirka spotted Orm and they headed his way, doing their best to look nonchalant. He had two sacks balanced on his head. This would have been difficult for a normal man, but Orm had no neck. His head just went straight into his shoulders. He was as broad as two men. His shirt had probably been white once, but it now looked yellow. Hirka hoped it was just the light from the torches.

He laughed when he spotted them.

"Ah, I wondered where you were, young misses!" He winked.

Sylja meandered over and smiled coquettishly. "Need help with anything?"

Orm sighed heavily. Hirka felt for him. He could get in a lot of trouble with Sylja's mother if she found out he gave them wine in exchange for help, but who could say no to Sylja? So the two girls moved a couple boxes of spices, some pork sausages from Smále, ten pairs of boots, and a box of books. Nothing much, but they were rewarded all the same. Orm took them aside and gave them a green bottle that had been almost completely hidden in his fist. He claimed it was the best wine from Himlifall's south-facing slopes. He pinched Sylja's cheek, then told them to get going before they got him into trouble.

Sylja tied the bottle to her waistband, letting it hang inside her skirt. Then they ran as fast as the bottle permitted up the rise between the quay and the blacksmith's house. They sat on the "bench," a depression in the rock that water and wind had carved out through generations, laughing and gasping for breath. Hirka removed the cork using her pocketknife and took a mouthful before handing the bottle to Sylja. The taste of preserved berries washed across her tongue and she closed her eyes. Orm hadn't been lying. It was good wine. Last time he'd given them something so sour it was barely drinkable, but that hadn't stopped them from drinking it.

Hirka smiled as warmth spread through her body. This was what the earth tasted like. Just like tea. *This is as close as I can get to binding.*

She took another swig that was even bigger than the first. Sylja was giggling already, gushing about the arms of one of the men on the quayside.

Hirka watched her. Sylja was the flower to her stone. The harp music to her washboard rattle. Sylja curtsied where Hirka beat a hasty retreat, and where Hirka would sweat, Sylja always came out smelling like flowers. No wonder she always got her way.

With Rime too?

Sylja had spoken to him, with that same smile and that same scent of flowers. Had he helped her? A weight settled like a stone in Hirka's stomach, and she could feel it growing. The wine certainly didn't help. She couldn't stop herself from asking, "Have you spoken to Rime since he—"

"Did I not tell you?!" Sylja interrupted, her eyes bright with scandal. "He came for dinner the other day. Mother was shocked that Ilume didn't come, but it didn't really matter. He's so handsome!"

Hirka couldn't even bring herself to nod. Sylja continued obliviously.

"But he's so peculiar, and so stubborn. Quite awkward, really. I don't think I could be interested in him. And he wouldn't leave me alone all evening!"

Hirka's breath hitched.

"It was really quite embarrassing, Hirka. You should have seen it!"

"Seen what?" Hirka heard herself ask. Why? She really didn't want to know the answer.

"You know ..." Sylja brought a hand to her shapely breast and laughed.

Hirka swallowed.

"What's the matter with you?" Sylja took the bottle from Hirka and drank the last of the wine. Hirka stared out across the black sea. If you traveled far enough, you came to Brott. Beyond Brott, there was nothing. How far would you have to travel to get to where she came from? Was it even possible to travel there?

"We're leaving." The tears started the moment she said it. She knew it was true, and it was as if it hadn't been true until she said it out loud.

"Huh?" Sylja slurred.

"We're going away." Hirka hugged her knees, making herself as small as she could. Her throat tightened, and suddenly her tears were soaking through the knees of her trousers.

Sylja sat up straight. "You certainly are not!"

Hirka couldn't help but laugh, even mid-sob. She dried her tears. It was so typical of Sylja to expect reality to bend to her will. As far as she was concerned, if she said they weren't leaving, they weren't leaving.

"We have to." Hirka knew the conversation was taking a dangerous turn. She couldn't answer the questions she knew were coming.

"Why?"

Hirka tried to get up. She needed to get out of there. She couldn't stay. She was a child of Odin. And she had lied to Rime. Her legs wouldn't cooperate. She took a couple unsteady steps before tumbling over. She lay on her side, looking at the empty bottle on the ground in front of her. Sylja asked again.

"Why?"

Everything looked green through the bottle.

"The Rite. We need to leave because of the Rite."

"Travel, you mean? Everyone travels to the Rite. Wait till you see my tail rings, Hirka! Pure gold and shaped like butterflies." Sylja beamed.

Hirka wiped her nose on the sleeve of her tunic. "Not travel. Leave."

Sylja seemed to realize that Hirka was being serious. She lay down beside her. "When?"

"I don't know."

Hirka watched Sylja's face distort through the green glass. Her nose had been pulled all the way up to her eyes and her mouth was half-open in a grimace.

It was as if she'd started to rot.

BETRAYAL

Hirka lifted her clothes out of the chest and laid them on the bed. She didn't have a lot. Two tunics, a shirt, and trousers. Some underwear and socks. Even a green dress Father had bought in a moment of weakness, but Hirka had never worn dresses.

Kuro's claws scraped against the wooden floor as he investigated the empty chest. The raven had never ventured inside before, but the conditions on this particular evening would have made any living creature seek shelter. Rain lashed at the cabin as it groaned under the onslaught of the wind. The oil lamps flickered, proving that not even Father could make walls keep out weather like this.

Hirka looked around the empty room. Everything she owned could fit in the big chest, but she was still going to leave a few things behind. She ran her fingers over her collection of stones. Large and small. Some of them rough against her fingers, others as smooth as Kuro's beak. She gathered them all up into her arms and went out into the hearth room. Father was sitting in his chair, waving a stick around in an attempt to close the roof hatch properly.

"I'm not taking these." Hirka put the stones down by the hearth. The embers danced in the draft from the chimney.

Father put the stick down and wiped his hands on a rag. "Shall I put the soup on?"

Just then Hirka thought she heard something. She didn't reply to Father. She looked up at the roof hatch, but it looked secure.

There it was again! Someone was knocking on the door. In this weather? Hirka felt the hairs on the back of her neck stand on end. Something was wrong. She could smell it.

She met her father's gaze. They looked around, both seized by the same thought. Their lives had been packed into chests and sacks. The walls were bare. Any idiot who came in would realize they were on the move. Hirka grabbed the sacks, getting ready to chuck them into her room, but Father stopped her.

"Wait, Hirka ..." The knocking was more insistent now. Father glanced at the long chest they used as a bench. That was where they kept the things they rarely used. Like his sword. Hirka's mind started to race. Could they climb out the bedroom window? No. The shutters were closed from the outside because of the weather. The roof hatch? She could manage it, but Father ...

She reached for her pocketknife without knowing what she was afraid of.

A woman's voice called from outside. Father wheeled himself over and opened the door a crack. A brown-clad figure squeezed through, along with a blast of wind and rain. Father closed the door and it was quiet again.

Their visitor lowered her hood. Hirka knew she ought to be relieved to see Ramoja, but her heart was still racing.

Ramoja took a couple steps forward as she pushed her braids out of her face. Her cloak was saturated with rain, stretched taut across her shoulders. Kuro cawed from his perch above the door. Ramoja smiled and nodded to the raven before speaking to Father or Hirka.

"I thought I was done for out there," she said. Father laughed, even though it wasn't particularly funny. Ramoja eyed the chests and sacks strewn around the room. The empty shelves. She closed her eyes for a moment, as if to collect herself. Then she turned to Father.

"I don't know where you're going, Thorrald," she said. "And it's none of my business either." Her words were slow and clear. It was like she was speaking in code. Trying to say something without actually saying it. "But if you're intending to avoid the Rite, there's something you should know. The Council already knows you're leaving."

Father stared at Ramoja, his eyes narrowed doubtfully. Hirka suddenly felt cold. She stepped back into the shadows. Ramoja glanced at her but carried on mercilessly. "If you'd hoped to slip away unnoticed, you're too late."

Father tightened his grip on his chair and hunched his shoulders as if he might stand up at any moment. "We have nothing to hide," he said hoarsely. "People travel all the time. What business of the Council's is it if ordinary people—"

"But she's not ordinary, is she?" Ramoja took a step closer to Father as her words burrowed into Hirka's chest. What was never supposed to happen, had happened. What no one was supposed to know, was known.

"It's too late, Thorrald. Don't leave unless you really have to. It might be the death of both of you."

"Why? Tell me what you know, woman!" Father growled.

"Kolkagga."

Father slumped in his chair. Hirka couldn't move. It was only a word, but it was weighted with fear from stories she could no longer remember. Kolkagga. The black shadows. Assassins. The Council's secret weapon. Specters that drained all life from those who defied the Seer. The already dead.

Nonsense! Tall tales used to frighten children!

But they were tall tales capable of making Father cower before her very eyes. Rumors Sylja had whispered about only a few days ago. Hirka pressed herself against the wall. The shadows suddenly seemed alive and listening. She felt trapped. She couldn't breathe.

Kolkagga.

Ramoja put her hood up again.

"I'm telling you like it is, Thorrald," she said. "The Rite is a point of honor for them, this year more than ever. They will send the black shadows."

"Why are you telling us this?" Father's voice was choked. Hirka stepped out of the shadows. Ramoja's face softened when she saw her.

"To settle a debt," she said.

"We can look after ourselves," Father replied. "No one will lay a hand on her. No one." His voice was unrecognizable. Hirka felt a sudden warmth blossom in her chest amid all the despair.

Ramoja's gaze swept over his wheeled chair. "I know you're strong, Thorrald. Other men would have withered away in their beds long ago. But that chair and your will are all you have to protect her with. It wouldn't be a fair fight, even against ordinary men. And Kolkagga are not ordinary men. You can't run from them."

Hirka waited for an outburst from Father, but it didn't come. He knew she was right. His lips pulled down into a grimace. "So there's nowhere we can go."

Ramoja had turned to leave, but hesitated. "The enemy of your enemy is your friend, Thorrald. If it means so much to you, there's only one place to go. You know that."

Ravnhov. She doesn't want to say it.

It occurred to Hirka that Ramoja was risking her own safety to tell them they were in danger. Hirka ran over to her. "Ramoja!"

Ramoja turned and Hirka searched for words, but she didn't know what to say. Nothing came out.

Ramoja smiled and nodded as if she'd said it anyway. Then she opened the door and disappeared out into the storm. The door didn't close properly behind her. It banged in the wind.

Hirka felt the rain on her face. She stared out the door as if all the monsters in the world had gathered outside. How could Ramoja know that they were leaving?

The ravens. Of course. She had access to the Council's letters. But how could the Council know?

Ilume.

The wind knocked the broom over. The lamp on the table went out. Hirka slammed the door shut and drew the bolt. She stood leaning against it. There was only one way Ilume could know about her: Rime had realized what she was and told his grandmother everything.

Because I lied. And in the grand scheme of Rime An-Elderin's life, I am nothing.

Hirka rattled the bolt and kicked the door. Then she kicked it again. And again. She kicked and kicked, wanting Father to stop her, but he didn't.

THE MIGHT

It was a gray morning. The storm had worn itself out during the night, but the occasional gust of wind still tore at Hirka as she made her way up Vargtind, as if to demonstrate that nature wouldn't give up that easily. The wind grew stronger the higher she climbed. The slope seemed steeper than before, the thicket pricklier, but she didn't care. She was fuming and needed to get up there. To get to Rime. It occurred to her that it would always be like this. He would always be elevated. She would always have to climb. She was Hirka. That was all. Hirka, Thorrald's girl. No. She wasn't even *that*. She was a child of Odin.

She climbed over the final crag and collapsed onto the flat ground. No one was there. Bushes grew around the foundations of the ruins, where the castle had once towered above Elveroa and the sea. That was all.

Where in Slokna's name was Rime? Had he left? Or maybe it was too early? Hirka looked down at the quay, but the fishing boats hadn't gone out during the night. Disappointed seagulls circled above empty barrels.

Rime had betrayed her. That was why he hadn't turned up: because he didn't dare face her.

Coward. He can rot in Slokna.

"Let me guess," said a husky voice behind her. She leaped to her feet and there he was. "You've worked out you're better off telling the truth?" He gave her a crooked smile and folded his arms across his chest.

His accusation caught her off guard. She'd stormed up here in a fit of rage. *She* ought to be the one folding her arms across her chest. *She* was the one who'd been betrayed. He'd ruined everything. Made it impossible for them to leave.

But she couldn't find any evidence of that in his face. His eyes were laughing. His smile was genuine. His lips could have belonged to one of Hlosnian's sculptures. Perfectly chiseled.

Hirka lowered her gaze. Rime hadn't betrayed her. If he knew she was one of Odin's kin, he wouldn't be standing in front of her like he was now. No one would smile at the rot. He still had no idea. The Council had found out in some other way.

So what was she doing here? She tried to slow her breathing, but her lungs weren't cooperating. The storm wasn't over. It had just moved inside her. What was she going to do? Rime couldn't help. No one could help.

They'll send the shadows after me.

She felt Rime's hand on her shoulder.

"Hey, take it easy. I'll try to help you."

"You're leaving soon ..." was all she could get out.

"Giving up before you've started?" he asked. "One point to me, then."

Hirka looked up at him and smiled. He smiled back.

"No, I didn't think it would be that simple," he said.

He asked her to breathe more deeply. Relax. Sit on the ground. Get up again. Run. Rest. Think. Concentrate.

Hirka could see that he finally believed her. That she couldn't bind. But no matter what he asked her to do, she still felt nothing.

If there was a life force flowing through Ym, it wasn't meant for the likes of her, that was for sure.

Rime paced back and forth with his hands behind his back. "It's not so much that you're not *feeling* it," he said, mostly to himself, it seemed. "It's that you don't even know where or what it is."

Here he was, an An-Elderin, looking at her as if she were missing a foot. *Or a tail.* Hirka felt powerless, as if she had lost every contest between them, all at once. As if she'd fallen when they climbed, drowned when they swam, stumbled when they ran. And here he was, pacing back and forth, rubbing it in. What was wrong with her?

It had been a long morning. Rime rolled his head to stretch the muscles in his neck. He clearly wasn't used to sitting still. "Have you tried with stone?" He came toward her again. There was optimism in his voice, but not in his eyes. "The Might can build up in stone …" The optimism faded from his voice as well. "Like a store. If you lay your palms on—"

"Rime—"

"Do what I do," he interrupted. And for the umpteenth time, he posed with his hands slightly out to the side, his head raised and his eyes closed. He looked like he was waiting for it to rain. Hirka watched his face relax. He looked like he could stand there forever. A beautiful statue. Filled with peace. He started to bind.

The only thing Hirka was filled with was disappointment. She would have given anything to share in that same peace, that same life. But she wasn't like him. He stood there in all his glory, elevated by his family's history and the Seer's blessings. The entire world embraced him. She had no place here. She was a fool for not realizing sooner. She knew that now.

"It's not meant for people like me." It was one of the most honest things she had ever said to him. She felt as if her heart had been laid bare, and it was terrifying. She turned to leave.

Rime gripped her shoulder and spun her around. For a moment, Hirka thought he had struck her. Her body was paralyzed and needed to fall, but it stayed standing despite itself. Suspended. Immobile. Blood pumped through her veins as if the Stryfe were ripping through her. Rime's hand was locked around her shoulder. Hirka could see the shock in his eyes. He stood as immobile as she did. It felt like her body might be torn to pieces. She was dying.

Then came time.

As Hirka looked on, the green leaves behind Rime turned yellow, red. They fell from the trees, withered and died. The snow came. It melted. New shoots emerged and everything turned green again. She watched the castle rise up on top of Vargtind, watched people come into the world, live and die. She watched a little boy chase girls and pull their tails. Become a father. Die. Autumn came. The castle fell. The heavens raged and wept. Ravens sailed past with rainbows in their black wings. Everything was blanketed with snow. Everything was eternal, contained within a moment. And all this she saw without looking away from Rime.

The Might surged through her to her very core. She was purged. Killed. Born. There was nowhere to hide, no matter how much she wanted to. She was seen. Scrutinized. Picked apart. She struggled in vain against the onslaught, but it just got more powerful. It plowed its way through blood vessels that were too narrow. Pain. Rime crying out. He fell. She fell.

Her heart was beating too fast. Much too fast. Her pulse hammered in her ears. She sat on the ground, gasping for breath. She fought to regain control. Earth. Earth beneath her fingers. The smell of grass. Decay. Rain. She looked at her hands, terrified she might be old. She wasn't. Her veins pulsed, expanding and contracting as she looked on. She was alive.

Hirka looked up at the sky. The sun hadn't moved.

A moment. An eternal moment. She'd bound the Might.

Rime was kneeling before her. He was so beautiful that her hand reached out to him as if with a will of its own. She smiled weakly before she slumped against him and everything went black.

Ghostly apparitions taunted her, and Hirka knew she was dreaming. There was no such thing as ghosts. Father was among them, and he was walking. He waved at her and disappeared. His voice was an echo from among the spectral figures.

Crones' talk!

Faceless beings with gaping mouths hissed viciously at her, but she couldn't quite make out the words. They came closer and closer. Hirka looked around, desperate to find a way out, but she was surrounded. She backed up against a dead tree. It was too fragile to climb. A white, shapeless hand reached out and suddenly Rime stood before her, holding a sword. He was a warrior. He looked like a shadow from another time.

His eyes narrowed to slits and he smiled coldly. His sword was narrow and colorless. She couldn't move. She just stood and watched as the blade plunged through her clothes, her skin, her flesh, and then into the tree trunk behind her. There it sat, the cold from the steel washing through her body.

There was a hole gaping inside her. She looked up at Rime, whose smile grew even wider. She needed to make him see! There was a hole inside her! He needed to get help. She felt something trickle from the corner of her mouth and saw red spots appear in the white snow.

Where was Rime? He had to help her! She fell to her knees and started digging in the snow until she saw his face. His lips were blue. His throat caved in on itself and wasted away. The skin peeled from his cheekbones. He was rotting. The wind howled and whipped up the snow around her. She couldn't see. She cried out, but all she could hear was the wind. She called for Rime. She had a hole inside her.

"Rime!" The snow covered what remained of his face more quickly than she could dig.

"Rime!"

A PLAN

"Rime!"

Hirka tried to get up, but someone was holding her down. She was still sitting on the ground. Rime had his hand around her shoulder.

"Just relax," he said. "You're exhausted."

He was right. Her arms ached. Her muscles were sore all the way down her back, as though she had been carrying vats of herring all day. They sat there for a long time, without doing anything other than looking. Creepers had grown between the stones and made cracks in what little was left of the castle wall. The wind had worn away all the corners. Nature had taken back what powerful men had once built. Yellowed leaves blew over the moss, as though nothing had happened. Had it all been a dream?

No. It was real. She had bound the Might.

Rime was stroking her shoulder with his thumb and speaking quietly, as if to a newborn. She could feel his chin on the top of her head. His jaw moving with each word as he tried to process what they had experienced. He seemed to be explaining it to himself as much as to her. Neither of them knew exactly what had happened. Though not the most mature reaction, she enjoyed the realization that it had taken as much out of him as it had her.

Rime had bound the Might and then grabbed hold of her. The result had been completely unlike anything he'd ever experienced.

They tried again, but quickly realized that Hirka still couldn't bind. Not on her own. It only took a tiny bit of the edge off the enjoyment Hirka felt in finally knowing what everyone was talking about. Finally being able to understand what the Might was. Even though it wasn't her own.

But Rime didn't think that she did understand. She still didn't know what most people felt when they bound the Might. What had just happened was stronger. He compared it to explaining the storm from the previous night to an inlander from Midtyms. It was wilder, more merciless, and difficult to control. He was cautious with his words. Pleaded with her to be careful, not to speak of it. Not to anyone. It had to stay between them.

Hirka glimpsed something new in Rime's eyes.

Curiosity. A chink in the An-Elderin family armor.

He couldn't explain what had happened and was like a little boy on an adventure—an adventure fraught with danger.

But they weren't able to stop themselves from experimenting. Hirka felt inebriated, as though Orm's wine were still coursing through her bloodstream. It made everything else seem unimportant. And best of all, what had previously been a weakness was now a source of amazement to Rime. She was no longer completely insignificant.

She listened as he explained. Most of what he said she barely understood, but she drank in his words like tea. They nourished her. Even Kuro seemed to enjoy them. He sat on a broken stone pillar nearby, with beady eyes and his head half-tucked under his feathers to avoid the wind.

Hirka couldn't bind, but when Rime did, she could experience the Might through him. The only requirement was that he had to be touching her. It didn't seem to matter to what extent. Whether he held both hands, or just one finger, the life flowed through her as though it had always been there.

She gradually got used to the feeling, and soon it was only mildly discomforting. The longer they continued, the longer she managed to hold onto that feeling, even when Rime took a few steps away from her. But never for more than a brief moment. As soon as Rime let go, the Might started to trickle out of her. Nothing she did could hold onto it. She was as leaky as a sieve, as Rime put it.

He was excited to discover that Hirka could actually feel when he bound the Might, even when he wasn't touching her. She couldn't remember having felt other people binding before. Nor could Rime. But she felt him now. It was as though he had shown her the Might for the first time, and now she could feel it firsthand. It certainly wasn't normal. He said the older members of the Council could feel it that way, those with the bluest blood in the land, but not ordinary people.

Hirka felt a stab of guilt. She wasn't ordinary people. She was something much, much worse. And she couldn't tell him that.

Before they climbed down from Vargtind, Rime promised to help her during the Rite. He had a plan. An insane plan. Hirka was fond of plans, but she felt her mouth go dry when she thought about it. She didn't even know if it was possible, but right now she felt larger than life, like there was nothing she couldn't do.

They stopped at the foot of Vargtind, where they had to part. Hirka still felt dizzy. She was going to go through the Rite, and Rime was going to help her. There was hope where before there had been none.

"What if the Ravenbearer is standing there for so long that …"

He gave her a crooked smile. "Hirka, there are thousands who are going to go through the Rite."

"But what if—"

"Hirka." He interrupted her, but his voice was gentle. "Do you trust me?"

"Of course."

She hadn't thought about it. Just answered. And she knew it was true. A few hours ago he had been her betrayer. Now he was the Seer Himself.

"Good." He started to walk away but turned around.

"As long as you do what we agreed."

Hirka nodded.

"Stick to the plan."

He smiled. Looked at her for a moment, head cocked. Then he left.

BLOODWEED

Hirka felt full of life, full of sounds and smells. It was as if she'd never truly lived until now. She ran all the way home. She needed to tell Father she could bind. That everything was going to be just fine.

Of course, she couldn't tell him the truth: that she could only bind with Rime's help. That wouldn't be good enough for Father. He was too scared after Ramoja's visit. But she'd convince him. She could describe the feeling in detail. No one who heard what she had to say would be in any doubt as to whether she could bind.

Hirka grew short of breath as she climbed the final slope. Lack of sleep was catching up with her. Kuro was sitting on the cabin roof looking out across Elveroa as if he owned it. She knew the feeling. She leaped up the steps to the door in one bound and went in.

"Father!"

He wasn't there, but one of the wheels of his chair was sticking out from behind the curtain by his bed. Was he sleeping? In the middle of the day? When she had such important news?

Hirka tore the curtain aside and immediately realized something was wrong. Father wasn't moving. Panic gripped her. Her heart felt as if it were trying to escape through her mouth. She dropped to her knees by the bed.

"Father!" Hirka shook him and he opened his eyes, agonizingly slowly. She hardly dared breathe. "Father …"

Father tried to smile, but all he managed was a twitch at the corner of his mouth. No. This couldn't be happening—everything was supposed to be fine!

"Father, I can bind!" Hirka heard her voice crack, but she continued all the same. She gripped Father's hand. It was cold. "I can bind!"

Father focused on her. Hirka could see how difficult it was for him to speak.

"Go. Now."

"I'm not lying, Father! I can bind!"

"That's good … Hirka," Father said, the words coming in short gasps.

The room grew hazy, and Father's face became like the ghosts she had dreamed about on Vargtind.

"I can bind."

Father's hand was limp.

"I can bind …"

But there was no one there to hear her. She squeezed Father's hand, but where there had once been life, there was now only death.

The room grew colder. Summer was over. The fire needed to be tended to, but Father couldn't do it. Not this time. Or next time. Father would never fetch them more firewood, never again. But that didn't mean he had to be cold.

Hirka rose unsteadily to her feet. She walked past the curtain and out into the small hearth room, which seemed darker than she could ever remember it being. She thought back to the previous morning, when she'd first awoken, before she'd remembered what she was. How blissfully unaware she had been for a brief moment—until reality had caught up with her. That was just how it would be from now on. If she ever managed to sleep again, she would always wake up to a new nightmare. Every time.

Hirka picked up a couple logs for the fire. Carefully, as if trying not to wake Father. She could hear drawn-out calls from the night warbler outside. It was late. Maybe if she could keep Father warm overnight, he'd get up in the morning, maneuver himself into his wheeled chair, and go about his day. He'd get flour all over the hearth room and push the sweat back from his brow, like always.

Hirka gazed at the place where he always sat. Black letters had been scratched onto the table in charcoal. Only one word. *Ravnhov.* Father's clumsy handwriting. He didn't write very often. About as often as he read. It made her want to smile despite herself. Father had known something was wrong. That he was going to die.

Hirka rubbed out the letters with her sleeve. She put the logs on the fire and blew on the embers. It crackled to life. She knew she ought to eat something, but she couldn't bring herself to try. She went back to Father, still lying motionless in bed. His gray woollen blanket was too thin. Hirka pulled a wolfskin rug out from under the bed. It was a bit dusty. She considered giving it a shake, but then she just pulled it up to Father's chin and lifted his hands so they were lying on top of it. They were cold. Big and cold.

Hirka kneeled down by the bed and tried to massage some warmth into them, then stopped. Of course. She was so stupid. Father was dead. Her lips formed a rueful smile.

She buried her face in the wolfskin in an attempt to escape the truth. But it wouldn't leave her alone. Would it stay with her forever, an unbearable companion until her dying day? *Or until Kolkagga catch up with me. The black shadows.*

The smell of wolf enveloped her. Nothing could kill a wolf, not completely. A hunter's arrow could stop it, his hands could skin it, and a merchant could take it to the end of the world to sell it as a rug. But it would always live on in the smell. For a brief moment, it was like when she had bound the Might with Rime. Father wasn't dead. The wolf wasn't dead. They were just something else. Hirka breathed in through her nose, as if trying to cling to meaning in a meaningless world. Wolf. And … metal?

Hirka lifted her face from the rug and stared at Father's hand, which she'd had tucked close to her. Surely not?

Smell his hands, then!

Cautiously, Hirka brought her nose to his hand. It was cold and smelled like him. Hirka's shoulders slumped in relief, but then she caught another whiff. A sweet, metallic tang she knew she recognized.

Hirka snatched back her hands, tucking them close to her body. Waves of disbelief rippled through her. She looked around to check the rows of jars lining the walls. But they weren't there. Of course. Everything had been packed up.

In a daze, she got up and pulled the curtain aside. There. In the red chest, between countless other jars and boxes, was a squat, black clay pot. Hirka picked it up. The pot had once been glazed and shiny, but not anymore. The lid was held in place by two wooden pins on either side. Hirka pulled them out and lifted it off.

The pot was empty. Only the nauseating metallic smell remained. Father had taken bloodweed.

The pot fell from her hands. It smashed against the floor. Thousands of brown and black ceramic pieces flew across the wooden floorboards. She needed to deal with this—and quickly. Hirka grabbed the brush and swept everything into the dustpan.

She opened the door as quietly as she could. It was dark outside. She climbed up to the clifftops without dropping a single shard. She knew she wasn't safe until she could hear the sea far below. And when she finally did, she scattered the pieces to the wind.

She carried the dustpan back down to the cabin but couldn't bring herself to go back in. Reality was in there. Out here it was night. Out here nothing had happened yet. Hirka walked out onto the ledge and looked down into the fog blanketing a sleeping Elveroa. No one knew Father was dead. No one knew what he'd done for her. He'd taken bloodweed, to make it easier for her to escape. Something Hirka had been about to tell him wasn't necessary.

Hirka fell to her knees in the scrub.

TO THE RAVENS

Time stood still. Hirka couldn't get back into her normal routine. She'd put everything back on the shelves, emptied thc chests and the sacks until the cabin looked the way it normally did. But no tea was sold, no amulets. No herbs were gathered. The flowerbeds weren't weeded. No salves or oils were delivered anywhere. Had the gulls not still been screeching, Hirka might have thought she was dead too.

A handful of acquaintances, some more familiar than others, came to pay their respects. Hirka welcomed them and said goodbye when they left. She heated soup, set out ale, and thanked them when they brought her more soup and ale.

Most of the people who visited had only dared make the trip because they were scared. The Hovel was still the Hovel, but without Thorrald's help, they knew they would have to travel a long way now to get salves for wounds, or tea that could ease the pains in joints and lungs. They smiled hopefully at Hirka. Surely her father had taught her what he knew? Hirka avoided answering. He'd been preparing her for this day all her life. But what could she promise them now?

In the evening, Ramoja and Vetle arrived. They brought Nora with them, the smithy's girl. They lit candles around Father's bed and washed and oiled him. Ramoja dried Father's hands, not knowing that Hirka had already done that—to remove all traces of bloodweed. Hirka pulled her feet up and rested her head on her knees.

The candles colored Father's body with warm light, as though he was just asleep. But against Nora's hands, he was obviously pale. Ramoja oiled Father's thin legs with gentle movements. She looked at Hirka several times and opened her mouth as though to say something, but then she didn't. In the end, Hirka said that she was going to speak with Sylja about living at Glimmeråsen after Father was cremated. It wasn't true, but at least it would spare Ramoja the guilt.

Ilume didn't come to the wake. Why would she? Councillors didn't make a fuss over ordinary people. Hirka had thought she would send Rime, but he didn't come either. Hirka found herself hoping that he had left. Both him and Ilume. What did they know about death? They got to live forever.

When people in Council families died, they weren't cremated like ordinary people. They were given to the ravens. Council families carried the life force in their very veins, and that had to live on. At some point in the future, Ilume would be cut up into bits and devoured by ravens. Become one with the sky, and the Seer.

Father, on the other hand, was anything but sacred. Father was just Father. But he had saved lives for as long as he lived. If anyone deserved to fly with the ravens for eternity, then it was him.

Hirka got out of bed. She was still wearing her clothes. She went out into the cool night. The trees whispered their warnings, but Hirka had made up her mind. She knew what she had to do.

She walked around the cabin to the lean-to that served—*had* served—as Father's workshop. The hinges creaked when she opened the door. There lay Father. In the middle of the room, on his workbench. He lay on the oiled linen cloth, which had to be wrapped around him before the cremation. Ramoja and Nora had dressed him in a simple black shirt, with no cord around the waist. His tail was hidden beneath him, reminding Hirka of how she looked to other people. Two arms, two feet, no tail.

Maybe she should take some of his tail? Hirka pulled her knife carefully out of its sheath. No, there wasn't enough flesh on the tail.

She heard a scream behind her.

Kolkagga! Hirka spun around with the knife in front of her. The door! She hadn't shut the door. *Stupid girl.* With her heart in her mouth, she shut the door behind her. She walked back to Father and swallowed hard. She had no idea what she should do. How much did she need for it to mean something? She couldn't take something that people would notice. She had to conceal it or be prepared to meet the Council in far worse circumstances than the Rite. After tonight she would be an outlaw.

Hirka pulled up Father's shirt. She placed the knife against his stomach. The blade quivered. His skin resisted, and she changed her mind. This was going to be more difficult than she had thought. She had been with Father several times when he'd had to slice open others—many of whom still lived, because of him. She had done it herself, under Father's watchful eye. But this was different. This was as dark as the night. Everything she breathed was black.

Hirka collected herself and moved the knife to his waist. She leaned on the blade and it sunk down into the skin. She held the wolfskin ready in her other hand, but no blood came from the cut. Even so, Father looked like he might wake up at any moment. As though he was just patiently waiting for Hirka to finish.

The first cut was the most difficult. After that it was like she was in a daze. In the end, Hirka stood with a fistful of Father. She plugged the wound with fur from the wolfskin rug and pulled down the shirt. Nobody would know what had happened.

The Seer sees. The Seer knows.

It didn't matter. If the Seer knew, then He would understand. He would agree that Father deserved to live on. And if He didn't understand, he wasn't the Seer she had heard about.

She took the scrap remaining from the wolfskin rug and wrapped it around the dead piece of flesh, Father's salvation. She wrapped her hand around the package. In the dark, it looked like a fuzzy club. She went back out into the night. The door was silent this time.

What have I done?

The wind had picked up now. The trees shook their leaves when she went past. They bent aside to get away from her. She was a desecrator of corpses. Hirka smiled crookedly to herself. What else could they expect? She was one of Odin's kin.

Hirka took long strides and looked around in the darkness. Would she find him? Maybe he was asleep? At the top of the cliff she unwrapped her sin and cut it up into smaller chunks, and then at last she heard wings flapping behind her. Good.

Kuro waited until she had pulled away before he began to feast. For a moment she worried he would save some of it for later, but he must have been hungry. Either that or he understood his job. Hirka squeezed the now-empty wolfskin into a ball and threw it into the sea. The waves crashed against the cliff. They were more amenable than the trees. The waves promised to conceal her misdeed, forever. She sat down on the grass and wiped her knife before she stuck it back in its sheath. She saw Kuro take to the skies. He disappeared above the trees. Along with Father.

It was done.

Heavy drops fell down on her hands. For a moment she thought it was rain, but it wasn't. She was crying. She felt exhaustion seize her. She climbed to her feet and walked down toward the cabin. All she wanted was to go to sleep, but she found herself stopping in front of the workshop. She had to go back in. She wiped her nose on her tunic sleeve before she opened the door.

The hinges groaned and she wriggled in through the opening. Everything looked like it had when she left. What had she expected?

The black-clad figure still lay in the middle of the room. Hirka went over and stared down at it. It had Father's face, but Father himself was long gone. There was nobody here now. Only an empty shell remained.

Suddenly it hit her. Children of Odin had to have fathers as well. And mothers. And for the first time, Hirka felt something other than panic while thinking about who she was. She felt a strange tingling she had no other word for than *curiosity*.

THE PYRE

Darkness observed the crowd gathered on the rocks at Svartskaret, inching as close as it dared to the torches burning at the water's edge. Rain drizzled down.

Hirka felt like a pocket of darkness in a pool of light. She looked up. The miller was carrying the bier along with Vidar, Iron Jarke, Annar, and Sylja's older brother, Leiv. Annar was probably only doing it for the sake of appearances. He didn't have the strength to carry much. Father was wrapped in linen. A shrouded figure on a wooden frame. It could have been anyone.

They inched forward. Hirka wished they could go faster, but they had to keep time with the monotonous drumming behind them. Who decided these things? Decreed the customs and how fast people should walk? Or was that just the way it was?

Hirka looked past the procession toward the pyre. The wood had been arranged just right, like two giant interlinked combs. Father would be set down on top of them. Dry kindling had been stacked on the ground beneath.

The men stopped and moved Father forward across their shoulders until he was lying where he was supposed to. Then they retreated into the crowd. Hirka turned to follow, but then there was a gentle hand on her shoulder. Ramoja gave her one of the torches.

Of course. She would have to light the pyre herself.

Hirka took the torch and held it to the rags they had woven

through the kindling. They had been dipped in oil, so the pyre was ablaze in only a moment, despite the rain. Hirka took a couple steps back as the heat hit her. She could see everyone's faces through the fire. She'd lived here for years but didn't feel like she knew anyone here now. That was what came of keeping to yourself. People never stopped being strangers. Kaisa and Sylja, both in black dresses. Nora. Vetle.

Rime!

He was standing diagonally opposite her, all in black and half-hidden by the flames. What was he doing here? He and Ilume were supposed to have left already. Had they been delayed? His white hair glowed against the dark sky and sea behind him. His eyes rested on Father's body, which was now hard to see for the flames. The fire crackled and snapped.

Rime looked up and met Hirka's gaze. He looked at her with raw, naked grief. The solidarity was so unexpected that she raised a hand to her heart in a futile attempt to keep him out. His eyes were fixed on hers. They cut through the flames and into her heart. Hirka could almost hear him talking. Not about grief, but about surviving.

We're alive. You and I, Hirka.

She felt arms around her. It was Ramoja, embracing her, pulling her close. Hirka looked away, and when she looked back, he wasn't looking at her anymore.

Father burned.

He burned until they could hear the sound of the waves over the fire again. People started to leave. They'd decided the flames had done their job. Kept the blind away and shown Thorrald the way to Slokna. So now they left her, crossing the bridge and heading back into the village. A solemnly dressed line of people, wending their way along the shore. You'd think they were the ones who'd died.

Hirka huffed out a laugh. Father wasn't sleeping in Slokna. He was in heaven. With the ravens. Or was he in both places?

He was everywhere.

Now it was up to the sea to claim what remained.

She, Ramoja, and Vetle were the last to leave. They followed the line of shadows to the inn and the ale. Hirka didn't really want to go. But Ramoja and the other women had been busy baking pretzels, honey bread, and cakes all day long. Hirka had been spared that work. The least she could do was show her face. She made a mental note to thank them.

There weren't many chairs left at the inn. Hirka and Vetle sat at the bar. Hirka couldn't remember the last time she'd voluntarily spent time with so many other people. What would Father have said?

Ramoja and Nora handed out ale and bread baked with dried fruit. The room was lit by a hundred candles. Children ran about while adults drank tankards of ale and talked among themselves. Hirka sat as if in a trance, oblivious to anything anyone was saying.

Until Kaisa mentioned Father.

Hirka didn't hear exactly what she'd said, but she heard Sylja's reply: "What do you mean?"

Kaisa raised her voice. "I mean that if he'd been a half-decent healer, he probably would have been able to save himself."

Hirka got up and walked over to Sylja's mother. "My father helped people."

Kaisa wouldn't look her in the eye. Instead, she leaned over to her daughter and whispered: "The wolves took her composure along with her tail."

It wasn't the first time Hirka had heard Kaisa say that about her, but she refused to let anyone talk about Father that way. Hirka didn't stop to think. It was as if her body took over, lifting her arm and upending the tankard. The contents poured over Kaisa, who shrieked as if she'd been stabbed. Her hair dripped with ale and stuck to her skin. Her dress was sopping wet to her waist. She gasped out a few unintelligible words. Sylja gaped. Vetle laughed, and Ramoja put a hand over his mouth.

Everyone was looking at Hirka, but she wasn't afraid. Her fury was burning hotter than Father's funeral pyre, and she couldn't contain herself.

"My father saved lives! He saved *you* from lung fever! He helped a lot of people who worked at Glimmeråsen. He built new stables for you." Hirka could hear her voice getting thicker, but she wouldn't cry. She needed to say this.

"And what did you give him in return, Kaisa? Where were you when that beam fell? He never walked again, and you wouldn't so much as look at him."

The silence was palpable. But it wasn't her that everyone was staring at now. They were staring at Kaisa. Hirka felt a stab of triumph amid the despair. The others knew. They knew it was true.

Kaisa of Glimmeråsen was speechless, but only for a moment. She looked around, realizing she would have to answer, and quickly. She put one hand on her hip and pointed at Hirka using the other. "Blindspawn! He never did teach you manners. Glimmeråsen can't be blamed for your father's foolishness."

Hirka lifted her fist, but someone grabbed her and dragged her toward the door. Rime. She had little choice but to go with him, Kaisa screeching behind her, "How dare you! You can leave, but you can't escape the reach of Glimmeråsen!"

"Her father was cremated today." Rime's voice was tense, but level, and it silenced Kaisa. The inn door slammed shut behind them, and after a moment of silence, Hirka heard everyone start talking again inside. That shouting match would keep them going for a while. She drew cold air into her lungs. She felt suffocated by the words she had just heard.

You can leave, but you can't escape the reach of Glimmeråsen!

How had Kaisa even known they'd been planning to leave? Then Hirka remembered. Sylja. Sylja down by the shore, through a wine bottle. Hirka had told her they were leaving. And what had Sylja done? Told her mother, apparently. And Kaisa had betrayed them.

Kaisa. Not Rime.

He tugged her along after him. The voices from the inn faded behind them. She was starting to worry that Rime would drag her all the way home, to the cabin. That empty, meaningless cabin. She tried to twist from his grasp, but he wasn't having it.

"Let go of me!" She aimed a kick at his shin but lost her footing. Rime caught her and put an arm around her. Then he started to bind. A dirty trick she couldn't fight. He pulled her toward him until she could bury her face in his chest. His hand cupped the back of her head. Hirka tried to hide her grief from the Might, but it was useless. It ripped through her, finding all her open wounds, pulling her apart and betraying her. When had she let Rime get so close? This was madness!

Stay away from the rot. It kills.

She started shaking. Rime wasn't only binding to comfort or calm her. He was making her a promise.

"I'll make sure I'm there for you."

Hirka laughed despairingly against his chest. If only he knew. Everything had changed. She wouldn't be going to the Rite. Under no circumstances. Never. Nothing in the world could make her turn up to something that had the power to hound Father into Slokna. He'd sacrificed everything for her. He'd known the Rite would be her downfall. That everyone would find out, recognize the rot. But he'd also known she'd never run while he lived—never leave him behind. In his own backward way, he'd been trying to help her.

She wouldn't give Rime the chance to do the same. What if the Seer found out? What if Kolkagga were sent after him? He could lose everything because of her. Just like Father had.

Hirka grudgingly tore herself away from him so he wouldn't see through her deception.

"One point to me if I beat you there."

THE DRAWING

Urd slammed the book closed. Dust fled over the balustrade and drifted down through the library's many levels. Taciturn men dressed in gray raised their eyes from their inane tasks and frowned at him as though he had pissed on the floor. They were called shepherds, he had been told. One of them stood a couple of steps away, his finger frozen on the spine of a book he had been busy putting into place. Urd bared his teeth at him. The pale figure backed away and disappeared between the massive bookcases.

Nothing. Absolutely nothing.

He had spent half the night in this useless place without finding anything at all he could use. And they called it a Seer's hall for the written word? What a joke! It was a hall for smug writers who worshipped their own ideas. Endless pages of tediousness. Rolls of parchment that smelled of mildew.

They had writings about practically everything. About the Seer, about the wars, about the glory of Mannfalla, about classical shoe stitching from Bokesj and deranged butterflies in Norrvarje that emerged in winter. The most absurd things! Words from yesterday, words from a thousand years ago. Urd found mentions of stone circles that hadn't been torn down after the war, yet he couldn't find something as sensible as a map. Or a list. He wasn't asking for much. A single book would suffice. Accursed Blindból, just one tiny book! One so small it could fit up your ass!

The raven rings. Was that so much to ask for?

Urd threw the book down on a haphazard pile of other books that had already disappointed him. He clenched his teeth so hard they ground together. What if everything was lost? Destroyed many generations ago, in a wave of hysteria? Knowledge forgotten and forbidden, knowledge about blindcraft. About binding the way the blind did. The way ymlings had also done once, as hard as they tried to repress that fact.

Urd had to find something he could use. It was getting urgent. They were restless. Every night worse than the last. Voices whispered from stone, eating their way into his head and making his blood vessels dilate. Other men would have lost their minds, thrown the stone fragments in the Ora where the water was deepest, and fallen to their knees in front of the Seer's hall. But Urd was a greater man. He controlled them.

He couldn't release them, of course. They would devour the world. Including his own part of it. That was the bloody problem with the blind. They were, well, blind.

The gong sounded outside. He had run out of time. The meeting was due to start at the next gong, so he had to get to the Council Chamber. This meeting was his first, and it was the last before Ilume returned. She was his biggest headache. The others he could handle. The question was whether he had enough to go on. A half-drunk informant's rumors of a gathering of nobles in Ravnhov. Hardly reliable, but worth using. What he really needed was nowhere to be found: a document that could prove that the stone circle in Ravnhov was more than a myth. He'd wanted the effect of throwing a map down on the table. Something he could point to and say: "There! *That's* where the blind come from!" If he could find that, then the Council would send every single man to Ravnhov. Kolkagga, guardsmen, merchants, even half dead fishermen. Anything that could crawl or walk.

But he'd find a way. Obviously. He *had* to find a way. Before the hourglass emptied again.

He flung his cloak over his shoulder and turned to leave. He heard one of the stacks come crashing down. A shepherd ran over like it was crystal that had fallen, not worthless books. Urd was struck by how idiotic the term shepherd was in this context. Books were dead things. Not something you needed to watch over.

He cast a glance back. The shepherd was crouched over, picking up books. He clasped them to his chest, thin arms cradling the load. One of the books lay on the floor, its pages splayed open. And in it, Urd glimpsed a drawing.

Curiosity seized him, and Urd took a couple of steps back to look. Urd picked up the book lying by the cringing shepherd's feet and flung it on the reading table. The drawing was faded, but detailed. In flaking gold, and brown that may once have been black.

Urd's heart beat faster in his chest. It wasn't a map. It was something completely different from what he had been looking for. But it was perfect. This he could use.

Urd pointed at the shepherd. "Make a copy of this for me before the hourglass turns."

The shepherd nervously shook his head. "It-it can't be done, fadri. Gretel is in the repository today and nobody can …"

Urd rolled his eyes. He would have to take the matter into his own hands. As usual. The shepherds spent their lives in the shadows, flitting between shelves, living to archive, to record. They had no clue what the world was really about. In the library in Eisvaldr, the blind did not exist. There were no enemies. No dangers. And wealth meant nothing. A book falling was about the most exciting thing that ever happened in this tower.

Urd grabbed the page where it met the spine and tore the drawing out. He smiled at the shepherd, who went pale and looked like his feet were going to give way beneath him.

Good. He'll learn to answer yes *next time.*

Urd walked down the stairs and left the library without looking at the shepherds who opened the doors for him. He crossed the open square outside and sought out the quickest way from among the multitude of bridges and stairs. He started up the nearest staircase, a winding stone snake, while he cursed generations of flawed town planning. Eisvaldr was a nightmare. A labyrinth. Towers and houses had been allowed to grow like weeds. The Council's unlimited resources meant people were able to start building the moment an idea occurred to them. Was he the only one who used his head in this city?

He reached the top and crossed the bridge over to the Rite Hall. The building was the largest and most central in Eisvaldr. Everything else in the city was built around it. *The world* was built around it. It had three levels, crowned with a spectacular dome decorated with tiles as small as fingernails. They shone in a thousand shades of red. People called this dome *mother's bosom*, an appropriate name given that it housed the Council Chamber. It was from here that Mannfalla extended its long arms. It was here that Urd now had a seat. And it was here that he was about to attend the meeting that would make him a legend.

Of all the days to be running late.

THE PENDANT

The room was almost bare, apart from all the chests containing his belongings. Rime had lived here since he was twelve, but he owned very little he'd call his own. Most of it was gifts and finery Ilume thought he needed. But Rime didn't need anything anymore.

He could hear Ilume's clipped commands from downstairs, followed by frantic activity. The servants carried the last of the chests out to the carts. Dust outlines indicated where the cabinets had stood. Rime opened the nearest chest. Clothes. Books. Two pocketknives, one of them with an ornate handle in silver and gold. It had never been used. Rime couldn't even remember where it had come from. He started rummaging deeper in the chest. Where had they packed that little box?

He opened the second chest. Paper. Writing implements. Ceremonial clothes. Belts. A Seer amulet. He ran his thumb over the raven. The chain had been too small for years. He'd meant to get a new one, but he'd never gotten around to it. Now he didn't need it anymore. He kept the Seer much closer now.

At the bottom of the chest, he spotted the box, encased in silk and soft against his fingers. The green was paler than he remembered. His mother's name was embroidered on the lid. *Gesa.*

He opened the box and found what he was looking for. A pendant on a leather strap—an oval shell fragment set in silver. A small part of the mounting had broken off. He turned the pendant in his hand.

Small lines had been scratched into the back using a knife. He felt strangely relieved to see them, as if they might have disappeared somehow. Or as if none of it had ever happened. A clumsy *R* with seven lines, and an *H* with eight lines. Well, he'd have to change that. He took out his pocketknife and scratched an eighth line for himself. *One point for pulling her up out of the Alldjup.*

Rime smiled. He put the pendant on and tucked it under his shirt, then pulled on his leather armor and strapped his swords into place. It was time to go.

Outside, they were all ready to leave, apart from Ilume. Typical. Always making everyone wait. Rime sat up front in the first of eight carts. It was quite the procession, with cooks, chambermaids, coachmen, a healer, and a contingent of guardsmen. A servant stood outside, smiling a bit too broadly. He had been tasked with selling what was left behind, an endeavor from which he would undoubtedly profit.

Ilume kept them waiting, and Rime tried not to get irritated. This was her revenge for the extra day she'd had to wait so he could attend Thorrald's funeral. Ilume herself had procured calming teas from Thorrald, remedies not even her own healer had access to. But honoring the man by going to his funeral? That would have been taking things a bit too far.

At long last, Ilume slipped out the door in her light traveling clothes. Rime got down from the cart and helped her up. She accepted his arm, presumably to make sure no one noticed any friction between them. Or maybe she was just having a good day. Rime took the opportunity to confirm two of his worst suspicions.

"There'll be plenty to do once we're back in Mannfalla," he said casually. "What with Urd in Insringin, and the blind on the loose."

"Fortunately, they're not your problem."

Rime smiled. That was all the confirmation he needed. "It's hard to say which will prove the greatest challenge."

Any trace of a smile on Ilume's face quickly faded.

"Drive!" Ilume said.

The procession started its long journey to Mannfalla.

A VICTORY

The sun streamed in through the windows of the Council Chamber and reflected off the domed ceiling. Twelve columns stood along the wall and accentuated the room's round shape. Each of them was adorned with oil lamps, even though there was more than enough daylight.

Around a massive stone table they stood; white chairs with backs as tall as men. A strip of gold ran around the edge of the table. Each family had its name in gold by each seat. The script was ancient. A runic predecessor to the one in use today, but still legible.

There were eleven people in the room. Eir—the Ravenbearer—was the first to take a seat at the end of the table. Urd quickly scanned the names around the tabletop so he could sit without giving the impression of searching for his place. He needed them to think of him as eternal. Someone who had always been here, and always would be here. He quickly swallowed his disappointment at not being one of those sitting closest to Eir. A detail. He had much to be happy about. This was the chair that had taken him a lifetime to win.

He leaned back into the soft cushions. They were also white, making them invisible against the chair. He folded his hands over his stomach. His name glistened in gold on the table in front of him. *Vanfarinn.* It was a challenge not to smile. It was as though the power that had belonged to his father flowed from the gold in the tabletop and into his body, where it belonged.

Urd controlled the urge to run his fingers across the letters. He had to remember that he belonged here. This was his place. He was sitting in this chamber as a councillor, as one of them.

Jarladin, Leivlugn, and Noldhe sat closest to Eir. Ilume's chair remained empty. Nobody took any notice of Urd. He was new, but clearly they had no intention of marking the occasion. He knew what they were thinking. Nobody had ever gotten in by a narrower margin. Nearly half of the councillors around this table wanted him gone. Still, before the day was done, he would start a war. Before the day was done, he would be a legend. A conqueror who would make all those who had sat in the chair before him pale in comparison. Including his father.

Three girls entered. They carried jugs of wine and trays of apples, nuts, and cakes. Urd swallowed. He hadn't been able to eat anything other than soup since winter. The beads on the girls' trousers jingled when they walked. Nobody in the chamber said anything until they had left the room and the jingling had faded down the stairs. It reminded Urd of someone or something, but he couldn't put his finger on who or what.

"Insringin is gathered for the forty-third time this year."

Eir had a strong voice. She was nearing eighty, but she looked as though time had forgotten her. Her flat nose bore witness to the family's roots in Blossa, but she had more than her roots to be embarrassed of. She wandered the gardens of Eisvaldr until the sun went down. She spoke to the ravens as though they were children. Urd used to think being so close to the Seer had made her a bit strange.

But Eir's strangeness was an illusion, he knew that very well now. She was going to be the toughest nut to crack today. She was never going to want to attack. His only hope was that she let the others vote without delaying the decision until Ilume's arrival.

Eir looked up from the papers and started to reel off what the Council was due to discuss. Urd only half listened. He had a more important agenda, and he had to size up the people he was sharing the table with. Every word he said today had to be right. Had to get through to them all.

To the right of Ilume's empty chair sat Leivlugn Taid, the Council's eldest member, only a handful of winters shy of a hundred. His cheeks had lost all their elasticity, practically hanging by his chin. He sat with his hands folded in his lap. It looked like he was barely able to keep his eyes open. The man would be raven fodder before the snow came, yet there he sat, with inconceivable power! Power he would not use in Urd's favor. The Taid family was known for their calm—or, as Urd preferred to call it, indecisiveness. Leivlugn Taid would certainly try to draw the matter out. He'd probably demand that the decision be put off until Ilume was back.

On Leivlugn's other side was Sigra. The Kleiv family's unpolished councillor. She was a little over fifty and, other than Urd, one of the youngest at the table. The woman had the face of a dog. Angular jaws. Hands that could have belonged to a man. Someone sharing a bed with this woman frequently enough to get twelve children out of her was nothing short of a miracle. But Urd smiled at her all the same. She would be the easiest. The Kleiv family was renowned for their hot-bloodedness. Overrepresented in the Council's army. Sigra was married to a mountain of a man who trained young warriors in Eisvaldr. Rumor had it that Sigra had won her seat on the Council in a fistfight with two brothers and an elder sister. Urd suppressed a shudder. He had also heard rumors that the Kleiv family had always wanted to challenge Ravnhov. There was little doubt as to what they thought of an independent region in Ym. Convincing her would be child's play.

Others wouldn't be much harder. Saulhe Jakinnin, for example, the man with the thin hair that was constantly falling into his face. Supposedly Mannfalla's richest and greediest man. It would be all too easy.

Jarladin An-Sarin was going to be a problem. The most respected man in Mannfalla. Steady gaze, strong as an ox, with dark skin and a perfectly trimmed white beard. His family had strategic connections with practically everyone of importance. Peace lilies, the An-Sarins had been called. Urd knew better. The family was strong and got what it wanted because they shared Urd's power of persuasion. But who was going to win today?

Garm Darkdaggar was asked to transcribe the meeting. A perfect role for a bureaucrat. The family consisted of legal experts and corridor walkers, but Garm was a man Urd could appreciate. Calculating. Garm would not let himself be ruled by sentimentality.

The first item on the agenda concerned a not-insignificant jarl who wanted a new hall for the Seer in his hometown. Urd was already bored and had no opinion on the matter. The majority raised their hand in support of the hall, so Urd did the same. What did he care? He was waiting for a more important point. The one that would lead him to victory.

"Two murders in as many days? It makes a mockery of us!" Sigra's masculine voice gave a splendid introduction to the next point. Urd made himself more comfortable. This was the moment. She leaned over the table. "I say send Kolkagga out at night to clear the streets!"

Noldhe responded with a cautious smile. "You always say that, Sigra. The Rite is just around the corner, the city is full of people, and they're still flocking in. Conflicts are bound to arise, and they do, every single year. What would you have us do? Kill everyone who gets drunk? Send Kolkagga after everyone who fights in the taverns? They have far more important matters to attend to."

"Which we hardly use them for!" Sigra leaned back and crossed her arms.

Several people spoke over each other, until Jarladin raised his voice. "The city is bursting at the seams, and more will come. We have no other option but to send more guardsmen out into the streets. Let's solve this as we do every year and move on."

Urd seized the opportunity.

"But this year is not like other years."

All eyes around the table fell on him, with expressions ranging from mild interest to clear annoyance. His first meeting as a member of Insringin, and he had just contradicted Jarladin.

They had better get used to it.

He waited for a moment. "This year is not like other years. This year we are faced with our downfall."

The reaction was not long in coming. Disbelief washed over the faces around him. Urd continued while he could. "This is the year Ravnhov sends the blind after us, while we discuss drunken rows in the taverns." Jarladin and Eir exchanged a quick glance. A silent dialogue about who was going to put him in his place. But they weren't going to get the chance. "We can avoid talking about it, but there isn't a soul in Mannfalla who doesn't know it. The blind are back, and they have made their mark in the north. Who among you think it is coincidental? Who among you think they found their way here on their own? Do you think—"

"Urd, this Council has discussed the rumors about the blind to death. We appreciate your involvement, but you probably wouldn't be as riled up if this weren't your first time."

Several people around the table chuckled audibly. Urd felt a twitching at the corner of his mouth. He couldn't allow himself to be provoked. He had to prove himself worthy. "I am here for the first time. A new servant of Mannfalla. A duty I undertake with humility. Have I not been asked to be here? Has the Council not invited me here to follow in my father's footsteps?"

Urd continued before anyone had time to consider the differences between him and his father.

"Rumors? Rumors about the blind? We have people in the pits

who have seen them. Who can describe them in monstrous detail. Half the kingdom has found its way here. They are flocking to Eisvaldr in pursuit of protection. Gifts and prayers to the Seer are stacked higher than the walls. Rumors?!" Urd could feel himself growing more fervent. "We stand faced with the threat that will decide our fate. The fate of all Mannfalla, not just those of us around this table. The blind have returned, and more and more people in Ravnhov are keeping their children away from the Rite. A direct provocation. A declaration of war! Or are we not talking about that, either?"

Eir looked like she'd forgotten how to breathe. She was stunned. She glanced at Ilume's empty chair, her eyes wild. Urd wanted to smile, but he controlled himself. This was just the beginning.

Eir asked everyone to calm down once more. The Council Chamber was seething. Old feuds and fears had risen to the surface. Urd stuck to his strategy. He received unexpected help from Jakinnin, who brought up Ravnhov's freedom from debt.

Urd was familiar with the matter. An age ago, the war against the blind had cost everyone dearly, but none more than Ravnhov. Entire villages had to be built anew. People suffered from illness and lack of food and water. Mannfalla had used its affluence to help them. Later came the conditions for that help: Ravnhov had to give up its dominion over the sky. Share the ravens and the knowledge that had been passed down for as long as anyone could remember. Tough to swallow for a region that trained the best ravens the world had seen. Adding insult to injury, they had to bury their gods and devote themselves to the Seer.

Ravnhov refused. But the money was gone, and so Mannfalla could impose whatever conditions they wanted—which they did, with a vengeance. Ravnhov had paid for fifteen generations but was finally able to celebrate its freedom in the year of the Seer 928. They had made good use of the seventy years that followed. Today Ravnhov could enjoy the surplus of ravens, stone, and steel. They were growing bigger and stronger. A fact that helped Urd's case now.

Nobody in the chamber doubted that Ravnhov posed a threat to Mannfalla. Not as a military power, but as an independent region. A blight on the Council's autocracy. A threat to everything that was and always had been.

"Ravnhov would never dare to defy Mannfalla," old Taid offered tediously.

"They defy us every day," Urd countered. "They keep their children from the Rite. In spite of the blind! Why do you think that is? They're in league! The blind are going to help Ravnhov to power!" Urd was impressed with himself. When he heard his own words, they seemed more convincing than they had done in his head.

"Poppycock!" Noldhe put her goblet down and leaned back in her chair. "Poppycock from start to finish. This Council has been discussing Ravnhov for generations. Are we going to sacrifice lives to a war of pride? We are better than that. We are Eisvaldr."

Urd took the floor before she could appeal to the hearts of the others. "We are Eisvaldr today. Tomorrow Ravnhov will be talking to its allies and by the next moon we will be gone."

"Which allies?" Darkdaggar put down his pen and rubbed his knuckles while he waited for Urd's answer.

Urd put on an air of surprise. "The nobles in the north, of course. I have it from reliable sources that they are riding toward Ravnhov. This is not difficult information to come by. I refuse to believe that the Council does not know this already."

He enjoyed seeing the unease spread across their faces. The rumor had meandered its way to him via an acquaintance of an acquaintance, and it was nothing more than a measly letter. An invitation to

Ravnhov that someone had turned down, but that was good enough for his purposes.

"Was that not why you took the life of the jarl in Skodd?" he added. An assumption, but he felt sure enough to use it. The silence that followed was confirmation enough.

"They have scoffed at us for a thousand years!" Sigra announced. "I say—"

"Send in Kolkagga?" Noldhe interrupted. "Your solution to everything? Kill them all?"

Urd leaned over the table. "Am I to understand that our … approaches … have not been successful?" He brought the question to the table with all the caution he could muster. He avoided mentioning Ilume's name but left it up to the Council to remember who it was that had failed.

He sat back again. He couldn't understand what was so difficult about it. Everyone could see that they had everything to gain from crushing Ravnhov. Still they did nothing. And people like this were the ones with all the power? It was heart-wrenching. He had lit the torch. Now all he could do was sit there like an idiot and wait. Wait until they were ripe. Until they had decided on their own that it was in Mannfalla's interest to march on Ravnhov.

He felt a stinging in his throat. He couldn't waste any more time. He got up and started to walk around the table. "Ravnhov has every reason to want to topple this Council. The chieftain who single-handedly carried the last of the debt to Mannfalla never returned. This Council was the last to see him alive. Do you think Ravnhov has forgotten that? Do you think Eirik has forgotten the dying day of Viljar, father of his father's father? Would he be called Eirik Viljarsón if they had forgiven us?"

"Sit down, Urd Vanfarinn! In this room, nobody stands above anyone else!" Eir's voice cut through murmurs of agreement. Urd wound his way back to his chair and met the gaze of Freid Vangard.

She had bags under her eyes. A seventy-year-old woman from a mediocre family who had never had a leading role in the Council. Urd smiled.

"Nobody above anyone else? Even though not everyone here has borne the Raven?"

"Why don't we try again?" An unexpected response from Miane Fell. The woman who had loved his father.

"Try what?" Freid Vangard asked, suddenly joining the debate. That could only mean one thing. Urd had succeeded in stirring something in her.

"To put an end to the chiefdom! Eirik is too strong. People follow him through thick and thin. And if Urd is right that he is in contact with the blind—"

"Bleakest Blindból, woman! Of course Ravnhov isn't in contact with the blind!" Tyrme Jekense remonstrated with a plump arm. Urd clenched his teeth. He'd been certain that he had Tyrme. He had forgiven his brother's debt and won his vote for this chair. Apparently, his loyalty went no further than that.

"You don't know that!" Sigra got straight to the point. Her eyes bored into Tyrme like a killer bear's. "For all you know, they could have unlocked the stone doors again. Why else would they hold their children back from the Rite?"

"If anyone had unlocked the raven rings, we would know about it." Eir was starting to sound tired. "You forget that Ilume had the stone whisperer with her. Had anyone used the stone way, Hlosnian would have known long ago."

Urd pricked up his ears. This was news to him. Stone whisperers? Those foolish, absentminded artists who did nothing other than make sculptures and Seer icons? He longed to ask but couldn't show his ignorance. He would have to return to the library—tonight.

"Elveroa is a long way from Ravnhov," Sigra replied. "There are limits to what an old man can feel. But that's neither here nor there.

Whether the blind have returned or not, Ravnhov must be brought to heel again!"

"Ravnhov has never been at heel," Leivlugn Taid muttered.

"Nor have they been any real threat," Noldhe responded. "And even if they were, we certainly wouldn't be within our rights to start a bloodbath. We must not forget who we are."

Urd knew that she was appealing to hearts around the table. Perfect. The time had come for him to strike. The stinging in his throat intensified. *Not now!*

He cleared his throat before he started. "No. We must not forget who we are," he repeated. "You know, I look around this room. I see our names in gold. I see a table abounding with fruit, nuts, cheese from every corner of the world and wine from the best vintages. I see oil lamps made of gold, and velvet on the chairs." He took a brief pause to allow people to look around.

"Perhaps this room tells us who we are. Affluent, comfortable, satiated. Perhaps we have forgotten what we used to be." He stood up again and dropped the drawing so that it fluttered down toward the table. It drifted back and forth before landing between the bowls of fruit. The others leaned forward to look. Eir too. He took the opportunity to walk around the table again while they were occupied.

"I found this drawing in the library. I wanted to become more familiar with our roots. I wanted to know how my father and my father's father had lived. I wanted to understand more about the position I have now been asked to fill. I am to be one of twelve, who together uphold a pact. An idea. An idea our forefathers have fought for. A free world. A safe world. And our forefathers devoted their lives to this idea."

Urd looked down at the drawing holding everyone's attention. It depicted the room they all found themselves in. The Council Chamber. Twelve warriors seated around a table, with the Raven behind them. The Seer. Apart from that, the room was bare. The faces were faded, so it was nearly impossible to make out their features. But it didn't matter. Everyone around the table had been brought up on stories about them, the twelve warriors who formed the Council after the world had been freed of the blind. Twelve warriors. Twelve families.

Their descendants still sat here today. But now they wore robes. Not swords.

"I see those warriors in this room today too," Urd continued. He had them now. He knew it. Felt it in every fiber of his being. "I see warriors. But they have lost their swords and are drowning in velvet and gold. They are sated and satisfied, in a room that was once bare. A room that was once about an idea, not about prosperity. While we wallow in luxury and idleness, Ravnhov can tear down what is left of that idea. I want to weep when I see this drawing. Weep! Because I will have to tell my future children that I occupied a seat at this table when we fell."

Urd sat down again. He bowed his head and rested his forehead on his hand. He glanced up surreptitiously to see what was happening around the table. Eir sat with her eyes shut and a face racked with doubt. But he doubted that it was because he had moved her. It was because she knew that he had won.

Jarladin An-Sarin was staring into space. He had a worried crease in his forehead. Urd's words had affected him. Sigra Kleiv's eyes were glistening, but strangely enough, that made her look more masculine. He knew that she had been with him the whole way. Noldhe Saurpassarid had put her hand over her mouth. She was touched, but still unwilling to attack. Garm Darkdaggar was the only one looking at Urd. He gave him a crooked smile, as though he was congratulating him. Urd nodded in return. Garm was a resource. He couldn't forget that. Garm was also the first to resume talking, since he was transcribing the meeting. He went straight to the vote.

"Raise your right hand, all those in—"

"Wait!" Eir held both hands above her head with her palms facing outward, as though she was trying to hold back a wall. "We cannot vote on whether or not to declare war without Ilume present."

Urd closed his eyes. This was what he had been afraid of. Only one option remained to him. If he didn't seize it, everything would crumble when Ilume returned. A divided Council could give the Ravenbearer two votes. That would topple him.

"Ilume's recent experience shows what comes of conversations with Ravnhov. I am certain that she would support the Council's decision, regardless of what it may be. But if the Council is uncertain, we have another option." Urd sighed. He had chanced everything. If this plan didn't work, he had also lost everything. But he didn't have to finish. Sigra Kleiv took the floor.

"The rumors of the blind are more than good reason to send warriors to the north. We do not need to declare war against Ravnhov. We declare war against the blind!"

Garm Darkdaggar interjected. "And we have a weapon that is stronger than a hundred thousand men. We have Kolkagga. Let them kill Eirik of Ravnhov while the world sleeps, and this war can be over before it begins."

Urd nodded and gestured to Garm with his open palm in acknowledgment of how wise these words were. But he had to act quickly to get a decision. "Shall we raise our hands for Sigra and Garm's proposal, or does this Council have no authority without Ilume?"

Eir set her steely eyes on him. He held her gaze. It no longer mattered, because he had won. Once Kolkagga had taken care of Eirik, the path would be clear. And even if they didn't succeed, Ravnhov would interpret any movement toward the north as a declaration of war. Especially in the wake of an attempted assassination.

Garm asked everyone to raise their hands for the proposal. Urd counted five hands. Six including his own. It was difficult not to smile. He had won. Ilume was going to be furious.

His father used to call him weak. If only he could see him now. See the power he had. Urd Vanfarinn. Councillor. Urd had accomplished more in a single meeting than his father had managed in a lifetime.

FIRE

Morning came. The seagulls shrieked down by the quay. Morning went. Hirka sat next to the birch stump and stared down at the road that snaked its way through the valley up toward Gardfjella. It was obscured by trees and hills in many places, especially up toward the Alldjup, but she had found a place where she could see most of it. Yet still it remained woefully empty.

Her stomach was empty too, but she couldn't bring herself to eat anything. She'd tried to choke down some dried apple and ham, but only Kuro had enjoyed it. And he'd taken off again. She was alone. Alone in a completely different way than before. More alone than she'd ever been. Father had traveled to Arfabu without her once. He'd been gone almost half a month, but she hadn't felt alone. She'd known he would come back. She'd been sure of it. He always came back.

Hirka hugged her knees tighter. It felt like rain. Summer had given up. Had she as well? Hirka didn't know. She didn't have anyone anymore. Sylja had betrayed her. She no longer had a home here. It had never been a home, really. Just a place they'd stayed for a long time. But even here, people had steered clear of them. Well, until they got ill. Or pregnant. Or had reason to be superstitious and wanted Seer charms and binding aids. And she and Father helped them all. Other people always talked about Father and her, but they never talked about other people.

What did Elveroa know about her? Nothing. Unless Rime had figured it out and told them. But he hadn't betrayed her before, so why would he now?

I'll never see him again.

Rime thought they'd see each other in Mannfalla. That he'd be helping her bind. But she wouldn't be there. She'd be on the run. Even through her grief, she was relieved that she wouldn't have to go through the Rite. But it came at a price. A price that might prove too high.

Kolkagga.

The black shadows with the power to make a man as full of life as Father choose death. Other people died. Other people got sick. Others gave up. Father lived. But he was no cowardly raven starver—he never backed down from a fight. That was just how he was. How he'd taught her to be. And if there were things in this world that could drive him straight into Slokna's embrace—

There!

Hirka's thoughts were interrupted by the appearance of a line of carts on the road. She got up for a better look. Eight carts and more people on horseback around the carts. It couldn't be anyone else. Rime and Ilume were leaving Elveroa.

Ilume would leave behind little more than the Seer's hall. Before she'd arrived, the people here had never attended messages. Sure, they'd prayed to the Seer and forged idols in His likeness, but Elveroa was so close to Ravnhov that no one had ever taken it that seriously. Hirka didn't even think the augur had been that zealous before Ilume came along. What would it be like now? She'd never find out.

The procession disappeared into the forest and Hirka went back into the cabin. She started packing. She took her time. Father's teas and herbs were relocated from pots and boxes to smaller hide or linen bags. She rolled some of them in paper. A few things had to be kept in sealed containers, but she tried to find boxes that were as small as possible. There was no way she could take everything. Dried tea and herbs they'd spent years collecting would have to be left behind.

She filled her travel bag. At the top, she made room for crisp bread, goat's cheese, and a jar of peas. She hung a cured elk sausage from the flap. All the money they had came to eight silver and five copper pieces. But she'd manage. She had things she could sell.

Then she waited.

Darkness fell and Elveroa settled in for the night. She waited a bit longer. She waited until she was sure everyone was asleep and that no one would see the flames. Then she poured oil around the room. Hesitantly at first. It felt unnatural. You didn't just slosh oil all over your home. But that's what she was doing. It spread across the floor, dripping down between the boards. The smell filled her nostrils, gluing them shut.

Her instinct took her to the chest bench, where she found Father's sword. She gripped the hilt and lifted it out. An unfamiliar heft. It was a simple sword from Ulvheim. People were tough in Ulvheim. If she held onto it, she might manage to do what she knew had to be done.

She plunged the sword into the hearth and swept the embers out onto the floor. The room was alight in an instant. For a moment her feet felt heavy, as if they wanted to stay where they were. She lifted the sword, but it was powerless against fire. Fire consumed everything. Even the rot.

She thrust the sword down between the floorboards before running out with her bag on her back. She wasn't dead like Father. She was alive, and Father had given everything to make sure she stayed that way.

She ran toward the Alldjup and didn't stop until she reached the top of the ridge. Then she looked back. The cabin was burning. The

Hovel, the cabin everyone had feared, was finally gone. But she and Father weren't superstitious. Perhaps they should have been?

Hirka watched as the flames, spiraling yellow into the darkness of night, consumed the closest thing she'd ever had to a home. She was far away, but it was like the flames were inside her. Like she had set herself alight.

Rime would think she was dead. Would he grieve? For a day? An hour?

Hirka squeezed her pendant in her fist. The worn wolf tooth with small lines scratched into it on both sides. Proof that for a time, at least, she'd been a normal girl.

She crossed the bridge over the Alldjup and ran into the forest, toward Ravnhov.

EISVALDR

Night had fallen, but the city was still full of life. The streets of Mannfalla had changed in the short time Rime had been gone. Normally it was peaceful after dark, with the exception of the occasional drunk. Or travelers arriving at inopportune times, like himself.

Now, though, it seemed the inns never closed. Minstrels could be heard through open windows. Their songs were bawdier at night, and the verses about willing milkmaids were encouraged with laughter and hollering. Destitute travelers slept in the parks and in the streets. Half the world had come. Rime wished it was just due to the Rite, but he knew that this time it was more than that.

He stayed his horse and looked over his shoulder. The carriages moved slowly across the cobblestones. Ilume sat behind the coachman with her eyes shut and her hands tucked into the sleeves of her tunic. But Rime didn't believe for one minute that she was asleep, so he decided against riding ahead. Several days on the open road had made him restless. It would have been liberating to slip away before they made it to Eisvaldr, but Ilume wouldn't let him off that easily. He accepted it, with the knowledge that it would be the last time.

They continued along the embankment, past the poorest parts of the city, where the stone houses were closest together. A blessing from the Seer amid the squalor, as they were so derelict that they needed each other for support. The air outside some of the more run-down inns was unmistakably saturated with the smell of opa.

A figure staggered toward them, then tumbled to the ground. Rime had to bring his horse to a sudden stop. The horse whinnied and pulled at the reins. Rime hopped down to help, but the man got back to his feet on his own. His age was obscured by a wild beard. One of his eyes was dead and white. His other eye appeared destined to suffer the same fate. He was bleeding from a scrape on his forehead. He looked at Rime and muttered an apology. Rime could tell straightaway that he wasn't drunk. Men had chased him, the man explained. Thrown rocks. "It's my eyes, master," he said. "They frighten folk. They think …" He didn't need to finish.

"They think you look like the blind." Rime shut his eyes and tried to swallow the weight of people's folly. So much meaningless suffering. Born of myths and legends. Born of fear.

He led the hapless man away from the road and pressed two silver pieces into his hand before he climbed back onto his horse.

"Don't make 'em like you anymore, young master!" the man shouted after him, before he continued on his way, ignorant of whom he had just met. Rime glanced back at the carriages again. They had caught up with him now, and Ilume's displeasure gleamed in her catlike eyes. Rime wasn't sure she ever slept.

They turned right and headed up the Catgut. Rising up before Rime was the journey's end: Eisvaldr. The city at the end of the city. Home to thousands of distinguished ymlings and their servants. The home of the Seer had grown until nobody, not even the privileged twelve of the inner circle, could say with certainty how big it was.

Rime's impatience wore thinner the closer they got. Soon. Soon he would be home. His *real* home. Just a quick stop at the family home with Ilume, then it was just a matter of how quickly she would let him leave.

They reached the wall that separated Eisvaldr from the rest of Mannfalla. Today it was only a wall in name. Archways had been built in generations ago, and now it was nothing more than a symbol. Two sleepy guardsmen straightened up when the carriages arrived. They bowed as deeply as their leather armor and chest plates permitted.

"Són-Rime."

Rime felt a twitch at the corner of his mouth. That was how he was doomed to be identified. Son of the Council. First son, and then—if time allowed—Rime. The guardsmen spotted Ilume and looked at each other nervously. They should really have greeted her first, but she had been obscured by shadow.

"Madra." They bowed again and drew back to either side, allowing the carriages to pass.

The An-Elderin family home was one of the oldest in Eisvaldr. It was grand, but different than other houses behind the wall, as it was built of stone that retained its natural color and shape. It looked like what it was named for: a sleeping dragon.

Rime rode up through the orchard but kept doubling back to the carriages. He wanted to go on. *Had* to go on. But Ilume would expect him to accompany her inside. She would likely also expect him to stay the night, but that was not going to happen.

The coachman helped Ilume down from the carriage and woke the servants, who had already been asleep for hours. They led the horses and carriages to the stable. Ilume gave orders for them to wait until the following day to unpack. Then she went inside. Rime followed her.

They were greeted by old Prete, who hurried along the hall with an oil lamp in his hand. Though he had clearly been asleep, his tunic hung straight and unwrinkled on his lean frame. "Ilume-madra."

He bowed and led them into the house. Prete updated Ilume on the household activities. His voice was low, but still echoed under the cavernous ceilings. Rime walked behind them and dimly registered that the furniture had been changed and the winter wing opened. He looked around the rooms he had grown up in and thought of Hirka. The cabin she lived in. He remembered how Thorrald had spoken to him. Openly, as though to a friend. Not someone's son. Not a master of the house. The hearth, the smell of fish soup. A family of only two.

In the An-Elderin family home, nobody sat close together. It didn't matter how many people lived here—Ilume, Rime, Uncle Dankan and all of his lot. The rooms were too big and too many. The floors too shiny. Rime turned as he caught a sudden movement out of the corner of his eye. Just a mirror. An eye in the house. The An-Elderin family home had seen him. Had always seen him. Every moment of every day, since he first came into this world. This wasn't a home; it was a place to be observed. A stage on which to be seen and adored.

Rime realized that he had been walking differently since he came in. His steps were shorter and stiffer. A memory forced itself upon him. He was five or six. Ilume teaching him to walk with his head held high. Forcing his chin up. A fingernail grazing his lip. The taste of blood. The memory faded as quickly as it had come.

Ilume stopped in the library and sent Prete back to bed. As vast as it was, the room seemed oppressive. Dark chairs upholstered with leather and floor-to-ceiling drapes absorbed what little light came from the lamps.

"You can take one of your old rooms until tomorrow." Ilume took off her cloak and draped it over one of the chairs. A thin servant scooped it up and disappeared as quickly as she had come. Ilume sat down, and Rime noticed that she was using one arm to support herself. He recognized her subtle attempt to manipulate him into staying, but he didn't take off his cloak.

"No."

Ilume cleared her throat. He waited for her to say something, even if to suggest that it would be easier to continue on after daybreak. But she didn't. It had been a long journey, and the tension between them had ebbed and flowed like the Might itself. Maybe she was more tired than he'd thought. Or angrier. For a moment he considered staying, but then he realized that had been the point of her remaining silent. She clearly wasn't finished with him, though it was equally clear that she wouldn't be saying anything more tonight.

"Good night, madra." Rime left the room.

He waited until he was out of the house, and then he started to run. No carriage or horse could take him where he had to go. He ran up the wide shopping streets toward the Seer's hall; a sheer white wall that rose before him. It sloped slightly inward, with thousands of narrow windows that had served as arrow slits in another time. His heart was racing. He nodded at the guardsmen at each of the gates he had to pass through. They nodded in return. Eisvaldr slept. But he was who he was, and he could go where he wanted.

Rime continued through the halls and out into the gardens on the other side of the intricate network of halls. He bowed in front of the Seer's tower, the one place he had never been allowed to enter. It was reserved for the twelve. The Seer dwelled somewhere within. A thought as dizzying now as when he had been a boy. He walked past the tower, stopped, and took in the sight of Blindból. A thousand forest-clad mountains were poking up in the valley, extending as far as Rime could see. In the darkness they looked gray, but he knew they were actually a brilliant green. These gardens and the view of Blindból were reserved for those closest to the Seer. The beauty was inaccessible unless you lived or worked in Eisvaldr. But even so, many of those who worked here took great pains to avoid looking at Blindból. Cursed mountains. Forbidden mountains. From where it was believed the blind had come, all that time ago.

It was almost dawn. Rime left Eisvaldr and set out for those forbidden mountains, along paths long forgotten by most. Up and down cliffs and slopes, through sparse pine forests, and over rope bridges that disappeared into the fog ahead of him.

Soon he would glimpse the outline of the camp. *His* camp. It was wild and beautifully situated among the trees atop one of the mountains. Soon he would be home, among his own. Where he wasn't Són-Rime, but simply himself.

Kolkagga.

THE WILD BOY

A sound woke Hirka. She jumped, but Kolkagga hadn't come for her this morning either. It was just Kuro. The raven was strutting around, feathers askew. Hirka sat up too quickly, hitting her head on the rock ledge above. The pain shot from the base of her skull down into her shoulders. She rubbed them until it let up slightly. Her back ached from sleeping on the uneven ground, but she hadn't had a choice. The rain had started in the evening, forcing her to take cover under the rocky outcrop. At least she was dry. She rolled up her jacket and crawled out of her hiding place.

It had stopped raining. The moss glittered with dew, and the mist was starting to retreat through the trees. Kuro flew up onto a branch and cawed irritably. If it hadn't been for his lamenting, Hirka wouldn't have been sure whether she was dead or alive. She had been walking through the dark spruce forest for so many days that she'd lost count. Seven? Eight? Always headed southeast. Toward Ravnhov. Her fear of Kolkagga kept her away from the roads, and away from people. The terrain was nearly impassable in many places. Like here. The forest floor was nothing but mossy stones. It would be all too easy to break an ankle. And what would she do then, all alone?

Father.

Every morning her heart sank when she remembered he was gone. Every evening she saw their cabin in flames. Everything they owned. Reduced to ashes. She'd broken the law by giving part of Father to the ravens, but for what? Had it really saved him? Nothing could save ordinary people from death. Father was in Slokna. Where everyone ended up sooner or later. Where everyone slept for eternity.

Everyone apart from people like Rime. They got to become one with the Might. A part of everything that was and everything that would be.

Rime.

She remembered his eyes blazing in the light from Father's funeral pyre. A longing for the Might flared up in her, gnawing at her chest and taking her back to when he had held her outside the inn. She quickly tried to think about something else. She ate the last of the cured sausage and a few underripe blueberries she'd picked the day before. She couldn't stay out here forever. She needed to get to Ravnhov.

Hirka climbed up onto the rock and surveyed the landscape. Hrafnfell. That was a sight to behold. She could see an opening through the trees to the south. That had to be the way to Ravnhov. If she stayed close to that, she'd probably be there before sunset. The ascent was difficult, and she didn't know what she'd do once she got there. She'd figure something out. She'd have to.

Hirka climbed back down and filled her waterskin with rainwater from a bark trough she'd fashioned. Kuro fluttered down from his branch and stood on the rock, hoping to get something to eat. She stoppered her waterskin and looked at him.

"You're on your own. You've eaten twice as much as me."

Kuro didn't reply. His feathers shone in all the colors of the rainbow. Everything was so simple for him. He could fly wherever he wanted, whenever he wanted. He had nothing to fear, and nothing holding him back. He was free.

Hirka suddenly realized nothing was holding her back either. She was painfully free to go wherever she wanted. Until she was caught. Or froze to death.

"What would I do without you?"

"Kooorp."

"Exactly."

Just as Hirka shouldered her bag and set off again, she heard a scream. She froze. She was used to sounds from the forest, but this was something else. *Kolkagga!* They'd found her. She couldn't bring herself to look around. Her body wouldn't cooperate. Her heart was in her mouth.

Fly! She shooed Kuro into the air and whirled around to face her enemy.

But no one was there. The danger was above her. An eagle! No black shadows. No mythical warriors pursuing her. Just a great eagle—with a wingspan wider than Hirka was tall.

As the winged monster came closer, she realized that it posed a very real threat. She tossed her bag aside and ducked down behind the rock, trying to make herself as small as possible. That was the wrong thing to do. The eagle zeroed in on her and drew its wings in, preparing to dive. Hirka jumped back up onto the rock and shrieked to deter it.

Kuro started flapping around it, cawing hysterically. *"Arka! Arka! Arka!"* The eagle snapped at the much smaller bird. Hirka shrieked for all she was worth, but the eagle had found its mark. It dove toward the raven with its beak wide open. Kuro was so small he would disappear down its gaping throat. There was nothing she could do!

"Kuro! *Hedra!*"

Kuro paused, flapping on the spot.

"*Hedra! Hedra!* Come here!" Kuro pulled his wings close to his body and plummeted toward her. The eagle didn't manage to turn as quickly. It circled round and came for them again.

In the name of the Seer, hurry!

Kuro missed Hirka's outstretched hand and flew straight into her chest. She wrapped her arms around him and turned her back to the enormous creature approaching them from the sky. She squeezed her eyes shut and crouched down. Something whizzed over her head. There was a thump. The eagle screeched just behind her. A piercing shriek of rage. What was happening? Hirka got up.

The eagle hopped around, confused, like it was sizing her up. Her hair was buffeted by the beating of its wings. A rock came flying through the air. It missed the eagle by a small margin, but came close enough to change its mind. It screeched again and disappeared over the treetops.

Hirka turned to see a man standing a short distance behind her on the slope. He was broad-chested and strong-armed, like Father, with brown hair sticking out in every direction. He was lightly dressed but had a jacket tied around his waist. Fur-lined sleeves protruded from where he had knotted it. He was carrying a bow and had a quiver of arrows on his back.

He came toward her and Hirka jumped reluctantly down from the rock. It felt like conceding an advantage, but he had helped her, after all. And he was the only ymling she'd seen in a week.

Ymling. Once again it struck her that she was a child of Odin. Not of Ym. She couldn't even call herself an ymling. The most everyday word you could think of. The word for all people.

He stopped. Hirka got the impression he was waiting to see whether she would run.

"Who are you, girl?" His voice was young. He was a boy with a man's body. Probably no more than two winters older than her. The question sounded like an accusation, but luckily he didn't wait for an answer. "Are you training ravens?"

It occurred to her that, for the first time, Kuro had come on command. True, he'd had a very good reason for coming, but all the same. She let go of the raven so that he could fly free again. Joy blossomed in her chest, but she did her best to look nonchalant. If he thought she trained ravens, that was his problem.

"I'm training this one," she replied, turning to pick up her bag, which had escaped the attack unscathed.

"You're the tailless girl."

Hirka whirled around to face him again. Her absent tail often came up when she met people brave enough to ask, but this time it didn't sound like a question. He stared at her. Hirka searched his face for the usual pity, but all she could see was curiosity.

"Yes," Hirka replied. "When I was little, some wolves attacked our—"

"Hundred northwest!" he suddenly shouted, without taking his eyes off her. Hirka heard a distant reply and more movement from the undergrowth.

"You've picked a bad time to be sneaking around in the forests, girl."

A hunting party, then? And one that couldn't tell the difference between travelers and targets? Hirka crossed her arms over her chest.

"Why? Do you get many two-legged elk around here?"

He looked at her as if she were an idiot. "Have you been living under a rock for the last year? No one travels to Ravnhov through the forests anymore." He pointed between the trees. "Walk up that way until you get to the rock face, then follow it south until you're on the road." He looked her up and down. "Friends of Ravnhov need not fear the road," he added. Hirka wasn't sure whether he was reassuring her or warning her, but before she could say anything, he turned and left.

Hirka stood bewildered next to the rock and watched him disappear between the trees. She opened her mouth to shout her thanks, but closed it again. She spotted one of the rocks that he had thrown at the eagle. Why throw rocks when you have arrows?

Hirka started her ascent. Kuro landed on her shoulder with a flap of his wings. Her woollen tunic didn't do much to protect her from his sharp talons, but it was nothing she couldn't tolerate. He'd come to her when she called. Her lingering fear gave way to wonder. Kuro was no longer just a raven who hung around scrounging honey bread. He was like her, an outsider, and even though they were two fundamentally different creatures, they had communicated with each other. Only one word, but it was a start. If she and the raven could understand each other, perhaps ymlings and emblings could as well.

After a while, she arrived at a vertical rock face, as the boy had said she would. Solid and gray with seams of white running through it. She followed it south. What had he meant by friends needn't fear the road? How could he know she was hiding?

Because you were picking your way through the forest like an idiot.

The trees thinned out, and Hirka climbed out onto the road to Ravnhov.

THE RAVEN'S BROOD

The road twisted up the mountain in gentle turns toward Ravnhov. Hirka walked with her shoulders hunched, feeling exposed and observed. Anyone could be sitting in the trees, watching her. Riders could appear behind her at any moment.

For the first couple of hours she jumped behind a tree every time she heard a noise. But then she reached the felled road marker: a stone pillar that would have been taller than her had it still been standing. It lay at the edge of the forest, cracked in half and overgrown with moss. The mark of the Seer was almost worn away. These road markers were all over the eleven kingdoms. Wherever there were people, there were road markers. This one had probably succumbed during a particularly snowy winter a long time ago. Or been toppled. The strange thing was that nobody had put it up again. She had reached a place where the Council no longer had sole dominion. After that she had stuck to the road. Maybe also because she was getting hungrier and hungrier. Not much else mattered when all you needed was something to eat.

Later in the day several carts trundled past. She pulled up her hood and walked close to the trees, with what she hoped looked like purposeful steps. She gave no indication of wanting a ride, and nobody stopped or asked.

Along the way she also saw men among the trees, building a log wall halfway up the mountainside. She had no idea what it was for.

But it meant that she was getting close to Ravnhov. Who would she meet there, and what would she say to them? Other than she was being hunted? A tailless girl on the run from the Council …

Evening drew in and the air was cooler. The slope grew steeper, and the trees more crooked. Hirka rounded a bend and saw an enormous stone wall some distance ahead of her. It extended from the mountainside, across the road, and into the forest. Stones of all shapes and sizes were firmly lodged in a mud-colored foundation. Two wooden poles supported a gate made of uncut logs.

Up on the wall, three men were talking loudly. One sat with his feet on the outside, picking rust off the hinges of the gate with a spear. Hirka stopped. They had swords, and the leather armor on their chests was worn. Warriors. Gatekeepers of Ravnhov. She reminded herself that she hadn't done anything wrong. At least not as far as *they* knew.

The wall seemed to grow bigger the closer she got. Rough weather had worn the stones smooth, but never managed to shake the barrier. Behind these walls she would be safe. If she even made it in. She couldn't see any doors in the large gate, and she couldn't bring herself to knock. That would be stupid.

Hirka looked up. The man who was sitting with his foot dangling over the edge had seen her, but he continued cleaning the hinges with what Hirka now realized was an angled scraper, presumably designed solely for this purpose. It grated against the metal. Flakes of grit and rust drifted down toward her, settling at her feet.

"How does it look from down there? Much rust left?" The voice was deep and Hirka involuntarily jumped back a step.

"Are you talking to me?"

The man above her stopped scraping and looked at her. He had eyebrows that had nearly grown together. "No, I'm talking to your wits, which you seem to have dropped."

"Those must be yours. Mine are in my bag," she replied, before realizing that provoking the people who would decide whether she was allowed in might not be the cleverest move. But he laughed, and looked over at his fellows, who had been following along.

"Are you wanting in, girl? Where are the rest?"

"The rest of what?"

He looked at her skeptically. "Did you come alone?"

"Yes."

"On foot?"

"Yes."

"From where?"

Hirka hesitated, but she saw no reason to conceal the truth. "Elveroa. Beyond Gardfjella, near—"

"People from all over the world pass through this gate, and you're trying to explain to me where Elveroa is? Who are you, child?"

Hirka tried to come up with a good answer. Should she tell them who her father was? That she was Hirka, daughter of Thorrald? That he was dead and she had nowhere else to go? But what if they asked why?

Then something occurred to her. Maybe they already knew about her? Like the boy in the forest?

"I'm Hirka. I'm … the tailless girl?"

That didn't seem to ring any bells. All three of them tilted their heads, and comically leaned to one side to see if her statement rang true.

"You going to the Rite, tailless?"

"Not unless I'm forced to, but that could very well happen."

They laughed loudly. She'd expected a comment like that would fall on good ground here.

"My kind of girl," one of the two in leather armor said.

"They're all your kind of girl," the other responded. "Including sheep." He raised his arm and signaled to someone behind the wall. The gate slowly screeched open.

"Welcome to Ravnhov, Hirka the tailless."

The crack between the massive doors grew. The town appeared, a throng of houses in stone and wood clinging to the mountainside. She had reached Ravnhov.

Hirka suddenly felt exhausted. This was everything she had feared and hoped for, and it seemed she was welcome. She had to stop herself from running through the gate. What if Kolkagga showed up now? What if she took an arrow in the back, just when safety was within reach? The thought was unbearable, and she couldn't let it go until the gate slammed shut behind her.

Hunger gnawed at her stomach. Now that she was here, she didn't know where to go. There were many streets, leading both up and farther into the town. Some of them were so narrow that she'd hardly be able to squeeze through. Houses were built close together, as though huddling for warmth. In some places they were leaning so close you couldn't see the sky. They had thick shutters and pointed roofs that were weighted with straw. There were a lot more people here than in Elveroa. Hirka tried to look purposeful, so she wouldn't end up in a conversation with anyone.

She spotted Kuro perched on a roof up one of the streets and decided that way was as good as any. Farther up the hill, she came across an inn. Carved letters fixed to the wall welcomed her to "The Raven's Brood." The *D* was missing. It had left behind a pale outline in the wood. Above the letters someone had painted a black, shapeless head with a screeching beak and red tongue. The doorstep had been worn gray and men were laughing inside.

She stopped. It was evening already, and she felt a growing reluctance to spend another night under the open skies. She wanted a hot bath. And a meal. It didn't need to be much. Just bread. Fresh bread. Maybe some hot stew. Her stomach grumbled. She went in.

The noise was deafening as soon as she entered. People were clustered around small tables and on benches along the walls. Tankards were slammed together. People were eating. The tavern in Elveroa had never been as busy as this. Hirka started to retreat, but then she spotted a fireplace in one of the walls, with five piglets roasting on a spit. Their ears were singed and the smell was irresistible. Her mouth watered. Hunger won out over her fear of people.

The fireplace bathed the guests in a warm glow. Hirka squeezed past a couple of large men and forced her way up to the bar. It was covered in scratches, from innumerable tankards that had been shoved back and forth. Hirka was working up the courage to order when an arm whisked her across the floor and behind the counter.

"You're too young for these lads. What are you doing here?"

Much to Hirka's surprise, the arm belonged to a woman. She was thin, but her muscles were clearly visible under her top, and she was balancing a tray of tankards like they weighed nothing. Her hair was gathered into a braid that swung back and forth as she emptied the tray and refilled it with fresh tankards overflowing with ale, all the while surveying Hirka with kind eyes. Someone shouted, "Maja!" from among the crowd, and she yelled back, "Hold your horses!"

"I'm after something to eat," Hirka answered, glancing at the piglets, their fat dripping into the fire.

"How much?"

"I've got money!"

"I mean, how much pork? One portion? Two?"

"Oh. Two. How much is that?"

"A small silver for two."

"Oh … Just one then. I'm not that hungry."

Maja shouted so loudly that Hirka backed up a little.

"Jorge! One portion at the end." The stooped man behind the counter nodded but didn't seem to be in any hurry. He finished pouring one tankard, then started on another.

"Won't be long," Maja said.

"Oh, wait! How much for a room?"

Maja laughed. "We'd be lucky to find you a pillow. You can try Langeli, but this close to the Rite they'll be full up too." She picked up the tray and was swallowed up by the crowd again. Hirka couldn't see any empty chairs, so she stood by the bar, her stomach rumbling. Finding a bed would have to wait.

Jorge mopped up the ale splatters on the counter with a cloth that was already sopping wet. He looked up and spotted Hirka. She smiled as widely as she could, and he appeared to remember her food. He pulled out a knife from under the counter and walked toward the fireplace. Then he returned and placed a wooden bowl with steaming meat in front of her. A square piece of pork with crackling and a strip of fat.

"Three copper pieces."

He held out his hand and Hirka dug out three small coins from her pouch.

"The knife."

"Eh?" Confused, Hirka picked up the fork she had been given.

"You can't come in here with a pocketknife. I'll have to keep it behind the counter till you leave."

"She's just a girl, Jorge! Are you worried she'll go on a rampage?"

Maja had appeared again. She pushed over a tall stool, and Hirka sat down. They could argue about her all they wanted. Hirka had no time for anything but food. Eating slowly to avoid burning herself was torture. When had she last eaten so well? Raw finger shells down by the quay, with Father?

Father.

The worst of her hunger abated, and she ate slower while she observed the people around her—carefully, so as not to fall off the stool. One leg was shorter than the others and every time she bent forward to take a bite of pork, it teetered back and forth.

A large man came in and walked straight up to the counter. The conversation around the nearest table died down as the five men followed him with their eyes. He leaned over the counter and raised one finger to Jorge, who slid over a tankard. The newcomer placed a copper on the counter and looked around the room.

A little younger than Father, Hirka thought, and just as much a working man. His hair was yellow as straw and short as freshly cut grass. Hirka continued gnawing on what little was left of her meat and tried to look like she belonged, without managing particularly well. Most of the patrons were grown men, and the few women looked old enough to have grandchildren, though she doubted any of them did.

The large man rotated the tankard and looked over his shoulder at the group who had been observing him since he came in. They were talking among themselves, but quietly. One of them was glaring, dark eyes twitching. Hirka felt uneasy, but none of this had anything to do with her. They weren't Kolkagga. They weren't guardsmen who would drag her to the assembly. She was worrying for nothing.

The dark-eyed man got up and walked toward the man at the counter. His fists were clenched, and he was clearly out for blood. Drops of ale glistened in his beard. The large man stood with his back turned, unable to see him coming.

"Look out!" Hirka shouted. It was all she could think to say without knowing his name. The large man turned and just managed to avoid the blow. It swiped past his chin and he raised his arms to defend himself. The two men crashed together and everyone flocked over. Jorge lost his grip on an ale barrel and it fell to the floor. It didn't break, but the cork in the tap hole shot out, and ale began to spill everywhere.

The large man managed to pull far enough away that he had room to retaliate. He landed a powerful blow on his opponent's jaw, sending him flying to the floor by Hirka's stool. She grabbed hold of the counter to avoid being taken down with him.

The room went quiet as people waited to see what would happen next. The dark-eyed man looked around wildly. People had formed a circle around them. Maja came running through the pool of ale with her skirts lifted.

The dark-eyed man stared at Hirka, then reached up and tore her pocketknife out of its sheath. Hirka lost her balance and fell off the stool. She heard someone screaming in pain. People shouting. Hirka tumbled to the floor between the two men. Her knife was planted in the thigh of the large man. He was the one screaming. The other one tried to get hold of the knife again, reaching across Hirka, who scrambled to get up.

She caught sight of Maja, standing on the counter with a bucket, which she poured over them. The icy water washed over Hirka's face. Maja shouted, "I don't want to see you here, Orvar! Do you hear! Never again!"

Orvar and the large man were soaking wet. People were laughing now. Three men took hold of Orvar and dragged him out of the inn. Hirka stared at the knife in the thigh of the large man. It was stuck, but not too deep. Blood started to seep into his clothes. Maja jumped down from the counter.

"Jorge, run and fetch Rinna! Are you all right, Villir?"

Villir stared at her in disbelief. Hirka tried not to laugh. Villir thought he was near death, but she'd seen far worse than this. Hirka stood up, cold water dripping from her clothes. She walked toward the fireplace.

"Come on."

Villir didn't follow, but merely pointed at the knife as though she hadn't seen it. She came back and stood right in front of him.

"Lean on me and we'll hobble over there. Don't bend your foot." Villir yelped as he eased himself into a low chair in front of the fire. Hirka managed to stretch out his leg and started to rummage through her bag.

"What are you doing, girl?"

"I have to stop the bleeding." She found what she needed but paused for a moment to look at him. "Or do you prefer it the way it is?"

The men around them started to laugh, and Maja shooed them out the door. Villir's forehead was dripping with water and sweat. Hirka smiled, but he didn't reciprocate. She had to distract him.

"So, what was all that about?" she asked.

"The man's a damned idiot!" Villir answered.

"Obviously," Hirka said as she ripped away his sodden trousers around the knife. "But apart from that?"

Maja answered for him. "Villir sent his girls to Mannfalla."

"Any respectable father would do the same!" Villir exclaimed. "There isn't a soul who hasn't heard that the blind are wreaking havoc again! Are we supposed to sacrifice our children just to stick it to Mannfalla?!"

"Orvar is," Maja said and shrugged.

"Orvar's got a brain like a waterskin."

Villir was fuming, and Hirka had found the perfect moment. She grabbed the knife and pulled. Villir screamed like a stuck pig, but the knife came out easy. She only had a second to act before the blood gushed out.

"Sit still!"

She found the pot of soldrop and vengethorn salve that would stop the bleeding and keep the wound clean. She had more than enough. The wound wasn't serious. She cleaned it and applied the salve. Then she wrapped linen around his thigh and pulled it tight. After a moment the salve started to sting and Villir moaned.

"You were lucky," Hirka said and got up. "You'll need a couple of stitches, but we'll get to that in a moment." Hirka pulled silk thread out of her bag. Villir looked terrified, so Maja fetched him a tankard of ale, which he nearly emptied in one go.

Jorge came running in. "Rinna's busy with Yme, delivering the baby!"

Hirka stood holding the knife and it dawned on her that all this was her fault. Jorge had asked her for her knife.

"Bloody Slokna does it ever sting! Blindcraft!" Villir moaned again.

"That means it's working," Hirka said.

It wasn't true, strictly speaking, but it usually helped to say so. The stinging just meant that it was stinging. There was no getting around it, but people preferred having a reason to suffer. Hirka warmed her hands by the fire to kill the worst of the germs.

"What else are you going to do?" Villir's voice was unsteady.

"Stitch you up," Hirka said, heating the needle over the flames.

"*You're* going to stitch me up?!"

"Do it yourself if you'd rather."

"Where's Rinna?" Villir looked at Jorge in desperation, but he shook his head.

Hirka was used to people thinking she was too young. "Listen, Villir, I've stitched up far worse before. But if you're afraid and you'd prefer to wait a while ..."

"I wouldn't say I'm afraid ... What's the worst that can happen?" Villir laughed nervously and looked around for confirmation, but he received none.

Hirka asked Maja to give Villir something stronger and he accepted it without grumbling. Hirka unwrapped the linen and stuck the needle through the lip of the wound. Villir flinched but didn't scream. It took five stitches, and Villir tried his best to be brave while she worked. Afterward they moved him closer to the fire so his clothes would dry.

Jorge cut off a couple pieces of pork, which he placed on the table, along with some bread rolls. They ate in silence for a moment. Until the door swung open and a woman came flying in. Her long blonde hair was all over the place and she was clutching a shawl around her.

"Villir!"

"Borgunn?"

"They said Orvar ran you through with a knife!"

Villir demonstratively stretched out his foot, putting on his best wounded soldier act. The woman took his face in her hands, then ran them over him to check that he was in one piece.

"Has Rinna been already?"

"No," Jorge answered. "Busy with a delivery. The girl here stitched him up."

"The girl? Who are you, girl?"

Everyone looked at Hirka. She swallowed a mouthful of food. It was the third time she'd been asked that question today. She was going to have to learn to answer. Maja's eyebrow was in danger of disappearing into her hairline, suggesting she'd been meaning to ask the same for some time. Borgunn stared at Hirka as though she had tried to steal her man.

Before Hirka had a chance to respond, the door swung open.

She froze on the stool. Three men in leather armor entered. Heavy swords hung by their sides. Behind them the evening had turned dark. The wind blew in and Borgunn's shawl fluttered between them and Hirka.

"Hirka?"

The voice came from the man standing closest. It was devoid of emotion. He was neither happy nor angry. It was just a question. All the same, Hirka felt her body go cold.

Stupid girl! Kolkagga are the Council's assassins. Why would they be in Ravnhov?!

Hirka nodded and swallowed again.

"You're Hirka?"

"Yes."

"You're the tailless girl?" Just as the gatekeepers had done, he tipped his head sideways to check whether it was true.

"Yes," Hirka answered.

"Eirik wants to see you. Follow me."

Eirik. The chieftain of Ravnhov? Why? What did he want with her?

"I have to pack my bag." That was the only thing she could think to say. The man didn't answer. Hirka got up and packed away her things. Her hands were shaking, but she managed to conceal it from the others. They didn't look scared. Just curious. She comforted herself with the fact that none of the three men bore the mark of the Council. She doubted anyone in Ravnhov did. In Ravnhov, you apparently risked getting a knife in the thigh just for sending your children to the Rite.

She slung her bag over her shoulder and walked out with the soldiers right behind her. It was dark. The only lights came from the homes clinging to the mountainside both above and below her. It was beautiful. One of the men gave her a shove on the shoulder. She took a breath and started to walk.

TEIN

The soldiers walked with Hirka between them. The tallest was a few paces ahead of her, carrying a lamp that swayed in time with his steps. She wanted to ask if she was a prisoner but couldn't work up the nerve. The road became steeper and the houses disappeared. Were they taking her up the mountain to kill her? Because she was the tailless girl?

Hirka bit her lip. An inn full of people was preferable to three men in the dark.

For a little while the light from the lamp was all that could be seen, but when they got higher up, more lights came into view. Hirka heard a familiar cawing. Ravens shifting restlessly in the dark. A lot of them. Strangely, the sound seemed to be coming from below.

They came to a sturdy wooden bridge over a wooded ravine. That had to be where the ravens were, in the trees directly below them. Hirka stopped to look, but the man to her left pressed his hand to her back to keep her moving.

The lights she had seen were torches guiding the way from the bridge to a large courtyard. A spruce tree stood in the middle of it, towering above the buildings. Two men in leather armor intercepted them and were asked to fetch Eirik.

Hirka felt her throat constrict. Should she run or stay put? Maybe she could jump down into the ravine? Land safely in the trees, climb down, and disappear?

Or end up hanging from one with a broken leg. Bad idea.

Though it was late, people from the chieftain's household were still walking between the buildings with lamps and bundles of wood or linen. Some were dealing with a cart that had just arrived. They unsaddled the horses and showed people inside.

"Ynge!"

A giant of a man strode toward them. He had broad shoulders, but one hung lower than the other, as if the arm on that side was heavier. His brown hair and beard made him look like he'd been dragged through a hedge backward. This had to be Eirik.

It occurred to Hirka that her own hair probably didn't look much better. She quickly smoothed her hand over it a couple times, but it didn't feel like it had any effect. The soldier with the lamp sent the others away and told Eirik he'd found Hirka in The Raven's Brood. He told him about Orvar and the knife, though he only got about half the story right. Hirka bit her lip so she wouldn't be tempted to correct him.

Eirik didn't take his eyes off Hirka the whole time he was talking to Ynge. "Make sure Grinn hears about Orvar," he rumbled. "Let him deal with it as he sees fit. A night or two in the cage, I imagine." Hirka gulped. A night with Orvar in the "cage" didn't appeal to her. Ynge nodded and took his leave.

Eirik quickly crouched down in front of Hirka. He was still almost as tall as her. He cocked his head. She knew what he was looking for, so she turned around for a moment.

He chuckled. "So you're the tailless girl?" His voice was gruff.

"Yes."

"Where are you from?"

Everything about him reminded her of a bear. Apart from his eyes. They sparkled blue in the light from the torches. Hirka had a feeling he already knew the answer, but she told him anyway.

"From Elveroa."

"Then you've been living among Council folks. A rare privilege." Eirik studied her.

She shrugged. "I hardly ever attend messages. Anyway, Ilume's gone back to Mannfalla now. There's no Council presence in Elveroa anymore."

Eirik's beard lifted slightly on one side, betraying a smile. "No. So I hear."

He got up and Hirka had to take a step back to take him all in. He called over a woman who was as shriveled as an old apple. She had a huge bunch of keys hanging from her waistband.

"Unngonna, this is Hirka. Get her a room in Friggsheim, a bath, and something to eat."

Hirka looked up at Eirik. Had she heard him right? Was this how they treated outlaws in Ravnhov—by giving them room and board?

"I've just eaten …"

Neither of them were listening.

"Eirik, with the moot feast tomorrow, the bathhouse is full of Meredir's half-drunk men. She can't—"

"Then she can use the round one."

Unngonna looked Hirka up and down skeptically, then gestured for her to follow. The keys rattled against her skirt as she walked. Eirik turned to Hirka.

"Follow the path closest to the rock face until you get to the river, and you'll find the bathhouse."

Hirka nodded. A bath sounded wonderful. It might even have been worth spending a night in the cage with Orvar. She turned to leave but was stopped by Eirik's huge hand on her shoulder. He had to lean down so far that his hair fell into his face. He winked. "Welcome to Ravnhov."

Hirka couldn't help but smile.

"We haven't got all night!" Unngonna shouted, and Hirka trotted after her.

Friggsheim was somewhat set apart from the rest of the buildings, and it turned out to be a longhouse full of small rooms. Unngonna had keys to them all. The chieftain's household in Ravnhov was like one big inn. Unngonna apologized for the room being small before taking her leave. Hirka just nodded. The room was bigger than the cabin in Elveroa. She had a chair and a nightstand with an oil lamp. A big bed with white linen. There was a lavender arrangement on the windowsill to keep vermin away. The window had yellow glass. Real glass. Was she dreaming? Perhaps she'd frozen to death in the forest and she was lying delirious in Slokna.

Hirka wanted to collapse onto the bed straightaway, but she couldn't. Not the way she looked. She tried to run a hand through her hair, but it got caught in the tangles. She needed a bath. She found the only change of clothes she had in her bag. She rolled them up in a towel and left the room as quietly as she could.

She could hear voices from the next room. One of the floorboards creaked when she stepped on it, and the discussion suddenly stopped. She hurried outside. It was chilly. Autumn was here, no doubt about it. She found the stone steps and followed them, as she had been told. She encountered no one along the way, so she walked faster until she came to a round wooden building by the river. It had no windows, so she couldn't see whether anyone was already inside. She stopped to listen. All she could hear was the river and the distant cries of the ravens. Hirka opened the door cautiously and peered in. There was no one else there. She went in and closed the door.

The bath took up half the floor. Hirka could see openings in the walls through which water from the river could flow. She'd never seen anything like it.

The water was still hot. She took off her clothes and climbed in. Her skin burned for a few moments until she got used to it. She swam a few strokes. She'd never imagined bathing could be so nice. Hirka let herself sink into the water until she could feel the bottom under her feet. Then she shot back up, breaking the surface again. She felt weightless. The flames from the lamp danced on the surface of the water. The river murmured outside. Everything seemed better now. All her worries about the Rite and the Council were being washed away.

There's still Kolkagga to think about.

She found some rocks under the water to sit on, and there were soaps and brushes on the shelves. People in Ravnhov thought of everything. She would be safe there. To Slokna with the Rite. She had escaped. She would never have to stand before the Council and the Seer. The relief was like a tight knot that had finally loosened. Hirka soaped herself, but when her fingers slid over the scar at the base of her spine, the thoughts she had been trying to push aside hit her like an avalanche.

The wolves that had never taken her tail. The truth about who she was. Father, who had given his own life to help her escape. Rime, who would be left waiting during the Rite. The disappointment in his wolf eyes.

Hirka ducked under the water again and held her breath until her lungs felt as though they might explode. Then she shot back up, broke the surface, and started coughing.

"Do people not bathe where you come from?"

Hirka jumped. The wild boy from the forest was standing in front of her at the edge of the bath. Completely naked. Hirka wriggled backward in the water until she found the wall and was able to sit down again. She tried to keep her body under the water so he couldn't see anything apart from her head.

"Do people not knock where *you* come from?" She started to comb her fingers through her wet hair to avoid looking at him, but she couldn't stop herself from glancing up. He grinned. His arms were folded across his chest and he was standing with his legs apart as if she were his girl and she'd seen it all before.

"Not when using their own bathhouses," he replied, stepping down into the water.

Hirka could feel her cheeks burning. "Unngonna said the other bathhouse was—"

"Has the raven recovered?" he interrupted.

He sat down opposite her and rested his arms on the edge. This boy had said no more than a few words to her, but he'd interrupted her almost every time he had. He was bound to do it again, so Hirka considered saying nothing.

But he knew about her, who she was, and Hirka wanted to know how.

"It was just a bit of a fright," she said.

He snorted. "Great eagles are nothing to be scared of."

Hirka suppressed the urge to sneer. "I'm not talking about the eagle. I'm talking about a wild man who started slinging stones at us."

The boy's arrogant smile faltered, and for a moment Hirka feared she'd gone too far. But then he threw his head back and burst out laughing. He could take a joke. That was at least one redeeming quality.

"Why didn't you shoot at it? You had a bow and arrows," she asked.

He looked at her. The pupils of his pale blue eyes had blown wide since he sat down. "You're not that bright, are you? What would you rather deal with? A great eagle, or an enraged and injured great eagle?" He ducked under the water. Hirka fought the impulse to cover herself. He stayed under for a few seconds before he resurfaced. Smiling.

"Are you going to the Rite?"

Hirka was already pretty sure it was safe to be honest about the Rite in this place. "No, I've—"

"I didn't go either. I was the first." He'd interrupted her again. Hirka weighed her irritation against her curiosity. Her curiosity won.

"The first to what?"

He smoothed his hair back with one hand, but it went straight back to sticking out in every direction. Apart from a thin braid starting at the base of his skull, which she hadn't noticed when she saw him in the forest.

"The first person in Ravnhov not to go through the Rite. I was supposed to. Two years ago. But I didn't. A lot of people here have decided against it since. But I was the first person to stand up to them." He looked at Hirka as if the words ought to mean something to her.

She assumed he was talking about the Council. But she asked anyway. "Stand up to who?"

"The traitors in Mannfalla." His eyes narrowed as if she was one of the people he was talking about.

"Why do you think they're traitors?"

He didn't reply. He grabbed some soap and turned it over in his hands a couple times. The soap bubbles gathered around his naked torso. He had arms like Father's. The boy was well built, no doubt about that. He was big. Bigger than Rime, but she'd wager Rime was stronger. Rime stood tall. He was subdued. He was lithe as a cat. The boy before her had stooped shoulders and bellowed like an ox. They were like night and day. And what was she?

The rot.

She was the rot, and here she was having a bath with a stranger. What if the rot could be carried by the water? Hirka forgot to breathe. But then she remembered swimming in the Stryfe with other children, Father washing her when she was little. It couldn't be dangerous. It just couldn't.

But she'd never shared a bath with a boy. And they were both naked. The song about the girl and the rot forced itself to the forefront of her mind. The girl who said *yes* in the final verse and died.

"Aren't you scared of the blind, then?" Hirka asked as she tried to think of a way to escape without him seeing her naked. He threw his head back and laughed again. The two actions were at odds with each other—like he was trying to convince them both that his laughter was genuine. He rested his hands on the back of his head, probably to make his arms look even bigger.

"Have you ever seen one of the blind?" he asked.

Hirka didn't reply. He would only interrupt her anyway, because he clearly had more to say. "Of course not. No one has seen the blind, girl. Not for hundreds of years! Guess why?"

"Hirka."

"What?"

"My name's Hirka. Not girl."

"No one's seen them because they don't exist! They're stories Mannfalla uses to keep people under their thumb. And it works. People from all over Midtyms, Norrvarje, Foggard, and Bik pass through here to be pawns in Mannfalla's game. People come all the way from the ice to go through the Rite! Every damn year." His pupils had contracted again. "Tell me, when has the Rite ever protected anyone from the blind?"

"Every day?" Hirka shrugged.

"How?!"

"If no one's seen the blind for hundreds of years, perhaps it's because the Rite works?" Hirka concealed a smile. She didn't really believe in the blind. Of course, until recently she hadn't believed in children of Odin either. But here she was, and she was one of them.

He gave her a look of horror. "No one's that stupid, girl. You sound like them."

Hirka lifted herself up onto the edge. She got up and stood tall. She didn't have a tail, but he knew that already. The water dripped from her body. She felt slightly sick as she turned her back on him. But she took her time. She walked over to her clothes and wrapped her towel around herself before looking at him again.

"Why not go, then, if you're so scared of the blind?" he asked, but he no longer looked as sure of himself.

Hirka turned away, picked up her clothes, and opened the door. "Thanks for the use of the bathhouse, boy."

"Tein."

Hirka walked through the door and closed it behind her.

"My name's Tein!" she heard him shout defiantly from inside.

You should be grateful to be alive, Tein. You've bathed with the rot.

THE IDOL

The mountains were teeming with plants. Just by following her nose, Hirka had already found vengethorn and soldrop. She had awoken early enough that Ravnhov still slumbered far below Protected by cliffs too steep to be climbed. Tein had been right. *No one travels to Ravnhov through the forests.*

How much did he know about her? Hirka was instinctively wary of people, but Tein clearly didn't know better than to get in a bath with her. And she *had* been well received here. So well that Father was probably grumbling with suspicion in Slokna. *Nobody gives without taking double in return,* he always said. Hirka didn't know what to think. All she knew was that she had been given food, a hot bath, and a bed—even though the town was bursting with strangers and the inns were full. Was this the home she'd always dreamed of?

She heard the screech of a raven. Then another. More joined in. Hirka looked down at the chieftain's household. It was situated on a plateau above the rest of the town; a cluster of stone buildings with wooden beams and pointed thatched roofs. The raven cries increased, and suddenly a black cloud streamed out of the ravine she had crossed the previous night. It grew above the houses. Hirka gaped.

The ravens of Ravnhov. Thousands of them. Tens of thousands. They darkened the sky above her. It was a sight for the gods. Her heart grew in her chest and she wanted to follow them. Follow them to the world's end.

But then the ravens disappeared to the north. She was left behind, earthbound. As wingless as she was tailless. It was time for her to head back. The ravens had probably woken the entire town.

She walked some distance before she noticed a path leading to a crevice in the cliff. She ought to continue down, but the draw was too great. The mountain lured her in. The chasm was no wider than her outstretched arms, but as high as five men. The sky was a pale snake far above her. The air quickly grew cooler. After two gentle turns, the chasm opened up into a space carved out of the mountain. Vertical stone walls surrounded her, forming a shaft that reached up into the heavens. Nearly perfectly round, and perhaps fifty paces across. The path continued around along the walls. Hirka stopped.

In the middle of the space stood a figure that could only be an idol. She glanced behind her, fearful of being seen. The Seer forbade idols. They attracted the blind, it was said. She continued on the path along the walls to avoid the idol. Forbidden or not, this place must have once been sacred. It felt disrespectful to get too close.

Someone had carved figures into the mountain, along the entire circle. There were pictures of ymlings taking in the harvest and slaughtering animals. Hunting. A woman surrounded by ravens. Someone lay dead at her feet. A man hanging upside down from a tree. An army of ymlings who—Hirka stopped. They had no tails! She moved closer and ran her fingers across the carvings. Were they like her? Children of Odin? No. They had fingers like claws. Eyes like empty hollows in their faces. *The blind.*

What was this? A story? How old could it be? She had nearly walked the entire way around. The last carvings were clearer. Newer. A man with a sword in his back. In front of him sat a figure on a throne, the Council's raven on his forehead. What had Tein called the Council? Traitors?

Hirka was drawn toward the idol. Nobody could see her here. What harm would it do to look? She walked toward the sculpture and looked up into a woman's face. She was of an indeterminate age, or maybe time had worn away the details. She sat naked astride a two-headed raven. She was voluptuous with large breasts, and Hirka couldn't help but glance down at her own, barely a handful. The raven looked like it was tearing itself in two, with each half wanting to go its own way. Hirka placed her hands on the beaks and pulled back in surprise.

One raven was cool. The other warm.

The sun. It had to be the sun. One of them probably spent more time in the shade.

The base of the sculpture was a pit, stained with blood. Some old and rusty. Some so new that she could still smell it. She felt a tingling in her body. *Stone has memory*, Rime had told her once.

Hirka found herself longing for the Might. Waiting for it. Praying for it. But Rime wasn't here. The Might wasn't here. Not for the likes of her.

Voices!

Hirka jumped behind the idol without thinking. She could hear people talking in the chasm. A man and a woman, heading her way. Why had she hidden? She'd done nothing wrong, but it was too late to show herself now. The echo faded, and the conversation grew clearer. They had entered the circle.

Hirka remained crouching with her back to the idol. Then she realized that she recognized both voices. The booming male voice was unmistakable. It was Eirik. And the other—

Ramoja?! What's Ramoja doing in Ravnhov?

"There's no doubt about it, Ramoja. He's chosen his path. Now he's killing for the people you thought he'd change. You should have known better," Eirik grumbled, though his tone sounded more consolatory than accusatory.

"Known better than to hope for change?" Ramoja sounded weary.

"Change is coming. That's as certain as the Might. But it's up to us, and we've waited long enough. I was willing to wait half a generation for your sake, Ramoja. But he can no longer help us. We could wait till the sun goes out, but what good would it do? While we sit here navel-gazing, the Council is sending agents and assassins across all of Ym. They're either making deals or killing, depending on what serves them best. They're on their way. Ravnhov cannot wait any longer!"

Hirka heard Ramoja's bracelets jangling. She'd probably rested her hand on Eirik to calm him. "Eirik ..." Her voice grew more fervent. "This has to be solved from Eisvaldr. From the inside. You know it's true, and I will not fail. But you need time to separate friend from foe. You can't afford to stand alone against Mannfalla."

Eirik grumbled and Hirka heard their footsteps in the grass. She clenched her teeth. Eirik and Ramoja were doing exactly what she had done. They were walking along the walls around the space. And here she was, sitting in the middle like an idiot. She crawled carefully around the idol in order to remain unseen.

"We're not alone. We have the tailless girl," Eirik said. Hirka froze.

"We know very little about her, Eirik. You can't pin your hopes on her."

"You said she would be our salvation!"

"*Could* be. We don't know. All we know is what I have seen and heard. She calms the ravens. They can smell that her blood is different, and she was strong enough to run from Mannfalla. It's a gift, Eirik. I thought we'd lost her in the fire."

Hirka's head was spinning. She rose up just high enough to glimpse Eirik and Ramoja between the raven's talons.

"And you think *that's* going to be enough for them tomorrow?" Eirik asked. He stopped and looked at Ramoja. She turned away from him, and Hirka quickly crouched down again.

"I can't attend the gathering, Eirik. You know that. Especially not now. Who would defend me if word got out? Not Rime. He is lost to us." They walked on.

"If they could just see you, Ramoja! That would win us more allies than anything else."

"I'm invisible in this war, Eirik. That's the way it has to be."

War! What war? Hirka crawled a little farther around. One of her knees cracked when she moved. She looked up, but they didn't seem to have heard. They walked calmly back toward the chasm.

"I heard Meredir has come. Does that mean Urmunai is with us?" Ramoja asked cautiously, as though she was afraid of the answer.

"Meredir is young," Eirik said. "He whiles away his days in his father's fortress with women and wine. Or men and wine, if what they say is true." They disappeared into the chasm. Hirka strained her neck to hear more.

"But he's coming to the gathering. That's something," Ramoja said.

"Not enough," Eirik answered.

The echo between the rock faces made it impossible for Hirka to hear the rest. She waited until it went quiet before she stood up. The blood rushed down through her legs and she had to shake them to stop the tingling.

She walked unsteadily toward the path. What had she actually heard? Ravnhov defying the Council and the Seer was nothing new. But this was more. Ravnhov was planning for war. And Ramoja was a part of it.

We have the tailless girl.

They planned to involve Hirka somehow. Said she could help. Where had they gotten that ridiculous notion from? Help *how*? What was it the ravens had said about her? Different blood? Had Ramoja realized what that meant, and told the chieftain of Ravnhov? But how would that be of any use to them? And how was someone like her supposed to help them win anything? The girl who avoided people at all costs. The girl who couldn't even bind.

What would Rime have said if he knew about this? And Ilume! Ilume An-Elderin. Ramoja worked for her, for the Council! And what had she meant about Rime being lost to them?

Hirka leaned against the rock face. She had to be mistaken. She'd only heard snatches of their conversation. She couldn't know what it was actually about. There was a reasonable explanation. There had to be. And she had to find it.

They had mentioned a gathering tomorrow. A gathering that Ramoja couldn't be seen at. But others were going to attend. And maybe they would talk about the tailless girl too. About her. She had to listen in on this gathering, whatever it took.

Hirka crept out through the chasm. She found the path down, and soon she saw the town below her, a hive of activity. More carts had arrived overnight. Men and women in dark blue aprons bustled across the courtyard with water, food, bed linen, and wood. The guard changed atop the walls. People carried in eggs from the hen houses, patched roofs with fresh straw, and set up stalls around the squares. Leather goods, baked goods, birdcages of all shapes, clothes, and weapons. Shields and swords.

After a thousand years of sleep, Ravnhov was about to wake up again.

THE FEAST

The music started long before the sun set. The moot feast in Ravnhov was quite the affair. If things had been like before, Hirka would have lain hidden on a rooftop and watched people being people from a safe distance. But nothing was the same anymore.

Torches illuminated the chieftain's household. Flutes and harps played songs about gods, love, and war. Whole lambs were roasted over open fires. Children with dirty faces ran around swiping things from platters without anyone chasing them off to bed. The evening air smelled of meat, ale, and spices.

The doors to the great hall opened and people crowded around to enter. Hirka was surrounded. Squashed. She managed to work her way over to the side.

"I see you're taking the stupid way in."

Hirka turned toward the voice. Tein was leaning against the corner.

"Not by choice," Hirka said, seizing the opportunity to break away from the crowd and walking over to him. He waved her after him around the back of the great hall and through the servants' entrance.

The hall had two floors. It was already packed, but people were still streaming in. The roof was supported by two rows of sturdy logs, at least fifty of them. Someone had decorated the banister on the second floor with flowers. Hirka counted four fireplaces with pigs over the flames. The tables were overflowing with ale, fruit, fish, and honey bread. People jostled each other as they squeezed onto the benches.

"There's no room in here, we'll have to go back out," Hirka said, relieved, and turned around.

Tein stopped her. "Oh, we can always find somewhere to sit," he said with a grin so self-assured that Hirka could practically smell the danger.

"WELCOME TO RAVNHOV!"

Eirik's voice boomed throughout the hall. He had climbed up onto one of the tables, and people cheered in response. "Now, now. Settle down," he called. "Ynge! For crying out loud, leave the food where it is until everyone's seated! We're not wild animals, no matter what Mannfalla might say!" People howled with laughter. They stomped their feet so their tankards shook.

Hirka smiled. No wonder Mannfalla was wary of this man. He'd won her over straightaway.

Eirik took a swig of ale before continuing. "Many of you are on your way to the Rite. Many of you attended the moot. And many of you are here for the first time. But fear not! I won't bore you with a long speech. All I'll say is, here we are! Here's Ravnhov! We've always been here. And we'll always be here!"

Everyone whooped and hollered. Tankards were bashed together, ale slopping everywhere. Eirik jumped down from the table but kept speaking. "We fear no one! Whether you're a wild man like us or a pale-faced Mannfaller, you're welcome here. In our house. On behalf of me, my beloved Solfrid …" Eirik put an arm around a buxom beauty next to him. "And Tein, my son and heir!" He reached out with his other arm. Tein walked over and embraced his father.

Hirka buried her face in her hands. He was Eirik's son. Her mind raced through everything she'd said to him. Would she have said the same things if she'd known?

As people started to settle down, Tein pulled Hirka over to sit at his family's table. He tore off long strips of meat with his fingers and stuffed them into his mouth. He never stopped grinning at her, not even while he was chewing.

She ate without saying a word. It wasn't that he hadn't told her who he was. That was easy enough to forgive. But seating her here, at the chieftain's table, in front of gawping visitors from half of Ym … Hirka's cheeks continued to burn through countless dishes and songs. The people became drunker and the songs bolder. Tein leaned over the table, pressed his forehead against hers, and winked.

Then a familiar song started up and her blood ran cold.

The girl and the rot coming down from on high
Lie with me tonight, lie with me tonight
The rot begged and pleaded 'til his face did glow
But no matter how he tried, the girl said no

Voices and people disappeared into a fog around her. All she could hear was the song. Why wasn't anyone else listening? Why were they just sitting there, drinking and bellowing? The girl in the song kept saying no, verse after verse.

Men were one thing, drunken men something else entirely, Father had said. Now she knew better. Men were just men. *She* was the one who was dangerous. Father had fought a futile battle to ensure she went unseen. To ensure no one would get the rot. How stupid could you get? Had he thought she'd live her entire life without lying with anyone? Everyone did it. Maybe even Sylja.

Sylja and Rime?

No. She'd have known. Not that it mattered. Hirka would never be able to touch Rime or anyone else. She was a monster. A disease. She was like the blind, who kept coming up in the many conversations around the table.

The girl and the rot at the parting of the ways
Lie with me today, lie with me today
The rot got down on his knees, praying for success
And on this day, the girl said yes

Hirka got up and ran toward the doors. She heard Tein shout behind her, but she pretended not to hear. There were even more people outside, but they didn't pay her any heed. They were dancing, eating, and drinking. A couple was sitting on a table, kissing, and one of the carts was rocking suspiciously. Hirka kept running until she'd crossed the yellow bridge. The torches had gone out. She stopped and squeezed her eyes shut. She needed to pull herself together. Nothing bad had happened. She'd shared a meal with people. That was all.

All Hirka wanted was to be left alone, but she could hear footsteps just behind her. Tein strode past and then turned to face her, smiling as he walked backward along the road.

"You haven't seen the ravenry yet."

The ravenry. It was only then that she noticed the low cawing. She followed Tein to some stone steps leading straight down into the ravine. It started getting cooler as soon as they started descending. The ravens cawed a little louder for a moment, but then fell silent. What was it Ramoja had said?

She calms the ravens. They can smell that her blood is different.

The ravenry in Ravnhov. A place of legends.

The wooded ravine was home to tens of thousands of ravens. She was surrounded by black shadows that watched her through narrowed eyes. Paths crisscrossed between the trees. They followed one of them until the ravine ended at a cliff. From here she looked out over the landscape toward Blindból and Mannfalla. The moon hung over the forest, almost full. She started to move toward the edge for a better look, but Tein grabbed her hand.

"What happened to your tail?"

Hirka breathed a sigh of relief. So he didn't know anything more about her. That meant Eirik and Ramoja didn't either. No one knew.

"Wolf," she said. Short sentences seemed like a good idea when talking to Tein, so he couldn't interrupt. He smiled and moved toward her. He stood so close that she could feel the warmth from his breath. Looking at him now, she didn't know how she hadn't realized who he was. He had his father's eyes. Just a paler blue. And they were bright now. Hirka knew what that meant, though she'd never seen it herself. She'd never been close to anyone in that way.

"I'll be king one day," he said, smiling like he'd won a competition. Like the ones she and Rime used to have. Hirka took a step back.

"There aren't any kings anymore," she said, looking away.

He chuckled, but he didn't sound amused. "Where do you think all the chieftains came from?" His arm muscles bulged under his white shirt. He started circling her as if they were going to fight. His voice grew rougher. "Do you think the kings just woke up one day and decided to disappear? Foggard, Norrvarje, Brinnlanda ... Do you think Mannfalla has always ruled the world, girl? The kings were here long before the Council, and it was the king of Foggard who held the blind back. Us! It was us! And we paid in blood. The Council grew strong while we lost our land, our leaders, and our lives."

The ravens above them shifted uneasily. Hirka looked at him, suddenly feeling like she knew who he was. Like she knew him. A wild boy, she'd thought at first, without realizing how right she was. There was a rawness to him, and it was both ugly and beautiful at the same time.

Tein carried within him the memories of things that had happened long before he was born, long before Eirik was born. He bore the weight of a thousand years of injustice.

Hirka tried to counter him, nonetheless. "The *Seer* held the blind ba—"

"The Seer?! He may have saved Mannfalla, but who did He save here? Ravnhov saved itself. Ravnhov has always saved itself." He lowered his voice and turned away. Tein wasn't much older than Hirka, but nevertheless, he wanted everyone to take up arms and defy Mannfalla so he could reclaim a lost kingdom he'd only heard about in stories. And it was clear that he wanted her help.

But Tein didn't know that she'd already fled from the Council. That she couldn't help if she wanted to. That she had no idea why Eirik and Ramoja thought she could.

"Always having to save yourself isn't a bad thing," Hirka said. "It's something to be proud of."

He straightened up, but didn't turn to face her. "They're back."

"Who's back?"

"Nábyrn. The deadborn. The blind."

Hirka said nothing. Only the previous evening he'd denied their very existence, but tonight the stories had flowed between the guests more quickly than the ale, so he had to have known.

Suddenly she understood. All that talk about saving themselves. The blind and lost kingdoms. Tein wasn't just angry. He was afraid. He was the first person in Ravnhov who hadn't gone through the Rite. What did he fear most? Mannfalla or the blind?

"Then let them come," she said, sounding bolder than she felt. "Remember what your father said: Ravnhov's here. It's always been here, and it always will be."

He turned to face her. It was as if a weight had been lifted from his shoulders. He beamed. He gripped her hair and searched her eyes for permission, clearly expecting to find it.

Tein was standing right in front of her. Warm and within reach. Hungry for life and so easy to be with that it was scary. But he wasn't what she wanted. He wasn't Rime.

She stepped away from him, but she smiled to take the sting out of it.

Tein smiled back, as if she'd made him a promise.

THE GATHERING

Hirka stole across the empty courtyard. Not even the ravens were awake. The fog lay like a blanket over Ravnhov. What remained of the feast bonfires reached into the gray sky like skeletal ruins.

She had no idea where or when Eirik and the nobles were going to hold the gathering he and Ramoja had spoken of. But if there was one thing she had learned since arriving, it was that Ravnhov hospitality knew no bounds. All she had to do was follow the food.

She squeezed into a gap between the great hall and Eirik's house. She sat there waiting until the ravens awoke. They dispersed northward, screeching all the way, and soon after she heard people coming and going. Unngonna shouted an order inside. Somebody ran. The door creaked and Hirka looked around the corner.

A girl in blue carried a tray of boiled eggs and pork up a path behind the great hall. Hirka followed her from a safe distance. The girl's footsteps stopped up ahead. A few moments later they suddenly returned, and Hirka barely managed to slip behind a spruce tree to avoid being seen. The girl passed, without the tray. The gathering had to be right around the corner.

The trees thinned out, and a ship-shaped stone building came into view on a mountain ledge. It kind of reminded her of the mountain ledge they'd lived on back home in Elveroa. But she wasn't at home. She was an eavesdropper in Ravnhov. It was a betrayal, but after the conversation she had heard, she had to. She had to know.

Hirka crouched down when she passed the windows at the back of the house. There was no movement inside, as far as she could see. She had to find a hiding place quickly, before people arrived. She looked up. The roof was covered with turf and small bushes. The chimney was wide enough that she could sit against it. Would she be able to hear what was being said through it? She had to take the chance.

Hirka placed her foot on a windowsill and pulled herself up onto the roof. The turf was moist with rain. She crawled up and sat down with her back against the chimney. Her clothes nearly blended in with the yellowish-green roof. Nobody would see her, but just to be safe, she ducked down between the bushes as best she could and pulled her hood over her head.

The girl returned and opened the door. From the chimney, Hirka heard a tankard being placed on the table. She smiled. With a little luck she would hear everything.

It felt like an eternity before she heard voices from the path. She made herself more comfortable. Her back was soaked, but it couldn't be helped. Eirik said something she couldn't quite make out, and the others laughed. The door opened again and Hirka heard a dozen or so people sit down around the table.

Her heart began to beat faster as she listened to the rumble of voices. Hirka was starting to regret her decision. This was not a meeting anyone was meant to overhear.

"Friends," Eirik started. Hirka settled in. "The time has come. Mannfalla's forces are moving north."

Hirka grabbed the turf below her. This was worse than she had thought, and it had come out of nowhere.

Are we at war?

She could clearly hear that the news made an impression on the unseen gathering. A woman's voice rose above the others. "Mannfalla is always moving, Eirik."

Fists and tankards were banged against the table. A new voice asked everyone to calm down and suggested a brief round of introductions. Hirka pressed against the chimney to hear who was present.

The woman who had made this suggestion introduced herself first. "I am Veila Insbrott, jarl of Trygge. Trygge in Brekka." Hirka knew the place well. Brekka was the largest island in Ym. Elveroa welcomed many ships from there. She'd never been there, but she knew that its towns did well on passing trade.

A new voice, a man. "I am Aug Barreson, jarl of Kleiv." He spoke with a sharp Kleivish accent.

"Leik Ramtanger, from Fross." A low voice.

"Rand Vargson from Ulvheim. One-Eye to my friends." This voice was younger, but rougher than the others. What if he was a relative? After all, he came from Ulvheim, like her. But then, he could only be related to Father.

I'm not related to anyone.

"Rand Vargson? Is everything all right with your father?" another voice asked.

More questions followed, so Rand quickly clarified, "I am the son of Varg Kallskaret, jarl of Norrvarje—chieftain, when we're not talking to Mannfalla. My father got into a fight with a mountain bear, and his leg is broken in three places. My mother and six men had to sit on him before he'd agree to send me in his place." The others laughed. "And I'm here with a simple message. Ulvheim stands with Ravnhov!" The laughter petered out. Hirka heard him sit down.

"Easy to promise," an amused voice said. "If Mannfalla comes, you can just sic your father on them!" The room broke out in laughter again. Hirka thought she heard a tremor in his voice when he continued. "I am Grinn Tvefjell. Jarl of Arfabu in Norrvarje. As you can see, I am but a small man with little strength to spare."

"You can say that again," Veila from Brekka replied. More laughter.

"Well, I suppose it's my turn now," said a new voice. He drew out his words as though they were frightfully important. "Meredir Beig. Jarl of Urmunai."

Meredir. The one Eirik said whiles away his days with wine.

Eirik took the floor again. "Three more were invited. Grynar in Ormanadas failed to respond. Audun Brinnvág from Skodd died in a fall." Hirka's ears pricked up. She'd heard about that! From Sylja. The day Ilume had announced the Rite. What was it she'd said? That somebody had seen shadows on the roof?

The jarl of Arfabu interrupted. "A fall? I knew Audun. He was unwavering. Both on his feet and in his support of Ravnhov. Is there anyone who doubts what killed him?" Nobody countered his speculation. Not even Eirik, who continued.

"We've also received a letter from Brinnlanda. From Ende."

This clearly came as a surprise.

"Nobody's had dealings with Ende in ages!" Leik from Fross said.

"Isa from Ende writes this," Eirik responded, unmoved. He cleared his throat and started to read: "'The ravens say nábyrn are back. The stone way is singing. The Might divides south and north, and the alliances are dead. In this new age, Brinnlanda stands with Ravnhov.'"

A new voice broke in. "And is anybody able to interpret this ditty?"

There was a commotion and somebody shouted that it was a forgery. Hirka sighed. This was going to be a long day.

The sun was high in the sky and Hirka was hungry. She'd heard a lot, but judging by the discussions, they were far from finished. She had learned that Mannfalla had moved its forces, but some of the nobles conceded that such a move could be considered reasonable in light of the rumors about the blind. She had also learned that most of them believed the blind to be pure fabrication, and a pretext for conquest.

Nobody could quite agree on anything.

Grinn, the nervous joker from Arfabu, claimed that everyone else had it easier than him. Arfabu lay right between the mountains on the border between Midtyms and Norrvarje, so he had regular contact with Mannfalla. It was clear to Hirka that he had no desire to enrage the Council, but at the same time he was bound to Ravnhov and the rest of the people of the north.

Rand from Ulvheim went on about Mannfalla's hegemony, and about how cowardice and greed prevented the others from acting. He was ashamed of the day his forefathers had bent the knee and become part of the alliance with Mannfalla. Someone pointed out that such utterances would have him sentenced to death, to which he responded: "We've been sentenced to death for generations."

Disagreements between the most powerful men and women of the northlands aside, one thing was certain: Hirka had done them a great disservice.

They hadn't even mentioned her. The discussion between Eirik and Ramoja seemed like a distant dream. Beneath this roof, men and women sat discussing things she wasn't meant to know. Frightening things. But things that had nothing to do with her.

Hirka heard a faint rustle behind the chimney. Kuro? She hadn't thought the raven would be able to find her here. It would be typical of him to want to keep her company right when she was trying to hide. What was ravenspeak for "go away"? She carefully bent forward—and froze.

She wasn't alone. At the end of the roof, right in front of her, crouched a figure with his back to her.

Hirka felt her body turn to ice. What kind of creature was this? A ghost? A man? Black from head to toe. Hirka could see neither skin nor hair. Even his tail was black.

He was holding something that looked like a knife, but it, too, was completely black. It was as though night itself had suddenly decided to climb up on the roof. Hirka pressed against the chimney. How had he gotten up here? Without a sound?

Hirka realized that he hadn't spotted her yet. Like a cat, he prowled toward the ridge of the roof. A silent and impossible dance. This had to be a nightmare. She had to wake up soon.

She heard the door open and people coming out. Somewhere beneath the icy fear, her instincts kicked in. She realized what was about to happen. Eirik and a couple of the others appeared on the path. The black figure raised his arm. Hirka didn't think. Panic ripped through her. She got up. The black figure threw his arm forward. The knife sliced through the air. Hirka screamed for all she was worth.

"EIRIK!"

The black figure spun around. It had eyes. Eirik turned on the path below. The knife sank into his chest. Pandemonium ensued. People running. Pointing at the roof. Hirka stared into the eyes of the black figure. An eternity passed. She heard shouts around her. But all she could see were the eyes.

I'm going to die.

She must have blinked, because all of a sudden, the creature was no longer there. She caught a glimpse of a black shadow out of the corner of her eye. She turned to see the figure leap off the roof and over the ledge.

The shouts from below had converged into a single terrified word.

"KOLKAGGA!"

Hirka stumbled and fell forward. Her body rolled down the turf roof. She managed to grab a hold of something that broke loose just as quickly. Then she had nothing beneath her. She fell. Her body hit the ground with a frightful thud. Pain. Her chest. Broken ribs?

Someone grabbed her.

Kolkagga!

She struck out wildly, but she was held down. Pain lanced through her frame. She tried to scream. No sound came out.

"Breathe, woman!" boomed the voice of Rand Vargson. She obeyed. After a couple of breaths she tried to talk. No sound came out at first. She stared up at the son of the chieftain from Ulvheim. He had a scar above one eye, long stubble, and short, wild hair.

"You look just like I imagined," Hirka said. His features blurred. Then she couldn't keep her eyes open any longer.

ILUME'S FURY

Urd's throat burned. Sweat streamed down his chest from under his collar. It was summoning him again. Soon it would be unbearable. He needed to get away from here. Now.

But Ilume was relentless. The old bat had barely made it inside the city walls before calling the families together. And they'd come! On command, like dutiful ravens. The Council sat around the table, willingly subjecting itself to her fury over the decisions that had been made in her absence. They sat with their eyes downcast, immobile and deflated. It was ridiculous.

Ilume's right to vent her fury was clearly sacred. No one questioned it. Her words carried incomprehensible weight in others' eyes. What in Slokna's name had she done to earn such respect? Not a damned thing, that's what!

Urd felt an involuntary stab of admiration before realizing it was his recent accomplishments she was railing against. He had managed to get the others on his side, but clearly they weren't going to lend him their voices now. Even though what he had managed to achieve was far more impressive than this performance.

Ilume leaned over the table on the Ravenbearer's right. Outside, the sun was sinking beneath the horizon, throwing long red shadows across her arms.

"An assassination?! We've wanted to take Eirik out since he was a child. And his father before him. But we've never sunk that low.

And now we send Kolkagga after him. Kolkagga?! A blatant declaration of war!"

Ilume sank down into her chair again and continued as if exhausted by her own tirade. "If your aim was to keep the peace, you've failed."

Urd seized his opportunity. "*Your*? This Council is one. Or are you not with us anymore?"

Ilume glared daggers at him. A good look on her. Piercing pupils ringed by gray. "I was on this Council the day you defiled the world with your birth, Urd Vanfarinn." There were several muffled gasps. Urd tried to reply, but his throat tightened. Ilume was able to continue uninterrupted. "The leaders from the north were gathered in Ravnhov. You have just given them a reason to rally around Eirik."

"Eirik's dead," Garm tried, but Ilume cut him off.

"If Eirik were dead, we'd know. Have you forgotten everything that's been said in this room in the last thirty years? Have you forgotten why we've let him live? Because he's more dangerous dead! You've made him into a martyr."

The pain in Urd's throat started to build. His muscles spasmed. Uncontrollably. He was out of time. He would have to find a way to bring the meeting to an end while also countering Ilume's attack on him.

"You clearly have no idea how they think. This will divide them. They'll blame each other. But perhaps you have another reason to be angry. Did you live near Ravnhov for long, Ilume?"

No one tried to conceal their gasps this time. Jarladin looked like he was about to get up. Urd moved in for the kill. "You've spent years in Elveroa with nothing to show for it. Without getting any closer to Ravnhov or managing to build a Seer's hall there. Where does your loyalty lie, Ilume? Are you afraid we'll succeed where you failed?"

"Urd!" Eir brought her fists down on the table. Her bangle hit the gold strip, the resultant clang reverberating around the edge. "This Council is one. We speak to each other as if we were one. Watch your language! This meeting is adjourned. We'll reconvene tomorrow."

Urd got up with his hand on his throat. The collar was warm. Breathing was painful. He walked as quickly as he dared across the bridge and toward the rooms reserved for his use in Eisvaldr. He stormed in and tore at the cupboard door. Locked. Of course it was locked. His hands shook. He fumbled in his coin purse for the key. Where had he put it? The pain was unbearable.

He emptied the purse onto the table, grabbed the key, and managed to insert it into the lock. His hands wouldn't cooperate. *There!* Damayanti's bottle was in a box on the middle shelf. The silver was tarnished black. He'd thought he had more time and decided against taking it with him. A mistake he'd never make again. He reached for the bottle.

"In a hurry, Urd?"

He snatched his hand back as if he'd burned it. Ilume's voice was as icy as a mountain stream. It wasn't really a question or a civility. She was outlined in the doorway. The door. He'd forgotten to close the door behind him. He'd been in too much of a rush. Damn it all to Slokna! He would have to be more cautious. If he was found practicing blindcraft in the Council's own halls, it would mean certain death for him.

"If you mean am I in a hurry to safeguard Mannfalla's sovereignty, then yes, I'm in a hurry."

He closed the cupboard again even though it pained him to lose sight of the bottle. He needed to get rid of her. Immediately. He clenched his fists to stop them from flying to his throat—or hers. "So if you'll excuse me—" he said drily.

But Ilume came into the room so they were standing face-to-face. The walls seemed to close in, as if the pillars were being drawn toward them. The rug became an island, and it wasn't big enough for both of them. She was shorter than him but still somehow managed to look down on him. He couldn't work out how. Blindcraft?

No. Not Ilume. Unfortunately. That would have made things so much easier.

"I know who you are, Urd."

Urd's lips pulled back into a sneer. "Such clairvoyance."

"*I know who you are.* Your father knew too. It was never his wish for you to succeed him."

Urd knew what she was trying to do, but he wouldn't let her. The seat was his and it would stay his. Until he got Eir's seat. Until he bore the Raven.

"My father's dying wish was to have honey cakes and an empty pisspot in the evenings." He smiled when her eyes widened. Had she thought he was beholden to his father's wishes? That Vanfarinn had enough power over him to control his life from eternity? She should have seen him in his final moments. Paralyzed by shock, a prisoner in his own bed. Unable to defend himself. He'd sounded off his entire life, but he met his death in silence.

"We all have wishes, Ilume. For example, I wish you'd leave me in peace, yet here you are."

"Here I am. And I know, Urd. You think you can bend them to your will, but you're a whelp. You think you can paint pretty pictures for them with honorable intentions, but no idiot will follow you when push comes to shove. You're alone, Urd. Alone between generations. Dead father. Damaged son. If you don't set your personal motives aside and start thinking about what's best for the eleven kingdoms, Insringin might have to learn more about its newest member."

Urd twitched. She was threatening him! Bitch. She dared threaten him? She had nothing. She knew nothing. She couldn't know.

He snarled. "Who are you to talk about generations, Ilume An-Elderin? What family do you have left? Weak binders, bakers, and historians! Women who throw themselves from walls. The only person who could have succeeded you has chosen Kolkagga. And he's the son of a traitor."

Urd laughed even though the pain ripped through his throat and down into his stomach. He tasted blood. "And who would be left if something were to happen to An-Elderin's great hope? They rarely live long, the black shadows."

Her eyes screamed that he wouldn't dare. But she also looked uncertain, much to Urd's glee. She had every reason to be uncertain, as his father should have been, had he had any sense at all. He could see she was thinking. Weighing his words.

"You'd be signing your own death warrant," Ilume said. She turned and left the room. Her robe danced around her. Urd stood where he was for a few seconds. He could feel her eyes boring into him as if she were still there. But he couldn't wait anymore. He closed the door, locked it, and tore the cupboard door open again. He raised the bottle to his lips and tipped a couple drops of raven blood down his throat.

The pain disappeared straightaway. But the respite was only temporary. Then came the spasms. Merciless. Worse than ever. The old wound opened, and it felt as if his throat were being shredded. It erupted against the collar. Urd fumbled at the small catch and managed to push it to one side. The collar flew open and clattered to the floor.

He fell to his knees on the rug, grabbing a cushion so no one would hear him. He pressed it to his face and screamed, blood gushing everywhere.

SLEEPLESS NIGHT

Rime allowed the night to envelop him. He was a shadow, no more. His sword was a contour that he stretched out in front of him in the darkness. Occasionally the moon peeked out to cast a pale light that glanced off the edge of the blade. Rime spun around and, using both hands, plunged the sword into an invisible enemy behind him.

Banahogg.

His body followed the sword's momentum in a curve over his head before he swung it down in front of him.

Beinlemja.

An owl alighted from the branch above him, wisely deciding to find another place to rest. Rime spun around again, letting the sword cleave the darkness around him before he defended himself against a counterattack by falling to one knee with his arms held out and back.

Ravnsveltar.

He knew he should be sleeping. Days started early for Kolkagga but sweat was tonic to his body. With each movement, his thoughts were normally driven further away. But not tonight. Tonight they had taken root. Something was happening. That certainty sat in his stomach, gnawing at his insides. Mannfalla hosted people from around the world during the Rite, and the rumors were spreading like wildfire.

Raudregn.

Rime knew that the Council was unsettled. He had heard snatches of conversations and quarrels in the corridors and seen signs of disquiet in Ilume's steely face. People from the north whispered about the blind.

Ormskira.

The Council had sent forces north, to strike the rumors dead once and for all, as they put it. But what fool would believe it was still a rumor when thousands of men were marching north? None.

Vargnott.

Kolkagga had been sent on more missions than normal. It had cost one of them their life. Maybe two, because Launhug was still missing, having not returned from a mission that none of the others knew anything about. But that wasn't their job. Kolkagga were nothing more than a weapon. They were told all they needed to know to serve the Seer. They were given a job, a target, and a place. Then they set out, in silence. Other people took care of the details. Rime had always known that was how it had to be, but it didn't make it any easier.

He took a deep breath and put everything he had into a spinning jump, but his knee touched the ground when he landed. His jaw clenched.

Blindring. Not perfect.

But it wasn't just the big things that were bothering him. He was restless. Unfocused. Had been ever since Elveroa. It was about more than men and women in high places with even loftier thoughts. It wasn't even the rumors of the blind that kept him up at night. It was Hirka.

He took a run-up and jumped. The ground became sky as he rotated, and he felt in every fiber of his being that he was going to succeed. He landed perfectly and indulged himself with a brief smile in the night.

Blindring.

Today was the first day of Heymana, the first harvest month, and the Rite had started. In eighteen days it would be Elveroa's turn—Elveroa and the other small settlements around Gardfjella. In eighteen days he would help Hirka. Had he fully understood the consequences of his own promise? He was going to help her conceal the truth from the Council. And, more importantly, from the Seer. What had he been thinking? He was Kolkagga! The Seer's way was the only way. The Seer's will was the only will. The Council was nothing.

He crouched down, letting his sword follow the ground before thrusting it up toward the heavens again, as though to kill a giant.

Myrkvalda.

A circle of irresolute councillors who did nothing other than regard one another with suspicion and spin their webs. Generation upon generation born into power and riches like it was the most natural thing in the world, with no greater ambition than to retain both. They had betrayed the Seer long ago.

Válbrinna.

Should he do the same? Betray himself—and his faith—to help a girl? Rime knew the answer. He was going to help her. It was the right thing to do. It reeked of desperation, and there was no guarantee it would work. But the Seer would understand. He had to understand. The Seer was the true path, how could He *not* understand?

Banadrake.

Rime wasn't worried about his decision. It was made. If he was punished, he would accept it, even if it meant death. That didn't bother him. What *did* bother him was that if he was punished, it would mean the Seer believed Hirka didn't deserve to live. Because she couldn't bind. Because she was unearthed, through no fault of her own. That would be unjust.

But that wouldn't happen. The Seer didn't make mistakes.

As a boy he'd believed that the Council never did anything unjust. That Ilume was infallible. But the Council made mistakes. The

Council had made enough mistakes to fill Mannfalla's sewers. The Council had let Urd Vanfarinn into the inner circle. Given him a chair for life. Nobody who did that was faultless.

A cold wind assaulted Rime's skin, giving him goose bumps. How could the Seer want someone like Urd in His inner circle? There had to be a good reason that Rime just couldn't see. Just as there had to have been a good reason the Seer saw fit to save Rime's life at birth. Why? What was his purpose in life? Was he right to choose Kolkagga?

Rime flung his sword high into the air and rolled forward on the ground in the cool grass, came up on one knee, caught the sword, and thrust it out in front of him like a spear. A soft thud. The sword was met with resistance from a tree. The vibrations in the blade radiated up his forearm.

Blodranda. A maneuver difficult enough in daylight. Foolhardy, people might say. But if that were true, he ought to have died a long time ago. He ought to have died before he was born. And again at the age of six, when they'd dug him out of the snow, almost as lifeless as his parents. But he had lived. And nothing he had done since had changed that. How was blodranda going to?

Rime felt his sword hand grow warm and moist. He had been a little late. A small cut. Nothing more.

That's why you're helping her. To get closer to Him. The Seer you've never spoken with, but who informs everything you do. To get answers.

Rime cleared his mind and pulled the sword out of the tree trunk, ready to try again.

He stopped suddenly. He'd seen a movement out of the corner of his eye. He remained in a crouched position and stared out across Blindból. The narrow mountains stuck up from the sea of fog. It was like something out of a story, an old battlefield for thousands of giants. All that was visible were the fingers reaching skyward in a final attempt to cling to life.

A bead of sweat ran down his forehead and settled in the corner of his eye. He didn't move. He had seen something. He was sure.

There! A figure on the rope bridge. Stooped over, walking in fits and starts, like a wounded animal.

Is that Launhug?

Rime started running. It was impossible to see who it was, but it was one of them. Wearing Kolkagga black. It had to be him. The figure noticed Rime and stopped, clinging to the ropes with both hands. The bridge swayed cautiously above the sea of fog. Rime refrained from sheathing his sword until he was certain.

"Launhug?"

It was as though his voice alone had the power to kill. The figure slumped down on all fours. His hands clung to the rope, which was now above his head. He was going to fall off! Rime ran out on the bridge and grabbed hold of the trembling body.

"Launhug?" He put his hands around his face and forced him to meet his gaze. All he could see was Launhug's eyes. They were round and shiny, as though all hope had run out of them. Launhug burst into tears. Rime had never seen Kolkagga cry.

He dragged Launhug across the bridge and back onto solid ground, where he collapsed in a heap, closed his eyes, and started sobbing. Rime pulled off his hood. Black hair clung to a pale face.

"Where?"

Launhug didn't answer.

"Launhug, where?!" Rime didn't wait for an answer. He ran his hand across his chest until he reached a point where Launhug flinched. A couple of ribs, right on the side. That was often where they broke. No wonder he was late getting back.

"Have you been running like this for long?"

Launhug nodded.

"Since Ravnhov," he managed to force out.

What was he doing in Ravnhov?

"Have you been sick?" A moment passed before Rime got his answer, then Launhug shook his head.

"I don't know. No."

His voice was hoarse. It was clear that he hadn't spoken to anyone since he'd left Blindból. But something wasn't right. His reaction was too volatile. A broken rib could be a nightmare of pain under certain circumstances, but they'd both experienced worse. They were Kolkagga. There was only one other explanation. Rime sat down in the grass next to the broken shadow.

"You failed."

Launhug tried to sit up, but Rime pushed him back down. He had given everything to get back to the camp. Now he needed rest.

But first, Rime had to see how serious the wound was. He unlaced Launhug's tunic, exposing his chest. Launhug didn't protest. He just lay there with his arm over his face. The skin on his side was hot and inflamed. Even in the dark Rime could see that it was red.

Launhug didn't react to Rime's investigation. He was whispering to himself. Hoarse reproaches, filled with hindsight. About everything that could have been different, if he'd just looked around. If he'd just waited until it was dark, like he'd planned. If he hadn't just jumped at the first chance he'd gotten.

Rime followed the swelling along his side up toward his shoulder. He noticed a round symbol on Launhug's arm, black with a figure depicted in the middle. Rime felt a chill run through him. He couldn't see the entire mark, as Launhug's sleeve covered part of it, but he didn't need to see more. He knew it well. It was a picture of Rime as a newborn. The child under the Seer's wings. The lucky child. The An-Elderin child. The symbol could be found all over the world, in the form of everything from amulets, icons, and bookmarks to decorations in Seer's halls.

He wasn't alone, naturally. The hallowed names and pictures of the Council families hung side by side on the market stalls, but the

An-Elderin child's ability to cheat death was a commodity in itself. Even as a permanent black mark inked into Launhug's skin. All the same, here he lay on the grass. Broken and exhausted. Rime's jaw clenched.

He noticed the cut on his own hand again and wiped the blood off in the grass. In his mind's eye, he glimpsed a red-haired girl near the Alldjup trying to hide her hand behind her back.

"It was her fault." Launhug was no longer sobbing. Instead he spoke in a monotone, as though he knew nothing he said would mean anything. He was probably right too. "There was nothing I could do."

"Launhug, you don't need—"

"Suddenly she was just standing there. She shouted out and everything was … lost."

Rime didn't stop him. Launhug had failed. He had to get it out of his system. Had to talk about it, even if he was sworn to silence.

"She must have been there the whole time! What was she doing there?"

Rime had no answer.

"How could I not have seen her? Her hair was flaming red, like dragonfire! She was standing right behind me, and she shouted."

Rime froze. "What did she shout?"

"EIRIK!!" Launhug screamed as though the name was a curse. Rime was happy they were some distance outside the camp, but the scouts were bound to have heard the shout. They'd be here shortly.

That was his mission. To assassinate Eirik.

Eirik of Ravnhov. The thorn in the Council's side. A man who had strayed from the Seer's path, they said. But he was a leader. Killing him wasn't only daring. It was an act of desperation.

"Was she old?" It bothered Rime that he couldn't help asking.

"Barely old enough for the Rite! Just a child! With wild eyes and a tunic like moss. There was no way I could have seen her!"

Rime smiled. So Hirka was on her way to the Rite. Via Ravnhov.

His smile faded. She had saved Eirik from Kolkagga. Launhug had failed because of her. The assassination had failed. Anything could happen now.

Launhug muttered something about outposts. Ravnhov erecting barriers at the foot of Bromfjell. Scouts keeping an eye on Mannfalla. And a gathering of powerful men. A meeting where he had lain in wait for Eirik. Meredir Beig. And a woman. Veila Insbrott. They were amassing allies.

"What was she doing there?! On the roof?" Launhug asked no one in particular.

Rime was certain he knew the answer. He smiled again. "She was listening."

"What?"

"She was listening in on the meeting."

Launhug took a deep breath, but stopped when the pain set in.

"I failed. Because of a child's scream. She fell, Rime! What if I've killed an innocent child?"

Rime felt another chill run through him. "Fell from the roof? Far?"

"Yes, but there were plenty of people there to help her. Maybe she … maybe …"

Rime brought his hand to his chest and felt the comforting shape of the shell with the marks. His marks, and Hirka's. She had survived a lot to get those marks. Climbed high and fallen far.

"She's survived worse, Launhug."

He heard footsteps running through the forest. The others had come to help. He got up and pulled Launhug to his feet.

Kolkagga were meant to follow the Seer's path. Not take the lives of innocents.

But then, they weren't meant to take the lives of their opponents, either, just because those opponents happened to be powerful.

Rime shook off the thought. Hirka had saved the life of Eirik of Ravnhov. A man the Seer had singled out as an enemy and wanted dead. What had she gotten herself mixed up in? Rime let his gaze follow the four black figures carrying Launhug between them. They disappeared noiselessly toward the camp. He stood looking out at the empty rope bridge. The gateway out of the mountains.

You'd better be alive, girl.

THE AGREEMENT

Hirka's feet were heavy. She wasn't looking forward to the conversation that awaited her, and she was dragging herself across the courtyard as if it had turned into a bog.

Eirik was drifting between life and death, they said. No one knew which path he would take. It all depended on whether Slokna would have him. None of it was fair. Why had the living shadow gone after Eirik but let Hirka live? Was it because Ravnhov was harboring her? Would she also be dead if the attempt on Eirik's life had gone as planned?

Since her fall, even the faintest sound had her on high alert. Kuro's beak on her window. The creaking of a gate. Unngonna's footsteps in the hall. It made no sense whatsoever, because noise was a good thing where Kolkagga were concerned. It was their silence that was dangerous.

If they're going to kill me, now would be a good time.

But the black shadows wouldn't save her from this meeting. She had to talk to Eirik. First confessions, then goodbyes. Father had taught her that nothing was free, but Ravnhov had welcomed her with open arms. They'd taken her in when she had nowhere else to go, and now they were being punished for it. She couldn't stay here.

Unngonna had wanted to confine Hirka to her bed, and the pain in Hirka's chest had agreed, but she had already spent an entire day in bed. That was long enough. They had brought her food and taken the same food away again untouched. She'd pretended to be sleeping to avoid having to say anything. After all, what would she have said? That she was sorry for eavesdropping on the meeting between the powerful leaders? That she hadn't meant to put Eirik's life in danger? That she was sorry she was what she was?

The rot who brought Kolkagga to Ravnhov.

The sky was a stormy gray. A flag fluttered in the wind on the roof of the great hall. She hadn't seen it before. It must have been raised during the day. Faded blue with three golden crowns. It looked to have withstood generations. What was it Tein had said?

Do you think the kings just woke up one day and decided to disappear?

Hirka stopped in front of Eirik's house. It was close to the great hall, with a wing connecting them. She forced herself to knock. The door opened a crack and a girl whose name she didn't know peered out at her. But the girl knew who she was.

"Hirka. We were so worried. It's good to see you up and about." She waved Hirka inside. A group of people had gathered by the hearth. "None of us have slept," the girl explained. "He's been burning up all night."

"Can I talk to him?" Hirka asked.

"You can *see* him. He's not doing much talking." The girl led her up some stairs, old but sound. "Have you eaten? We've got some hot stew downstairs," the girl said.

Hirka shook her head. "Thanks, but I'm not—"

"Here." The girl stopped in front of a dark wooden door decorated with iron nails.

Unngonna came out with her keys clinking on her hip. She moved aside to let Hirka in. "Let him sleep," she said. Then they left Hirka alone in the gloom with a giant on his deathbed.

Eirik lay snoring in a shaft of light from a narrow window. The glass depicted a blue shield decorated with three crowns. The shades of blue varied, as if they had been replacing pieces of glass for generations without ever finding quite the same color. A wood carving above his bed depicted a two-headed raven with outstretched wings set against a pattern of copulating mythical creatures. Its intricate details seemed out of place against the bare stone of the wall. Beams crossed the ceiling like in a funeral ship.

Hirka sat on a chair by the bed. Eirik was flushed and sweaty, the blanket plastered to his stomach. Someone had applied a bandage diagonally across his hairy chest and around one of his shoulders. The knife had entered just above his heart, between his ribs. It smelled foul. Worryingly foul.

Suddenly the room was silent. Eirik had stopped snoring. Hirka leaned toward the edge of the bed and stared at him fearfully.

In the Seer's name, don't die!

One of his eyelids sprang open and a round eye stared at her. Hirka jumped back in her chair. "Is she gone?" Eirik's voice was an uncharacteristic whisper. Hirka looked around, but there was no one else there. "Who?"

"Unngonna." He tried to prop himself up on his elbow but gave up with a pained growl. The bandage changed color from white to yellowish green. Hirka's jaw clenched. He didn't try to sit up again, but he kept talking, breathing heavily. "She's trying to kill me! Washing and changing bandages and refusing a poor creature a drink."

He gazed hopefully at a tankard on a table by the fire. Hirka got up and filled it with ale. He drank the lot, then let his arm flop toward the floor with a sigh of pleasure. Hirka refilled it before sitting down again. Good ale was very nutritious. And it would dull his pain. But not hers. She shifted restlessly in her chair. She couldn't get comfortable. Finally she opened her mouth to speak, but Eirik beat her to it.

"They didn't catch him, I'm told."

She shook her head. "No. He disappeared over the ledge."

"Well, he is Kolkagga, I suppose."

Hirka nodded. She was starting to realize what that meant.

"Eirik ..." Hirka swallowed. "I've enjoyed my time here." It wasn't what she had meant to say, but it was what came out.

Eirik chuckled, but then had to stop and clutch at his chest. "Of course you have." He said it without arrogance. "You're in Ravnhov!"

Hirka was starting to realize what that meant as well. But she couldn't keep beating around the bush. "Eirik, I've done you all wrong! I was listening in on the meeting. I know it was nothing to do with me, but ..." She forced herself to continue while she still had the courage. "I'm not who you think I am. And it's my fault Kolkagga came here. It's my fault that ... that you're lying here." She tailed off in a hoarse whisper.

Eirik reached out so the tankard bumped against her knee. He threw another glance at the ale. Hirka topped him up again and then sat back down to continue.

"Codswallop! Utter nonsense, from start to finish," the giant of a man rumbled over the brim of his tankard. His voice had regained some of its strength. "You saved my life, girl! Kolkagga don't miss. If you hadn't shouted, that knife would have ended up through my neck." He had to rest between almost every word. "The Council has always had it in for me, but this is the first time they've sent Kolkagga. That must mean they're getting desperate!" He took another swig, chuckling into the tankard so the foam clung to his lips.

"The first time?"

Eirik tried to turn toward her. He cursed through clenched teeth and Hirka got up to help. She rescued the tankard and set it down on the floor. He gripped her hand and she was forced to crouch down by the bed. His grizzled hair clung to his face. His eyes were bright. Hirka knew he would need help if he was going to survive.

"Have they given you yellowbell?" Of course, it was a stupid question. She assumed they'd done everything they could.

Eirik scoffed. "Just let them try! Listen to me, girl—"

Hirka's eyes widened. "You haven't taken any medicines?!"

Eirik pulled her closer. His eyes bored into her. The smell of the ale mixed with the smell of the wound. "I know you're strong in the Might. Ramoja's told me all about it."

It had to be the fever talking. This was even worse than she'd feared.

He went on. "You'll stand up to Mannfalla, Hirka. I know you will."

She jumped when he used her name. So he knew who he was talking to, at least. She pulled her hand back. The fog she'd been living in started to lift. Pieces of the puzzle started falling into place. Confusion. Then clarity. Ramoja's words up by the idol. What was it she'd said? They thought … they thought Hirka wanted to escape the Rite because she was a skilled binder and she wanted to hide it from the Council. They thought she could bind like she had blue blood! That she was so strong the ravens talked about it. Like in the old stories. She felt the warmth drain from her body. And Eirik thought she could somehow help him protect Ravnhov from Mannfalla.

Hirka started to laugh. The whole situation was absurd. Upside down. She'd been terrified that people would smell the rot. Realize she was unearthed. That she couldn't bind at all! And now they thought she was a miracle among binders. A weapon in the war that would make Tein king.

Eirik gripped her arm again. "You'll stand up to Mannfalla, right?" His voice had taken on a different tone. It wasn't an order or a question. It was a prayer. The man before her wasn't a chieftain who feared death. He was a father who feared for his son's life. Who feared what would happen if he didn't survive.

"Yes, Eirik. I'll stand up to Mannfalla."

The wind had picked up outside. The chieftain indulged in a sweaty smile. His eyelids drooped. "Stay with us, Hirka."

Hirka knew what she had to do. It was clear as Vargtind early in the morning. For the first time in as long as she could remember, she was sure what was needed of her. There was no other way. She'd done too much harm. Father was in Slokna because of her. Eirik was drifting between life and death. Rime had promised to help, and she'd promised to be there. That was enough. Tein had made her realize what she was missing. The Might. Rime. His white hair. His chiseled features. His arm around her shoulders and the last words she'd heard him say.

I'll make sure I'm there for you.

She needed to go to Mannfalla. To the Rite.

"No. I can't stay. Not now. I'll come back, Eirik. But it'll cost you." She heard the words, but they didn't belong to her. She was just playing the part.

But Eirik was a practical man. He knew most things came at a cost. "What do you need?" He had closed his eyes, perhaps afraid she would ask for something he couldn't give. Lying like this, his face reminded her of Father's. The slackness that came before death.

Hirka clenched her teeth. As sure as she was unearthed, Tein would not lose his father to Slokna. Not this time.

She considered her words carefully. "I'll come back, and I'll do everything I can for Ravnhov. But only if you do everything you can for Tein."

Eirik opened his eyes again. He frowned, his bushy eyebrows pulling together, suspicious now. "I already do everything for Tein."

Hirka leaned forward and whispered, "Take yellowbell."

He stared at her in horror. It was as if she'd asked him to drown himself. "Take yellowbell and break your fever. Live for Tein. Then I'll stop Mannfalla."

"Not even Rinna has yellowbell."

"I'll get some if you promise to take it."

She sensed optimism. He thought for a moment. Weighed his fear of folk healers and plants against her promise to save Ravnhov. Hirka's heart started pounding. She had to be crazy. She had come here to lay her cards on the table, and now she was making matters worse. But if it would keep Eirik alive, it was worth it. If she could rescue him from the clutches of Slokna, perhaps her lies would no longer be lies. Surely the best thing anyone could do for Ravnhov was to keep the man Mannfalla hated alive?

"Do we have a deal, Eirik Viljarsón?"

Eirik nodded. "I swear you're all trying to kill me! But we have a deal, tailless."

The door opened. Unngonna came in with another girl on her heels. "Is he awake? Is he any better? I heard talking."

Hirka got up, but couldn't answer. The lump in her throat grew. She'd done good. And she'd done bad. And she was leaving them. Eirik lay still as if playing dead. The only thing that gave him away were the creases in his forehead. Unngonna laid a wet cloth on it as Hirka smuggled the tankard back onto the table.

There was no one down by the hearth now. She followed an errand boy through the wing connecting the house to the great hall. There, she stopped and stared. The hall was packed with people. She hadn't heard them. It was so quiet.

The calm before the storm.

There were servants and warriors. People from the town. Some spoke quietly. Some polished silverware. One of the boys was washing a round wooden shield decorated with the three crowns. Two of the fireplaces were lit. Half the town was there, just waiting. Waiting for news about Eirik. She spotted Solfrid and Tein, but she couldn't bring herself to speak to them. If she did, her mask would slip and all the lies would come out. She walked out into the autumn evening and let the storm come.

Seer preserve me!

They thought she was like the Seer. That she would be Ravnhov's salvation. But she was the rot.

A SKILLED BINDER

Day and night had become one. Hirka had hung around the darkest taverns in Ravnhov for days until she found what she needed. A traveler with the same inking as Father—an evenshade flower. But he hadn't been like Father in any other way. He had been wiry with cold eyes. He'd taken what little money she had left, and acted like he was doing her a favor. He'd offered to sell her opa as well. Hirka had left without replying.

But she had gotten hold of yellowbell, and people knew better than to ask where it came from. She had given the chieftain as much as she dared, but his fever hadn't gone down, and the wound was still inflamed and red. At least he wasn't getting hotter.

She had slept in short bursts, nodding off at Eirik's bedside, waking every hour to apply soldrop and greenstem to his wound. She had sent out half the household to look for ylir root to clean it. They had found a small amount among Rinna's supplies, but the old midwife had been far from gracious when she realized the circumstances. Ravnhov's most renowned healer had never been allowed to lay her hands on Eirik, and she made no attempt to hide what she thought of a young girl, barely old enough for the Rite, doing the job. Had it not been for Solfrid's appeals on behalf of her husband, they would have received nothing more than curses from Rinna.

Ravnhov was anxiously waiting for news from Eirik's room, but

Hirka didn't have anything for them. Only time would tell. She had done what she could.

The ravens flew above the great hall like a black, shrieking blanket. Hirka woke with a start in the chair beside Eirik's bed. It was early, but she couldn't stay any longer. Light fell through the stained-glass window and drew three crooked crowns on the floor. One stretched across the edge of the bed and Eirik's shoulder. She made sure his condition hadn't worsened before she left. There was only one thing she had to do today.

She had to leave Ravnhov.

She had also worked out how. Keeping one eye on Eirik and the other on the stables over the past few days had paid off. Ramoja was still in town, but Hirka knew that the ravener couldn't stay. Vetle also had to go through the Rite, and that meant that they would have to travel soon. Sure enough, the previous evening the servants had carried raven cages into the stable where the carts were kept. And it hadn't been difficult to find out where Ramoja was staying while she was in Ravnhov. Every afternoon one of the blue-clad housemaids carried a pot of spiced tea to a guest cabin on the mountainside. The smell was unmistakable.

Hirka followed the path up to Ramoja's cabin. Kuro sat on her shoulder. He was an important player in the performance she was about to put on. As she approached, she heard Vetle singing inside. A children's song that made her smile, about all the men who went to Bromfjell to kill the dragon. The song started with twenty men, then there were only nineteen, then eighteen, and in the end only one. Whether the last man succeeded or not nobody knew, because there was nobody left to sing about it.

Hirka stopped outside. She had a difficult task ahead of her. If Ramoja was the source of Eirik's delusions, then she wouldn't take Hirka to Mannfalla willingly. Hirka would have to exploit the misunderstanding. That was all she had. And she would have to conceal her own doubt. Show no signs of fear. Only then would she have the authority she needed. It was just a matter of believing her own words. Having Kuro with her would help. Ramoja respected ravens more than people.

The morning was bright and clear. Hirka looked out over Ravnhov, at the chieftain's household on the plateau between the mountaintops. The crooked houses huddled together in defiance of the weather. The surrounding wall, the forest beyond, and Gardfjella in the distant west.

She was going to miss this place. The way you miss something you've only just been given, that you never thought you would have. She would miss its hardy people. The women with strong arms, which they deployed when the menfolk got home late from the taverns and inns. She was going to miss the continuous murmuring of the ravens in the ravine, how they disappeared in a commotion of feathers every morning and returned every evening. She was going to miss the rain, the way it collected in puddles on the road, and in barrels at the corners of buildings.

She would even miss their disdain for Mannfalla. The feeling of having a common enemy. Someone to blame. Now she was going to be on her own again. And she wouldn't be able to talk to anyone anymore. Still, she had to leave. The Council had already swung its knife while she'd been there. Maybe to strike her. To strike those who protected her. She wasn't going to let that happen again.

She shivered. What if the knife was never intended to kill anyone? *Kolkagga never fail*—she'd heard that far too many times. Maybe they'd just wanted to smoke her out? To make sure she crossed Ravnhov's well-protected borders and set off on her own? It wasn't outside the realms of possibility.

The low door opened and Ramoja came out. She was carrying two large cloth sacks, one under each arm. The light clothes she always wore had been exchanged for a long leather jacket lined with fur, the fur poking out from the hood like a halo around her dark face.

Hirka straightened up and looked at her.

Steady now. Remember you're the one she thinks is a skilled binder.

Ramoja dropped one of the sacks on the ground. She bent down and picked it up slowly, presumably to avoid looking at Hirka. A moment passed before Ramoja straightened up again. She closed her eyes for a few seconds.

"I didn't mean to startle you," Hirka said.

"No, no. That ..." She searched for words for a moment. Turned and pointed at the raven ravine. "We—I ... had to come here to ..."

"You're a ravener, Ramoja. Nobody knows more about ravens than the people here in Ravnhov, so I expect you come here a lot. I don't see anything unusual about it, and I have no interest in telling anyone that you've been here either."

Ramoja gave her a look that was difficult to interpret. Hirka responded with what she hoped was a calm and confident smile. She continued before Ramoja had time to reconsider.

"I'm coming with you to Mannfalla."

"Hirka, there's nothing to be gained from—"

"I'm coming with you to Mannfalla. I've promised Eirik I'll help. I can't do it from here."

Ramoja had dark rings under her eyes. In the cabin behind her, the dragon had taken all but the last man in Vetle's tone-deaf song. Hirka, on the other hand, did her best to strike the right chord. She held her arms out a little to the side, her back straight and chin down. She had to look strong, and she had to make herself clear. As if on command, Kuro adjusted his grip on her shoulder and shook his wings.

"I don't know how you found out, Ramoja. But you know what I am. You know what I can do. I can't tell you what's going to happen, but it has to happen from Mannfalla. Trust me."

Relief washed over Ramoja's face. She dropped the sacks on the ground. Her eyes glistened and she embraced Hirka. Kuro felt redundant and flew over the roof.

"I knew it," she whispered over and over again into Hirka's hair.

SVARTELD'S MERCY

Rime held his sword arm straight as he circled master Svarteld. Wrist locked. Firm grip on the hilt. Svarteld's eyes gleamed in his dark face, deceptively calm.

Rime tracked him with his blade. He tried to hold it steady so it was centered on his master at all times. The task required his full attention, which was a challenge after the conversation he'd had with Ilume earlier in the day.

The master, on the other hand, could allow himself to be distracted. He kept looking past Rime, out at the blanket of fog drifting between the mountains. But Rime had been training with him for three years and wouldn't let himself be fooled. If he turned to look, his master would have an opening to attack. And Rime couldn't afford to make mistakes. First he had to perform, then he could ask for the help he needed.

Rime was tense. Training with master Svarteld was an awakening. The Might hung watchfully in the air, a palpable presence that heightened all his senses until it was almost unbearable. He could feel the wind cooling the sweat on his brow. Hear the sound of insects in the grass outside. Rime glimpsed the old pine trees outside for only a fraction of a moment, yet he could see every single needle on every single twig. Muted sea green. Swaying.

He was barefoot and could have read stories from the wooden floor the way a blind man reads with his fingers. Kolkagga had been leaving marks on this floor for hundreds of years. It was all chronicled here, in nicks and scratches. Victories and losses, progress and humiliation. Etched forever into oiled oak that wouldn't be bested, that refused to fade or crack. Like Ilume.

Let Ilume be Ilume and do your job!

Rime snapped back to reality and saw what he had to do. Svarteld had a tendency to jump over his opponents and attack from behind. Rime didn't intend to give him that opportunity. He lifted his shoulders and launched himself into brotnahogg, a maneuver he usually performed faultlessly. He held his sword at throat height, having learned from past mistakes. To his surprise, Svarteld came toward him instead of pulling back. Then he was gone. Rime felt a sword chop at his neck. Pain radiated down his spine and out into his tail.

Dead. If they'd been using proper swords, he'd have been dead. Again. But even the blunt training swords could do a lot of damage. Due to his miscalculation, his white collar was now stained red. He had attacked too high, expecting Svarteld to jump. The master had made the most of the opening, dropping to the floor and spinning around until he had Rime precisely where he wanted him. Defenseless, with his back to him.

Rime leaned on his sword as if it were a cane and caught his breath. Blood dripped from his neck down onto the wooden floor. He could have been a carpenter. Wouldn't that have been easier? A crow laughed at him from the pine tree outside. Rime cut off that train of thought. He groaned.

"Várkunn, master."

"What are you apologizing for? You still have your sword, don't you?"

Svarteld wasn't even out of breath, but he was visibly irritated. He wasn't one for apologies. The opportunity to ask for help was moving out of reach.

Rime straightened up and turned toward him. The master had lived through half a century, but you would never have guessed. He had a young man's body, strong and lean, and not so much as a hair on his dark brown head. He studied Rime with a critical eye, from top to toe, as he'd done the first time they met.

Svarteld had been hard on him from the get-go. An heir to the Council as Kolkagga? A spoiled Són who fancied himself a warrior? Svarteld had done his best to get rid of him. But Rime hadn't given up. And he'd hardly put a foot wrong. He was one of the best. Just not today.

"If you're going to apologize for something, apologize for not being here," Svarteld said.

"Sorry?"

"Be here when you're here or go somewhere else."

Rime knew what he meant but didn't want to admit it. "I'm h—"

The master's sword was suddenly resting against Rime's throat. The steel was cold against his skin, but all the same Rime flushed with humiliation. The master was right. He wasn't present. His mind was on other things.

Ilume. Hirka. And the Rite.

Earlier today Ilume's voice had been sharper than Svarteld's sword, and just as merciless. He'd sought her out in Eisvaldr to arrange to be on guard duty on Elveroa's Rite day. He had to keep his promise to Hirka. He had to be there for her.

He had told Ilume he wanted to see everyone again. Vetle, Sylja, Hirka. He'd lingered on Hirka's name to test Ilume's reaction. To see whether she knew Hirka was in Ravnhov. After all, Launhug had submitted a report detailing his failure, and Ilume might also have thought of Hirka when she heard about the red-haired girl on the roof.

Ilume had refused. What did they need more guardsmen for? They had enough people for that. His services wouldn't be required.

And if he just wanted to see his old acquaintances again, he really had made the wrong choice. Kolkagga didn't exist. Kolkagga were already dead.

That was when she had sent him reeling. Ilume had continued to flick through her letters as she said: "Ramoja sent a raven. The Hovel burned to the ground the day we left. The girl's probably dead. I forgot to mention it."

He had been staggered by her indifference, rendered speechless. She had glanced up and given him an inquisitive look. "What? Was it important?" Rime had left the room to stop himself from doing something he would later regret.

Svarteld lowered his sword again. He shook his head and headed for the door. Rime followed him outside, ready for the inevitable punishment.

"You were in Mannfalla today." Svarteld could even make questions sound like commands.

"Eisvaldr, master. Visiting Ilume."

"Ah," Svarteld said, as if that explained everything. Rime could see the shadow of a smile on his face. They looked out at the mountains. There was a sheer drop only a couple steps farther. Beneath them, crows sailed between the sprawling peaks, bobbing in and out of the fog in an attempt to organize themselves for the evening. The sweat in Rime's hair dried in the wind.

"You were her last hope," Svarteld said without looking at him.

Rime swallowed, unsure what to do with the sudden intimacy that statement created. "Master, the An-Elderin family is bigger than me and Ilume."

Svarteld chuckled. He stood shoulder to shoulder with Rime, his arms folded across his chest. "Your mother is dead. Her brother, Tuve, is lost. Only your father's brother, Dankan, is still alive. He might live under Ilume's roof, but Neilin keeps his balls in a dish on her bedside table. Their firstborn died. Their youngest is often sick and Illunde is illegitimate. Apart from that, all you've got is the usual assortment of parasites with negligible blood ties to the family."

Rime was taken aback. He'd never heard anyone apart from Ilume talk about their family that way. It was an ice-cold summary that would have gotten anyone else burned on the walls. But every word was true, and the master wasn't finished.

"You're the one who inherited the blue blood. You're the one who has the Might. It came to you through Gesa. It came to Gesa through Ilume. It came to Ilume through Storm."

It came to Storm through Yng. It came to Yng through ...

Rime could continue down the family line for a thousand years. To the first Elderin. He'd learned to do that before he'd learned to read or write. He knew it shouldn't come as a surprise that the master had such knowledge. He was Kolkagga's leader. He'd been the long arm of the Seer and the Council for longer than Rime had been alive.

"She almost lost you when you were born. She almost lost you when you were six. Now you're eighteen and she's lost you forever."

The master's words gave him chills. Images came to him unbidden. Ice. Cold fingers. Heavy snow. They were only flashes, but a memory all the same. He had been dug out of the snow and survived. His parents hadn't been so lucky. He felt a kind of detached grief over it—more like he was remembering a time of grief than actually grieving for something he remembered. It was what it was. As it had always been. Ilume had lost her daughter, Gesa, along with Gesa's husband. But she had managed to hold onto Rime. Until now.

The master started along the paved path along the edge of the cliff. Rime followed him until they reached the outskirts of the camp. Kolkagga had several camps spread around Blindból, but this was the biggest and the closest to Mannfalla. Together they comprised the Council's invisible network of assassins, controlling the entire mountain region between Mannfalla and Ravnhov. Stories about bloody encounters between Kolkagga and warriors from the northlands were rife, but Rime had never run into anyone while out on a mission.

Svarteld and Rime stopped on the path and looked down at Kolkagga getting ready for the evening. Hundreds of torches had already been lit. They were fixed to poles in front of the cabins, low wooden buildings shared by a minimum of four men. They each had their own room and shared a hearth in the middle of the building. Apart from that, Kolkagga had next to nothing. They slept on straw mats on the floor with their black outfits rolled up as pillows. They had weapons, woollen blankets, and little else.

Out here you had to rely on yourself and your own knowledge. You only had what you needed to survive. The An-Elderin family home—the sleeping dragon—was the polar opposite. Before becoming Kolkagga, Rime had never gone hungry and never known real pain. He had never wanted for anything. Yet still he'd had nothing.

Svarteld looked at Rime. "You swore the Oath," he said. Rime was momentarily confused until he remembered what they had been talking about. Ilume and how he'd been her only hope, her intended successor. It suddenly occurred to Rime that the reason his master was so hard on him might be different than what he had thought. He really had done his best to make Rime give up before he swore the Oath, to send him back to Eisvaldr with his tail between his legs. Why?

Because if anything were to happen to Rime An-Elderin, Kolkagga would have to pay the price. They would have to face Ilume's fury. Svarteld would rather have Rime on the Council than see him die in Blindból.

But he could have refused to let Rime swear the Oath. He could always have found a reason. It would undoubtedly have made life easier for him, yet the master had accepted him, nevertheless.

Rime felt a new warmth blossom in his chest. He meant something to Svarteld. Something worth the problems that might come later. It was as if he had seen straight into the master's heart for a brief moment. It made him feel braver. Perhaps he could find a solution to the problem he'd been trying to solve all day. He'd made Hirka a promise, and he would keep it. He would make sure he was on duty on her Rite day, and Ilume would never find out about it.

"Master, I need a favor."

If Svarteld was surprised, he hid it well. He pointed back toward the training hall.

"Clean your blood off the floor. Then we'll talk."

MANNFALLA

The conversations in the cart were colored by the landscape. Through the spruce forests, Ramoja was bold, talking about things nobody was supposed to hear. About how you can't always choose and how your path can seem predetermined. How you wake up one day and wonder where you were when the choice had been made. Like missing a trial and receiving your sentence at the door. The more she went on, the clearer it became that she felt the need to downplay her role in the festering conflict between Ravnhov and Mannfalla.

Hirka heard Father whisper from Slokna, *Idiots choose sides. Be on your own side and you'll live longer.*

As they came down from Hrafnfell, the spruce forest thinned and gave way to the occasional birch. Hirka and Ramoja grew more guarded, chose their words more carefully, almost as if trying to draw a veil over everything that had been said. Hirka had said as little as possible, keeping her mouth shut and smiling mysteriously whenever the conversation turned to the Might.

Ramoja believed the Might was strong in Hirka, and that she didn't want to use it to serve the Council. She believed that Hirka was a blue blood who could bind the dragon forth, as had been said since ancient times. Making Hirka a pawn in a far bigger game. A fantasy. What would the ravener have said if she knew how insignificant Hirka really was? Unearthed and mightless. An outsider. What would Eirik and Tein have said? Tein, whom she hadn't seen since his father had been attacked. She had expected him to storm into the room while she was working to bring down Eirik's fever, but she had remained alone at the chieftain's bedside. She hadn't asked about him either.

In the lowlands, people were starting to bring in the harvest, perhaps earlier than usual since the Rite had been brought forward by nearly an entire month. Nobody looked worried. They just worked as they'd always done. Children chased birds or picked up the grain their parents had dropped. A couple of them pulled at each other's tails. Hirka looked at them longingly. What if she just jumped off the cart? She could find a family. Work, eat, and turn in with them, in a house so full of people that it blocked everything else out. But the moment passed and on they rolled, without anyone giving them so much as a second glance.

The weather grew worse after a couple of days. The open countryside of Midtyms lay between Tyrimfjella in the east and Blindból in the west. The wind came in fierce gusts and swept dust from the road over them. They wrapped scarves around their faces or sat inside the cart with the ravens, which grew more irritable with every day they spent cooped up in the small cages.

They started encountering more and more people on the road. People who had seen the army inching its way northward. People resting around road markers. The Seer protected travelers, and His mark could be seen everywhere. People also put up their own. They passed a farm where a pair of antlers that had been painted black hung on the gate. Someone had covered the antlers with thin leather strips to make them look like the Seer's protective wings. They fluttered bleakly in the wind. It looked more like a starving raven had flown into the gate and died.

Hirka grew more and more uneasy. She tried to hide it by taking on small tasks: word games with Vetle, looking after the ravens, sweeping sand out of the cart. Nothing helped.

Rime haunted her thoughts. He was going to be there. He was going to help. Was he not An-Elderin? The Seer's favorite? That had to count for something. At night she prayed quietly that the Seer would prove worthy of the faith Rime had in Him. That He would be a wise, merciful, and loving Seer. The one who had saved them from the blind. The one who protected those who could not protect themselves.

Crones' talk, Father whispered from Slokna.

They reached a village so big that Hirka thought they had reached their destination. So this was Mannfalla? Big, but not as bad as she'd expected. She almost felt relieved—until Ramoja cleared up the misunderstanding. This was just one of many villages located around the actual city.

"You'll see Mannfalla when we get over that ridge," Ramoja said and pointed.

The cart climbed upward until the houses gave way to hilly terrain and tea plants. A couple of older women with wrinkled brows walked between the orderly rows of green, making notes in small books. They touched the plants, smelled them, and walked on.

The terrain leveled out toward the top of the ridge, and suddenly enormous camps appeared. Tents, carts, horses, and campfires. Some families had hunkered down under the open sky without any kind of shelter. Ramoja looked almost stunned. "There are more than ever."

"Do they live here? Who are they?" Hirka asked, climbing over the back of the bench to sit next to Ramoja.

Ramoja shrugged. "People. Families whose children have to go through the Rite. There isn't enough room for everyone in the city, and not everyone can afford to stay there. There's always a lot, but this ..."

Hirka remembered hearing some men, reeking of ale, talking at the feast in Ravnhov. Rumors of the blind. Mannfalla's warriors heading north. War and superstition driving more and more people to the capital.

Ramoja urged the horses on, past roadside peddlers selling jewelry depicting the Seer. Guardsmen dressed in white and brown were directing people away from the roads and handing out what Hirka thought was food, but what Ramoja said was soap. It was the most important protection Mannfalla had against illness when the city was overcrowded. Hirka remembered Father's story about the woman she had thought was her mother.

Maiande was a girl in Ulvheim who I … knew for a while. She made soaps and knew to sell them to weak men at the taverns. They spent more on soaps than on ale. You'd have struggled to find cleaner drunkards.

Hirka forgot her fear for a moment and held her hand out to one of the guardsmen. He gave her a piece of soap without stopping or deigning to look at her. It looked like a flattened egg in her hand. The mark of the Council was stamped into the bottom. It was hard to tell whether it was to remind them of who was behind the good deed or to boost its cleansing power.

The cart rolled over the hillcrest and Mannfalla appeared below them, an incredible sight that left no doubt in Hirka's mind that they had finally arrived. She stood up and held onto the roof of the cart so as not to fall. Everything she had heard about Mannfalla was true. The city could have housed half the world. Houses of all imaginable shapes and colors were stacked on top of one another, in some places organized in streets, in other places more haphazardly, as if by a landslide. The buildings formed a horseshoe around the Ora, which was dotted with ships and narrow boats that didn't seem to do anything other than sail back and forth between the riverbanks. Gray spires poked up all over the city.

"This is nuts," Hirka said, sinking back down onto the seat.

"Nuts!" Vetle echoed.

"What's that over there? Out on the river?" Hirka pointed at a group of houses that appeared to be floating in the middle of the river. A maze of jetties jutted out in every direction. It was like looking at a giant crow's nest.

"It's a fishing camp. In a month the redfins will start swimming upstream, and then they'll be busy." Ramoja nodded at the fishing camp. "The fishermen sleep and eat out there, or at least they try to."

"Don't they live in the city?"

"Yes, but they're afraid of missing shoals of fish, so they prefer not to go ashore. It's good food and good money."

The road sloped down toward the city, and the camps disappeared behind them. They rounded a small hill and the whole city came into view, twice as big as it had first appeared. And now Hirka could see the wall.

Her eyes widened. She'd heard the stories. She knew it was meant to be tall, but she'd thought tall as in the walls of the Alldjup. Not tall as in Vargtind. The legendary white wall that divided Mannfalla in two stood like a luminous bridge, barring the mountain pass leading into Blindból. On the outside lay the city in all its motley glory. On the inside lay Eisvaldr, the home of the Seer. A city in its own right, almost as large as the one outside. On the inside everything was white, apart from a couple of red roofs and domes. The largest of them was shiny and gleamed in the sun.

"Eisvaldr," Ramoja said.

"All of that?" Hirka asked, trying to stifle her horror. The cart continued stolidly onward.

"All of that. Eisvaldr is a city at the end of the city. A thousand years ago, it was just the wall against Blindból. Then the home of the Seer was built inside. Then came the Rite Hall, the Council's headquarters. Eisvaldr grew and grew. Today all of the Council families have their houses inside the walls." Ramoja gave a crooked smile. "Every time I come here, the houses are a little bigger, the gardens a little nicer, and the embellishments a little more lavish. They stopped being homes a long time ago."

"What do you mean? Does nobody live there?"

"Oh, yes. Several councillors have practically their entire family under one roof. But the house's primary function is to impress other families."

Hirka shrugged. "So a bit like everywhere else."

Ramoja smiled and looked at her. "True. Here there's just more to choose from."

They came down to the western city gate, which was almost hidden behind all the various stalls. People shouted, pointed, and quarreled. They held up pots, clothes, and decorative items of iron, brass, silver, and gold. There was screeching from cages and squealing from pens. Ducks, geese, chickens, and sheep. Black pigs and goats with decorations on their horns.

Guardsmen patrolled atop the city wall. Hirka stared at the ground to hide her face, but they weren't stopping anyone. They had enough to do just keeping peddlers and animals off the road.

Their cart rolled through the gate, a huge arch of dark wood that probably hadn't been closed for hundreds of years. Other carts creaked through in a steady stream. Inside the walls, the streets were wide but teeming with life. A smoky, charred smell came from the stalls selling food right on the street. People bought roasted nuts, stews, and grilled pieces of redfish spiced with seeds that they ate from cones while they walked. Large wooden crates and sacks were filled to the brim with dried fruit, vegetables, and spices in all imaginable colors.

Hirka tried to be polite to everyone who approached the cart. "No, thank you, I don't wear bangles," or, "That's lovely, but I don't need a vase." More to the point, she didn't have any money. Who could afford all this? Hirka had never seen so many things in one place. She had no idea what half of what the merchants held up to her even was.

Ramoja laughed at her and told her to look straight ahead so she didn't have to reply to everyone. "They can see that you're curious, Hirka."

So she looked up instead. Many of the houses had windows with colored glass. Some were left open, and from one of them hung an expensive-looking rug with a hunting motif in red and gold. From another hung a simple straw mat that looked about ready to fall apart. People wearing shoes of colored leather with metal buckles walked past people sitting barefoot, begging. Hirka saw a young boy slip his hands into a stranger's pockets and sneak off into a dark alley with his loot. Hirka expected people to run after him, but nobody saw him. He was simply able to disappear. Invisible among thousands. Hirka stared after him in amazement.

Ramoja had to urge the horses onward when, confused by the crowds and with no clear path forward, they slowed to a stop. The smell of food, manure, and sweat was everywhere. But it gradually faded as they approached Eisvaldr. The stalls gave way to shops with hanging signs, like the inns had. The houses became bigger and more handsome. Family crests marked the entrances and there were carved eaves framing the roofs, which gradually went from being flat to sloped and covered with good black tiles. Each one perfectly shaped. The roof edges were furnished with small gutters made of the same kind of stone. In places Hirka could see the wall towering above the rooftops, even though it was some distance away.

Some houses had private gardens with tall gates and hedges that ran along paved paths up to the front door. One of them had a man guarding the gate. He was wearing red leather with a silver breastplate. Two throwing axes with red straps around the shaft hung from his belt. Hirka tried to meet his gaze, but he just stared straight ahead as they rolled past.

"Do Council folk live here?"

"No," Ramoja answered. "The Council families stay within the wall. It's mostly merchants living here."

"Wow, they must be richer than Glimmeråsen!"

Ramoja laughed. "Most of them could buy Glimmeråsen a thousand times over."

"Seriously?"

"Seriously."

Hirka had never understood Sylja's dreams of Mannfalla. In Hirka's world, Sylja already had unimaginable wealth. More than most could dream of, or need. But here there were people who were richer than Glimmeråsen. And here there were people poorer than Hirka.

Mannfalla accommodated everything and everyone. Poor and rich. Overt and covert. Merchants and thieves, side by side. Nobody stuck out, because everyone did. She'd had nightmares about an entire city running after her. After the child of Odin. But in Mannfalla she was insignificant. Hirka smiled. In Mannfalla she could do anything.

Except Kolkagga are after me and I have nowhere to stay.

Ramoja caught her off guard by asking about that very thing: where she was staying. Ramoja herself was going to stay at a ravenry on the eastern bank of the river with some other raveners. They'd all come for the Rite, so there wouldn't be room for Hirka.

"I have to meet someone. I can't say who or where," Hirka had replied, with a clean conscience. Strictly speaking, it wasn't a lie. It looked like she was going to be meeting a lot of people. And she had no idea where. She had assured Ramoja that she had all she needed, including money and a meeting place.

The cart rolled out into an open square. At the opposite end towered Eisvaldr in all its glory. Ravens flew in and out through open archways in the wall, which was clad with polished white stone.

Hirka's jaw dropped. What manner of fear had prompted such an undertaking? Shutting off an entire mountain pass at the entrance to Blindból. The mountains it was said the blind came from.

But no living soul had seen the wall closed. It was a gateway. A window to another world. Through the archways Hirka could see that the streets on the other side were paved with the same white stone. Spires and domes glittered. And even though guardsmen stood watch at every single archway, carts continued to roll in and out of Eisvaldr.

Vetle held his stone figure up to the sky to make it look like it was walking atop the wall. The new Jomar became a giant who could crush the entire city.

"Do you see that red dome?" Ramoja pointed, and Hirka followed her gaze.

"Barely," Hirka teased. The dome crowned the largest and most central building on the other side of the wall.

Ramoja winked at her. "It's the center of the world."

"You mean ...?"

"Mother's bosom. The Council Chamber. The home of the Seer is right behind it."

Hirka felt her confidence drain away. It was like getting hit by the bucket of water Maja had poured over the men at The Raven's Brood to stop them from killing each other. This was Mannfalla. She was here. Now. And she was looking at Eisvaldr, up at the home of the Seer. The most sacred of all halls. The home of the Rite. She had to do something.

"Stop!"

"Here?" Ramoja stopped the horses. Hirka looked around frantically, then remembered an inn they'd passed on the corner. It looked expensive, but that didn't matter. She wasn't planning on staying there, and anyway, Ramoja thought she was meeting someone.

"Over there."

Ramoja looked at the inn. Hirka slung her bag over her shoulder and jumped down from the cart. Vetle wanted to jump off with her, but Ramoja held him back with promises that he would soon see Hirka again. Hirka smiled, but her heart sank. She doubted that she was ever going to see either of them again.

Kuro had kept his distance the entire trip, but now he circled high above them. At least that was something.

"Thanks for the company, Ramoja."

Ramoja wrinkled her brow. "Are you sure it's here? Do you have everything you need?"

"Positive."

"And you know what you're doing?"

"Always."

Hirka was surprised at the confidence in her own voice. It was a stark contrast to how she actually felt. But Mannfalla appeared to be full of contrasts, so what harm could a couple more do?

Hirka reached up to Vetle and gave him a hug. His fair curls tickled her and he took his time letting go. Ramoja snapped the reins and the cart continued east across the square.

Hirka stood outside The White Square Inn and felt her heart sink. Alone again. Not like in the forest near Ravnhov, where Kuro had been all she'd had. This time there were more people around her than she'd ever seen. But all the same, she was alone.

Hirka straightened up a little. This wasn't so bad, she reminded herself. She had feared Mannfalla every single day since long before Father died. Sometimes it had been so bad that she'd woken up in the middle of the night, sweaty and afraid after dreams about Kolkagga. Merciless black-clad warriors who threw themselves at her the moment she ventured inside the walls. She'd been afraid she would be stopped, arrested, executed. But it hadn't happened yet.

Yes, she was afraid, alone, and in possession of no more than what she carried on her back. And her only company was an aloof raven who had his own business to attend to. But Mannfalla was the best hiding place she could have hoped for. She could lose herself in the city where she had thought she would be like a fish out of water.

She just couldn't stay *here*.

Hirka turned her back on Eisvaldr's majesty and walked down the street, past the merchants' houses, and down toward the river, where the houses were smaller and more ramshackle. Where the streets had a stronger smell and the people shouted louder. Here she could disappear.

THE SLEEPING DRAGON

"A silver piece for two scrawny chickens?! Do I look like I was born yesterday?"

Hirka put her hands on her hips and glowered at the downy-lipped woman manning the stall. The woman raised an eyebrow and reappraised her. Hirka started to turn away.

"Wait."

Hirka smiled and turned back toward the stall. The mustachioed woman slapped a third chicken down on the counter next to the other two. She looked both ways, as if to reassure herself no one had noticed, as she tied them together. Hirka nodded, pleased, and left the silver piece on the counter. She grabbed the chickens and went over to Lindri, who was waiting by the next stall.

He ruffled her hair with a wrinkled hand. "You learn fast, Red."

"Always."

Lindri took the chickens and slung them over his sloped shoulder, even though he was almost as skinny as Hirka. Just a bit taller. "There's no limit to what they'll try during the Rite. Prices double overnight! Do they think people get stupider just because there are more of them?"

"People *do* get stupider when there are more of them," Hirka replied.

Lindri laughed. His lower teeth stuck out, crooked like the ruins on Vargtind. "You're all right, Red. You're all right."

Hirka grinned. Lindri had liked her straightaway, from the moment she'd come into his teahouse only three days previously, looking for somewhere to stay in the overcrowded city. He'd dismissed her before she'd even opened her mouth. If it was work or lodging she was after, she was out of luck.

Her first night in Mannfalla had been fast approaching. Her feet had ached from walking up and down the streets looking for somewhere to sleep. But it was futile during the Rite. Hungry and exhausted, she had heard the sound of a wind chime coming from an alley by the river. A melodious invitation from among the houses. She had followed the sound and found herself at Lindri's. He ran a teahouse that would have brought tears to Father's eyes. Wooden drawers lined the walls. Every herb had its place. Even the counter was made of drawers. The tables were low and people sat on stools covered by gray sheepskins and drank from cups without handles, like the ones Ramoja had. The urge to stay had been overwhelming.

Lindri was almost seventy winters, and she had noticed that he often massaged his wrists and elbows. It slowed him down, and it was clearly an effort to climb up to the top drawer to fetch what customers wanted. So Hirka had started serving people while negotiating a bed.

"My dear girl, I haven't so much as a stool to sleep on!"

"I don't need a stool. I need a bed. And it looks like you could do with one too."

"What do you mean by that?"

Hirka had wiped the counter with a cloth that only made it dirtier. "Sore joints?"

"What of it?"

"I have a salve made from ylir root. For the pain. And I've been loosening stiff joints since I learned to walk."

"*You're* a healer?! You're just a child! Have you even been through the Rite?"

"Yes. Well, in a few days."

Lindri had given her a skeptical look as he rubbed his wrist. That was when she had dealt the final blow: "Where I come from, it doesn't matter how old you are, only what you can do. I'd like to help you, but you'll have to lie down. And since you don't have anywhere to do that ..."

For a moment she'd feared Lindri would throw her out. He'd jutted out his chin as if he couldn't believe her audacity. But then he'd started to laugh. A wheezy screech of a laugh.

"I like you, Red."

That evening, Lindri had applied her salve to his joints and slept better than he had in five years, apparently. And Hirka had been allowed to use his granddaughter's room. The granddaughter was older than Hirka, but according to Lindri, she was as lazy as she was sullen. Lindri said he was glad she didn't visit often because everything she touched turned into more work. But he made as much use of Hirka as he could. She'd been going to bed exhausted in the evenings and had started dreaming of her own teahouse. She would offer rooms and people would come to stay for days at a time. They would eat well, sleep well, and get well if they needed to.

But then she'd remembered who she was. She was a child of Odin and she was in Mannfalla. A couple days before the Rite. What was the point of dreaming when she didn't even know whether she would live to see the next moon?

"Are you coming?"

Lindri snapped her out of her torpor. She'd stopped without even noticing. She looked up at the red dome. It was close. Tall windows ran all the way around, just beneath where it started to curve. All of them had stained glass with motifs she couldn't make out from where she was standing. The Council met behind those windows. And if what she'd heard was true, the Seer resided in a floating tower somewhere behind the red dome. Out toward Blindból. Perhaps He could see her right now. They said He saw everything. The hairs on her arms stood on end.

"I'm not used to this many people," she said by way of an apology. "It's almost impossible to get anywhere."

"You're telling me, Red. Keep hold of your coin purse. Come on, we'll try a different way."

Lindri put a hand on her shoulder and steered her into a side street. He was still a bit bowlegged, but his pain had abated somewhat. They entered a quieter street running parallel to the main street in Eisvaldr, but closer to the eastern ridge. From here, they could see the Council families' magnificent homes. Structures fit for gods that could have housed a hundred men with room to spare.

Hirka spotted something and stopped. A mountain of a house built of gray stone towered above them. White flowers whose name Hirka didn't know climbed up the walls and around leaded windows that were taller than a grown man. The hillside was covered in fruit trees. A row of torches blazed along the roadside even though it was still light. White flower petals fell as she watched, settling on the ground like snow. She could hear some kind of music—random notes from small bells caught in the wind.

Every stone in the walls was a different size, making them look like scales on a lizard's skin. And the roof looked like it had been there for eons. Dark tiles in various sizes reinforced the impression of something living. Hirka couldn't take her eyes off it. Any minute now the roof would lift up slightly and the stones would pull apart from each other, as if it were an immense dragon drawing breath.

Hirka realized she was holding her own breath.

"They call it the sleeping dragon. It's where the An-Elderins live," Lindri said. He needn't have bothered. Hirka already knew. Lindri leaned closer to Hirka so no one would overhear him. "If it hadn't been called that since the dawn of time, it would be tempting to think it had something to do with Ilume-madra."

Hirka twitched on hearing her name.

"She's one of the twelve. The head of the family. Surely you learned about the families at school, Red?"

Hirka nodded absently. She stood there listening to the silver bells chime. The wind whipped at her hair, blowing it into her face. Red curls against white flower petals.

"Yes. We learned about them at school."

Hirka had learned most things from Father. She'd never gone to normal school. And now she had to learn everything herself. Get by on her own. Would Rime be there during the Rite, when she'd need help the most? Was he here now? Was he behind one of the windows up there?

Guardsmen patrolled the road up to the impregnable building. No one was allowed too close. What lay within was valuable. Pure. Sacred. It was the An-Elderin family home.

Why would he help? Why would *anyone* who lived like this so much as spare a thought for someone like her? A lump formed in Hirka's throat. People in Elveroa were generally on equal footing. Some had more than others, but it was a small place. Children played together, though Ilume had done her utmost to keep Rime away from them all.

This was something else entirely. What she was looking at here wasn't a house. It was a castle. From a legend. A story. Nobody growing up here would play with children outside the wall. Maybe with merchants' children, but what about the scrawny kids roughhousing down by the river? The urchins living on rooftops? She doubted they ever crossed paths.

It suddenly dawned on her why people romanticized Mannfalla. Maybe it didn't have anything to do with greed after all, and it was just a question of being on the inside. Somewhere children could be safe and didn't have to steal and live on sagging roofs by the river.

Eisvaldr had never held any appeal for Hirka. The Council's schools were of no interest to her. She didn't even have the Might, so she didn't have the slightest hope of being chosen or offered a place in this city. She'd had all she needed where she was. Until Rime had left to come back here.

She remembered that day at the Alldjup. Rime, back after three years. A warrior. A guardsman. Bearing arms, jaw set. A grown man. So utterly beautiful that it was infuriating. She'd been angry that he had come, angry that he had outgrown her, angry at the Rite and everything he represented. The distance between them had been greater than the span of the Alldjup. And now it was even greater still.

Hirka stared at the house, which sat, unapproachable, high above her. She wanted to curl up into a ball. Her chest felt like it might explode.

"Come on," Lindri said. "The chicken soup won't make itself."

THE HEALER GIRL

Slabba was a complete idiot. He didn't see the usefulness of anything at all, not least information. Urd sat down in the carriage and shut the door so hard the hinges rattled. "Ora Square!" he shouted to the coachman above. For a moment he didn't recognize his own voice. It sounded hollow and dry.

The carriage started to move straightaway. Urd opened his leather pouch and pulled out a bottle. A plain, nondescript item containing an elixir from the Council's so-called best doctors. A remedy for sore throats. Urd sniggered. If only they'd known what they were dealing with. They were helpless in the face of what ailed him.

To be fair, the bravest among the doctors had asked to examine him, but Urd had stopped his hand before it got anywhere near his covered neck.

Urd drained the bottle. Sweet mint mixed with the persistent taste of rotting flesh. It was better than nothing, and it did provide a brief respite from the pain. He leaned back and closed his eyes. The carriage crawled onward. The sound of the city's people, horses, and merchants filtered in.

Slabba.

The fat merchant hadn't realized the value of what he had said. It had tumbled out of him as an anecdote. His brother's wife had suffered from serious headaches for years. They came and went but were often so bad that she was bedridden. She had tried everything.

Slabba had rattled off a long list of ridiculous remedies, from standing on your head to eating nothing other than vegetables. As though Urd had any interest whatsoever in this woman's more or less imagined history of maladies.

But the other day she had been to see a young girl with a flair for healing, and she was convinced that she was cured. The girl had just arrived in Mannfalla, but according to Slabba she was already being spoken of in the best circles.

You wouldn't recognize a good circle if it hit you in the face, Urd had thought. That was when Slabba, in all his ignorance, had really shocked him. "They call her the tailless girl. Wolfgirl. I've heard Ravengirl too."

"People will believe any—" Urd interrupted himself. "Tailless?"

"Tailless! They say a wolf bit off her tail when she was a child."

"Is she a dancer? From Urmunai?"

"No, no! She comes from the northeast and doesn't have so much as a stump. And her hair is red as blood, they say."

"Is she old?" Urd had yawned, to give the impression that the answer was of no significance.

"Rite-ready, they say. That's why she's here."

Slabba had continued to bore him with a list of afflictions he was considering consulting the girl about. A rash. Tired legs. And his digestion wasn't up to scratch. Urd had felt his upper lip curl in disgust. Slabba's digestion was not something he cared to know about.

The carriage juddered over uneven cobblestones. The farther from Eisvaldr you got, the worse the roads became. Urd opened his eyes again. He pulled the curtain aside and looked out at the street. They had a way to go still.

A Rite-ready, tailless girl. Who stood out enough to be a topic of conversation in women's boudoirs around the city. He shivered. A mixture of joy and anger. Joy because he had been given this opportunity to neutralize her before she attracted the attention of the Council. Anger because it could actually be her.

The chances were infinitesimally low. The child who had been used was dead. Had to be dead. Most likely frozen to death on the mountainside in the world of the blind, long before anyone found her. She wasn't here, in any case. The Voice had assured him of that. She couldn't be here.

Urd shifted uneasily in his seat. He hated feeling like there were loose ends to tie up. Elements he couldn't control. Once upon a time he, too, had been young, fresh from the Rite, and not known what he was doing. He was still suffering the consequences, and it was starting to dawn on him that it was going to get worse. Much worse.

The carriage was approaching the square by the river. It was easy to hear. They were a rowdy bunch down here. Sellers shouted louder from the stalls, the dogs barked in the streets, and people let their children run wild. There was a sharp smell of fish, dung, and spices. The carriage crept forward through narrow, crowded streets. Had he taken one of the Council's black carriages, the crowd would have parted like their lives depended on it. But just now, nobody could know who he was.

The carriage came to a stop, and Urd made sure that the gray silk scarf he had tied around his head was secure across his forehead. The ends hung down his back. It made him look like a ponce. A conceited idiot. But it did the job. It hid the mark that nobody was to see today.

He got out and placed two copper pieces in the coachman's outstretched hand. "Where can I buy a cloak?" he asked.

The coachman raised his bushy eyebrows and let his eyes roam over Urd's body. "For you?"

"No, for a dog! Of course for me. Where?"

"There are a lot of stalls here," the coachman replied, apparently without taking any offense. "But I don't think you'll find any that are … suitable. The shops farther up have finer wares. Where are you from?"

Urd didn't reply. It was to his advantage that he had been taken for an out-of-towner. The coachman was about the same size as him. His cloak was made of faded red wool. Nobody would look twice at it. It was perfect. Urd topped off the coin in his hand with a small silver piece. "I'll take yours."

The coachman didn't need to be asked twice. He undid the cloak and gave it to Urd. "Sorry about the smell. It's the horses, they—"

"Doesn't matter."

The carriage crawled off, the coachman shouting inquiringly to passersby. "Eisvaldr? Uptown? Ride to Eisvaldr?"

Urd reluctantly put on the foul-smelling cloak, pulled up the hood, and walked across the square toward Lindri's teahouse.

The girl had wild, bloodred hair. She had tried to tame it by gathering the tangles into small braids that hung to the middle of her back. They were secured with makeshift woollen ties. Her hair was shorter in the front, seemingly haphazardly trimmed.

She was so simply dressed it was almost embarrassing. A green tunic perilously close to coming apart at the seams. The neckline had been mended a number of times with thread of a yellower shade than the tunic itself. The color was just different enough to be annoying. The sleeves were wide, and she had folded them up several times.

Hanging from her belt were two leather purses. Not that it was a proper belt. It was a slim strip of leather which she had wrapped around her waist a couple of times. Dangling around her neck was a scratched animal tooth that had begun to yellow.

She sat bent over Urd's ankle, examining the wound. A cut he had made before coming, as a pretext for seeing her. She was a little skinny and moved like a cat. Limber and steady. She looked up at him. Her eyes were big and green above a small nose. He studied them intensely, searching for the slightest sign that could reveal that she was not like everyone else. That she didn't belong here.

"When did this happen?" she asked.

"Two days ago. It won't heal. What's your name?"

"I've put some salve on it. Just keep it clean and dry, then it will take care of itself."

She had a clear voice, but her dialect was difficult to place. She was from the north, but where, exactly? And she hadn't answered the question about her name. He fought off the impulse to grab her by the neck and force it out of her.

"Where are you from?" he asked.

She smiled. A sudden and broad smile that was surprisingly beautiful. "Foggard."

"Ravnhov?"

"Thereabouts."

"Have you been in Mannfalla long?"

She glanced at him before she replied. "Almost two weeks."

She kept her herbs in a piece of cloth, each in its own small pocket. She rolled it back up and wound a strap around it. Urd glanced at the door. It was closed, but the key was in it. He could lock it. Throw the girl into a corner. Force her to talk.

But he could hear laughter and conversations from downstairs. The teahouse was half-full of people. They'd seen him come in. He couldn't go back out and leave behind the body of a young girl.

"What happened to your tail?"

She smiled again and raised a hand to the tooth around her neck. "A wolf got it. But Father got the wolf."

"That must have hurt!"

"I was just a small child. I don't remember any of it."

"How do you know that was what happened, then?"

"Father doesn't—didn't—lie. And you can still see it. The scar, I mean."

"Ah."

The room was small and bare. The walls were made of untreated oak, as was the entire teahouse, actually. A wide bench that doubled as a bed. The chair with a woven back that he sat on. A pitiful knotted brown rug on the floor. A hollowed-out stone as a washbasin, and a water jug on a stool by the door. A lopsided table. That was it.

A sudden shadow made Urd jump.

"That's just Kuro."

A small raven was perched on the window ledge, staring at him as though he was in the way. With dark, narrow eyes. Small, black feathers lifted from its throat in time with its breathing.

How could a girl from the north afford her own raven? Maybe she had inherited it from her father?

Something wasn't right. Urd could feel it in every fiber of his being. He started to sweat. *The Ravengirl. The tailless girl.*

She pulled up his socks. Her hands were warm.

"It's nothing serious. A clean cut. Would you like me to have a look at your neck?"

Urd stood up so quickly that he got dizzy. He grabbed his neck, but the collar was still in place. The wide gold band covered his entire neck. She hadn't seen anything. Nobody had seen anything. So how could she know?

He stared at her. "What, this? A mere trinket. There's nothing wrong with my neck."

"If you say so."

It was her! It had to be her. Holy Seer in Slokna, he'd found the key! Damayanti had been right, after all. Without realizing it, he'd had help. Had he really thought that he alone had the ability to control the gateways? That he had become strong enough overnight to open them without a key?

Fury swelled in his chest. He'd been lied to. The Voice had told him it had been him and him alone. But here she was. In Ym. Living proof of all that he had done. Of all that he was doing still. *A child of Odin.* What abilities did children of Odin have? None that he'd heard of. Yet somehow she knew …

He put three small silver pieces on the lopsided table and walked toward the door.

"Three is too much," she said.

"Thanks for your help," he replied and left the room.

The teahouse was full now. People were kneeling around all of the low tables, drinking from steaming ceramic bowls, as though none of them had anything better to do. Urd pulled up his hood and hurried outside, along the alley, and out to the street. He needed air. He had to have air. But all he got was the foul stench of fish and sweat. People from all over the world, stinking like animals. Crammed together. He plowed through the crowd until he found a carriage. Two men were about to get in, but he pushed past them.

"Two silver pieces to Eisvaldr!"

The coachman smirked at the two men. "Sorry, lads. Money talks."

Urd climbed inside and shut the door on their protests.

The Rite. She was here for the Rite. But when was it her turn? The Rite was taking place every morning now. Children in and children out again. Hopeful parents who left either disappointed or celebrating. Lives were changed from one hour to the next in Eisvaldr. Had she only said where she came from, he could have known for certain. It could be tomorrow. Or in a week. Either way, he had no time to lose.

The rot was in Ym.

What if she didn't know what she was? What if she took a lover?! Lovers? She would leave behind a trail of rotting corpses, and there wouldn't be a shadow of doubt about what she was. Urd could hear his heart pounding in his chest. He would have to use Hassin. Hassin had served the family for many years and was loyal to Vanfarinn. He could take her in the night, quiet and unnoticed. Nobody would ever know that she had existed.

Urd leaned back and closed his eyes. All he could see was the raven on the window ledge. A stark, black creature that stared at him as though *he* were the animal. And her hair. A tangle of red cascading down her back. She definitely wasn't like other people. It had to be her.

But blood would be spilled soon enough, flowing red just like her hair, and she would be gone. The muscles in his throat relaxed a little. He could breathe normally.

Yes. Hassin could take care of the problem.

Hassin always took care of the problem.

Hirka closed her bag and slung it onto her back. It wasn't heavy. She owned very little and that would always be the case, the way things were going. It didn't really matter. She didn't need much. All she really needed was a place to keep the few things she did own. A place she never had to run from.

She looked around the room, but she hadn't forgotten anything. She squeezed past Kuro on the window ledge, and then climbed out on the roof. It was dusk, and it was going to be even colder tonight. And she had no idea where she was going.

Hirka sat down and looked out across Mannfalla. Kuro walked impatiently around her, scratching the roof tiles. She could hear muffled conversations in the teahouse below her. Now and again, when someone opened the door, the noise got louder. A long-legged dog strolled along the riverside, sniffing everything that might prove edible. There wasn't much, so he continued up the street.

The sky was a dark orange where the sun had set. Stars were twinkling, as were the lamps on the fishing boats on the Ora. Hirka drew up her knees and wrapped her arms around them. They were stiff and reluctant. She was tired. She wanted to climb back through the window and lie down, but she couldn't.

He had lied. The stranger.

He had come with a fresh cut on his ankle and claimed it was from days ago. Why? And he had expensive shoes and the finest socks money could buy, but a tattered cloak that smelled of horses. His eyes hadn't moved from her at all. They had been locked on every single movement she made.

He'd asked where she was from, and what had happened to her tail. A lot of people did that, but there was something about the way he asked. Hirka couldn't put her finger on it, but there was something about him that scared her. Something didn't smell right.

He'd looked normal enough. A little younger than Father. Maybe thirty winters, give or take. Smooth, blond hair. Oiled and short, apart from three thick braids at the back. Trimmed beard that followed his sharp jawline and perfectly surrounded pale lips. Golden eyes that reflected the gold collar around his neck.

But his voice had been rough, and he had alternated between pleasant and sinister. As though he were a stallholder one moment and a damned gatekeeper the next. He had tried to show restraint, but his smile had never reached his eyes. He was unstable. He had swallowed heavily and often. Several times he had grabbed his throat and shaken his head, but he had gone as pale as one of the blind when she had asked if she should look at it.

Hirka sighed. Seer knew she had seen a lot of strange people over the past few days. He was no stranger than some of the others. But she couldn't help but feel unsettled. In two days she was going to stand in front of the Council and the Seer. Until then, she had to find somewhere else to stay. She couldn't stay with Lindri. What if he and his granddaughter ended up like Eirik? Because of her?

Two nights. She could manage that. Mannfalla was a big city. She was bound to find somewhere to sleep. She got up and continued stealthily across the roofs, with Kuro flying close behind.

THE RITE

Hirka sat by the riverbank, rubbing her arms in an attempt to keep warm. It was early in the morning and she hadn't gotten much sleep under the bridge. Mist drifted across the river, the yellow lights from the fishing boats twinkling like stars. Scattered sounds came from the houses behind her. Stalls were being set up. Someone was poking around in a henhouse. A gong sounded six times in a tower up near Eisvaldr. Other towers echoed it. The same sounds she'd heard every day since arriving here. Nothing was different, and everything was different. Today was her Rite day.

Hirka crawled closer to the river and splashed cold water on her face. She drank, but not much. The water of the Ora didn't taste clean. Not like in Ravnhov, where it came straight from the ice. She caught sight of her own reflection and thought back on when she had done the same in Elveroa. It felt like a lifetime ago. She'd expected to see something other than herself. Something monstrous and frightening. But she hadn't. Not then, and not now.

Her mind wandered to Sylja and how she would look today. The girl who hadn't talked about anything except the Rite for as long as Hirka had known her. She would be wearing a dress with a billowing skirt embroidered with gold thread. Gold tail rings and braided hair scented with lavender. Hirka stared at her own red tresses. She tried to smooth them into place with wet fingers, but they resisted.

Hirka walked up the Catgut into the city. It was still quiet. No one was up unless they had to be. She bought a chunk of bread and two cubes of soft cheese from a boy who was younger than her. He was wheeling his wares up the street to sell to the stallholders, who would sell them on. He had dirty fingers, but a broad smile. His pockets clinked with coins. She'd left most of what she'd earned for Lindri, but she still had enough that she wouldn't go hungry for a couple days. She sat on a bench outside a saddler's and ate. Unsurprisingly, Kuro came fluttering out of nowhere and settled down right next to her.

It was strange having to think about money. She'd thought about little other than the Rite in the last few months. About this day. It had been like she couldn't imagine a time afterward. But soon all this would be behind her. The Seer would realize she hadn't done anything wrong. Maybe then she'd be able to get on with her life.

Or maybe these were her final hours. Maybe this was her lot.

Would she see Rime one last time?

A door opened and Hirka jumped, but it was just the saddler. A small man wearing baggy trousers with his sleeves rolled up to his elbows. He nodded at her and started sweeping the street in front of his stall with practiced movements. Hirka watched him until he went back inside. He'd probably had the stall his entire life. Perhaps his father had owned it before him. A lump formed in her throat, so she got up and continued on.

The gong struck eight.

It was easy to find her way. The Catgut went right up to Eisvaldr. But you could get there from anywhere in the city. All you really had to do was head for where the streets were wider and the houses grander, and sooner or later you'd end up by the wall.

Hirka stopped for a moment where she had left Ramoja and Vetle on that first day. Just looking into Eisvaldr had been scary enough. Later she had visited with Lindri. Seen the sleeping dragon—Rime's house.

Now she was to stand before the Seer beneath the red dome, which glittered in the distance in the early morning sun. She walked past bunches of flowers, many more than there had been just a couple of days ago. People from all over had made offerings and prayed to the Seer here. Hirka didn't have anything. Should she have brought something? Was that what you were supposed to do? No one had said anything about that. And where was she supposed to go? She wished Father were here so she could ask him.

She joined the scattered but steady stream of people heading toward the red dome. This was it. What if she ran into someone from home? Both Sylja and Kolgrim would be here. And lots of the others from the north side she didn't know so well. The last thing she'd done was burn the cabin down and disappear. She'd never thought she'd see any of them again. She tried to make herself as small as possible in the crowd. She was getting quite good at it.

The red dome got bigger as she got closer. People forged relentlessly onward. The street became a wide staircase. The steps were bone white and worn low in the middle where people had been walking for a thousand years. There were guardsmen on both sides of the staircase, all the way up, wearing black with golden chainmail and helmets that covered their faces. She felt like they were all staring at her. What if Rime wasn't here? What if all these guardsmen surrounded her? They had swords in black scabbards, with gold straps around the hilts. Hirka looked for Kuro, but he was nowhere to be seen.

She tried to temper her growing panic. She'd made her choice. She couldn't live in the forest like an animal without even knowing who she was. *What* she was. Was she supposed to spend her life looking for Kolkagga behind every bush, never having a place to call home? How would she live with herself when people had died for her sake? Father. Eirik.

No, Eirik would survive. He had to.

A gong sounded, deep and resonant beneath her feet. Every step took her closer to a pulsating center, somewhere inside the round building with the red dome. Mother's bosom. Everyone streamed through a doorway and into a tunnel. Hirka felt like she was being swallowed alive.

They were funneled through the dark and into the hall. When they emerged, the light was almost blinding, and Hirka had to shield her eyes until they adjusted. People were welcomed by men and women in gray tunics carrying heavy books in which they recorded the arrivals. Ahead of her, people stated their names and where they were from. Some were directed to the left of the round room, others to the right. Panicking, she looked for a way out, but by then she was already standing in front of one of the men in gray.

She tried to tell him her name, but it got stuck in her throat and she had to repeat herself. She told him she was from Elveroa. He waved her to the right with a pale hand and she followed the others, relieved to be one of many. One in the crowd.

Where was Rime?

Low benches were arranged like tree rings, facing the center of the room. She sat at the back, where there were more empty seats, while others pushed as far forward as possible. Monotonous chanting mixed with the strikes from the gong, the sound seeming to come from everywhere at once. She could smell some kind of smoke. Everything was new. Surreal.

She'd expected to see a vaulted ceiling, but it seemed there was another floor between them and the dome. The ceiling was still high, though. It was decorated with gleaming gold tiles and colorful motifs. She stared up at the details, which seemed to become more numerous the longer she looked. So many of them, and so interwoven that she wouldn't have thought it was possible. She wished she could lose herself among the plants and people. Maybe she could stand on one of the benches in the back row and reach the lamps hanging along the wall. From there, she could pull herself up onto one of the window ledges. But even then, she'd still only be halfway up the smooth, white walls. They were also decorated with motifs, but they were paler and more difficult to make out.

There were three aisles between the benches leading into the center of the room. Several guardsmen lined these on both sides. They stood as if carved from stone.

How am I going to find Rime?

A girl and her mother sat down next to Hirka. The girl was wearing a shimmering orange dress. Hirka smiled, but the girl didn't smile back. She was holding her head high, moving it unusually slowly as she looked around, as if afraid her carefully pinned hair might come loose.

Hirka's body felt leaden. If she was asked to get up now, she wouldn't be able to. She stared down at the floor. It was ancient. There were pictures here as well, made of small fragments of tile. The motif had faded, in some places so much that she couldn't make out what it was supposed to depict. She looked along the rows of benches and saw that the motifs varied in different parts of the room. Mythical beasts, plants, words, and creatures she'd never seen before.

The gong stopped sounding. Conversations turned to whispers as people squashed together on the benches. Hirka stared at a platform on the other side of the room. It was raised above the crowd, by at least the height of a man, accessible from steps on either side. It was empty apart from twelve chairs in a semicircle. There were three doors in the wall at the back of the platform. A large, blood-red double door in the middle, flanked by two smaller doors. That was where they'd come from. That was where they'd sit. The Council. The Ravenbearer. The Seer.

Where is Rime?!

She edged her way along the bench to get closer to the exit. She could still change her mind. If she didn't find Rime, then—

The outer doors banged shut, putting an end to that train of thought. It was too late. She'd have to go through with it, even if her courage had failed her. Hirka's blood ran cold.

The doors at the back of the platform opened and everyone immediately stopped talking. Only the chanting continued. It seemed more intense now, more high-pitched. People bowed as the Council entered. The benches were so low that some people managed to get their heads right down on the floor.

Through the doors, she could see the landscape beyond Eisvaldr. Blindból. The edge of the forest-clad mountains. The Council came toward them across a narrow bridge extending all the way from the doors of the floating tower. It hung in thin air, only tethered to this world by the fragile bridge. An impossibility. The bridge was too long and too narrow to support it. It was more like a string stopping it from floating away. The Seer's tower, held up by His will alone.

Hirka didn't dare swallow. Twelve figures took their places on the chairs, one by one. They seemed almost to glide across the floor in their black robes. The hoods hanging loosely over their heads were lined with gold, which caught the sunlight from the windows. The light framed their faces, making it almost impossible to see what they really looked like. Though Hirka had seen paintings of most of them, they looked completely different in real life. But she recognized one of them straightaway: Ilume.

The red doors closed with a metallic clang.

The Ravenbearer sat in the middle. She looked like all the others, but with the world's most important distinction: she carried a black staff, on which He sat. The Seer. He gleamed bluish black. Larger and more powerful than Kuro. He was sitting too far away for Hirka to see His eyes, but all the same she could feel them deep in her soul. She tried to think about everything that was good and just. Everything she'd done right. Everything she'd done for others.

I haven't done anything wrong. I'm not a monster. Where is Rime?!

One of the people in gray shouted, "Sinnabukt, Mylde, and Hanssheim!"

People stood in a couple places. She could see mothers and fathers hugging their young hopefuls before sending them over to the Council. They walked between the guardsmen, up to the steps, where it looked like they had to repeat their names to another person in gray before climbing up onto the platform and kneeling before the Council.

They were all the same age as her, but they walked with their backs straight and their chins up. Excited. Some smiling. A couple of them seemed nervous and had their heads bowed, but they had nothing to fear. They were all wearing their finest clothes, and they could all bind. The only thing they had to fear was disappointment at having to go home with their families without being accepted by one of the Council's schools, as many of them hoped to be. That was the worst thing that could happen to them today. Hirka would be happy to get out of here with her life. Rime was nowhere to be seen.

Her throat was dry. She felt dizzy. Nothing seemed like it was actually happening. But it was real enough. She could feel the bench she was sitting on. The tiny fragments of tile in the floor. She could see the flames in the oil lamps dancing erratically.

No one from Sinnabukt, Mylde, or Hanssheim was selected by the schools. Everyone went down the steps on the opposite side of the platform. Another person in gray waited for them there. He dipped his thumb into a dish and pressed it to each of their foreheads. They went on their way with a black mark that would fade after a few days. They had been blessed. Protected. Accepted.

Another group was called up and the Rite played out again. Everyone went up to kneel before the Council. The Ravenbearer walked from one person to the next and laid a hand on their heads to give them the Seer's protection from the blind. Hirka didn't know how.

Perhaps He sent the Might through the staff, into the Ravenbearer and on to each of them.

She prayed and prayed that Rime would come. She looked around for him, along every single bench. She was filled with hope every time she saw fair hair, but it was never as white as Rime's. He wasn't there.

"Elveroa, Gardly, and Vargbo!" one of the people in gray shouted, and Hirka felt her feet tremble. She was surprised that they actually supported her when she stood. Her heart was pounding like she'd just run all the way here. She squeezed past the people on the benches and out into the aisle. Was that Kolgrim at the front? And there was Sylja, among a group of unfamiliar faces. She was wearing a deep blue dress and cloak, and a belt around her waist linked together by golden discs. Her tail was covered in jewelry and rings. Blue stones sparkled. Her hair was smooth and oiled, apart from two thin braids on either side of her face, like the ones Ilume wore.

Sylja's eyes swept past Hirka, but quickly returned, as if they'd been deceiving her. Her eyes widened like she'd seen a ghost. Hirka winked at her, not sure where the impulse had come from. Sylja quickly turned around again. The girl had been going over this day in her mind since she was old enough to walk, so Hirka doubted she would let herself be distracted. Even if a friend suddenly appeared out of nowhere after her house had burned down.

They lined up in pairs and approached the Council. The Seer. Hirka's feet walked as if of their own accord, and she had to remind herself why she was here. That no matter what happened today, a life on the run from Kolkagga would be worse. If all went well, she would finally find peace. Belong. Everything would be okay. Everything had to be okay. It would soon be over.

A guardsman grabbed her hand. She jumped and tried to snatch it away from him, but it was no use. They'd seen her. Found her. She was going to die!

But then a tingling warmth washed through her. It was the Might, coursing through her, feeling its way to her fear and doubt, digging deep to find out all her secrets.

Rime!

She met his gaze behind his golden helmet. Pale gray wolf eyes. Rime's eyes. He was there and holding onto her. A weight lifted from her shoulders. Hirka tried to drink in as much of the Might as she could, but she was pushed forward by the people behind her. She clung to Rime's hand, but in the end she had to let go.

The Might lingered within her. A warm certainty that drove her toward the steps. The room felt suddenly alive, like a pulsating cage. She wanted to tear down the walls and let it loose. It was strong. It was wild. It made her thirst. She was saved! All she had to do was make sure she was among the first to face the Council.

No sooner had that thought occurred to her than pain shot through her foot. Someone had stepped on her. Hirka saw Sylja climb the steps ahead of her and glimpsed a pair of high heels, like the ones women wore at weddings.

It was an accident. Keep moving.

The warmth and thirst was still there, but Hirka's heart sank when she saw how many of the others were already in place before the Council. She had to go all the way to the end before she could kneel like everyone else.

The Ravenbearer stood up. The black staff was taller than she was, the Seer looking down on all of them. Nevertheless, she bore Him with ease. Everyone bowed, their foreheads against the floor. Hirka did the same. The floor was cold against her skin. The Might trickled slowly and relentlessly out of her body. They sat up again. The Ravenbearer walked from one person to the next. Slowly. Painfully slowly.

For the Seer's sake!

Hirka didn't dare close her eyes. She also didn't dare look at the

Council, who were sitting only a few steps away. All she could see was the black robe out of the corner of her eye, coming closer and closer. Hirka's blood ran cold, chilling her to the core.

She had nothing. The warmth was gone. The Might was gone. All she had was emptiness. She was nothing. She felt her eyes grow moist. What was she doing? Why was she even there?

The Ravenbearer laid a hand on the head of the person next to her, whispered, "Ungi verja," which meant "Protect the children" in old ymish, and made the sign of the Seer. Then she stopped in front of Hirka.

Hirka didn't look at her. She didn't dare look at the Seer either. She just stared into the Ravenbearer's robe. It was black as night.

"Bind the Might," the Ravenbearer whispered, as if Hirka had just forgotten what she was supposed to do.

Hirka closed her eyes and felt a tear fall. She knew what she was being asked for, but she couldn't.

"Bind the Might, child," the Ravenbearer whispered again.

Hirka shook her head. "I can't."

The words were leaden. As soon as she got them out, she felt lighter. She'd said it. She couldn't bind, and she'd said so. Simple as that. Time stood still. Someone coughed, but no one said anything.

At long last the Ravenbearer laid a hand on her head, and a cold washed through her, a tingling from the Might. A pale imitation of the Might in Rime. This wasn't as demanding. It looked inside her, but Hirka was able to hide from it. With Rime she was laid bare.

The Might was suddenly cut off as if with a knife. The hand on her head was torn away. The Ravenbearer took two steps back. Hirka heard a half-smothered gasp, almost childlike. The other young people leaned forward to see what was happening.

"You're—you're hollow." The voice came from the Ravenbearer, but her unwavering patience was gone. This was a scared old woman.

One of the Council stood. "Hollow?" one of the others said. Hirka thought it might have been Ilume.

"Empty! Unearthed!" the Ravenbearer gasped. One of the other girls on the platform started to cry. Hirka opened her eyes and looked up at the Ravenbearer, at her flat nose and deep-set eyes, which were staring at her fearfully as if she were one of the blind. The Ravenbearer put her hand over her mouth. Her little finger trembled. The Seer shifted restlessly atop the staff.

Hirka felt like she needed to explain. She reached up toward the Seer. He had to understand. Or what about Ilume? Ilume could explain. But she looked just as disbelieving as the others. Like Father when he'd realized he would never walk again.

More councillors had stood up. She recognized another one of them now. The stranger! The man who had lied to her at the teahouse, now bearing the mark of the Council on his forehead.

"Seer preserve us! A child of Odin. A daughter of Embla." The Ravenbearer clutched at the staff. "The rot! The rot in Ym!"

"Eir!" Ilume's voice. Sharp, admonishing.

Someone gripped the staff to help Eir, leading her away from Hirka. The words *child of Odin* ripped through the rows of young hopefuls like fire through dry grass. The boy sitting closest to her got up and backed away. The others weren't slow to do the same.

"Just let me explain …" Hirka started, but she couldn't hear her own voice. Utter chaos had descended. People rose to their feet, some shouting, others hurrying out of the hall. She could hear the echoes of words. Words just as strange to her as they were to everyone else in the room. *Daughter of Embla. Unearthed. Menskr. Rot.*

Hirka got up. She couldn't feel her feet. It was as if she were floating above the crowd. They stared at her. Pointed. Shouted. So many eyes. Explaining to this many people was impossible. If she could explain to just one of them …

She could hear the councillors talking loudly behind her. One of them was trying to stifle her sobs. She thought it was the Ravenbearer. Eir. The world's holiest and most powerful woman was crying. Because she'd touched Hirka. Touched the rot. Plumbed the depths of her body with the Might.

Guardsmen surrounded the platform. Hirka laughed in disbelief. This was ludicrous. Didn't they understand that she hadn't done anything wrong? This was just one big misunderstanding. She'd never hurt anyone. She *saved* lives. That was what she did. As often as she could. Hirka took a deep breath. The air tasted like hundreds of different perfumes and oils.

This is a dream.

From where she now stood, Hirka could see the entire floor. As people fled the scene, she realized that the individual motifs came together in the shape of one enormous star. The points extended all the way out to the walls. The work must have taken a lifetime. It lay there, eternal and still, as the world crumbled around it.

The others had fled the platform. A group of guardsmen came up the steps on both sides. They seemed to be running. It was difficult to tell. It was all happening so interminably slow. Their breastplates gleamed. They had drawn their swords. Their eyes moved between her and the Council. All they needed was the order to kill.

Hirka's feet failed her. She felt herself falling. Falling from the rooftop in Ravnhov, unable to look away from the dark figure with the knife. Falling at the Alldjup, the weight of Vetle on her back.

Someone grabbed her and pulled her back. They didn't need to pull. She was happy to comply. But first she had to see Rime. Hirka tore herself loose and ran back toward the edge of the platform. People screamed and backed away, as if expecting her to bind them straight to Slokna.

Rime!

He stood looking at her with his helmet in his hand. His white hair spilled over his shoulders. Wolf eyes stared up at her, wide with shock. Perhaps he was thinking about all the times he'd touched her. Touched the rot. Sylja spotted him and grabbed his arm, as if to save herself from the horrifying creature on the platform. *The abomination. A child of Odin.*

He didn't react. He just stood there with his helmet in his hand, as if on a battlefield. She met his gaze.

One point to you if you pull me up.

A heavy blow landed on her back. Pain radiated out into her fingers and she fell to her knees. Someone grabbed her and pulled her back again before she could fall farther. Away from the people. Away from Rime. It was pandemonium—and she could do nothing to stop it. She was caught in an iron grip. Guardsmen with cold steel gauntlets. She saw red doors close in front of her and chaos turned to silence.

THE VOICE

Urd ran into the nearest bathhouse, catching two young men in the act. The two servants ran off, still in a state of undress, shirt tails flapping behind them.

How much time did he have? None. No time at all. Just the few moments the Council would spend running around like headless chickens out there. He could hear the clinking of chainmail in the corridors. Half the guardsmen in Eisvaldr were on their way to the Rite Hall, as if they would make any difference in all the chaos. Ilume had ordered people out and closed the hall, while Garm had declared that nobody was to leave the room. The guardsmen hadn't known what to do. Sigra was probably already on her way down to the vaults to execute the girl, as any good Kleiv was wont to do. As for Eir, she had completely lost the power of speech. She'd just sat there, as though staring into Slokna, while the world fell apart around her.

He had been so close. He had touched the girl at the teahouse. Could have put his hands around her neck there and then, on suspicion alone. Now it had been confirmed. She was exactly what he'd been afraid of.

Urd kneeled down on the blue tiles in front of the pool and tore off the collar. His hands were shaking, but he managed to pull out Damayanti's bottle from the inside of his robe. He swallowed the splash of raven blood that was left. It wasn't much, but it would have to do. It felt as though every drop of blood in his body was surging toward his throat. First an intense, hot stinging. Then pain. He stifled a scream with his hand. Blood seeped between his fingers and dripped into the water.

His throat began to move. He could feel the raven's beak opening and closing. The wound was torn open again. The wound that would never heal. The wound that was starting to rot. To think that he had once thought he could still be saved. He laughed. A choked, gurgling sound that nearly made him vomit. His nostrils were assaulted by a smell he knew only too well. Nauseating, metallic. Then came the Voice. Half inside and half outside of him. As though it were his own.

THIS BETTER BE IMPORTANT, VANFARINN.

The Voice was hollow and metallic. He always spoke slowly. Agonizingly slowly. Every word tore at Urd's throat. The hairs on his arms stood on end. His body's natural defenses, which constantly had to be suppressed.

"I found her! I found the gift! The stone offering! She's *here*. Not just here in Ym, she's *here*. In the Rite Hall!" A moment's silence. Then the conclusion.

YOU ARE MISTAKEN.

In the midst of all his pain and fear, Urd felt a spark of satisfaction. The Voice was not infallible. He wasn't so all-knowing that he couldn't be shocked, like they all had been. Urd clung to that fragile sense of security.

"I swear. She's Rite-ready, tailless, and unearthed. Not only have I seen her, I've touched her hand. She's real and she's here!" Urd gasped for air. If anyone came in and found him like this, on his knees, his throat torn open, up to his elbows in blood … but he had no choice. He had to know what to do. Now. Before the Council reconvened.

The Voice didn't respond straightaway. The pause ought to have been immensely satisfying, but the wait was unbearable. The water gurgled through the channels leading to and from the pool. The light played on both walls. Malevolently flirtatious, daring him to come closer. To look. Urd leaned over the edge and stared at his own reflection. He gave a start. It had gotten worse. Again. The skin on his throat was sallow, bruised yellow and green, like he'd been throttled. Blood dripped from a gaping hole in his throat where the raven beak was pressing through. You could see it inside, if you looked close enough. He never did, despite the fact that he'd lived with it for half his life.

ISOLATE HER! BEFORE ANYONE REALIZES.

Urd squeezed his eyes shut. This was what he had feared. But there was no point in holding back.

"They know. Everyone knows. The Ravenbearer laid hands on her. She knows what she is. Everyone knows what she is! The Rite Hall is full of people, and the girl has been thrown in the pits. I tried to kill her. I sent Hassin, but she had already—"

KILL?!

Urd jumped. He coughed and spat up more blood.

WE HAVE SUCCEEDED BECAUSE SHE LIVES! THE RAVEN RINGS LIVE AND DIE WITH HER! YOU HAVE ONE TASK, VANFARINN. PROTECT HER LIFE WITH YOUR OWN UNTIL YOU HEAR FROM ME.

Urd put his hands on his head and curled up on the floor. It was an impossible task. The Council would act rashly. They were going to kill her, if for no other reason than out of fear of the blind.

The Voice withdrew, and the relief was instant. The wound in Urd's throat closed. The muscles relaxed. Urd hung over the edge of the pool, waiting until he had the strength to stand. The pain was worse each time. All was lost, he couldn't pretend otherwise. Had he been like everyone else, the signs would have been wasted. But he was better than them. More alert. Always thinking several steps ahead.

The girl was here. She should never have been here, at least not alive. But the Voice knew. Damayanti knew.

The raven rings live and die with her.

Urd had been lied to. Betrayed. But for how long? Since he had taken the chair? Or always? The certainty was suddenly all-consuming. Stark. Painful. He battled his instincts. All he wanted to do was lie down on his side and block out all sound. Find his strength again. His calm. Think back and see everything in this new light.

But he had work to do. He had to find the rest of the Council. They were probably assembled in the dome already. Urd used the Might to get to his feet. He washed his hands and his neck. He closed the collar and checked that his clothes were clean. The blood slowly dissipated in the water. It flowed through the channels and out the sluices, draining into the gutters of Eisvaldr.

SPY

An embling? A child of Odin?

Seer preserve us all! Why didn't you say anything?

But Rime knew Hirka never would have told anyone, especially not him, a son of the Council. One of *them*. Why would she trust him? Nevertheless, she had asked him for help. She must have been terrified. And not without cause. Rime had feared she was dead—broken by a fall in Ravnhov. A fate that might soon prove to have been preferable. Rime had no time to spare. He had to act *now*.

The Rite Hall was awash with a chaos never before seen within its walls. Black-and-gold-clad guardsmen tried to maintain order while people shouted and shook their fists like they were at the market. The guardsmen at the western entrance had been told to keep the doors closed, but the eastern entrance was wide open to the stream of panicking people who wanted to get away. Away and out into the city to spread the terrible news. Menskr in Ym. Perhaps the blind as well.

Children of Odin and the blind weren't the same thing at all, but Rime had learned never to underestimate people's depressing ability to lump things together in stressful situations. You only had to look around. A merchant with his son in tow tore a woman away from the crowded exit, trying to get past. The woman didn't put up a fight. She dropped her thin shawl and was knocked off her feet. She lay there with a hand on her chest, doubtless clutching a Seer amulet.

Rime threw his helmet aside, ran over, and tackled the merchant to the ground. He pressed his knee into the man's back and held him down.

"Open the doors! Open all the doors! Now!" Rime drew on the Might and heard his own voice carry across the room. He didn't have the authority to give such an order, but the guardsmen obeyed anyway. He might have been new to the guard, but he was still Ilume's grandson. For once Rime was glad of the advantages that afforded him.

The merchant stopped squirming when he heard the order. No one was going to be shut in. They were free to leave the hall, and most of them did so, more than willingly. But some refused to go. They had closed in on the guardsmen in front of the steps. They wanted answers. They wanted to know what would happen. Who was the child of Odin? What was she doing here? Would the Seer protect them? Rime couldn't blame them. He needed answers too.

He ran up the steps and through the red doors. He put the shouting mob in the Rite Hall behind him and hurried onward. He needed to get up into the dome. And he needed to get there before the Council convened.

The corridor was open on one side with archways facing onto one of the many gardens that were half-outside and half-inside. Rime spotted Noldhe, Leivlugn, and Jarladin in a frantic group, surrounded by guardsmen receiving contradictory and ill-considered orders. He couldn't see the rest of the Council. His heart sank. Was he too late? Had they managed to convene already? No one was going to take any notice of yet another running guardsman, so Rime darted past them, through the garden, and up the stone steps. As he'd hoped, the guardsmen outside the Council Chamber had long since been summoned to the Rite Hall. The door was unguarded. He opened it and looked in. The room was empty. The coast was clear.

Rime shrugged off his chainmail. He needed to be rid of any steel. His gauntlets, sabatons. Anything that would make noise. He hesitated for a moment with the sword in his hand. He couldn't be without it. He might need it.

Against your own family? Against Ilume? The Council?

No. He'd rather take what was coming to him. This thought brought a familiar calm. He was safe to act as he needed to. He had devoted his life to serving the Seer. He was Kolkagga. He was already dead. Dead men had little to fear.

He was just about to chuck his armor into a storeroom when he realized that the Council would be sitting for a long time. A very long time. Servants would come in with food and wine, and they would use the storeroom, so he would have to find another solution.

The garden.

He threw his armor over the railing. It landed in a heap behind a dense clump of trees. It would be safe there for a while. He couldn't bring himself to leave his sword, so he took it with him. He slipped into the dome room and closed the door behind him.

The room was unfurnished apart from the table in the middle, surrounded by twelve white chairs. Narrow windows ran all the way around. They extended from the floor right up to the vaulted ceiling. Daylight pushed itself through in concentrated shafts. There was only one place to hide. Under the table.

Gold glinted along the edge of the solid stone tabletop. Twelve family names. Rime gave a lopsided smile. In theory, anyone could sit around this table, if they were skilled in binding the Might, worked hard, and distinguished themselves during their schooling and service in Eisvaldr. But it was a false hope. This table and these names had all but never changed.

The tabletop was scarred in two places, from the edge into the middle. You had to look closely to tell, but one section of the table had been replaced a little over three hundred years ago when the

Jakinnin family became part of the Council. Probably the most affluent family in Mannfalla. Simple as that.

Rime found his own name. An-Elderin. He laid a hand on the back of the chair that had been intended for him. The chair he would never sit on.

Someone's coming!

Rime ducked under the table and immediately realized he had a problem. If he had a clear view of the door, they'd have a clear view of him. He would have to get closer to the tabletop itself, hang beneath it. It rested on two pedestals—solid stone crosses almost six feet apart.

He pushed himself up on his arms and hooked his feet over one of the crosses. He stuck his arms through the other so he could rest on his elbows. He hung there with his back to the tabletop and his face to the floor. He had to tense every single muscle in his body. The stone dug into his forearms, which he had to press out to the sides to hold himself up. He pulled his tail up after him.

Rime thought about what he had been through while training under Svarteld in the last few years. He'd run for days on end. Held swords out to both sides until he'd thought his arms would drop off. He'd been positioned much like this, straight as a plank with his stomach muscles tensed and all his body weight on his arms. And just when he'd thought he was going to break in two, Svarteld had told him to continue on just one arm.

He was Kolkagga.

But even so, Rime knew this was going to be impossible. The situation in Eisvaldr was critical. The Council's discussion wouldn't be over by the time the gong next sounded. Perhaps not even by the one after that. They would sit here until the day was done. Perhaps into the night.

He started to lower one of his feet back down to the floor, but quickly pulled it back up again when the door opened. Familiar voices, talking over one another as they took their places around the table. He heard the voices of Jarladin, Leivlugn, and Noldhe. More soon joined them.

Now he had no way out. He had to stay hidden.

The Seer will know I'm here. He'll sense me.

Truth be told, Rime didn't know what powers the Seer had. It was said He was omniscient, but what did that really mean? Could He see through stone? See Rime's body beneath the tabletop? Would Rime be exposed as soon as He entered the room? If that was the case, then so be it. The Seer would also see that Rime wasn't acting out of defiance. Either way, he'd made his choice, and in one way or another it would cost him.

"Where's Eir? Isn't Eir coming?" Noldhe's nervous voice.

"She's with the ravens. She's on her way," a voice replied.

Ilume.

Rime watched the swish of their robes as they took their places around the table, one by one. Someone paced to and fro next to the table instead of sitting.

"Is the hall empty?"

"The doors were supposed to be closed! How could you let people leave?! The whole city will be panicking soon."

"The city's already panicking, Sigra."

"How many guardsmen have been posted in the vaults?"

"No more than before, unless you've given them different orders."

"Has anyone seen Urd?"

The door opened and the last two councillors came in. Urd and Eir sat down. Rime was surrounded. Unseen, but surrounded. He took a deep breath. He'd have given anything to be able to bind. It would have helped hold him up, but those around the table who were most attuned to the Might would perhaps feel it. Like Hirka could. It was too risky.

Where is the Seer?

Rime squeezed his shoulder blades together and prepared his body for a trial he wasn't likely to recover from anytime soon.

Sweat dripped from Rime's forehead down onto the floor. The drips exploded on red-flecked granite and settled like dew. His hair hung in front of his face. Every time he breathed out it tickled his chin. His abdominal muscles burned.

But at least he needn't have worried about anyone hearing him. The Council tore into each other like never before. They were divided. Fragmented. Broken.

Crises separate friend from foe.

Rime hung beneath the table, listening to the world come undone.

"We don't know what she is or who she is. We have no other choice but to detain her." Noldhe's voice trembled.

"Lock her up?! And wait for the blind? Wait for her to destroy us?"

Sigra Kleiv. Impatient. Bloodthirsty.

"Destroy us? How? Sons and daughters of Embla are mightless!"

"She's already caused widespread panic! What more do we need?"

"What we need is to complete the Rite. Think about it. The city is bursting at the seams. You heard the guardsmen. The merchants guild is already railing against us. They want answers, and they have the means to challenge us. They won't stand for the Rite being put off while we're dithering."

"Touching of you to think of the practical aspects of the matter first, Saulhe, but pray tell, have you forgotten we have the rot sitting in one of our pits?"

"*Someone* here has to use their head!"

They all started talking over each other and didn't stop until someone slammed their fists down on the table. It was Jarladin

An-Sarin. Rime remembered him well. A gaze that never faltered. When Rime was little, he had thought of Jarladin as an ox because his nostrils were so big. His strong jaw was now hidden behind a white beard. He was a good friend of Ilume's. His voice was deep and made people listen.

"Show your mettle, dear councillors! We know that postponing the Rite will have consequences. We know the city is overflowing with people telling tall tales about the blind in every corner."

"Tall tales? Surely you don't still think they're tall tales?!"

Jarladin continued unperturbed. "It doesn't matter what we think at this point. We know that the nobility and the merchants won't want to wait for us. But let's acknowledge the severity of the situation. This is critical, but that's why we're here. This is our job! If we can't do it, no one can."

Rime smiled to himself under the table, but not for long. It suddenly occurred to him how different his own fate would have been if everyone around this table had been like Jarladin. If Rime could have had an ounce of faith in them.

Leivlugn Taid spoke up. He was allowed to speak uninterrupted despite his low voice and how long it took him to say anything. His words were drawn out, as if he had to dust them off first.

"The girl makes it clear that the gateways to Ym are open. Odin's kin? The blind? What you're all failing to consider is whether we ought to cancel the Rite entirely under such circumstances. We might turn out to have greater need of binders than ever before."

There was silence for a moment.

Greater need of binders? What does he mean?

Rime shifted his arms uncomfortably, but the edge just dug in even more. His stomach felt like it might tear. He would have to lower his feet soon. Just for a moment, before his muscles started to cramp. He clenched his teeth.

"A good theory, Leivlugn, but when did we last discover anyone with blue blood? I was a child the last time anyone exhibited a strong affinity for the Might, and that was old Vanfarinn. One of us!"

"Oh, come now. We've rejected a lot of people who could have been something."

"*Something* won't help us now, Leivlugn."

Sigra interjected, "What will help us now is destroying the gateways and killing the embling. That's our only option! She's brought the blind back, and there might be hordes of them!"

"Ludicrous!"

Rime's ears pricked up. Urd's hoarse voice had interrupted Sigra—in defense of Hirka. Rime couldn't picture him as anyone's savior. Where was he going with this?

"The girl's just a child! A mightless, unearthed child. If she's done anything, it's as nothing more than a pawn. Think about it! This has Ravnhov written all over it. They want to distract us, cause panic! And they've succeeded. We were right to send forces north, but they're wasting time. Sleeping in camps. Why are we waiting until it's too late to attack?"

"Urd, not even *you* can think Ravnhov is in possession of knowledge like this? Knowledge we ourselves have lost. That our forefathers had lost. And even if it were possible, not even Ravnhov would be stupid enough to open the stone doors. It would be suicide!"

"There's an intact raven ring somewhere in Ravnhov! Where else could they be coming from?"

"In the Seer's name, Urd, nábyrn sightings have been reported from places across all the kingdoms. They're coming from places where none of us even knew there were circles."

"Good heavens, how can we be so uninformed—so oblivious?! Some of us have pretty much lived with this girl without seeing what she was. Ilume, the truth was almost in your lap! Neighbors told you the tailless girl wanted to run from the Rite. What more did you need?"

Rime had been about to rest his feet on the ground, but quickly changed his mind. Urd had just attacked Ilume and risen to his feet. Something was about to happen.

But he's right. None of us knew who she was.

Ilume got up as well.

"That's enough, Urd Vanfarinn. Nothing you're saying is helpful. No one has seen the rot in our era, and no one here had any reason to check her. The very notion is absurd. Everyone around this table thought Odin's kin were a myth until today. Everyone! And the girl wasn't the only one who wanted to avoid the Rite. Foggard is full of Ravnhov sympathizers. Anyway, the girl was presumed dead after the fire."

Ilume wore her mask well, but Rime could see right through it—as could Urd, it seemed.

"Feeling defensive, Ilume? Are you saying you couldn't see what was right under your nose?" Urd started to pace the length of the table. Rime pushed himself as close to the tabletop as he could to avoid being seen. His body burned from shoulder to ankle.

"Are you saying you couldn't spot a traitor? Though I suppose you never could—not even among your own."

"Urd Vanfarinn!" Eir snapped. The councillors around the table started mumbling.

Traitors? Among her own?

Were they talking about him? Did they consider him a traitor because he'd chosen Kolkagga? Ilume would see it that way, he was painfully aware of that. But the rest of the Council? Nothing could have pleased them more. Less power to An-Elderin meant more power to them.

Ilume spoke again, her voice cool—albeit slightly strained. "Forgive him, Eir. He's tired and scared. We all are."

Urd snorted, but to Rime's relief, he sat down again before continuing. "We agree that the rot has to be neutralized. It is crucial that the Council appears decisive on this matter, before panic spreads through the kingdoms. But my dear friends, we haven't even interrogated the girl yet." A murmur of agreement rippled around the table. "Let's take a break. We need to eat before we continue. Then we should at least question the girl before consigning her to the flames. The longer we sit here, the longer she has to polish her lies."

Urd had created the conditions for a temporary adjournment. Rime needed it more than they did—if he was ever going to walk again.

There was agreement around the table that the girl had to die. And it had to happen publicly and send a clear message to Ravnhov. The assassination of Eirik had failed and they still needed to be put in their place. Hirka was doomed.

The Council got up and left the room. Rime heard them wash their hands in the silver basin outside the door. It had always been that way. They washed their hands of their own decisions as if their hands weren't stained with blood every single day.

The door closed and Rime forced his feet to cooperate. He coaxed them down onto the floor, then sat crouched under the table, fending off the cramps. And the nausea. That gnawing feeling that something was horribly wrong.

The Seer hadn't attended the meeting. Rime's mind raced mercilessly, unstoppably. He couldn't believe the Seer didn't care about worldly matters. Were these details that didn't even warrant His presence?

Then came the fear.

Why hadn't the Seer been here? This had to be the biggest threat against Mannfalla in living memory. What if the Council had excluded Him? Decided to have the meeting without Him?

A chill ran down Rime's spine. He needed to get out of here. Quickly. If anyone found him, he would be as doomed as Hirka.

PAIN

I'm still alive.

The cramped pit was quiet, but Hirka could hear an echoing between her ears. Voices and shouts from the Rite Hall. *Unearthed. Daughter of Embla. The rot.* But she was alive. Shaking all over, but nobody had run her through with a sword. Or burned her on the spot. The Seer hadn't damned her. He had just stared at her through narrow, all-knowing eyes. Like He had always known that she would come, even though she didn't belong here.

Rime had tried to help her.

And now he knows what you are.

Hirka pressed herself up against the wall, at the bottom of a pit that sloped down into the root of the mountain. Daylight came in via a narrow opening at the top of the pit. The light formed a perfect square in front of her, right where the ground began to slope upward. It wasn't so steep that she couldn't walk up it, but she wouldn't get any farther than the grating, which covered the entire opening. It looked flimsy, but that was a cruel illusion. The bars were razor-sharp. Hirka had crawled up several times and cut herself as soon as she tried to stick her hand out. She wasn't going anywhere.

What was going to happen to her?

None of it seemed real. The Rite. The shouting in the hall. The trembling Ravenbearer with the Seer on a staff. Hirka saw it over and over again in her mind, but it remained unreal. A painful ache in her stomach. Some people had blamed her for opening the gateways. For the return of the blind. She'd never seen any of the blind, nor had anyone else she knew. But she had seen images of them, in the rock face in Ravnhov.

Crones' talk! Which gateways was she supposed to have opened? Gateways to the blind? Raven rings? Old stories she'd heard as a child. She remembered them. Tales of Odin, who passed through stone and stole a pair of ravens from the king of Ravnhov. Of blind tracks and blind trails. Paths leading to circles of stone where people disappeared and never came back. *More crones' talk!*

But Father had found her by one of them. A stone circle in Sigdskau, up near Ulvheim. She could see Father's face clearly, as though he was right in front of her. Red in the light from the hearth while he talked.

You were no more than a few days old. Someone had wrapped you in a blanket that blended in with the snow. You would have been easy to miss. A pale face barely the size of my fist in an ocean of frost.

Father had been right all along. He had wanted to flee. From Elveroa, from the Council, from Kolkagga. He had feared for her life. He hadn't sacrificed his own life only for her to end up in a pit in Eisvaldr waiting to die.

The grating opened with a screech. She saw the silhouettes of four guardsmen in the opening. One of them told her to get up. Hirka hesitated. Maybe waiting to die wasn't as bad as *not* having to wait any longer.

"I said *get up*," the guardsman shouted.

Hirka stood and walked up to them. As soon as she was within arm's reach, she was forced to the ground. Someone tied her hands behind her back. From her position on the ground, she saw that she was in a vault with at least six pits, three on either side. Sunlight came in through an arched iron door that was covered in spikes, some of them rusty. She could see flowers outside, delicate and swaying between the guardsmen's feet. They disappeared suddenly behind white robes.

Councillors.

Someone blindfolded her. Everything went black.

I'm going to die.

She was pulled back to her feet and felt something sharp dig into her back. She stifled a scream and started to walk forward. One of the guardsmen barked directions at her, but they were difficult to follow when she couldn't see. There were two steps. At one point she felt wind on her face and got the feeling that she was high up. A raven shrieked nearby.

Kuro?

Then they were inside again. Someone kicked the back of her knee so she collapsed. She forgot that her hands were bound, and she tried to catch herself. She lost her balance and her shoulder collided with the stone floor. Someone pulled her up into a sitting position. She raised her head and tried to look under the blindfold, but it was no use. Even though the room wasn't cold, she was shaking all over.

There was a faint smell of burnt oil, but she didn't know whether the lamps were lit or not. A heavy door closed behind her. The room went completely quiet, but she knew she wasn't alone. She could feel people staring at her.

"How did you get here?"

Hirka turned her head toward the woman's severe voice. "I was brought here by the guardsmen. Could I get something to drink?"

"Here to Ym! How did you get here, child of Odin?"

"Uh … I don't know. I think I was born here."

"Liar!" The hostile voice of a man. Another jab in the back. Hirka gasped.

"It's not a lie! I've always been here."

"Who are you working with?"

"Working with? I … I'm alone. I'm not working with anyone. I—"

"Ravnhov? Are you collaborating with Ravnhov?"

"No! What would I—"

It was the first thing Hirka said that felt untrue. She was sitting here in front of councillors, blindfolded, with a sword to her back. She only had one choice, and it was to be honest. She had nothing to lose in telling them everything she knew. It was barely anything, anyway. But if they had seen her by Eirik's bed, promising to help, they wouldn't have thought it was barely anything.

"How do you know about the stone doors?"

"Stone doors?"

"The blind paths! The gates! How do you use them?"

It was as if she didn't speak or understand her own language anymore. Nobody was listening to her. "I don't use them. I don't know how. I had no idea—"

"Then who let you in? How long ago was it?"

"I've been here my whole life!"

Hirka's entire body sagged. She just wanted to curl up into a ball and disappear inside herself. Escape. Maybe she could ask them to get Ilume. Ilume could explain.

"I've been here my whole life. Father found me. He didn't know—"

"Girl, we know you tried to flee from the Rite. Why? Why did you not want the Seer's protection against the blind? Is it because you have no reason to fear them? Because you're one of them?"

"I've never even seen one! I didn't even know the blind were real. I thought—"

"Why did you want to shun the Rite?"

Another jab in the back. Hirka clenched her teeth. She was completely helpless. No answer she provided could satisfy them. A new realization flooded through her like poison in her veins. A certainty that made everything worse.

The Council feared the blind as much as everyone else. All they wanted was a simple explanation, and she was it. The world's most powerful men and women had lost control. A chill ran down her spine as the truth sunk in. The Council was without counsel.

"I don't know anything. I haven't done anything. I'm … nobody."

"Then why did you burn down your own home and disappear? Why did you want to shun the Rite?"

Hirka tried to laugh, but the sound got stuck in her throat. "If you had just found out that you weren't from this world, that you were like me, would *you* have come?"

It was quiet for a moment. Someone whispered from her right, but she couldn't hear what they were saying. Was she surrounded?

"Have you spread the rot?"

Hirka turned her head toward the voice. Images of Rime entered her mind unbidden. Wolf eyes. The warmth from the Might. His husky voice. How he looked strong, even when he was doing nothing more than simply standing there.

"I've never been with anyone," she answered quietly, hearing sorrow in her own voice.

And nor can I ever be.

"You are unearthed, but you had traces of the Might in you. Why?"

Hirka stopped breathing for a moment. If she answered truthfully, Rime would have to face the consequences. She fumbled for another answer.

"I don't know. Maybe from the Seer?"

A loud snort came from somewhere in front of her.

"I can't bind! I swear!"

"I'll give you one more chance. It's the last one you'll get, girl."

Calm, level words. As if he was talking about everyday things. As if her life didn't depend on it. She wished she could see. The voice came closer. He leaned forward.

"Why did you not want to attend the Rite?"

"Because I was scared."

"Of what?"

"Of all of you! I was scared of you. I couldn't bind, and I had just found out that I was ... that I ... Father said it could cost me my life. That Kolkagga would come after me. I was scared!"

"Kolkagga? Where have you heard such tales, embling?"

Hirka straightened up.

"They're not tales! I've seen them! I saw them in Ravnhov!"

The moment she said it, she realized her mistake. Her life lay in the Council's and the Seer's hands, and she had just said that she had been to the place they feared most, and seen something they had worked for centuries to keep in the shadows. She could have bitten off her own tongue.

It was quiet. Scarily quiet. Hirka turned in every direction in the hope of hearing something, but nobody said a word. Then someone started to whisper. Voices rose. Discussions. She could hear fragments of words. Eirik. The gathering in Ravnhov. Then suddenly it went quiet again, as if someone had said "stop."

"It was you."

Hirka started. The voice came from above. Someone stood bent over her. She raised her face, but still there was only darkness. "It was you. On the roof in Ravnhov. You're the reason Eirik's still alive. You're a traitor!"

Eirik's alive!

The voice came right up to her face.

"Did you know that Eirik of Ravnhov has turned his back on the Seer? That he worships false gods? The gods of the blind from before the war? Did you know that he denies people protection against the blind?"

"People do what they want. He's no traitor!"

Another jab in the back. Deeper. The pain radiated through her body. Hirka screamed. Her back was hot and wet with blood.

"You're tailless and unearthed! You burned down your own home and tried to flee from the Seer. You're in league with Ravnhov, and people who lived near you testify to your disrepute. You've been trading in illegal drugs for many years. Did you kill your father?"

Hirka couldn't cope any longer. There was no use explaining. She had to ask them to find Ilume. It was her only hope. "Get Ilume-madra. Please. I'm a perfectly normal girl. I'm no one important. Get Ilume-madra! She'll explain."

It was quiet for a moment. Then a familiar voice came from her left.

"I'm already here."

Hirka screamed. Her despair gave way to a rage she didn't think was possible. *People mean danger. People have always meant danger*, Father whispered from Slokna and she screamed even louder. Someone grabbed her and she kicked out. Thrashed like the fish on the quayside. Tugged at her bindings, but they wouldn't come loose. Bit someone. She didn't know who. Didn't care, either. She was going to scream until they understood. Until everyone understood.

THE FINAL STRAW

Rime ran through Eisvaldr. No one batted an eyelid, not today. Servants stepped aside in the corridors and bowed until he had passed. He had to find Ilume before the Council reconvened. He had to look her in the eyes. Reassure himself that she hadn't completely lost her mind. Not even Ilume could sentence a child to death in the name of the Seer.

He cut through the gardens on the west side. Polished stones reflected colors from various flowers brought from all over the world. Conifers stood in perfectly tended clusters. If an uninvited shoot suddenly reared its head in these gardens, it was immediately torn out by its roots. Eisvaldr didn't tolerate anything unplanned.

That had become frighteningly clear today. Rime had heard things he wasn't supposed to hear, and his heart beat faster the more he thought about it. The twelve had sentenced Hirka to death in the Seer's absence. Where was He? Why hadn't He stopped this madness? They had to know she couldn't have helped the blind into Ym. They had to! The very notion was ridiculous and did nothing more than make the Council look desperate.

And that was what made Rime's blood boil. They *did* know. But they were doing it anyway. To shock Ravnhov. To appease the baying mobs. To maintain the illusion of control. And they were doing it without consulting the Seer they supposedly served.

And then there were Leivlugn's cryptic words.

What you're all failing to consider is whether we ought to cancel the Rite entirely under such circumstances. We might turn out to have greater need of binders than ever before.

Meaningless utterances. Strong binders were rare, but they were all selected during the Rite to be schooled in Eisvaldr—along with binders who weren't nearly so strong, but who had bought their way in.

Urd had actually fought for Hirka's life while Rime was under the table. His sudden benevolence was suspicious at best. Urd didn't fight for anyone other than himself—that much Rime knew. He had something to gain from keeping Hirka alive. But what? The man's megalomania had already worsened the conflict with Ravnhov. Why curb it now? Rime intended to find out.

Urd had a quality that most of the others in the inner circle lacked. He was direct. He didn't embellish things until they were completely devoid of substance. But he was tactical. He had gotten where he was today because he was the best tactician of them all. And he openly accused Ilume of having traitorous children.

Me? Mother? Uncle Dankan?

The gardens were arranged across different levels and Rime had reached a ledge. The steps were a short distance away, but he didn't have time. He bound the Might and jumped. He landed softly and painlessly. He was getting better. A lot better. From here he could see the openings in the rock that led into the pits.

Hirka.

Guardsmen flanked one of the many towers. So he was right. They'd just dragged her into the closest assembly room for questioning. Rime ducked under a balcony and continued up the steps. He came to a wide bridge with a canopy, which crossed over to the tower in question. A double door carved from dark wood led into a room that was said to have been the Council's most important assembly room once upon a time. Before the red dome had been built.

A silver basin sat on a pedestal outside the door, as in many other places in Eisvaldr. The Seer's immediate forgiveness and absolution, available anywhere at all in the form of water. Practical.

The door opened and four guardsmen came out, Hirka dangling between them. The blood drained from Rime's face. She wasn't moving. Her slight frame hung limply between the hulking men in black steel. They dragged her over the bridge. Her head lolled against her chest. She was blindfolded and her hands were tied behind her back. Her woollen tunic had been ripped to shreds. Rime had never seen it fully intact, but now one of the sleeves was about to fall off.

They approached Rime. One of the guardsmen recognized him and nodded. Rime silently prayed he wouldn't say his name. Hirka couldn't know he was there. How would he live with himself if she knew he was there? That he had seen her and not done anything? He was close enough to touch her now. It was a struggle not to. Overpowering the guardsmen would have been child's play. Then he could take her somewhere far away from here. Away from the corruption of Eisvaldr.

Does such a place even exist?

They passed him and he turned to watch them go. Something dark had seeped through Hirka's tunic and stained her bound arms red. Anger rose in him, growing into something so incomprehensibly vast that he could no longer control it. The Might flooded through him unbidden. Unrestrained.

Ilume!

He ran over the bridge and tore the door open. But he was too late. The Council had already left the tower room. Two startled serving girls stopped in their tracks when he came in, then bowed and continued to clear away fruit and empty goblets.

He stood in the doorway, staring at the red blood trails on the floor. Marks left by her knees. Rime had been wrong. Painfully wrong. He'd thought he could make them see reason, but all reason had abandoned the Council. Eisvaldr was its own enemy. A viper's nest. He hated this place like nothing else. He raised his fist and knocked the silver basin off its pedestal. He heard himself howl. Water was thrown everywhere as the bowl flew through the air. It clattered against the floor and lay there vibrating against the tiles.

The girls came running and immediately kneeled down to wipe up the mess, but Rime yelled at them.

"LEAVE IT! LET THEM CLEAN UP THE BLOOD THEMSELVES!"

He needed to find Ilume. To put an end to everything that could still be ended.

A FOOL

Urd paced around his bed, in bigger and bigger circles, but his usual calm wouldn't come. His thoughts refused to fall into place. He had bought himself precious time, but he didn't have enough information to use it. Not anymore. The Voice had confirmed old fears. Suspicions of the most unpleasant kind. There was knowledge out there—certainties—of which he hadn't been told. A slip of the tongue? Or had it been deliberate?

We have succeeded because she lives.

Urd could hear his teeth grinding. *Enough!* He had to know more! But how?

He walked over to the table and steadied himself on the corners. In the middle lay the round piece of slate. Deceptively plain, apart from the stone fragments arranged in a ring along the outer edge. Had it not been for the bloodstained groove in the middle, people would have said it was an ornament. A game. Or a toy. The stones seemed powerless now. They no longer looked like a weapon. Not in the way they used to.

He uncorked the bottle of raven blood and poured a couple of drops into the groove. Then he drew upon the Might. Let it fill him completely. The whispering returned. Agitated voices like in a nightmare. Demanding. Spiteful. The blood shook before it moved. Then it drew toward him and stopped between two stones, the way it was supposed to. As it had always done. The voices became more forceful. They rushed inside of him. More real. The sign that he had succeeded.

Urd clenched his teeth. For the first time he felt afraid to act. But the truth was already out. He went over to the window and dripped two drops of raven blood on the sill. Precious drops. Sacred blood that would have seen him burned faster than the embling if anyone had known. Then he drew upon the Might again. The whispering from the unknown intensified once more. Provoked him. Tugged at his heartstrings. Made his blood run cold. The raven blood started to move. It drew toward him and ran down toward the floor in a narrow rivulet. Ran into his shoe.

Betrayed! He'd been betrayed. Made to look a fool.

What were these stones? Picked up by the riverbank? Children's toys? How had he ever believed that they would let him open the stone doors? Was it even possible to open them from a distance? Using fragments of stones from circles no one knew the locations of? A ridiculous thought. The magnitude of his own stupidity was too much to swallow. He screamed and swept the stone slab off the table with both hands. It shattered against the floor. He screamed again.

Damayanti. That dancing whore!

Urd threw his cloak over his shoulders and ran out. He headed toward the hall square and shouted for one of the Council's black carriages. He leaped inside and asked the coachman to drive him to Damayanti's whorehouse. The coachman's eyes widened. Urd bared his teeth at him. He had no time for idiots. Had no time to be cautious or to put on a mask of propriety. And why should he? He was Urd Vanfarinn. Couldn't they see that he was a busy man?

A condemned man.

Damayanti's place hadn't opened yet. He pounded on the door until a terrified girl let him in. She bowed when she saw the mark on his forehead. He pushed her aside and tore up the stairs, into Damayanti's room. She was standing by her bed, looking over three different outfits with a critical eye.

"I think the red one would—"

He grabbed her by the neck and forced her up against the wall. Her eyes opened wide, as though she knew what fear was. Urd knew. And he was going to show her. *Lying whore of the blind!* She had messed with the wrong man this time. Urd pressed himself so close that he could taste her fear. He had to be quick. Before she managed to draw upon the Might. Because truth be told, he didn't know how strong Damayanti was. Or what kind of blindcraft she commanded. He hissed through his raw throat.

"You've betrayed me! Taken me for a fool!"

She didn't protest. She tried to wrench herself free from his grasp. His nails cut into her chest, making her gasp.

"The stone way cannot be opened from a distance, can it? You have to be where the stones are. I haven't been there. Not in over fifteen years. That means that *you* have. Where have you been, Damayanti? Eh? Where did you let in the blind? Were you surprised when you managed it, hmm? Did you realize what it meant? That the girl was alive? That the stone sacrifice lived? When were you going to share your secrets, Damayanti? When?!"

She relaxed in his grasp. As though she knew she'd lost. But her eyes were blazing. No longer out of fear. "I am all that stands between you and death, Urd Vanfarinn."

Urd tightened his grip on her neck. She was right. But that also meant that he had nothing to lose. "I don't need to kill you to cause you pain, whore! Where have you been, Damayanti? You've found it, haven't you? The lost stone circle in Blindból. The first. The greatest of all the raven rings."

She shook her head. He wanted more than anything to use the Might to bind her into oblivion, but he didn't know what she could do with his Might. He hated being afraid. All he had at his disposal was brute force. He banged her head against the wall.

"Where is it?! Answer me!"

"It's not that one." She swallowed. "Not the lost one. Another one. Let go of me!"

"In the north? Where?"

"The blind way … to Bromfjell."

Bromfjell. Right near Ravnhov.

Urd let go. She slumped down and grabbed her neck. Her gaze fell on his own neck, an impulse she obviously was unable to control. Did she truly think her pain could ever be measured against his? He made a move toward her, to scare her. It worked.

"Give me everything you've got, whore, or die here. Die now. I've nothing to lose, and you know it."

Damayanti opened the cabinet and he stood behind her to make sure he was getting all the bottles she had. He grabbed them greedily. His life depended on them. Then he pulled Damayanti close and kissed her with all the power he had left in him.

"Isn't everything so much better when everyone's nice to each other?" he whispered in her ear and turned to leave.

"Send my regards to Slokna," he heard behind him.

"Oh, we're going to a far worse place, my dear. That's the one thing we can both be sure of."

THE PUPPET MAKER

Hirka lay down carefully on the part of the floor that sloped upward. It was too painful to sit with her back against the wall. But here she could lie on her side and look up at the light coming in at the top of the pit. A man in gray had removed the ropes around her arms while the guardsmen stood around them, spears at the ready.

He'd washed her hands and back in silence. She'd sensed traces of the Might in him. He'd granted her a brief respite from the pain, but she hadn't said anything. Ordinary people couldn't sense others binding, and the last thing she needed now was to stand out even more.

Ilume had been her last hope. She'd been so sure that Ilume would explain. That she would enter the room and shout: "Stop! What are you doing? This is Hirka! I know her from Elveroa and she's just a normal girl. She used to get into all sorts of scrapes with my grandson. She's a healer!"

But Ilume had been one of them. And that hadn't even been the worst part. The worst part was thinking they might be right. She didn't belong here. She was a danger to ordinary people. Maybe it was true, maybe she *had* let the blind into Ym. She realized to her surprise that she perhaps hadn't believed in what she was. That deep down she'd hoped the Seer would find another explanation for why she couldn't bind. Say it was all okay. That she was an ymling, just like everyone else. But she wasn't. She really wasn't.

Hirka pictured herself as a newborn, lying in the snow by the stone circle. She was no longer able to differentiate between actual memories and those she had conjured later. Everything was so distinct yet indistinct, all at the same time. She pushed herself up to drink from a pot of water that had been left on the floor in the corner. It tasted of soil. She spat it out again and coughed.

"Don't drink the water."

Hirka jumped and looked around. She was still alone. Was she finally starting to crack? She looked up at the light. A tiny head had been pushed between the bars at the top of the wall. It was brown, bearded, and wearing a golden crown. Small hands had been raised to either side of its mouth as if it were shouting. Two thin sticks attached to its hands disappeared somewhere behind the wall.

Hirka crawled farther up toward the bars. It was a puppet. Its head was made of wood and no larger than her hand, but someone had put their heart and soul into the details. Big, blue eyes with bushy eyebrows. Pale lips and a beard made of black wool. The crown looked like it was made of copper. The same color had been used for the embroidery on its blue robe. Its eyelids were also wooden, and they moved up and down as it moved.

"Don't drink the water. They forget to change it."

Hirka cocked her head. The puppet was astonishingly lifelike. She reached out to touch it, but it ducked behind the wall.

"Wait! Who are you?" The puppet had to belong to the prisoner in the pit next to hers. It reappeared with its chin up and its arms crossed.

"I am Oldar, the last king of Foggard."

Hirka smiled at the pride in its voice. Ravnhov in a nutshell. The puppet disappeared again and another took its place, this one even more beautiful. A warrior with real rings in its tiny chainmail. Broad-chested with steel pauldrons.

"Try asking him who stopped the deadborn."

The new puppet had a more powerful voice, even though it came from the same man.

"I'm sure he tried his best," Hirka said, smiling.

Hirka picked up the thread straightaway. The war against the blind. The kings in the north who had had to swear allegiance to the Seer after He helped the twelve warriors defeat the blind. The twelve warriors who became the first Council. Hirka craned her neck to see who was holding the puppets, but it was impossible. The warrior leaned closer to the bars. He had golden hair fixed in waves down his back.

"We went into Blindból alone. We asked the people to build the wall behind us, in case we should fail. We went in, and we won!" That wasn't how Hirka remembered the story. She'd heard that the people had built the wall out of fear, after the warriors had left.

"So who are you?"

"I'm Eldrin the Warrior! One of the Twelve!"

Eldrin. Rime's ancestor.

Hirka bit her lip and looked down at the floor. This was Eisvaldr. This was Rime's home. Ilume's home. The world was ruled from here. And it had been for a thousand years.

Hirka knew that many people were envious of Rime's position. It had never bothered her before, but now she felt a sharp pain in her chest. Rime had roots. She was alone. She had absolutely no one. All she'd had was Father. And now she didn't even have him. No family and no history. She couldn't even call this world her own.

Rime An-Elderin's family, on the other hand, could be traced all the way back to the war. Blessed and embraced by the Seer. It had to be nice, having a history like that. Being a descendant of the legendary warriors who had saved the world. But that had been a thousand years ago. What were they now? Malicious. Unthinking. Full of hate. They could rot in Slokna, every one of them.

"But who are *you*? Who's behind the puppets?"

There was silence for a moment. Some rummaging behind the wall. A new puppet appeared between the bars. It was pale and naked, its eyes closed.

"I'm the puppet maker."

Hirka smiled. She didn't know who she was talking to, but he clearly couldn't speak for himself. He needed the puppets. She sent a warm thought to the guardsmen who had let him keep them. But then she realized that was probably so he could entertain the guardsmen during long shifts. They could rot in Slokna too.

"Why are you here?" she asked, more angrily than she meant to.

"Because I saw them."

"Saw who?"

"I saw. I know."

"Okay … what do you know?" Hirka kicked at the floor absentmindedly. She doubted he knew anything. Just like she didn't know anything. Neither did the Council.

"Thank you, thank you." The puppet bowed.

"Er … don't mention it. What do you know?"

"I saw."

"What did you see?"

"I saw them die."

"Who died, puppet maker?"

"The king and Odin."

"Wait. You saw the king and Odin die?"

"We'd just eaten. All I heard was the cuckoo in the tree."

"You mean friends of yours? Friends who were playing the king and Odin?" Hirka didn't get a response. "What happened to them?"

"I'm no liar!"

Hirka barked out a bitter laugh. "Neither am I, puppet man, but no one cares. What happened?"

"They hunger for it. Did you know that? They hunger for the Might. They've hungered for it for a thousand years. That's why they came. Some people say they were here before us. That they were the ones who built the stone doors. They came and went as they pleased. Before us."

The hair on the back of her neck stood on end. She asked even though she knew the answer.

"Who?"

The puppet opened its eyes. They were deep-set and nothing more than a white membrane. The effect was intense. Simple, but horribly real.

One of the blind.

Hirka leapt up and grabbed the bars. They bit into her fingers, and she snatched her hands back. *Blackest Blindból!*

"Wait! Have you seen them? You've seen the blind? Where? Where did they come from?"

"They came through stone."

"Where? Where are the stones?"

"There are a lot. A lot."

"What happened when they came? What did they do?"

The puppet disappeared again.

"Answer me!"

No response. Hirka kicked the wall, to little avail.

"Answer me! They're saying I brought them here!"

"Don't drink the water."

Hirka slid down the slope again, where she sat with her arms folded around her chest.

"I know," she whispered. "They forget to change it."

GESA'S GARDEN

Rime walked up toward the An-Elderin family home. The sleeping dragon. The house he no longer called home. The lanterns along the road were lit, yellow dots snaking their way through the evening dark, showing him the way.

The Council had hardly left the dome all day, but now they had adjourned for the evening. Rime had come close to bursting in at several points, but he couldn't bring himself to do it. There was little point risking his life needlessly, though he supposed that was all he had done today, without quite knowing why. But Ilume had the answers. And this time he wasn't going to hold his tongue.

He didn't get a chance to knock. Prete opened the door for him.

"Són-Rime. Come in. Come in." Prete had an anxious warmth in his eyes, which Rime presumed was due to the news that the rot had spread. "It's good to see you, Són-Rime. Your uncle and his family are gathered in the library. They're with friends. Nobody is sure what to do under the circumstances. I'll inform them that you're here."

"No, Prete. I can't stay. I have to speak with Ilume."

"Certainly, certainly. I saw Ilume-madra in Gesa's garden, but I can see whether she's come back inside."

"That's fine, Prete. I'll take a look. Thank you."

Rime walked through the north wing and out into the part of the garden that was named after Gesa, the mother he barely remembered. Ilume was standing with her back to him, between the sivberry trees. A lantern decorated with dragons made the leaves shine like silver. They whispered in the wind. Whispered about the waning summer, and whether it was time to shed their white flowers. He moved closer and the leaves settled down, as though to listen to what was coming.

A creek ran through the garden, one of the only things here that wasn't man-made. His mother had wanted it left untouched. Ilume stood motionless in front of it. She was still wearing her robes. Rime realized that she had to be exhausted. He couldn't remember a more intense day. It couldn't have been easy for the Council either, but he felt no sympathy, no tenderness. All he could feel was the Might, simmering away, waiting to fill the emptiness inside him.

"What are you going to do with Hirka?" he asked.

Ilume turned toward him. Her pallor matched her robes, making her face look like furrowed porcelain. Her piercing eyes were all that showed signs of life. The mark of the black raven was stark against her forehead.

"You should be in Blindból now."

Rime didn't reply. He stood wondering whether he'd ever looked at her that closely before. Had he seen how old she was? Was she old enough to have lost her wits? No. Rime knew better than to entertain that thought.

"You were here." Her words were cutting. "You were here this morning, during the Rite, even though I'd told you no." Ilume's eyes had widened. After all these years, she was still able to don a mask of incredulity. Incredulity that he would even consider opposing her. Or that he would choose another path.

Rime was done with masks. He couldn't take it anymore. "What do you intend to do with her?"

He knew the answer, but he had to hear it from her. He wanted her to own up. To admit that they had completely lost control.

"She is the rot, Rime."

"Answer me!" He realized that he was speaking through clenched teeth.

"What do you think? She doesn't belong here. She has brought fear and chaos! She has let the blind in. As long as she lives, everyone's lives are in danger. You're a fool if you don't—"

"You must really be desperate!" Rime laughed. "What a load of old tripe! Let the blind in? She's just a girl! I've known her since I was twelve!"

Ilume lifted her chin so that she could look down on him. Rime could see the twitching in the corner of her mouth that revealed what she thought about him "knowing" anyone outside the wall. But then her eyes narrowed again, as though she had realized something.

"You knew! You knew what she was, and you kept it from me!"

"Don't blame me for what you failed to see, Ilume."

Her mouth twitched. He was hitting where it hurt, and he knew it. This was an accusation that had been looming over her all day.

"This is not a game you should be playing, Rime."

"But that's just it, Ilume. I'm not playing. You're all happy to play. Play for the people and for Ravnhov. Turn the world on its head, without listening to the Seer! Let people into the schools in exchange for money, without giving a damn whether they're strong in the Might. I don't care. Roll around in your privilege if you want, but you're not executing a young girl just to set an example for an imaginary enemy. Not as long as I live."

Rime could see the weight of the day welling up in her. This woman's words had been law since the day he was born. Defying her was like defying an avalanche. He had to stop himself from taking a step back, out of habit. She pointed at him as though he were one of the undead.

"You've made your choice! You refused the chair. You betrayed me! Betrayed us! I hold the dust in the streets in greater esteem than your opinions, Kolkagga. You're already dead."

Her whole body was shaking. White sivberry flowers fell like snow around her, around both of them. Rime could see them hitting the surface of the creek and getting washed away. Drowning. Disappearing. Soon the trees would be bare. Winter was coming.

He looked at Ilume and he understood. She had lost her daughter, and now she had lost him. The An-Elderin family was going to lose its position of power on the Council. And she blamed him. Blamed him with every bone in her body, to the very tip of her accusatory finger that was shaking in righteous indignation.

She stepped closer. Tendons stood out from her neck. Small silver hairs had escaped the otherwise flawless braids, but Ilume hadn't given up. Ilume stood her ground. She always stood her ground. And now she was standing her ground right in front of him. He realized that he'd hoped—and maybe expected—to see shame in her eyes. Shame at what the Council was going to do. At what they were. But that would never happen.

All his life he had been told that he was worth more than other people. Better than other people. Stronger blood and stronger in the Might. The child the Seer had waited for. The lucky child. He'd been born to lead the people, the country, the eleven kingdoms. Rime had woken up from this lie, but Ilume still believed. Ilume doled out life and death as if it were the most natural thing. Because she was who she was. And now she was losing more than she could bear: her name.

But it was no longer in Rime's power to do anything about her loss. She wasn't a woman anymore. She wasn't his mother's mother. She was one of them. One of the twelve he could no longer tolerate. He had known that as far back as his Rite day at the age of fifteen, when he had chosen to study with Kolkagga. What Ilume had said was true. His words no longer meant anything. He was already dead.

"I'd rather be dead than an An-Elderin," he said.

He saw the blow coming, as he had seen it in the Seer's hall in Elveroa. Back then he had let her strike him, but back then he hadn't had the image of Hirka burned into his retina. Hirka. Half dead, hanging between guardsmen, weighed down by chains. Hirka, with dark rust-colored stains on her tunic.

He grabbed Ilume's arm before her hand reached his cheek. He held it firmly. They stood face-to-face. Her eyes had narrowed into hateful slits. He realized that she was binding in an attempt to overcome him, but it wasn't a fair fight. He was stronger than her.

Svarteld had taught him self-control. Composure. To live as though he were already dead. But still it was a struggle to keep from squeezing harder. He could have squeezed her wrist until her fingers fell off. Until she couldn't point anymore. Or do more damage.

But he didn't do that. Because he understood why she wanted to strike him. He was never going to be one of them. And if he had become one of them, he would still have been a threat to the house's history. She wanted to hit him because he despised everything she had worked for. And because the sleeping dragon was never going to wake up. The house of An-Elderin was dead.

He let go of her hand, turned his back on her, and left.

She shouted after him. Her voice was like a child's. Screaming, inconsolable. "Where do you think you're going?!"

"I'm going to wash my hands," he replied.

TYRINN

Hirka crumbled the bread into the gruel and tried to shape it into small cakes. There wasn't much bread, so she only ended up with five, but that would have to do. She climbed up onto the lid of her toilet bucket, reached up toward the narrow opening in the top of the wall, and threw two sticky cakes out onto the ground. She didn't dare shout. Not yet.

She had heard ravens—of course, there were thousands of them in Mannfalla, particularly in Eisvaldr. But one of them was Kuro. He was out there somewhere. He was her only hope. The lid creaked under her weight. She crossed her fingers in the sign of the Seer, hoping the bucket would hold. If not, it would be an unpleasant day, to put it mildly. She craned her neck and looked out.

Kuro! Come, Kuro! Food!

Something furry darted over and started sniffing optimistically at the food. A rat. Again. She reached out with her fingers and hissed at the rat.

"*Ssss!* Scram!"

The animal took hardly any notice of her. She pulled her arm out of her sleeve and tried to whip it between the bars. The rat moved a little farther away and continued gnawing at her precious food.

"Hey, stop that! Kuro! Hedra! Hedra!"

The grating at the top of the slope opened. Hirka whirled around. A guardsman stood in the opening. "What are you doing, girl?" He stared at her. His eyes raked up and down her body. It suddenly dawned on her that she was half naked. She quickly shoved her arm back in its sleeve and tugged her tunic down over her exposed stomach.

"Hunting rats," she said, climbing down from the bucket.

He took another couple steps into the pit. Hirka folded her arms over her chest. She felt her skin pucker into goose pimples. His eyes had taken on a glassy sheen she didn't like. He was almost twice her height and twice as many winters old. His face was angular and sunburned. Sylja would have said he was handsome. She liked his type. Strong, conceited, and mouthy. Dangerous.

I'm not afraid.

"Is it true what they say?" he asked.

"I doubt it. People say some crazy things."

He gave a joyless bark of laughter. "You've got some nerve … Odinspawn."

"I've got plenty of it."

He stopped right in front of her. She could feel his breath on her forehead.

"Are you like other women?"

He grabbed at her crotch. She seized his wrist and twisted until he shrieked in pain. She didn't pull away. Her heart was pounding, but she couldn't let him see that she was afraid. Men like him thrived on fear.

He straightened up. His eyes were narrower. He was furious. Hirka tried to smile, but she wasn't sure she'd managed.

"I'm a child of Odin. I can do things you wouldn't believe. Touch me again and I'll see to it that you rot."

He looked uncertain for a moment, then he laughed again. Just as joylessly as last time. He pushed her up against the wall. "If you could spread the rot just by talking, half of Eisvaldr would be in Slokna by now. Besides, I heard you have a scar where your tail used to be. You're lying." He brought one hand to her throat. The other slid down to her chest.

A cacophony of shrieks made the guardsman back away. Kuro was outside the bars, wings spread, screeching. The guardsman stood looking between Hirka and the raven for a moment before baring his teeth like an animal and retreating out of the pit. Hirka hissed at him until he was gone.

She slid down the wall and sat with her arms folded across her chest. She could feel her heart pounding through her tunic. At least there was one thing she could thank the Seer for. The respect people had for the ravens. Hirka gripped her own throat, trying to get rid of the feeling of his hands.

What if he came back? She was tired, but she didn't dare close her eyes. She sat chatting with Kuro, but after a while he flew away. The night was the longest since she'd arrived here. She didn't feel any calmer until daylight returned and she heard the changing of the guard above her. Finally she could rest her head on her knees and sleep.

The sound of scraping metal woke her again. She looked up at the bars in the narrow window. An armored boot. It was him. The guardsman.

He's standing outside!

A shutter slammed down. She heard the sound of bolts on the outside. He was barring the window. Shutting Kuro out. Despair welled up inside her. She got up and banged on the shutter, but it was designed to hold. It wouldn't budge. Hirka realized that no one would see him now. The coast would be clear for him this evening, when he came back on duty. Kuro wouldn't be able to scare him off this time. She was alone.

Hirka shuddered. She could only hope that the rot acted quickly. Before he managed to hurt her. That his flesh would slough off before her very eyes. Her own thoughts scared her. She'd never known a man the way Sylja had. Father had made sure of that. Not that she'd wanted to. Most of the boys and men she'd met were idiots. Untrustworthy, lying idiots. Apart from Father, of course.

And Rime.

She sank down onto the floor again and squeezed the wolf tooth with the small marks on each side. If Rime came and took her away from this place, he could have a hundred points. A thousand! As many as he wanted. If only he came.

Hirka kicked the wall as hard as she could. Several times. No one was going to save her. The only person she could rely on was herself. She would have to find her own way out.

And quickly.

Hirka sharpened the piece of wood against the floor. She stopped to study it before carrying on. All she could hear was the sound of her work. There was nothing but silence from the pit next to hers. There hadn't been a peep out of the man with the puppets since the guards changed. She was worried the guardsman had put dreamwort in his food. But that was a rare and expensive plant. Maybe he'd used something else. She couldn't smell anything suspicious in her own food, but she'd refrained from eating it just in case.

She'd broken the piece of wood off the toilet bucket lid and was fashioning a weapon. Hirka stopped again and scrutinized her handmade knife. It wasn't very good. Shorter than the length of her hand, but sharp now. It had a curve at the end that would have to serve as a handle. She jabbed it into the air a couple of times. It didn't feel right. Her fists had served her well her entire life. Kolgrim could attest to that. But a weapon? Against a person? It was her job to patch people up, not slash them to ribbons.

But that was before. Before the Rite. Before the welts on her back.

She let her arm drop. She wasn't going to kill anyone. Just scare him. Keep him away from her, far enough away that she could ... what? She looked around. There was nowhere to run. In her darkest moments she had considered giving in. Maybe it would tell her something she never would have known otherwise—whether the rot was crones' talk or not. And how bad could it be? She could squeeze her eyes shut and count to a thousand. Then she could open them again and see whether he'd rotted. But what would be worse? Finding that he had rotted, or finding that he hadn't?

He'd walked past several times now, together with another guardsman. They watched her. Restless. Waiting as the daylight waned. Yellowing, reddening. Then it was gone.

She saw the outlines of two men when the grating was opened. A third man was pushed down toward her. He was filthy, wearing tattered clothes. This wasn't a guardsman. Another prisoner?

Hirka straightened up and tried to be confident. "Have they told you what I am?"

He came closer. He was big. Bigger than the guardsman. His hair was dark and slicked back with grease. Hirka swallowed. "I'm a child of Odin! If you touch me, you'll rot!"

He laughed in a manner suggesting he hadn't used his voice in a while. "I've heard all sorts from unwilling women, but that's a new one."

"Why do you think they've sent you down here instead of coming themselves? They've sent you to the tailless embling to see if you rot. Use your head, man!"

He hesitated, tilting his head to one side to see if she was telling the truth. Hirka dared to hope. He might not have heard about her specifically, but he'd heard the stories. He looked up at the two others behind the grating. The guardsman from the evening before called down into the pit, "The girl's full of shit! She has a scar on her back that proves it. How long have you been in here, Tyrinn? Don't you miss women and ale?"

Tyrinn lunged at Hirka. He pressed her up against the wall, a hand on her throat. In a panic, she swung the piece of wood at him and felt it catch against his skin. He loosened his grip and swore. Blood dripped from a cut just below his eye. He wiped it with his hand and crowded her up against the wall again. Hirka's breath caught in her chest. She ducked under his arms and jabbed her elbow at his temple but managed nothing more than a glancing blow. He grabbed her hand and twisted. Hirka shrieked in pain and her wooden knife clattered to the floor. Then she fell as well.

He pressed down on her chest, pinning her with his entire bodyweight. Hirka felt like she might suffocate. She gasped for breath. She tried to lift her knees to kick him off, but he was too heavy. Much too heavy. She tried to grab his feet so she could tip him, but her arms weren't long enough. She couldn't reach. He started to fumble with his belt and panic gripped her. He was going to do it. He was going to take her by force.

Rime!

Tyrinn clamped a hand over her mouth. It tasted of sour sweat.

"I'll snap your neck if you scream," he hissed above her. Hirka screamed. He hit her hard in the jaw. A hand groped her breast under her tunic. She lashed out blindly. Scratched. A knee pushed between her feet and up toward her crotch. She twisted to the side and groped for her wooden knife. A mistake. He pressed her head against the floor. She lay helpless on her stomach with the nauseating weight of him on top of her. He tore her trousers down and laughed when he saw the scar. She no longer had the upper hand. His fear was gone.

He pulled her head back with one hand. The other pushed between her thighs, cold fingers fumbling where no one had been before.

"Is this it, hm? Is this the rot?" He hissed in her ear. Hirka bit his hand and threw her head from side to side like a wild animal. She thought she heard a finger break. But he didn't cry out. He didn't react. Nothing happened. His weight lifted from her body. His hands let go. Hirka kicked and hit something soft. Still he didn't cry out. She quickly rolled over, pulled herself up against the wall, and stared at him.

He kneeled before her. The shadow of another man loomed behind him. He had a hand on the criminal's head. Tyrinn sat still, his mouth hanging open. His eyes had rolled back into his head. Hirka could feel something in the earth beneath her. Cold and hot at the same time. Her skin pulsated. Time stopped.

The Might. This was the Might, and it felt like ice in her veins. Merciless, yet indifferent to her.

Tyrinn started to laugh like a child. Then he screamed. Blood vessels rose to the surface in his face. They grew thicker. One of them ruptured.

"Stop!" Hirka sobbed.

Her assailant fell to the floor. Blood and saliva ran from the corners of his mouth. He lay there like a butchered animal. Dead. One of his eyes was blood-red. His manhood jutted out of his trousers. A pale column of flesh that might have been inside her now, if it hadn't been for … Hirka tore her eyes away from him.

The other person stood hunched over with his back to her. He leaned against the wall, breathing heavily. Holding his throat. It wasn't Rime. Hirka felt the Might slowly dissipate, as if sinking back into the earth it had come from. She pulled her trousers back on. Reflexively, she grabbed the wooden knife and hid it in her shoe. Then she got up.

The man turned to face her and pulled his hood down. He smiled, but it didn't reach his eyes. He bore the mark of the Council on his forehead.

She knew him. She'd seen him twice. He'd lied to her at Lindri's teahouse. He was the reason she had run from there. And she'd seen him during the Rite. He was one of the twelve. A member of the Council. The same Council that had thrown her in here.

"You're one of them." Hirka moved closer to check that her eyes weren't deceiving her.

"Regrettably," he replied, heading for the grating. The guardsmen were lying outside, slumped over each other. Immobile heaps. The councillor unsheathed a knife belonging to the one on top before coming down toward her again. Hirka backed away. Would he kill her now? But he walked past her. He lifted his hand and brought the knife down into the prisoner's back. A quick and almost practiced movement. The dead body spasmed. Hirka stared. He had stabbed a dead man. A dead man. She tried to swallow her disgust, but it stuck in her throat.

The councillor turned to face her. His blond hair had been combed back. His eyes glinted coldly. His expression was still exactly the same, as if he hadn't just stabbed a dead man in the back.

"Listen to me, embling. We don't have much time. All that awaits you here is death. You only have one chance, and that's coming with me." His voice was just as hollow as before. Almost gurgling. It sounded like it took a lot of effort for him to speak normally. Only three grains of sand ago she would have seized any opportunity to get out of here, but now she hesitated.

"You're one of them. How—"

"They don't understand! They'll kill you, but that'll make everything even worse. You need to go back where you came from, embling." He gripped her arm and pulled her after him.

"Wait! Where are we going? I can't just ... What if the Seer's right? What if it's my fault the blind are back? I need—"

"You need to get out of here! And I'm going to help you. Get on my back and hide under my cloak."

She stared at the dead man and shuddered. What was worse? Being locked in with his corpse or breaking out with the man who had killed him?

Breaking out. I'll have more options then.

She climbed up onto the stranger's back and he threw his cloak over both of them. It smelled of horse. Hirka could feel the coolness of the metal collar around his neck. It had a clasp on the side. The skin was red around the edges. Who was he? What was wrong with him?

He left the pit and headed for the exit. The moonlight reflected off the nails in the door. The outlines of domes and towers emerged from the darkness outside.

"Wait! The man with the puppets!"

Hirka twisted back, but the councillor neither replied nor stopped.

KOLKAGGA'S MISSION

The night was cold. Unforgiving. Rime stood straight-backed, watching his breath freeze in front of him. The torches cast a restless light over the ranks of Kolkagga who had been woken by the gong, hours before daybreak. Some were still pulling their clothes on while they waited for Svarteld.

Rime had been the first to rise. He hadn't slept anyway. He heard a second gong in the distance, and it sent shivers down his spine. They were waking all the camps. This was serious.

The master lived on a small rise to the east of the camp. Light shone through the folding doors and revealed the outline of two men in discussion. The door was pushed aside. Svarteld came out and stood before Kolkagga. He unrolled a small piece of paper, which he studied for a moment. Then he started giving orders in a mechanical voice.

"The child of Odin has escaped. She's got a few hours' head start. She has killed two men and a fellow prisoner. She is considered a serious threat to all. The Seer commands us to find her and annihilate her."

Rime's jaw dropped. He quickly remembered himself and clenched his teeth. What in Slokna had she done? Killed and fled? Hirka? Impossible. She had to understand that doing so would only expedite her death.

The master's voice carried across the entire camp. Monotonous.

Unaffected. As though it was a perfectly normal mission. "The girl is fifteen winters and has no tail. She is small and has fiery red hair. Comes from Foggard, but she has a mixed dialect."

Rime closed his eyes. They were wrong. Her hair wasn't fiery red. It was deep red. Like blood.

"The mission will continue as long as necessary. The Council has given it the highest priority. I repeat: highest priority. The rot is on the loose in Ym. Change, pack, and meet your group leaders by the long bridge for instructions."

Kolkagga dispersed. Rime pushed the door aside and went back inside. He got undressed and stood naked. He stared at the black outfit he'd been using as a pillow. It was all he'd cared about for the past three years. He was Kolkagga. A black shadow. Already dead.

The Seer's word was his law.

His skin tingled with goose bumps. Rime put on the clothes that made him invisible in the night. Then he went outside. He only made it a couple of steps before he ran into the master, who was standing outside observing him.

"Master?"

"You grew up with this girl?"

Rime hesitated. "We both lived in Elveroa for a few years."

"Ilume-madra has not exempted you from this mission." The master looked at him as though he wanted Rime to provide an explanation.

"That would be unlike her," he replied.

"I could exempt you, if you want. Do you want me to?"

"No."

Svarteld nodded in approval. Rime felt the master's eyes on his back as he walked toward the long bridge. They were assembled there. Kolkagga. A hundred men. Dark outlines in the night. And out there between the mountains there were more camps. More men. Black-clad. Lethal. Unstoppable.

And now they had just one job. One mission. *Find her.* Rime felt the cold creep down his neck and wash through his chest. Restless. Merciless. A cold certainty. Hirka only had one hope.

He had to find her first.

HOUSE OF VANFARINN

The upholstered leather chair could have held three of her, but all the same Hirka made herself as small as possible under the woollen blanket. Flames danced in a fireplace big enough to stand upright in. It was made of black stone with green veins running through it. Veins like the ones that had stood out in her assailant's face before he died. Urd-fadri sat before her. Urd Vanfarinn. Son of Spurn Vanfarinn, and his successor on the Council. Her savior. She shuddered.

Her clothes had been returned to her. Dry now after an ice-cold flight through the waterways from the pool. They had emerged in the gutters outside the buildings of Eisvaldr, but still within its wall. Urd had taken them up the forest-covered mountainside, which had kept them hidden all the way to the Vanfarinn family home—a castle-like structure in polished green marble.

Large paintings hung on the wall behind Urd. Portraits of an extensive family, though Hirka hadn't seen much life in the house. She'd heard Urd dismiss the servants, everyone apart from a family guardsman—the only person who had seen her.

Hirka was no longer in a pit, but she felt anything but free. The man before her wore a mask of concern. The wooden puppets in the pit next to hers had been more convincing, even though she didn't doubt that the councillor had plenty to be concerned about. One of his feet bounced up and down. Up and down.

"What will happen to you?" Hirka asked.

He swapped his expression of mild concern for a smile that was probably supposed to be reassuring.

"Nothing will happen to you, embling."

"Not me. You. What will happen to *you*, now you've helped me?"

He raised a sculpted eyebrow as if surprised by the question. His beard was perfectly groomed as well. How was that possible? Hirka's hair stuck out in every direction. A red haystack. His looked like it was glued to his scalp.

"No one knows I've helped you, and either way, it's a risk I'm willing to take. It's what's best for Ym. For everyone." He raised his hands in a self-sacrificing gesture, as if to indicate that he was willing to die for the Seer.

"And if they realize it was you? Surely you spoke out in my defense when my fate was being discussed?"

His eyes narrowed again. He cocked his head slightly and regarded her with interest. She had a feeling that was something he hadn't even considered. "There were other dissenting voices. And even if the Council does find out, there won't be anything they can do about it. They're running around like headless chickens. They're fools who can't see farther than the ends of their own noses. They think burning you on the walls or chopping your head off will help them sleep at night."

He was quick-tempered. Hirka took note of this and his clear disgust for the Council he was part of.

"They want you dead, embling." Hirka wasn't used to such statements being leveled at her, but she said nothing. "Dead. Understand?"

"I'm glad you're doing this for me."

The councillor didn't correct her. A moment ago he'd said he was doing it for Ym, for everyone, but now it was suddenly for her? Well, if this man wanted what was best for her, she'd be a turnip's uncle. He leaned forward and caressed her throat.

"Just look at that throat … so untouched. So pure. It would be such a pity if they brought a sword down on it—or burned it."

Hirka tried to suppress another shudder. Maybe she could sneak out at sunrise. He was part of the Council. Surely, he would have to return to the Seer's hall? He couldn't sit here watching her.

There were two knocks at the door and a guardsman came in. He was a young man, but he had bags under his eyes. He handed Hirka a black bowl of meat stew. Hirka was so hungry that she felt sick. She thanked him and took it. The guardsman nodded at both of them and left. A wonderful smell spread throughout the room. But it was mixed with something else. Something she recognized. Sharp. Earthy.

Dreamwort.

There was no doubt in her mind. Of course. Urd was the reason why the man with the puppets had been sleeping when she was attacked. Where would normal guardsmen get dreamwort from? It wasn't a plant you could buy just anywhere. You had to know someone. Have money. And this man had more than enough money. She knew that thanks to Sylja. The Vanfarinn family owned a lock in the canal through Skarrleid in the south. Everyone who passed through it had to pay. It had been that way for generations.

"Aren't you having any?" Hirka asked.

"I've already eaten."

"Oh …"

Why would he give her dreamwort? Hirka pictured the body again. The bulge and his open fly. The blood running from the corners of his mouth. The knife in his back. The two guardsmen heaped on top of each other like dirty laundry. If Urd wanted to kill her, she'd already be dead. All he needed to do was wait until she was executed. So what he wanted was for her to fall asleep. But that was enough for Hirka. Every nerve in her body told her she couldn't be helpless near this man. She chewed the stew without swallowing. Then she nodded in the direction of the paintings. "Who are they?"

He turned to look and she quickly took a fistful of stew and pulled it beneath the blanket. She shoved it down between the cushion and the back of the chair. It was hot and unpleasant and would make a real mess. But she'd be far away before he found it.

"My father," he replied, somewhat bitterly. "And my mother, Meire. She lives in Skarrleid. That's where my family's from originally." Hirka wasn't listening. She was making the best use of the time she could. Smuggling stew under the blanket and behind the cushion. He no longer seemed as restless. He was talking and waiting. Waiting for her to fall asleep.

The history of the Vanfarinn family was well known to those who were interested in such things. She'd heard parts of it. The family were originally called Drafna, after one of the first twelve to enter Blindból. Quarrels had divided them, and the eldest son had told his brother that he was *villfaren*—a lost cause. The younger had taken the insult and turned it into a new family name. When the Drafna family had died out, Vanfarinn laid claim to the seat on the Council. Those with the wickedest tongues called them the bastards.

But Hirka had never heard the story as Urd told it. He held that they had been robbed of their seat on the Council for generations. An injustice corrected by an adulated forefather who squinted down at her from a faded painting on the wall. He was hanging next to Spurn, Urd's recently deceased father. And Gridd, his father's father. And Malj, his father's father's father.

Hirka yawned. It wasn't all an act, as she'd spent most of the past few days awake. She put down the half-empty bowl and leaned her head against the arm of the chair. Now that she would appear drowsy enough, she chanced her luck.

"What happened to your throat?" She made a point of slurring her speech.

"Nothing," he replied.

"Do you know how to send me … home?"

"Of course."

"How do you know that? No one else knows how I got here."

"I do."

He wasn't giving anything away, so deciding she might as well play the part, Hirka closed her eyes.

I fell asleep!

Hirka tried to sit up, but her hands and feet were tied. She had been gagged with coarse linen. Dry. Dusty. She couldn't swallow. She'd hardly touched the food, but she'd still fallen asleep! It had to have been the exhaustion. Or a really quite astonishing quantity of dreamwort. Where was she?

She could see shafts of light in the darkness. She was in a confined space. She couldn't stretch her legs out. She heard a horse whinny. She was in a cart. What had woken her? Was she in a crate? Voices outside. A muffled argument.

"I can't have her here, Urd. The guardsmen are searching the city, they'll find her, I can't—"

"You won't have her here. You'll take her to the stone circle. Are you deaf?" Urd's voice was hoarser than before. "Get her out of the city tonight."

"Seer have mercy, Urd ..."

"Tonight, Slabba. Now."

"We'll be stopped at the city walls. They'll—"

"I thought you knew every gatekeeper in this city?"

Slabba hesitated. "What if she wakes up?"

"She won't wake up, you half-wit! Not for ages. I need to attend the Council meeting tomorrow, but I'll be there after. Just get the girl to the circle."

"She's the rot! I can't drive around wi—"

"Slabba." Urd's voice was suddenly low and intense. Hirka's ears pricked up. She could hear this Slabba sweating just as much as she was. "I don't have time for this. The blind are waiting and the Council is hysterical!"

"The blind?!" Slabba squealed like a pig.

"Be quiet!"

"What—what are you going to do to her?"

"The girl was never supposed to be here. She was a stone offering. A gift for the blind, and now they're looking for her. They're searching for a tailless girl. They know she's here. When they have her, I—we—will have what we need."

"In Slokna's name, Urd. This can't be worth it! The blind?! This wasn't part of the agreement. I've never—"

Hirka heard a gurgling sound, like Urd had gripped Slabba by the throat. "Either you get her out of the city and help me, or you take her place as a gift to the deadborn. Which would you prefer, Slabba?" Slabba didn't reply, but she assumed he was nodding for all he was worth.

Hirka couldn't breathe. She couldn't panic. Not now. Not here. She had a mouthful of linen. She needed to breathe evenly. Calmly.

She heard Slabba give orders to other men. Footsteps. A lot of footsteps. Several men. The cart started to move.

Somewhere nearby, a raven shrieked.

ATTACKED

Hirka lay curled up in the crate watching light flicker in the cracks between the boards. It was cold and she missed her cloak. And her bag, with all her herbs and tea. Everything she owned. It was probably somewhere in the vaults.

As the cart rolled over cobblestones, she started to curse how small she was in the grander scheme of things. She had nothing. No family. No home. *Hirka the tailless girl. Daughter of gods know who.*

She enjoyed using the word "gods" instead of "Seer." He hadn't raised a finger to help her, and right now it was the only way of defying Him. And she might never get another chance. She was meant to be a gift to the blind. An offering. A worm on a hook, in exchange for Seer knows what.

Gods. Gods *know what.*

But there was one thing she had learned since the new moon. As long as there was life, there was hope, and she was still alive. Confined, cold, and hungry, but alive. And as long as she was alive, anything could happen. She just had to keep her head. Look for opportunities and seize them. If only she had …

The knife!

She pulled up her knees and arched her back as much as the small crate allowed. Luckily her arms were bound at the front. Urd clearly hadn't expected any trouble from her, knocked out by dreamwort as she was meant to be. She stretched her fingers toward her feet, all the while keeping in mind the fact that the councillor had excessive faith in his own abilities. She reached as far as the fold on her boots. A little more. Just a little more.

There! She grasped the makeshift knife eagerly, got it up to her mouth and clamped her teeth around the end. It didn't take long to saw through the ropes. Her wrists were hot and clammy, but free. She wanted to have a go at her feet, but the cramped crate made it difficult to reach them.

She took a break and lay there, gauging the cart's movements. When would be the right time to escape? At the city walls? No. The guardsmen would drag her back again, if they didn't just club her to death on the spot. It would have to be outside the walls. The question was how.

She started to work on the knots by her feet. The trick was not to make them tighter. Urd expected her to sleep through the night. Hirka could feel the weight of the lid above her. She hated being in enclosed spaces! Her knees hit the side when she tried to pull them up, and there wasn't enough room to turn around. She had managed to prop herself up enough that she could push at the lid with her head, but it had been no use. It didn't feel locked, just weighted down.

She dug her thumb into the knot by her ankles and found a weak spot. She pulled on the rope and felt it loosen. She tugged at it until she was free. Then she pushed the lid open a crack and stuck her hand out in the darkness. Blankets. There were blankets piled on top of the crate. She tugged on them and they thumped to the floor, but the cart continued on as before.

So she was alone in the cart. That made things easier. Finally something was going her way. Hirka climbed out of the crate and started to feel her way around. It was pitch-black. Night. It had been a long time since she had seen a flicker of light through the wooden boards. So they were outside the city walls. Maybe.

There were more blankets in the cart. A couple of oil lamps, with no oil. Several crates like the one she had been held captive in. *A merchant's cart.* But nothing she could use to escape. Apart from the wooden knife.

The image of her assailant forced its way back into her thoughts. The way he had lain twitching on the floor of the pit. But his fate would have been far worse had he managed to have her. The rot.

It was his fault. Not yours.

Hirka pressed her ear against the front wall and listened. At least two horses in front and just as many behind. Maybe more. That complicated matters. But she could hear wind in the trees. A couple of crows. The smell of fairy's kiss and moss. The forest. At least here she had a hope of getting away. Maybe she could get up on the roof so that—

Her thoughts were interrupted by two heavy thuds. Whinnying horses. The cart lurched to a sudden stop. She fell against the wall but managed to stay on her feet. Shouting. What was happening? She had to know what was happening! Hirka's hands skittered along the boards in search of an opening. Someone screamed outside.

"KOLKAGGA!"

The hysterical scream sounded as though the man didn't actually believe what he was seeing. Panic erupted outside.

Hirka felt a cold grip her. They were here. They'd finally found her. The black shadows. Her hands started to tingle and were difficult to raise. She fumbled for the latch, but her fingers wouldn't obey. She kicked at it. It gave way and the tailboard crashed to the ground and lay there like a ramp.

Hirka saw one of the riders on the ground. She ran down the ramp, which bounced beneath her. With a wave of nausea she realized that another rider was lying motionless under the tailboard. She didn't stop. She ran away from the cart. Away from the shouts.

But there were no longer any shouts. Just the sound of someone riding off at a tremendous speed.

Don't look! Run! Just run!

But Hirka couldn't help but look. She turned. A black figure was crouched on the roof of the cart, staring by turns at her and the man fleeing on horseback.

Not me! Go after him! He's bigger!

"HIRKA!"

All hope was lost. It was her they wanted. She ran up a slope. Her feet threatened to give out on her and she pulled at the moss to drag herself up. She could hear him coming after her. She tasted blood. A strong hand grabbed her by the tunic, which tore at the neck, and she fell onto her back. She wanted to scream, but she couldn't.

NO! No …

She lay in the moss with the weight of a black monster on her. It sat astride her and pinned her arms to the ground. It was like being back in the pit again. But this time he wouldn't budge. He locked her hips between his knees, and he had a firm grip on her wrists. White eyes sparkled like ice in the darkness.

Wolf eyes.

Rime?

The shadow tore off a black hood and stared at her. A white ponytail fell down into her face.

"Rime? RIME!" Was he really here? Her chest collapsed with relief. *Rime.*

He let go of her. She raised her hands to his jaw. Ran them over his face as if to confirm what her eyes were seeing. It was him. He had come. He had saved her! Dressed as Kolkagga, he had scared Slabba's men off. She laughed, but it sounded more like a sob.

"Rime! You scared the wits out of me! And out of them!" Hirka glanced over at the motionless figures by the cart. The laughter caught in her throat. It was too dark to see the faces over there, but there was no sign of life. They could have been rocks on the road, had she not known better. Her elation withered.

"Rime, what have you done?" She took her hand away from his face. He stared at her. She searched his eyes for regret over what had just happened, but she couldn't find any.

His voice was hoarse. Cold as the night. "They'd have killed *you* if they'd had the chance."

Hirka swallowed. That wasn't true. What he was saying wasn't true. These were not the men who had hog-tied her and thrown her into a wooden crate. They were probably ordinary men. Men with a job to do. Now they were dead.

"We can't stay here. We have to move." Rime got up and pulled her to her feet. Hirka hesitated. She had a lot she wanted to say. Rime had saved her. Not just now—he had been there during the Rite too. She had seen his face when the Ravenbearer revealed the truth about her. The truth that swept through the hall like wildfire.

"Rime, I couldn't tell—"

"Of course not. Some things can't be told. It's fine." He sounded like he meant it. As though it didn't have anything to do with him. Maybe it was all an act? Or maybe he had other things to think about. He had just killed, after all.

Determined to take his mind off it, Hirka started to talk. Unsteadily at first, like a newborn calf. Trying to create a sense of order, to make sense of everything she had seen and heard. She told him about Urd. About the man with the puppets. And about the blind. It gradually got easier and she found her own voice again. Talked faster and faster. She asked questions she tried to answer herself. Questions about the stone circles, and about what Urd wanted her for.

Rime didn't respond. He let her purge herself while they plowed onward between tall conifers. Occasionally she glanced up at his back to make sure that he was still listening. He never turned toward her. All she could see was his white hair. Most of it was gathered in a ponytail that fell down over what looked like a flat, square rucksack. It was as black as his clothes and held in place by wide black straps that crossed his chest.

White fairy's kiss glittered like stars on the forest floor. They were bigger here than back home in Elveroa. Hirka stopped again.

"Where are we going?" She hadn't thought about that until now.

"To higher ground, while we can still get the lay of the land."

"No! Rime, we have to go back. The Council has to be told about Urd! And about the blind!"

"The Council knows about the blind, Hirka."

"What about Urd? They don't know that he's the one who—"

"It doesn't make a difference to them. They'll do what they stand to gain the most from, regardless."

"But … if we can explain to them that—"

Rime stopped and looked at her. She stopped too.

"I've grown up with them, Hirka. I've seen them play with people's lives and futures. The Council won't help you. The Council has condemned you to death. As long as they get what they want, the truth doesn't matter. They wouldn't be where they are now if it did."

He kept walking. Hirka swallowed. He was right. Of course. She was naive, thinking a simple solution could be found. Had she not personally tried to explain herself to these powerful people? She had bled for it. Her words were worth nothing.

But Rime could explain! He was one of them.

"They'll listen to you!"

Rime was some distance ahead of her. He disappeared between two enormous boulders. Hirka hurried after him. "Rime?" Where was he? Not even the moonlight reached between the boulders. They were slick with moss. She felt her way forward.

"Here."

She looked up in the direction of the voice. Rime was on top of one of the boulders. It was the size of a small mountain. He reached out to her and helped her up far enough so that she could get a foothold. Then he continued up. Jumped toward the top and pulled himself up. He reached down to help her when he was at the top, but Hirka made it up on her own. She didn't sit down either. Didn't want him to think she was tired, though in truth she was close to blacking out. She was starving.

They were standing on the highest boulder in the area. There were a lot of them, scattered here and there, as though the gods had played dice and never cleaned up after themselves. The game now lay here, forgotten and overgrown with moss. The moon hung above the forest. The sky was bruised. In the distance she could see the sprawling mountaintops of Blindból. It didn't look like they had gone that far.

"They'll listen to you," she repeated.

"Hirka, let me try to explain the position we're in. The Council couldn't care less whether or not you broke the law. You were in Ravnhov and prevented them from assassinating Eirik. They probably would have succeeded, had it not been for you. That alone is reason to kill you. You've escaped from the pits and you've killed—"

"I haven't killed. Urd killed them! He—"

Hirka shut her mouth. Rime looked at her. He knew she hadn't killed anyone. "I get it," she whispered. "I didn't kill them, but that doesn't matter."

"You're learning." Rime drew his sword from its scabbard and chopped a couple branches off a tree that had grown up between the boulders. He started to weave them together into a large mat. Maybe he was settling in for the night. Hirka didn't know what else to do, so she helped. They sat in silence for a moment before she dared to ask. "Who were they?"

"Who?"

"The guardsmen who died in the pits."

"There are thousands of guardsmen in Mannfalla. I didn't know them."

Hirka couldn't bear to ask about the others. The ones lying by the cart. She had to look on the bright side. She was alive. Rime wasn't saying more than he had to, so it was up to her to lighten the mood. "That was a great idea. You really scared them. Dressing up as Kolkagga and hounding them over stock and stone."

She laughed. Rime didn't. He got up and hopped down from the boulder with the woven mat in his hands. Hirka didn't have time to remind him how high up they were. She leaned over the edge, but he was walking around, apparently unhurt, on the ground below. He camouflaged the mat with moss and grass, positioning it right up against the boulder. He stepped on it and the twigs gave a couple of cracks.

A warning system. He climbed back up to her, but she didn't have to ask who he was expecting.

Kolkagga. Actual Kolkagga.

"And those clothes! Where in the Seer's name did you get those clothes?" She laughed again, but something didn't smell right. She suddenly didn't feel so well.

"You talk too much," he said. He turned his back to her and chopped off a couple more branches. Hirka stared at him while he finished chopping. Then he sheathed his sword again. Quickly. Without looking. As though he had done it hundreds of times a day, all his life. Hirka pulled the sleeves of her tunic over her hands to keep warm, but it didn't help. The cold she was feeling came from within, pushing an unwelcome suspicion to the surface.

Rime started to weave another mat out of twigs. An eternity passed before he next spoke. "The clothes are mine."

Hirka got up and took a couple of steps back. The figure in front of her didn't meet her gaze. The clothes were his. His own. He didn't need to dress up. Didn't need to get them from anywhere.

The truth came so hard and fast that the wind was knocked out of her.

"You're one of them! You're Kolkagga!"

"Lower your voice! Do you want half the world to know where we are?"

"You killed. You kill …"

"You're alive, aren't you?" He said it as a matter of fact. Completely devoid of feelings. Was this a nightmare? Was she going to wake up?

"I'm alive because three men are dead!"

And Father. And Eirik, nearly. The prisoner. The guards. I'm alive because others have died.

"Would you rather be dead?!" Rime hissed. He grabbed a hold of her and pushed her firmly to the ground again. Hirka didn't answer. She curled up into a ball and gnawed on her tunic.

He was one of them.

Rime was Kolkagga.

SLABBA'S SLIP UP

Urd woke with a start. He'd heard something. He was sure of it. He raised a hand to his throat, but that wasn't it. The same gnawing pain as always, but no Voice. He sat up, tangled in sweat-drenched bed linen. Had he slept at all? When had he last slept?

His dreams weren't like they used to be. They were dark and disturbing. They stayed with him. Urd's hands were clammy. They were here. They'd come. Time was up.

No! It couldn't be. He had protection! He swung his feet down onto the cool stone floor. A narrow arrow slit let a shaft of moonlight into the room. Urd's eyes swept the floor. He could see a circle of deeper darkness around his bed. The stone tiles reflected the moonlight, but where it fell on the circle of raven's blood, it disappeared. It was absorbed. The protection was intact. The blind couldn't reach him here. None of them.

What in Slokna's name was he thinking?! What was he? A petrified child? One of Damayanti's trembling girls? Had he lost his mind? What did a man like him have to fear? Nothing!

Someone knocked three times and he jumped up. The knocking grew louder and a familiar voice stuttered: "U-Urd-fadri?"

Urd grabbed the robe hanging over the armchair and threw it on. He tied the belt around his waist as he headed for the door. He unlocked and opened it. The unoiled hinges creaked, as they were supposed to. If anyone tried anything, he'd hear them coming.

"This better be a matter of life and death!"

Rendar stood before him with bags under his eyes. He'd fallen asleep at his post. Rendar would have to go, he was good for nothing. Too young, like so many of the guardsmen. And nowhere near as ambitious as he ought to be.

"There's—there's a man outside." Rendar hugged his helmet to his chest.

"A man?" Urd raised an eyebrow. Could he have been any less specific? Doubtless his parents were siblings.

"He s-says it's urgent."

Urd sighed. His patience was wearing thin. "Who is it? I assume he has a name and a face?"

"I … He wouldn't tell me his name. He's … big."

Rendar threw his arms out to illustrate a man of significant girth.

Slabba. Blackest Blindból! What is he doing here?

Something must have gone wrong. Slabba ought to have been halfway to Ravnhov with the girl by now. Urd stalked along the corridors with Rendar on his heels. The young guardsman was all but clueless when it came to his duties, including discretion. Urd stopped for a moment and stared at him.

He waited until Rendar had taken the hint and withdrawn before continuing to the doors in the entryway. The bolt had been drawn back and one of them was ajar. The idiot had probably just mumbled "wait here" before rushing to wake him. Risking his life! He'd make sure he didn't forget that anytime soon.

He could see Slabba through the chink of the door. He opened it and somehow managed to pull him inside before slamming the doors and locking them.

"Never, I said! Never set foot here!"

Slabba was quivering like pudding. He didn't look at all well. His skin was pale, almost green. He was sweatier than usual, not that that said much. "It's all gone to Slokna! We're done for!"

"Hush!" Urd hissed, pulling the wreck of a man into the sitting room. The wine goblets were still on the table by the fire. Both his and Hirka's. Slabba collapsed into the chair the girl had been sitting in. "Could I trouble you for a drink?"

"What are you doing here, Slabba? Where's the girl?"

"Kolkagga have her!"

"Have you completely lost your—"

"Kolkagga, Urd! He attacked us before we'd even made it to the Blackwood."

"*He ...?*"

Slabba got up and started pacing around the room, rubbing his arms. "He killed two of my men. I'm lucky to be alive! What am I going to do, Urd? What are we going to do?! They have her. They're going to work out who owns the cart. I'm a dead man! *We're* dead men, both of us!"

"Idiot! If Kolkagga had her I'd know by now. No one's brought her in, Slabba. No one."

"I'm telling the truth! If I wasn't, I'd have told you there were five of them, but he was alone. One man, Urd! One! All in black, out of nowhere. He was suddenly just there. On the roof of the cart!"

"And what did you and your men do, Slabba? Piss yourselves?"

"He was Kolkagga!"

Urd didn't reply. For once in his life, Slabba had a point. If it really had been one of the black shadows, even *ten* of Slabba's men wouldn't have made a difference.

"Could I please have a drink? I need a drink."

Urd shut out Slabba's irritating, girlish voice. He needed to think. What had happened? If Kolkagga had found the girl, why hadn't they brought her in yet? Why didn't the Council know anything? Kolkagga would have made it back to the city in a fraction of the time it had taken Slabba. So why?

Slabba must have blabbed. He'd cracked and confessed. Now

he was standing here lying to mislead Urd. That was the only explanation.

"How could they have known the girl was in the cart, Slabba?"

"Because she jumped out! She scampered up a slope and into the forest like a rabbit."

Urd locked eyes with him. Searched for a tell in his gaze. For the slightest indication of a lie. It had to be there. The girl had been tied up in the crate with enough dreamwort in her system to knock out a horse. She couldn't have run anywhere.

Slabba sobbed and turned away from Urd, as if that would conceal the fact that he was falling apart. Muck dripped from the mustard-colored tunic that was pulled taut across his buttocks. Urd wrinkled his nose. What in Slokna's name was wrong with him? Had he soiled himself? Urd followed the trail of muck from Slabba to the chair he'd been sitting on. The chair Hirka had been sitting on. It wasn't muck. It was stew. It oozed out across the chair. Squeezed out of the blanket she'd had wrapped around her.

The truth hit him like a spear. She had tricked him. She had tricked *him*! That cursed rot had tricked him! Urd got up and swept the goblets off the table. They clattered to the floor and rolled over to the fireplace. Slabba took an uncertain step back toward the wall.

"Come!" Urd said, heading for the door.

"Where? Where are we going?"

"To find something to drink."

Slabba followed him. They walked through the house and out into the back garden. It hadn't been tended since Urd's father had died. But the view of the river and Blindból never failed to impress.

"Don't worry, Slabba. It's a minor setback. We'll sort it out."

"Sort it out?! How? You've lost her! I didn't even know what she was when you asked me to take her. I thought she was a relative. I thought you were joking!"

Urd started to bare his teeth but then managed to smile. Slabba had already started covering his back. He was lost. He would no longer be of any use. "Let's take things one step at a time, Slabba. First of all, who saw you come here?"

"No one. I swear! I wouldn't have come if there was any chance of being seen."

"Good. Do you have any meetings set up for tomorrow?"

"No. I'm going to pay that damned tea merchant in the Catgut a visit. I swear he hides the best teas under the counter and just gives me brackish water! What's the plan?"

"I'll show you. Can you see what I've hidden there?" Urd leaned over the edge and stared down into the river far below. Slabba followed his lead, like a sock puppet. Urd pushed him with both hands. It took astonishingly little effort. Slabba's heavy torso did the job itself. He had no way of regaining his footing to avert disaster. He didn't say anything either. Just flailed helplessly. And fell.

A moment later, Urd heard Slabba scream just before his body hit the rocks below. Silence descended. Then there was a splash. Urd wrinkled his nose. Slabba had always been tardy. Even when it came to his own death scream. At least now he had one less thing to worry about. As did Slabba's wife. She was young enough to be his daughter and probably would have thrown herself at Urd's feet in gratitude if she had been here. Now there was a thought. Perhaps he would pay her a visit when Slabba's body washed up in the slums. To offer his condolences, of course.

The fat merchant had made his last mistake. As had the girl with the red hair. He was Urd Vanfarinn. His family had an army of three hundred guardsmen. Loyal men who had served the family for generations. Now they would all make themselves useful.

But first he had to make the most important decision of his life. Should he tell the Voice that he had lost the girl or not? Urd could hear the dogs whimpering at the front of the house.

It had started to rain.

THE SHADOW

Rime was Kolkagga. The Seer's assassin. He was everything Hirka feared and fled from. He was the reason for all the sleepless nights. The reason she froze at every sound from the woods. He was the reason Father was resting in Slokna. He was Eirik's fever. Tein's bloodthirst. He was death.

She had nearly cried with relief when she saw him. Relief because there was someone who wanted to help her in this fight. Not just someone. Rime. And now here he was. Kolkagga. A confirmation of the truth she couldn't escape. The Council was never going to listen to her. Or spare her life.

There wasn't even rage or malice behind their desire to kill. They didn't hate her. Maybe it was born of fear. She was an outsider, after all. But they wanted to rid themselves of her as easily as they breathed, simply because it was the most expedient thing to do. They wanted to maintain stability. Pull out the weed. Purge the kingdoms of the rot.

Hirka straightened up. The wounds inflicted by the Council's sword still smarted. Had she only had her bag, she could have rubbed something on them. They'd get infected if she wasn't careful.

"So they've really sent Kolkagga after me?"

"Yes."

"To kill me?"

"Yes."

"That's not how the world works. You can't just kill people willy-nilly." She sounded like a child, but she wasn't anymore. After all, she'd been to the Rite. Hirka smiled bitterly in the dark.

"The Seer gives and the Seer takes," Rime replied.

"Gives what, Rime?!" She got up. The moon was behind him. Outlining him, as if to show her where he was. As if to warn her. Be careful. Here he is. With broad shoulders and powerful thighs, made to catch anything that tried to run away. He turned to face her.

"He gives the answer to all questions," he said mechanically.

"Cursed crones' talk! He gives answers so you never *ask* questions!" Hirka's words were like an echo from Father in Slokna. Rime hesitated, but she didn't think it was because he was considering what she had said. More because he was considering what he was going to say. But the Seer's sovereignty didn't concern her anymore. It was dead to her. No words would ever change that.

"I can show you what He has given *me*, Rime." Hirka lifted her tunic and turned her back on him. She was burning now. Burning to show him what the Raven really was. How unwilling the holiest of the holy was to intervene.

"This is what He has given me! Do you think I'm sorry to be cut off from His mercy? Do you?!" She let go of the tunic and looked at him again. He had tensed his jaw. His eyes had narrowed in anger, as though the wounds on her back were her own fault.

"The Council's misdeeds are not His. We follow His word, not theirs."

"So what in Slokna are you doing here, Rime?!" She tried to make him see how illogical he was being. How he couldn't see what was right in front of him. "If you follow His word, and He wants me dead, why are we here? Why am I still alive?!"

"I DON'T KNOW!"

His shout echoed between the boulders. Frightened crows alighted from the edge of the forest. He looked like a ghost, standing there. One of the blind. Pale against the black sky. He was a shadow. A figment of her imagination. Had she gone mad? Maybe she'd wake up soon. Maybe she was still in the cramped pit in the vault in Eisvaldr, dreaming that Rime had saved her.

An even darker truth revealed itself to her. Rime hadn't come to save her. The Seer had asked him to kill her, and here he stood, at war with himself. Hesitating. But he didn't know why he was hesitating, why he couldn't bring himself to kill her or hand her over to the Council. So far he'd followed orders. He'd caught her. The question was: where would he go from here?

Hirka wanted to scream, to scream that Rime was an idiot for being willing to kill, in the Seer's name or otherwise. But she couldn't scream. She hadn't realized it until now, but she was bargaining for her life.

The man before her was not thinking clearly. He was an animal. A wolf. Right now he was as likely to kill her as not. It was down to the flip of a coin. She was at the mercy of his inner turmoil. His conviction. His faith. She promised herself that she would never believe in anything or anyone, as long as she lived.

Hirka swallowed. Her words had to be chosen with great care. She took a step closer to him. "I've only seen the Seer once," Hirka said. "And all He did was lock me in a pit. He could have killed me on the spot. But He didn't. Wouldn't I already be dead, if that's what the Seer had wanted?"

Rime closed his eyes and bowed his head. The weight lifted from his shoulders. He nodded.

"I've never taken a life," she said, bolder now that she'd seen him land on the right side. "I've eased suffering. Stitched people up. Talked them through their pain. You've killed them. Which of us has best served the Seer, Rime?"

"Get some sleep. We have to be up before daybreak."

THE TAIL

The sun crept out from behind the mountains, giving the world back its colors. But some of them were unrecognizable. Hirka stared at her reflection in the river. Her hair was dripping brown, colored by tree bark. She tightened her grip around Rime's knife.

"I'm going to look like a boy …"

"You already look like a boy," Rime replied.

The words hurt her more than they should have. He was crouched on the riverbank, his elbows resting on his knees, tall reeds hiding him from view. His scabbards stuck out behind him on each side. He had changed his clothes. He was no longer Kolkagga, he was Rime An-Elderin. The guardsman who had pulled her up out of the Alldjup, wearing the same light-colored shirt with slits in the sides. His bag was on the ground. That had changed color too. It was brown now, like her hair. A trick, a bag that could be turned inside out to blend in. It was starting to dawn on her where the stories about Kolkagga came from. The warriors no one could see. Invisible at night, invisible during the day.

Kuro had reappeared. Once again she'd thought he was gone for good, but the raven never let her down. He was currently eyeing up a bundle next to Rime's bag. Hirka hoped it was something to eat.

Rime looked at her. Hirka lifted the knife and started to hack at her hair, cutting away big handfuls at a time. She looked like an animal. The shoulder of her woollen tunic was torn. She wanted to say she couldn't even remember the last time she'd had a proper night's sleep, but her reluctance to show weakness stopped her. If only she could sink under the water, into a soundless world. Like in the bathhouse in Ravnhov.

She found herself thinking about Tein. What would he say if he could see her now? With Rime An-Elderin. With Kolkagga.

"Finish up. We need to get moving," Rime said, getting up.

"Where are we going?"

"Mannfalla."

She looked at him. Had he lost his mind? He seemed fine, apart from what he had just said. His eyes were clearer than they had been only a few hours ago. Calmer. He was no longer a starving, confused wolf. He knew what he was doing.

"Mannfalla? Sure, that sounds brilliant, Rime. Let's go there. I've got loads of friends there. Urd, the Council … even the Seer! His love for me knows no bounds." She crossed her fingers in the sign of the Seer, like an augur.

"Don't forget Kolkagga," he replied with a straight face. He started picking up her hair from the ground. "Kolkagga have been looking for you for more than a day. They'll have looked under every tile in the city by now. From now on they'll spread themselves out from Mannfalla like a hail of arrows. Out here we're easy prey. However, if we survive in Mannfalla until tomorrow, then we'll have a chance. It'll buy us some time."

"But they have guardsmen on all the gates. Probably more than usual just now. Even if we were stupid enough to try, there's no way we'd get *into* Mannfalla."

"You're forgetting the most important thing."

"What? That you're Rime An-Elderin? The holy idiot? The good luck charm who thinks with his little toe and goes wherever he wants?" She rolled her eyes.

He got up and gripped her shoulders. The sudden show of intimacy felt threatening. It niggled at something close to her heart that was better off left alone. "Use your head. They expect outlaws to *leave* the city. It might well be impossible to get out, but not *in*."

"We don't know that for sure," she mumbled, dropping one final fistful of hair on the ground.

"We don't know anything for sure. But we have one thing that works in our favor." He let go of her shoulders, but the heat from his hands lingered. "No one will know what I've done yet, or that we're together."

"Urd has to know, doesn't he?" she asked, thinking about the third rider who had made a run for it while Rime watched her from the roof of the cart.

"He only knows it was Kolkagga, not that it was me. And he won't tell anyone what little he knows. Even a holy idiot can work that much out."

Hirka could feel her cheeks burning. She should have thought of that. Urd couldn't tell anyone about her or what he had done. It was a relief to realize.

"The only thing he can do is send his family guardsmen out to find you," Rime continued. "But that's nothing to worry about. There's only a couple hundred of them. Kolkagga would find you first anyway."

She stared at him, but nothing suggested he was trying to be funny. Hirka adjusted the cloak around her shoulders. It was his, and almost brushed the ground when she wore it. "My hair's still wet," she said. "It'll stain your cloak."

Rime reached out and ran his fingers through her hair. "It'll dry as we walk," he said. She swallowed and nodded.

"The city gates are just beyond the ridge. The road's a couple hundred paces east. We'll run into a lot of people."

Hirka nodded again. She knew that. Rime continued.

"The cloak helps. It hides your tail." His cheeks colored slightly for a moment.

Hirka smiled. "You mean it hides the fact that I don't have a tail?"

"It does, but that's not enough."

"It'll have to be."

"They're looking for a tailless, red-haired girl. They'll be paying particularly close attention to people's tails."

Hirka bit her lip. He was right. She would have asked to see her tail if she were guarding the city gates. It was the easiest way of ruling people out.

"Then let's not go together," she said. "If they catch me, you can't be with me. There's no other way."

"There is."

"Oh?"

Rime turned away from her before answering. "You need to have a tail."

Hirka laughed. "What, do you expect me to *grow* one?" No sooner were the words out of her mouth than she realized what he was getting at. She backed away. Rime picked up the bundle by his bag. He opened it and threw it down on the ground.

Hirka swallowed. A tail lay before her, in a coil that loosened as she watched. Fine hairs were all too visible against the bloodless skin. It tapered into a brown tangle. There should have been a man attached to the other end, but all she could see was a bloody stump. The insides bulged around the tailbone, which protruded from the center like a cracked egg.

An image of one of the men who had accompanied the cart pushed to the forefront of Hirka's mind. A man lying on the ground as she ran away. It was his. The tail was his. Part of his body, without ... its owner.

She turned away and closed her eyes. She'd thought there was food in the bundle. Emergency rations. Her stomach churned, threatening to expel the mushrooms they'd eaten for breakfast. She was such a child. What had she expected? Rime had tidied up during the night. Of course he had. He couldn't leave bodies and carts lying on the side of the road. They'd attract half the guardsmen in Mannfalla. They might as well have left a map showing where they were hiding. But what had he done? Apart from carving one of them up?

The nausea wouldn't abate. Rime spoke again. He sounded indifferent, as if he were talking about a cured ham.

"It was hanging upside down overnight. It won't bleed anymore. We'll thread it through the tail hole in your trousers so they'll see it if you're asked to lift the cloak." He hesitated for a moment. "It's not like he needs it anymore," he added.

Hirka opened her eyes again and looked at him. He met her gaze, but it was as if he were looking at her from far away. As if he were here and she were in Ravnhov, several days apart. If he felt anything, it was impossible to see from here.

"Well, that's simple enough," Hirka said tersely.

Rime nodded and took the knife from her. Hirka turned around. She stared up at the sky. If only the sun would rise quicker. She longed for its warmth. She could feel it already. No. That was Rime's hands. Warm against her hips. He kneeled down behind her.

"I'm attaching a strip of cloth to the end," he said. "We'll need to tie it around your waist to carry the weight."

Hirka nodded. She swallowed again and again. Rime's hand loosened her belt and she felt his fingers on her back. A dead man's tail was pulled across her skin and threaded through the hole in the trousers she had inherited. A hole she'd never had any use for. The tail was cold and heavy. It seemed to get heavier and heavier. It was too heavy to carry. Too heavy.

Hirka felt something force its way up her throat. Unstoppable. She fell to her knees in the undergrowth and heaved. Nothing came up, no matter how much her stomach twisted. Bile ran from the corners of her mouth. She sobbed. Everything she'd been through was threatening to overwhelm her.

She raised herself up onto her hands and tried to crawl away, but she couldn't move. Rime had locked his arms around her. He was on his knees behind her, holding her firmly. He put one of his hands over her mouth and pulled her head back. She twitched. The man in the vaults had done the same. But this wasn't him. This was Rime. She felt his lips against her ear. His breath. He spoke.

"Everyone dies. It doesn't change anything. Everything dies. As sure as you're alive right now. Nothing changes, Hirka. We're torn apart and put back together, as something new. You're the sky, you're the earth, water, and fire. Living and dead. We're all dead. Already dead."

Hirka sobbed again. Rime was a new weight on her back. Like Vetle when they'd been hanging over the Alldjup. "I'm no one!" Hirka didn't recognize her own voice. It forced its way out, half-smothered by Rime's hand. "Slokna has taken everything I care about. I don't have a father, a home, not even my hair! I'm … a gift for the blind. I'm wearing a dead man's tail, a man who died so I could … Father …"

Rime tightened his grip, almost lifting her from the ground.

"We're already dead. All of us. Nothing can hurt us. Do you understand, Hirka?" She felt her body let go. The weight of what he was saying lodged itself in her chest. She understood. She slumped in his arms as if dead. The hand over her mouth loosened its grip. Warmth spread through her body. Warmth and the strength to lift her head. He was binding.

"Do you understand, Hirka?"

She nodded. "Already dead."

She became one with the Might. She turned to dust. She dissipated and was scattered. The wind gripped her and she rose up through the forest, through the landscape, through Slokna, and into the stars. She was a wind of sand and dust, and she blew through Rime. He gathered her up and made her whole again. Until she ended up back where she'd started. In a very real world, surrounded by reeds reaching out to the newly risen sun.

Already dead. Nothing could hurt someone who knew nothing would last. There was nothing left to fear. Rime got up behind her, pulling her up with him. She felt weightless in the Might's grip. It flowed through her and disappeared down into the earth. Would it settle there and rot, now that it had been through her?

"Who are you?" His question was abrupt, but not without warmth. She knew he was trying to bring her back, but she couldn't make herself say it in front of him. He asked again. "Who are you, Hirka?"

"I'm the rot," she said, hollow with grief. "Everything I touch rots and dies."

He laughed. How could he laugh at that, twist the knife even deeper? Was that what Kolkagga did? Rime spun her around. "That was a bit dramatic, even for you." His words brought her back to reality. Showed her the fool in her, like a reflection. The weight of the world lessened and she smiled.

"I'm Hirka. Hirka Has-No-Tail."

"Are you alive, Hirka?"

"Yes, I'm alive."

"Good." He bent down and pressed his lips to hers. So suddenly and unexpectedly that it was over before she'd had time to react. He gave her a crooked smile. "One point to me if I start to rot."

She could feel herself gaping and tried to pull herself together. Her lips tingled. He had kissed her. Rime An-Elderin had kissed her. Quickly. It was like it hadn't even happened. But it had! She hadn't imagined it. He tightened the strip of fabric around her waist and let go. The weight of the tail made her wobble, but she managed to stay on her feet.

"Anyway, from what I've heard it takes a lot more than that, Hirka Has-a-Tail." He walked over to the river and spread her hair across the surface of the water. It floated away like rust-colored grass and disappeared.

Hirka swallowed, unable to stop herself from thinking about what he meant by "a lot more."

SHADOWS IN MANNFALLA

The walls appeared when they rounded the ridge. It was plain to see that the guardsmen had more to do than usual, running to and fro, searching carts and groups of people who were leaving to work in the tea gardens or to travel home after the Rite. But unlike previous years, most people seemed to be staying put. Nothing was as normal.

Every girl who left the city was being made to show their tail. Hirka gulped. Rime had been right. She pulled her cloak closer around her. The dead tail pulled at the strip of cloth around her waist. A sickening weight.

They approached the gate from the north. They'd agreed to walk right through like ordinary people. Rime would be a familiar face to many of the guards, so they were unlikely to run into any trouble. They walked side by side and tried to have a casual conversation about fish. About the redfins that were on their way up the Ora.

Hirka's heart was pounding in her chest. Was everyone staring at them? The two guardsmen leaning their heads together and whispering by the stall? The one standing on the wall looking down?

To Hirka's relief, none of the people ahead of them were stopped. Rime had been right once again. Nobody cared who was coming in. She saw his eyes darting around as they passed through. He spotted a middle-aged guardsman and raised his hand in greeting. The guardsman returned his greeting and continued searching a cart transporting animals out of the city. Hirka's shoulders didn't relax until they had made it through and the gate was out of sight.

They followed the Catgut up toward the square in front of Eisvaldr. Hirka had been here many times before, but something was different now. The stalls had crept out farther onto the street. She and Rime had to squeeze past sellers promising protection against both the blind and Odin's kin. Talismans and raven icons, silver jewelry, bone and mother-of-pearl. Incense and scented oils that were saturated with the Might, or so they claimed.

A scrawny man had his arms full of necklaces that had all been blessed in Eisvaldr. Many by the Seer himself, he promised. Guaranteed to be effective. A child of Odin would be forced to keep its distance from this jewelry.

"I doubt it," Hirka said and kept walking.

"You're marked!" he shouted defiantly after her.

A few people looked at her and drew away a little. Hirka could hardly believe her own eyes. What was wrong with them? The city had become completely consumed by fear. And by greed. She saw Rime a little in front of her and tried to push through the crowd, but suddenly everything came to a stop. No movement. She ended up with her nose against a man's back. He turned and glowered at her. What was going on?

Hirka strained her neck to see. An older woman was standing above the crowd. Probably standing on a box that Hirka couldn't see. She had long hair that had lost its luster several decades ago. It framed her face in wisps. She spoke with an unexpected vigor that carried easily.

"And she will be the first! She has opened the door. She is the vanguard." A couple of people standing at the front voiced their assent by repeating the final words of her every sentence, like an uncritical echo. "Vanguard! Vanguard!"

"The child of Odin comes first. Mark my words! The blind are her slaves! And with her she brings all the ashes of Slokna!"

"Slokna! Slokna!" the words were vacuously repeated by those in the first row.

Hirka tried to retreat, but she was stuck. Unbelievable! The old woman was talking about her. As if she were their enemy—one of the blind! Behind the old woman, a notice bearing the Council seal had been posted. A drawing. The text was impossible to read from where she was standing, but it wasn't necessary. Hirka knew what it said.

She stared at the drawing. Black ink on paper. The only splash of color was the hair. Red as blood. It was meant to be her. It was unmistakable. Hirka looked around, expecting the crowd to set upon her at any moment, but they were listening to the old woman, enraptured. They drank in every word, clueless to the fact that the one they feared stood among them.

It was like in her dreams. Last night she had stood on a mountaintop, surrounded by snow but with the blood boiling in her veins, and the blind had swarmed around her. Millions of them. They came every time she fell asleep. The dreams grew worse every night. The thirst grew stronger. Someone else's thirst. But they didn't see. Just like now. She'd feared crowds her entire life, but here she stood, safer than anywhere else and exactly what they were afraid of.

Hirka felt someone grab her. She tried to tear her hand away, then realized it was Rime. He pulled her through the crowd and farther up the street. Another notice was posted farther ahead. Two girls stood in front of it, pointing.

"Come!" Rime pulled her into an alley. They squeezed between a pile of sacks that smelled of moldering vegetation.

"That's me." Hirka stared out at the street, peering under Rime's arm, which he rested against the wall behind her. "That's me! They're saying I brought the blind here!" Hirka laughed. It was so absurd that it was impossible to be scared. Rime was more scared than her.

"I know! Let me think. We can't stay here."

A woman with a tub of wet clothes came walking along the alley. She nodded and squeezed past them. Hirka dared not say anything until she had passed them and was out on the street. "They're looking for me, Rime."

"And in doing that they actually admit they lost you. That's a first." Rime curled his upper lip as though he had eaten something he didn't like. "We have to find somewhere to hide. Somewhere people won't ask questions."

Hirka smiled. She grabbed Rime and dragged him back onto the street. "Come! I know where to go."

THE RAVENRY

Mannfalla's oldest ravenry was located high up in the east of the city. It was a longhouse intersected by a smaller wing in the middle. The walls leaned over the ridge. It was as if it were looking down on the rest of the city through narrow slits that didn't reveal any of its inner workings. It was like a fortress. Built from stone that blended in with the gray sky.

Hirka heard Rime stop on the path behind her. She turned to look at him. He'd laughed at her when she'd told him where they were going. He'd said that seeking out Ramoja was like knocking on the door of the red dome. Reluctantly, Hirka had told him the truth about the ravener. It couldn't hurt anymore. After all, Rime was a traitor now too.

So she'd told him. About Ramoja in Ravnhov, and about the gathering where Eirik had been stabbed. Rime had asked more questions than Hirka was able to answer. It pained her to destroy his perception of someone he'd grown up with. A friend of the family. Ilume's right hand. No wonder he was hesitating. She didn't feel great about it either. The last time she'd seen Ramoja, Hirka had been playing the part of Ravnhov's mighty salvation. Now she was an unearthed embling on the lam.

Hirka gave Rime an encouraging smile and hurried onward before she could change her mind. The murmuring of the ravens got louder the closer they got. There was no one in the courtyard. The porch doors were open, so they went in. Hirka knocked on the inner door.

"What if the others—"

Hirka shushed him. Rime had taken the lead so far, but now it was up to her. He had his doubts about her story, but he hadn't been in Ravnhov. Hirka had. She knew. Ramoja was no threat to them. She wouldn't give them up. Rime was probably the more likely threat in Ramoja's eyes. That's why he was wearing his cloak inside out, so no one could see the embroidered mark of the raven over his heart. His hood was pulled forward so his face was in shadow. Hirka swallowed. She opened her own cloak at the throat. It was tight. Picked up in a hurry from a cheap stall.

"Hirka! It's Hirka! Mama, it's Hirka!"

Hirka took a step back and eyed the peephatch in the door. The voice could only belong to one person. Hirka smiled. The door was flung open and Vetle threw himself at her, almost knocking her over. Ramoja appeared and extricated Hirka from his grasp. She sent Vetle into the kitchen, warning him not to tell anyone other than Joar and Knute that they had a visitor. It was a secret. Vetle nodded solemnly.

Ramoja looked out across the courtyard and spotted Rime.

"I have a friend with me, and we've come alone, Ramoja."

"In the Seer's name, Hirka ..." Ramoja stared at Hirka as if she had come back from Slokna.

Hirka did nothing. She just bit her lip while she waited for Ramoja's next move. It was up to her to decide what their relationship was now. Now that Hirka was an outlaw. Now that she was the rot.

Ramoja pulled Hirka into a hug, her bangles jangling.

"There were three men here searching the house barely an hour ago! No stone in the city has been left unturned looking for you. Where've you been, child?" She pushed Hirka away to get a look at her and ran a hand through her newly cut hair. Her eyes flickered as if it were too much to take in all at once.

"Joar!" she shouted without looking away from Hirka. A young man appeared in the corridor. "Joar, send the kitchen and the rest of the household home for the day. Tell them it's so they can recover from the guardsmen ransacking the place. And bar the doors." Joar nodded and disappeared with Vetle on his heels.

Hirka savored their welcome as if it were the Might. The unconditional consideration. The willingness to act, to protect her. The knowledge that Ramoja had been worried about her, even after the Rite. After she had found out what Hirka really was. And not least after she must have realized Hirka couldn't bind and would never be able to save Ravnhov.

"Ramoja, we have a long story to tell. But there's something you need to know first." Hirka looked at Rime. He lowered his hood. It pooled around his neck.

Ramoja's eyes widened. Then she lifted her hand and slapped him. Rime clenched his jaw, but he didn't move apart from that.

Hirka's mouth fell open. It was all going wrong before it had even started.

"I know what you are, Rime An-Elderin," Ramoja said through clenched teeth. "You're a murderer. Already dead. Kolkagga!"

Hirka gripped Ramoja's arm. "He saved my life!"

More people came out onto the porch. They spread out along the walls.

"Of course he did! To use you as a puppet. To find out what you know and use you to bring him here."

"No! No, you don't understand!" Hirka tugged at her tunic.

Rime had had enough. "There's no point in me being here," he said, turning to leave. Six men and two women were standing between him and the door. One of them slid the bolt across. The others had already drawn their swords. Swords that were nothing like

Rime's. These were plain steel. Clumsily wrought, like the one Father had in the chest. They were raveners. Ordinary people. Rime would kill them all if he had to. Hirka couldn't let that happen.

"Rime, stop!"

He stopped, to the obvious surprise of the others.

"They can't let you go, Rime. Think about it. They know I've brought you here because of Ramoja. They have no way of knowing you won't come back with every guardsman in the city. They have no way of knowing, Rime ... Please." Hirka stared at his back. The others stood as immobile as the beams supporting the building. The only sound was the ravens.

Rime turned to Ramoja. "How do you know what I am, Ramoja? Where did you hear that secret? From Ravnhov? You've been serving them behind our backs, yet here you are judging me for my choices. Who *are* you, Ramoja? Who is this woman who has spent a lifetime at my grandmother's side with her heart in Ravnhov?"

Hirka didn't dare breathe. Ramoja's dark cheeks glowed. There wasn't a good answer to Rime's accusations. He was right, and he had more to say. "You're threatening me because you know what I am. Because you're as disdainful as only a traitor can be. You're an outlaw, Ramoja. You've betrayed Mannfalla."

The air was thick with accusations. There wasn't room for two winners here. Hirka looked despairingly at the bolt locking the door. What had she done?

"Rime!" Vetle came running out onto the porch, past his mother and into Rime's arms. Ramoja reached out for him, a silent scream on her lips. Rime put an arm around Vetle's chest. Ramoja looked like she might fall apart. She'd lost the upper hand.

Hirka's despair grew. This wasn't right! This wasn't what she had intended. None of the people in this room were enemies. Everyone here had betrayed someone, in one way or another. But too much had been said and done to bring them together now.

"Rime ..." Hirka didn't dare speak in more than a whisper. It was a quiet plea. He looked at her. Looked at the others. Then he pushed Vetle away.

"Go to your mother."

Vetle looked around, confused. The boy was aware enough to realize something was wrong. Ramoja met him halfway and pulled him close to her. Hirka took a deep breath. This was the only chance she had. This brief moment.

"You're a traitor, Ramoja. You've betrayed the Council and Mannfalla. But so has he." Hirka pointed at Rime. "He can walk out of that door whenever he wants, and you know that. You all know that."

Hirka surveyed the sweaty faces around her. Some were old, some young. But they were all afraid. They might be able to stop one Kolkagga between them, but it was far from a sure thing. And few of them would come out of it unscathed if they tried, that much was certain. They had a lot to lose, and it was easy to read in their eyes.

Hirka continued. "He can leave whenever he likes. Believe me. I've seen him. He can leave, but he's choosing not to. Because he's in just as deep as you are. We've all made the same choice." She knew she was taking a chance. She didn't know these ymlings. She just had to assume there was a reason they were willing to protect Ramoja. "He's choosing not to leave because everyone in this room has taken the same path."

Hirka took off her cloak. She let it fall to the floor. "And I don't know what it's like for you ordinary folks, but I can assure you that being on the run makes emblings tired and hungry." She untied the strip of fabric around her waist that was holding the tail in place. "And I refuse to take another step wearing a dead man's tail."

She let the tail fall to the floor and folded her arms across her chest. She had done what she could. The others stared at the tail. She recognized the reactions on every single face. The same disgust she had felt. Some eyes widened. Others closed. One woman put her hand over her mouth. Hirka said a silent prayer, hoping they'd realize what she'd been through. That the coiled piece of dead flesh on the floor would explain what sort of situation she and Rime were in.

Vetle reached out to touch the tail, but Ramoja stopped him. She nodded to the others. Hirka heard swords sliding back into scabbards. She closed her eyes in relief, and breathed out for what felt like the first time since they had arrived. Ramoja took a step toward Rime.

"How will we ever be able to trust you?" It wasn't an accusation. It was a genuine question. She wanted an answer.

Rime met Ramoja's mournful gaze. "You can trust me because I don't trust Urd." He looked between Ramoja and Vetle. Hirka didn't understand what Urd had to do with anything at that precise moment, but his words seemed to have an effect.

Ramoja stared at Rime.

"I've always known," he replied to her unasked question.

She lifted her chin. "Let's eat," she said, and it was the most beautiful thing Hirka had heard in days.

ON A KNIFE'S EDGE

Rime ate in silence while Hirka shared the whole story with the others. She was inexhaustible. She talked with her mouth full, unable to decide what was more important: eating or talking. He'd never seen her like this.

She described a deluge of events that had randomly befallen her, and how she'd had little choice but to take things as they came. But that wasn't the way it had happened. Rime could hear what she couldn't hear for herself: the decisions she'd made. Not because she'd had to, or because she'd hesitated until she'd been forced into action. Hirka had made decisions simply because they were the right thing to do. Difficult decisions. Dangerous decisions. Like traveling to Ravnhov. Like leaving Ravnhov to stand face-to-face with the Seer. Like warning Eirik.

What would Rime have done? Why had he chosen Kolkagga? To serve the Seer? To fight the system from a safe distance? Really? Or had he made the simplest choice of all? Rime felt an unease growing in his chest. A warning. These thoughts were taking him down a path he'd prefer to avoid.

Hirka related the events with sensitivity and humor. From her days in the pit, the interrogation by the Council, the fall from the roof in Ravnhov, to carrying around a dead man's tail. Laughter came easily to those around the table. Had Rime not been able to see the pain in her eyes, he would have thought she was unmarked by everything that had happened. But he knew better. He had held her when it had been too much for her. Now she was talking like she couldn't wait to see what would happen next.

He remembered the look in her eyes when she had realized that he was Kolkagga. How the light in them had gone out. Since then she'd barely spoken to him, and then only reluctantly and flatly. As though he was some kind of monster, that she had no choice but to walk next to.

Rime finished the food in his bowl and soaked up the remains with a piece of bread. He tried to ignore the fact that he was being stared at. The group around the table made little effort to conceal their glances. Nervous. Scrutinizing.

They stared at Hirka, too, but more out of curiosity. They leaned back when they spoke to their neighbors, a blatant excuse to look behind her back. The tailless girl. He assumed she was used to it. But he was happy that nobody avoided sitting close to her. Near the rot.

Vetle sat right beside her. Next to his bowl sat the stone figure with the broken tail. "I have no idea," Hirka responded to a question from Joar, the youngest of the men. "All I know is that Urd has brought the blin—" She looked at Vetle and found another way of putting it. "He brought *them* here. The first. I swear."

The blind had many names. Nábyrn. The deadborn. The nameless. The first. The songless, Rime had also heard.

"He's not acting alone," Knute replied. "The Council knows. They're using it as a pretext to attack Ravnhov."

Rime knew that the raveners had few illusions about the powers that be in Eisvaldr, but Knute was wrong. All the same, he didn't say anything.

"The Council doesn't know a thing," Hirka answered. "I got these scars on my back because they wanted to know how *I* brought the blind here. That's how little they know. And Urd came to me and got me out of the pits on his own. He's *sick*. And not just in the head. I think there's something seriously wrong with him."

Ramoja got up from the table. "We've sent the help home, so we'll have to manage on our own tonight. Letters from the city will arrive over the course of the night. Will you see to them, Knute?"

Knute nodded. Letters had to come and go as normal, particularly now that they were harboring a good deal more than just ravens and raveners. Rime could tell that this lot meant business. They weren't just a bunch of disgruntled, overtaxed merchants, or families with children whose Rites never led to anything more than a brief visit to Mannfalla. These people discussed their problems so openly that they had to have been doing it for a long time. They knew each other so well they could have entire conversations without speaking a word.

Hirka had been right. Ramoja had betrayed the Council. But she was doing more than that. She was leading a group of men and women who wanted to topple them.

Rime felt his anger rise to the surface. An anger he had no right to feel. He stared out the narrow peephatch in the wall. Far below them lay Mannfalla. Sunlight broke through the clouds, making the wall shine. It was always the first thing to catch the light in the morning, and the last thing to let it go in the evening. The rest of the city had to make do with the wall's inclination to reflect it. People entered Eisvaldr through the tall archways, moving from darkness into light. The red dome was pale, as if asleep. The irony made Rime smile crookedly. The dome had never seen more activity in living memory. Inside sat twelve families deciding the fate of the world, simply because that's what they'd always done. And they did it for their own benefit.

He was meant to have joined them in a few years. Taken over Ilume's chair. The youngest ever, she'd said. He was the An-Elderin who had renounced his seat out of pure contempt, and now he felt anger at Ramoja's betrayal. He felt his blood boil because someone wanted to remove the twelve. Wasn't that what he'd always wanted himself?

The difference was that Rime had always respected the fact that the inner circle was the will of the Seer. Inherently flawed, but still His choice. So there were no alternatives.

"Vetle, it's time to go up to our room," Ramoja said. "You can play up there for a while."

Vetle voiced his displeasure loudly, but he let himself be convinced by Hirka's promise to play word games with him later that evening. Ramoja asked the rest of them to gather in the letter room, telling them she'd join them in a moment.

They sat in silence while they waited for Ramoja in the cross-shaped room at the center of the building, which had doors at all four cardinal points. Heavy beams crossed the ceiling like in a funeral ship. There was one window. It was bigger than any of the others, and revealed more of Mannfalla, but the frame was crooked. As if the walls had leaned outward and forgotten to take the glass with them. The walls were covered in shelves and drawers, all filled with letters and ivory and metal sleeves. There were also gloves, leather straps, oils, and feather trimmers. Letters were received here throughout the day, then marked, sorted, and delivered. Or collected and distributed to the city's inhabitants. At least those who could afford to pay for the service. The poor seldom used ravens.

Normally there'd be people working in the room, but Ramoja had sent them all home for the day. Nobody was to see her two guests. The slightest rumor of strangers or a tailless girl would be the end of them all.

Hirka had spotted the beams and started to climb. She sat on one of them with her legs dangling down. Two of the others sat down at a table that was hinged to the wall so that it could be folded up. The others stayed standing with their arms crossed, leaning against beams and walls. Rime remained on his feet too. Sitting down made you vulnerable. If anything were to happen, valuable time was wasted getting to your feet.

The ravens quieted down behind the closed door he was standing next to. They had started to make noise as soon as they heard people. Now maybe they'd noticed him, even though there was a door between them. It wasn't impossible. The Might grew stronger in him every day. He assumed that the ravens were the reason Ramoja had chosen a room with only two seats. With hundreds of ravens in the adjoining room, nobody could overhear what was being said.

Rime was very aware that he was being observed. They were six men and two women, not including Ramoja. Joar stood to his right. He was a broad-shouldered fellow with brown curls, maybe four winters older than Rime. Knute had seen twice as many winters, and his arms bore the most obvious signs of years spent in the company of ravens.

Rime had noticed their dialects. They came from every corner of Ym. A secret group within the worldwide raveners guild. The best raveners in the eleven kingdoms. The elite of their trade. Few knew the Council's secrets better than those who handled the letters. But how they had come together, and what kept the nine of them together, was more difficult to determine.

Ramoja came in. She asked Lea, who was closest to the window, to secure the hasps. The wind had picked up. An oil lamp hanging from a beam flickered in the draft.

"Does *he* have to be here?" asked Torje, a slim fellow from the north, with hair trimmed close to his head. There was no need to clarify to whom he was referring.

"He has already sacrificed more than all of us," Ramoja answered.

"If the girl is telling the truth," Lea said.

"I'm not lying," Hirka answered from her perch.

Rime was tense. Restless. He didn't have time to waste. He'd thought he had put the world behind him when he'd chosen Kolkagga. Now he'd been thrown right back into the middle of it—as an outlaw. Kolkagga were still on the hunt for Hirka, and it wouldn't be long before he was missed. It would be time to report back soon, and he would be absent. Nobody would have heard from him. How long would it take for the Council to start putting two and two together? He didn't have time to stand here arguing with treasonous raveners.

"Why would she lie? Use your head. Her face is plastered all over the city. She's been condemned to death and has no one to turn to. She's a child of Odin. An embling." Rime addressed each of them in turn. "If you woke up tomorrow and found out that you were in the same boat, what would you do? Where would you go?"

Several of them glanced up at Hirka. Rime continued. "And why would I pose a threat to you? I became Kolkagga to *escape* Eisvaldr. To escape having to deal with the twelve families. You think you know them, but you have no idea ..." He shook his head. "Still, I know enough to have you burned alive, each and every one of you, if that's what I wanted. And I could have taken every single life in this room, and nobody would have held me responsible for it. So tell me: why would any of us here speak with forked tongues?"

Nobody answered for a moment. Only Torje was willing to challenge him. "Because you still don't know who we are. You don't know what we're going to do, or when. You don't know whether there are *more* of us." The stress on that word was meant to suggest that there were a great many more. That was a lie. A strategic bluff, thrown out there to intimidate him, in case he was still loyal to the Council.

"What does it matter if I know or don't know?" Rime took a step toward Torje. "Nothing the guild is planning can make the situation we're in any better or any worse."

"We can eradicate all of you! Is that worse?"

"Torje!" Ramoja's voice came like the flick of a whip. Torje backed off with a snarl. His hand was at his hip even though none of them carried their swords. Rime felt the same reflex but managed to restrain himself.

We can eradicate all of you.

It didn't matter to Torje or anyone else here what he had or hadn't done. He was and always would be Rime An-Elderin. A symbol. An enemy, with a name they despised.

"At least then you'd have done something useful before you died," he replied and stared at Torje until the Northlander looked away.

"Slokna take me, you're all so dense!" came from above. Hirka smacked her forehead. "We're all in the same boat here! Can't you see that?"

Ramoja broke in. "Hirka is right. We have to assume that we have the same goal, and that it will cost all of us our lives if we fail. Rime, you and I have chosen our paths. You serve the Council as an assassin, as their weapon. I don't know where your loyalty lies when all is said and done. In any case, it's too late. The Council is going to fall." The others muttered in agreement around her. Ramoja continued. "If you want to honor your parents, do not try to stop us."

She was obviously trying to bait him, but Rime was too curious not to bite. "My parents had the same regard for the Council as everyone else."

"I doubt that, Rime. Ilume is good at keeping secrets. I had no better friend than your mother. Your parents died near Urmunai, taken by the snow, it was said." Rime pricked up his ears. "And maybe the snow did take them. We'll never know. What I do know is that they weren't going to Urmunai. Gesa woke me the night they left. You were asleep in your father's arms. Her eyes were like glass. There was something in them that I'd never seen before. I asked what was wrong, but she didn't say. All she told me was that you were leaving. For good."

"To go where?" Rime could feel himself growing restless. He knew what was coming.

"To Ravnhov."

Rime studied Ramoja's face for signs of deceit. She had a lot to gain from lying, but he found himself believing her. "What does it matter where they died?" His voice was sharper than he had intended it to be.

"Knowing where might not be important, but surely knowing *why* has to mean something?"

"You're making it sound like someone brought the snow down on us intentionally. There is no *why*."

"Come on, Rime! You said so yourself, use your head. They showed up at my home in the middle of the night to say goodbye before fleeing to the only sanctuary in the eleven kingdoms."

"Ilume would never have allowed it."

"Ilume didn't know. I kept my word to Gesa. I never told anyone that they had come to me first. Not just for her sake, but also to save my own skin. Had I said anything, it would have revealed that I knew their trip to Urmunai was a fabrication. Trust me, I have good reasons for never telling a soul about this."

"Why? Why would they want to leave Eisvaldr?"

"Why would *you*, Rime?" The warmth in Ramoja's eyes had returned. They revealed that she'd finally understood why he had chosen to be Kolkagga. It wasn't a thirst for blood. It was a necessity. Rime barely recognized his own voice when he answered.

"Because it would have cost more to stay."

Torje approached Rime and began to speak. Rime realized that he had suddenly become a new weight on the raveners' scales. An ally in the fight. Torje trembled with indignation, assuming that they had to be talking about murder.

"The Council has served its last lie! Blood will be repaid with blood!"

"Wait!" Rime grabbed his arm. "Not now. You can't do anything now, while the Rite is still on. Rumors or no rumors! The blind are in Ym and people need all the protection they can get."

Rime could picture a Mannfalla controlled by the blind. Destruction. Powerlessness. A place without the Might, and without life. He couldn't let anyone set out from Mannfalla unprotected now that he knew the blind were real.

The others glanced uncertainly at one another. At Ramoja. He had a point.

Hirka hopped down from the roof beam. She cocked her head. Her eyes were full of wonder. "How does the Council actually protect people? I felt no protection on the day of my Rite. But I felt the Might."

"You can feel the Might?" Lea's eyes widened.

Rime concealed a smile. They really knew nothing about Hirka. Had it been up to him, it would have stayed that way. She'd be safer that way. "She can feel the Might," he affirmed.

Torje was still skeptical. Or he was the only one willing to express his doubt. He may have been too quick to judge, but at least he said what he thought. Rime felt a seed of respect for something he had seen far too little of in his life.

"Even blue-blooded folk can barely feel the Might. You're lying, girl!"

Hirka hissed at him. "I can't feel it in chickens like you! But when it's strong, I can feel it. In Rime. In the Ravenbearer. In Urd." She shuddered. "When the Ravenbearer offered us protection on the day of the Rite, it felt cold. The same as when Urd killed the prisoner who ... when he killed him. Using the Might! He put his hand on the man's head and I felt the Might fill the room. Fill me. Not like with Rime. It was painful. Destructive. Familiar, yet unfamiliar. It's hard to explain. Everything was drawn toward the man's body. It was shaking. His eyes ..." Rime watched her swallow. "His eyes rolled back into his head. And he fell. There was blood. In his mouth. He …" Hirka looked at her hand as though she had done it herself. "Urd was leaning against the wall. He was panting. I wanted …"

Rime heard a sob behind him. Ramoja had wrapped her arms around herself and was slumping to her knees. He grabbed her before she collapsed entirely.

"Vetle … In the Seer's name …" She gasped, burying her face in Rime's shoulder. Lea came over and pulled her away pointedly, as though Rime's mere presence was going to make things worse.

Rime didn't pay them much notice. He was too busy staring at Hirka. When Urd had killed, the Might had felt the same to her as when she'd been offered protection at the Rite. An echo from the meeting he'd overheard in the dome came to him.

Maybe we ought to cancel the Rite entirely with the blind on the loose.

Why? Why?!

Because the Rite had never protected anyone.

Rime's blood ran cold. It was like being hit by an avalanche. An unstoppable certainty plowing through him. Ugly. Arrogant. Ice-cold.

"They've never protected anyone. They're taking the Might from people …" Rime's words made everyone stop. Those who were sitting stood up. Then everyone started talking at once.

But Rime didn't pay them any notice. He needed to think. Finish his thoughts. Had to fit the pieces together. This was too much to take in. Far too much. "Nobody skilled in the Might has been born in generations, not outside the twelve families. Of course not! They aren't protecting anyone. They've never protected anything other than their own sovereign rule."

Rime slumped onto a chair by the window and gripped the table. He stared at it. Dark wood. Born of the Might. Aged through the Might. Power in every growth ring. Every knot. "We've taken the

Might from people. To be the strongest. So as to never allow other families in."

He looked up at the others. They looked at him with concern, as though he was sick. Even Torje. It looked like there were more of them now. Or was he seeing double? "We've been burning the Might out of all of them." He looked at Hirka. At Ramoja's puffy eyes. Vetle had never been strong in the Might, even though he should have been. Now Rime knew why. "For how long?"

Ramoja put a hand on his shoulder. Hirka looked from one person to the next in confusion. It was too much for them too. They looked like they were going to fall. He couldn't let them fall.

Get up, Rime!

Rime looked around, but the voice came from within. Master Svarteld's disdain for fatigued muscles. There was no weakness in the master's world. No body over mind. Only mind over body.

It's your damned body! Get up!

Rime stood up. "I know that the Council is reeling. If we wish to see them fall, there has never been a better time for it. Not in generations," he said. "But you'll have to wait a little longer."

"Don't you dare, An-Elderin," Torje said. "This may be as new to you as it is to us, but it makes our cause infinitely stronger."

"Torje, do what you have to do, but I need answers first."

"Nobody can give you answers, Rime." It was Ramoja, her face drawn. "I've hoped for answers my entire life. Vetle's entire life. Nobody can give you what you want. No one can offer a good reason for why things are the way they are."

Hirka took a step forward. "He can," she said.

"Who?" Ramoja asked.

Hirka didn't need to say it. Rime answered for her. "The Seer."

Hirka moved toward him, her gaze shifting between wonder and certainty. He smiled cautiously. She understood. He could see that she understood. Torje snorted and Rime could hear the others laughing awkwardly. Rime didn't take his eyes off Hirka. Nor she him. He had to make the others understand.

"The Seer has the answers. He knows. He knows why."

Lea flung out her arms. "Nobody outside the Council has ever spoken with Him. Not even *you*, apparently. And you're the child He saved at birth. The An-Elderin child."

Torje chimed in. "And if you're going to get Him to talk, what makes you believe He'll give you answers? The Council is a viper's nest of lies and greed. That has to be at His behest?"

Several of them made the sign of the Raven on their chest. That surprised Rime. Their contempt for the Council ought to have extended to Him as well, to the Seer. But then, he didn't feel that way, so why should they?

"You're right, both of you. But I *know* they're acting without Him."

"What are you trying to say?" Knute put a tankard of ale down on the window ledge. The wind outside caused small ripples on the brown surface.

"I'm saying that the Council has been making decisions without Him. For how long, I don't know, but at least since Vanfarinn's death. The Seer would not have admitted Urd to the inner circle."

"But I saw Him," Hirka said. "I looked Him in the eyes during the Rite."

"So we know that He lives. And I'll get my answers."

Ramoja sighed. "Rime, what answer could He give that would satisfy you? No answer can justify an eternity of suppression and corruption. No answer can explain why they've stamped out the Might, if that's what they've done. None, Rime."

"Maybe. But I'm going to get my answers, regardless."

"We don't have the people or the time to waste on getting answers. Not even with a thousand men could you succeed in gaining an audience with Him," Torje said.

"You don't need a thousand men and you don't need time. I'll do it myself." Rime could feel power in his words, as though he were binding. As soon as the words were spoken, they were true. He was right. That was what he had to do. He had to see Him. The Seer he had lived and killed for. The beginning and the end. He who had all the answers. And if He turned out to be like the rest of the Council, it would be Rime's final act. But that didn't matter. Either way, he had already given his life to Him.

Torje slammed his fist into the wall. The ravens started to chatter. "Don't listen to him, he's going to ruin everything!"

"You've nothing to lose. I'll do it alone, and I'll do it tonight. Are you so thirsty for blood that you can't wait *one* night?"

None of them responded. A moment passed before Lea asked, "What did you have in mind?"

Rime nodded at her gratefully. He'd been given the time he'd asked for. "I'm going to break into the Seer's tower."

He left the room. He needed rest. Quiet. He heard the raveners talking over one another. They thought he had lost his mind. Maybe they were right. The problem was, he was relying on Hirka sharing in his madness. His Might became a storm when it was allowed to flow through her. Without her, he would never be strong enough to reach the Seer.

Hirka had spent the worst days of her life in Eisvaldr. Imprisoned. Bloodied. Condemned. Why would she ever set foot there again? She had rejected the Seer, so what could he offer that would convince her to follow him into almost certain death?

Torje's voice rose above the din. "Is he crazy?"

"The craziest of them all," Hirka replied. "If he thinks he's going alone, that is."

That's when Rime knew he was in danger. Because suddenly the rot seemed a small price to pay to be close to her.

RAMOJA'S STORY

It was early evening. Outside, the wind tossed the ravens around like scraps of cloth, but they were always quick to right themselves. To regain control between the towers of Mannfalla.

Hirka hadn't been able to sleep. It wasn't just her fear of the dreams that kept her awake. It was the thought of what they were planning to do that night. That would have kept anyone up—apart from Rime. He was asleep, which was a relief, because she'd been starting to wonder whether not needing sleep was some bizarre Kolkagga thing.

Ramoja had let them use a narrow room in the loft. It had two bunks, with one fixed to the wall above the other, like on a ship. Rime had claimed the lower bunk, and Hirka noticed his breathing grew quieter as she left the room. Even in his sleep, he was aware of people coming and going.

She climbed down from the loft and followed the sound of Vetle's chattering until she found the kitchen in the east wing, where Ramoja offered her some tea. Hirka asked for chamomile, or something else that might calm her nerves, though she doubted anything would help.

They sat at the corner of the long table. Ramoja's black hair shone in the light from the embers under the pot. Vetle sat at the other end of the table, drawing with a stubby piece of charcoal on a scrap of paper. Hirka sat watching him. He was drawing a raven. Hirka had seen his drawings before, but she was always surprised to rediscover that he drew better than she could. It was so easy to forget they were the same age.

"What happened to him?"

Hirka knew Ramoja would tell her. She had never asked because she had assumed Vetle had always been the way he was, since birth. But watching his mother shrink into herself earlier in the day had made her think again.

Ramoja moved a candle with two wicks closer to Vetle so he had better light to draw by. "You've seen it yourself. The Might sapped the life out of him. He was two summers old."

"But who? Who would want to hurt Vetle?"

"His father."

Hirka had never given much thought to the fact that Vetle was fatherless. It had just always been that way. Some people in Elveroa had whispered about it. Sylja had called Vetle a bastard and Hirka had told her she couldn't know that for sure. Maybe his father was dead. She wanted to ask, but she didn't need to.

"Urd is … his father," Ramoja whispered.

Hirka's eyes widened.

It couldn't be true! The boy sat drawing by the fire, without a care in the world. She couldn't see any of Urd's narrow, angular features in him. Vetle was a warm, happy boy. His nose was on the broad side, like Ramoja's. Not sharp like Urd's. The only feature he had perhaps inherited from Urd was the councillor's corn-yellow hair.

Ramoja had told her without using Vetle's name. As if it pained her to mention him and Urd in the same sentence. Hirka knew something worse was coming. Something she understood all too well. Her hand settled on top of Ramoja's.

"He raped you …"

Ramoja's eyes glistened with tears. She lowered her gaze to the table.

"There are a lot of things I'd have done differently today. I wouldn't have smiled at him like I did before he ... He clearly wanted me. I enjoyed the attention, like you do when you're young." Ramoja looked at Hirka and smiled when she remembered she was talking to a girl who was yet to see her sixteenth winter.

"You don't understand people when you're young, Hirka. You don't see the dangers. Today I might have noticed something off in his eyes. In the way we looked at each other. Today I might have realized what he was capable of. Today I might have been able to—"

"Stop it? See it coming?"

Ramoja smiled. She looked grateful that Hirka understood where she was coming from. It didn't make Hirka any less angry. Her ribs were still tender from her brutal encounter with Tyrinn. "You can't know. You can never know. It's not something you *see* in people, Ramoja!"

Vetle looked up for a moment, but finishing his drawing was more important than listening to their boring chitchat.

Ramoja laughed guardedly. "You sound like Rime's mother. Gesa was the only person I told, and she was furious. It was the day Jarladin was sworn into the Council. I tried to stop her, but she stormed off to tell Ilume what had happened. I remember her pearl earrings dancing as she turned on her heel, her gray silk skirt rustling as she swept along the corridor. She was going to make sure Urd paid. She knew it might cost Vanfarinn his seat on the Council, and cause a scandal they couldn't recover from, but that didn't matter to Gesa."

Hirka's chest felt tight as she realized what was coming. Ramoja's voice was hoarse now. "Gesa went to her mother. She told Ilume what Urd had done. Ilume was upset. Shocked, of course, but ..."

"But nothing happened." Hirka knew how things were. All too well.

Ramoja nodded. "Vanfarinn kept his chair. Ilume thought making a fuss would just be punishing the father for the sins of the son.

Vanfarinn was a good man. For the Council. For the people. The stability of the kingdoms would have been compromised."

Hirka understood. Ilume had let Ramoja pay the price so the people would retain their faith in Eisvaldr, in the Seer himself. Hirka would meet Him that night. She and Rime. Maybe He would kill them or send them into exile. Only time would tell. The list of things the Almighty had to answer for was growing, as far as she was concerned.

"Something happened that night, Hirka. It was more than Ilume's dismissiveness, that much I know for certain. Gesa wanted to get away from here. Away from the family, away from Eisvaldr. Everything. For almost thirteen years, I've wondered whether she only left for my sake. Because she and Ilume ended up in an argument about how Urd's crime should be dealt with. All Gesa told me was that she and Allvard were taking Rime to Ravnhov. A couple days later we found out that Gesa and Allvard An-Elderin had died in an avalanche near Urmunai. The boy was the only survivor. Little Rime, only six years old. The fabled child. Chosen by the Seer. They say a wolf dug him out of the snow."

Hirka shuddered. *Wolf eyes.* "And Rime knows all this? Has he always known?"

"Oh, no. He never knew they'd run, or where they were going. It's never been anything other than a tragic accident to him."

"What do *you* think it was?"

Ramoja turned her cup in her hands. She didn't answer Hirka's question. She kept talking about Rime. "I thought the secret about Vetle was between me and Ilume. No one else. But Rime has always haunted the corridors of Eisvaldr. And Elveroa. He's picked up on a lot. He probably knows what Urd did to Vetle as well. He might not have realized before, but today he put two and two together. When you talked about how Urd had used the Might to kill."

"Urd wanted to kill Vetle?!"

"I've been trying to work that out for over a decade as well. But I don't think so. He had nothing to fear. I hadn't told anyone what he'd done. Two years had passed and he must have known I was never going to say anything. He probably just wanted to make sure no one would find out. During the Rite, for example."

Hirka understood. "A boy with as strong an affinity for the Might as the twelve families. Everyone would wonder ..."

Ramoja nodded. "I didn't know it was possible to take the Might from anyone. I've never heard of anyone being able to do such a thing. But then again, the Might's a rare gift in itself. For a while, I thought *you* had it. That you could do more with it than anyone else. That raven came to you of its own free will. You were always hanging out with Rime, as if you shared the same secret. The ravens said your blood was different. And when I saw you with Kolgrim in the square that day, when that rock shattered, I thought ..."

Hirka sighed. Ramoja thought she had seen her break Kolgrim's rock, but that had been Hlosnian, the stone carver. Not her. The ravener had seen a girl who could use the Might to shatter a rock, and who wanted to run from the Rite ... Hirka was too tired to explain.

"Sometimes I wonder whether he wanted to kill him," Ramoja went on. "Other times, I think he just wanted to show me what he *could* do. Show me that he could take away the most precious thing I have if he wanted to. If he had killed—"

"Then you'd have shouted the truth from the rooftops. He wanted to make sure you still had something to lose." Hirka's skin crawled at the unwelcome thought, and at the fear she might be right. How could someone live that way? Like one of the blind! Completely without conscience.

Ramoja nodded. "I've never told anyone else. But I talked to Ilume about it. Rime might have overheard. He's always been a sharp one. Perceptive."

"That didn't stop you from slapping him."

Ramoja dragged her hands over her face. "He's always been like family. Him and Ilume. When the Council wanted to get closer to Ravnhov, she asked me to come with her. They needed a ravener, and she could have chosen anyone, but she chose me. I don't know why. Maybe she felt guilty for what had happened with Vetle. Maybe she could have prevented it if she'd taken it seriously when Gesa first came to her. Maybe she just considered me a link to the daughter she no longer had."

Or maybe she just wanted to make sure you didn't say anything while she was away. Hirka thought about a board game Lindri's customers played. Each player started on their own side of the board with various wooden counters. The idea was to use them strategically to take over the opponent's side. Hirka almost always lost because she took the most direct route. It was like announcing your intentions. She knew better than that now. Ramoja continued.

"Ilume said the best thing for me and Vetle would be to get away, and it was difficult to disagree. So we moved to Elveroa. We never went a day without seeing each other. Particularly at first, when the ravenry was being built. The first Elveroa had ever seen. Rime was so young. Back then."

"Before he became Kolkagga," Hirka said.

Ramoja nodded again. She poured more tea into their cups from a cast-iron pot. It was tepid, but neither of them cared. "Eirik told me about that when I got to Ravnhov. I'm not the only spy in Eisvaldr. Others had sent letters about Rime's decision."

"He let you down." Hirka knew exactly how Ramoja felt. She thought back to Ramoja and Eirik's conversation at the icon in Ravnhov. They had been talking about Rime.

He's chosen his path. Now he's killing for the people you thought he'd change.

"Rime was all I had left of Gesa. I've been around him since he was born. Ilume was convinced he was going to be one of the youngest and strongest Insringin had ever seen. It seemed predestined. I started to believe in her. In him. He was strong, and he had always questioned everything. I dared to see change in his eyes. The possibility that the game would end and justice would prevail. And what did he do? He made sure it would never happen. Kolkagga. Already dead in the service of the Seer. A shadow. An assassin. For *them*!"

Hirka's skin prickled as she listened to Ramoja's story, pieces of the puzzle falling inexorably into place. Rime. The Council. The Might. If Rime was right, then no wonder Mannfalla was reacting to Ravnhov holding people back from the Rite. What if the Might flourished among the enemy? Among those who shunned the Seer? The world would be divided. Everything would change.

Would this be her last night? The Seer could kill them both if He wanted to. All she had to cling to was her faith in His unconditional love. That and Rime's convictions.

"Have you forgiven him?" Hirka asked.

"Rime? Yes. I can't blame him for his decision, for dashing my hope that he'd make good on the Council's mistakes. Collecting mistakes is a dangerous pastime. You end up with so many. Did you know that Ravnhov used to be the only place that had raveners?"

Hirka shook her head.

"Until Eisvaldr sent Kolkagga in to abduct men and women who used the Might to forge bonds with the ravens. That's why Mannfalla has the same knowledge today."

"That's impossible!"

"That's what I thought too. That's what I've thought many times. And that's what I thought when the letter arrived saying that Urd would take his father's place in the Council. That's when I knew for certain. The Council was never meant to serve anyone other than themselves."

Once again, the pieces fell into place. The letter that arrived that time she was at Ramoja's. How she had collapsed. Was that when she'd found out?

Ramoja continued, her voice cooler. "Their time needs to end. Even if it means bloodshed."

Hirka put her hand on Ramoja's arm again. "It won't come to that. We'll get all the answers tonight, Ramoja."

Ramoja smiled in a way that suggested she was glad someone had faith in the plan, even if she didn't personally. They sat in silence for a while. All they could hear was the wind in the trees outside, and Vetle's charcoal scraping back and forth across the paper as he colored.

"He's risked everything for you, you know," Ramoja said after a while.

"Who?"

Ramoja raised both her eyebrows as if it were unnecessary of Hirka to ask. It was.

"I can tell you have as much contempt for his decision as I do, Hirka. But he sacrificed everything for you."

"He'd already sacrificed everything for Kolkagga," Hirka replied drily.

"Not his life. Not his name. No matter what he'd done, he'd still have been Rime An-Elderin. But not anymore. Now he's even turned his back on Kolkagga, and *no one* turns their back on Kolkagga. He's sealed his fate, Hirka. The time he has left is the time he spends with you. And the last thing he needs is contempt."

"I don't have any contempt for him. Quite the opposite! I … I don't have contempt for him."

"Yet you sneer when you look at the swords he carries. You turn your back on him every time the conversation turns to life or death."

"He kills people! And you want to kill people too. Death has never solved anything. Death is just death. It's never made anything better, and it never will. A lack of respect for life contradicts everything the Seer has said."

"Well, you'll be able to ask Him about that tonight," Ramoja said.

Vetle had put down his charcoal. He held up his drawing and cocked his head, appraising his depiction of the Creator with dissatisfaction.

THE SEER

Eisvaldr was founded on a compromise. The city at the end of the city was the home of the Seer, an open place for prayer and work. The city of the people. At the same time it was meant to protect the twelve families and the secrets they guarded. The city of the Council. Stronghold and public square in an unlikely embrace. On this particular night that was an advantage.

The first part—the wall itself—was no obstacle. People came and went through the archways as they pleased. Guardsmen patrolled either side, met in the middle, and exchanged a few words before continuing. They didn't stop anyone, nor would they inquire about people's business in the middle of the night.

Night was the time for the most wretched of souls. The desperate and the sleepless. They came with their hoods pulled over their heads. Alone, or leaning on a companion. They followed the gleaming flagstones, which took them all the way up to the walls of the hall complex. There they fell to their knees with their hands on the stone, or they hung their prayer ribbons on the wooden boards, along with tens of thousands of others, all equally unreadable in the dark. The walls of the complex surrounded the Rite Hall and all the towers and bridges of Eisvaldr. They were the height of several men, and well-guarded. For that reason, they weren't an option for Hirka and Rime.

Hirka felt like a bowstring. Tense. Pent-up. Rime looked back to see if she was keeping up. They struggled up the ridge on the eastern side. Much higher than she had been the night Urd had broken her out. It was steep. Hirka used branches to help pull herself up.

The plan was to follow the ridge toward Blindból, and reach the red dome from the inside of the walls. They walked in silence, well aware that Kolkagga were still searching for them. Rime stopped up ahead. At first she thought it was because she was lagging behind, but then she realized with relief that they had reached the top.

Hirka stopped and looked upon Blindból for the first time. The place nobody ventured. Even if it were allowed, they wouldn't dare. The place was a gateway to ancient times. No roads. No people. But it wasn't the wildness that kept people away. Blindból was the place the blind had once come from. Cursed mountains. Forbidden mountains. Reaching up toward the moon. Hundreds of them. Greater than people. Greater than the old gods. So much so that her entire life would pale into insignificance if she kept walking.

"What's out there? The blind?"

"No," Rime whispered. "Just mountains. And Kolkagga."

Hirka gave him a questioning look. He smiled with moonlight in his gray eyes. "That's where we live and train. Kolkagga live in Blindból."

Of course. What better place to station an invisible army than somewhere no one set foot. The clouds rolled across the sky. There would be a storm tonight.

Rime grabbed her arm and pulled her in a different direction. Down toward a rocky outcrop that overlooked the gardens of Eisvaldr. Hirka swallowed. They were on the inside. It looked different than she had expected, though she wasn't sure of what she had envisaged. Eisvaldr was all that stood between the otherworldly Blindból and the people of Mannfalla. The valley beyond ought to have been … desolate. Terrifying. Something to indicate that it was the battlefield where the Seer had fought the blind a thousand years ago. But this was no battlefield. The area directly behind the hall complex and a good way into the valley was a swaying carpet of tea plants and herb gardens. Paths and white stone steps stood out in the night.

Diagonally below she could see the outlines of doors carved into the mountainside. The moonlight revealed spikes, and with a shudder, Hirka recognized them. The doors to the pits, where the prisoners were held. The cluster of nearby towers must have been where she'd been interrogated. The place where they'd gouged her back. Dragged her on her knees, blindfolded, for no other reason than being born. Hirka felt a stinging pain in her back, and her courage faltered. The power that was concentrated in this place didn't answer to anyone. They could treat her however they wanted. And if she was captured, they wouldn't hesitate to act.

What if the Seer already knew? He had been one of the blind, after all. One who had taken the form of the raven and turned His back on His own kind to save the children of Ym from destruction. What if He had changed His mind after a thousand years and wanted the blind to come back? An invasion. Hirka quickly buried the thought. It made her head spin. Because what could you do against gods with evil intentions?

Rime had continued along the outcrop. She sped up and pulled him back. "My bag," she whispered. He gave her a questioning look and turned his ear to her. "My bag! They took all my things. It's in there, in the guardroom. In the vaults."

Rime looked at her in disbelief. Moments passed before he asked, "And?"

"All my things! The herbs. The teas. All I have left of Father."

His look left no room for doubt. Her things were lost. Going back for them would be ridiculous and was out of the question.

Hirka chewed on her lower lip. The bag was all she owned. All she was. And they'd taken it from her. Dumped it in a corner. Now all that stood between her and the bag was an inattentive guard, halfway to dreamland. She continued, more forceful this time.

"It looks like a green sausage with straps. There's a shell hanging from the tie at the top, and—"

"Forget it!"

"But it's right down there."

"All right, then I guess you can go down and get it yourself," he said.

"I'm not Kolkagga," she muttered. "I'm not the mystical warrior from the shadows with immense powers who—"

"Wait here. I swear, you're a nightmare."

Hirka stared at his back as he disappeared into the darkness. She kneeled and peeked over the edge of the outcrop, but she couldn't see him. The wind shook the trees behind her and suddenly she realized what she had done. She'd sent off her only protection against other Kolkagga. The ones who were still hunting her.

She crawled between some trees and tried to sink into the forest floor. As if that would help if they came. And why wouldn't they? They lived there, in the mountains. Trained there. She sat turning that thought over in her mind until it was unbearable. She was just about to shout for Rime when her bag thumped onto the ground in front of her.

Hirka hugged it close. She'd gotten a part of herself back. Something they'd taken from her. It wasn't much, but it was hers.

She started to fiddle with the flap to check that everything was there, but clearly there was a limit to Rime's patience. He pulled her to her feet and dragged her back to the outcrop. Hirka slung the bag on her back while he pointed at a white dome beneath them. Then he pointed at a tower with steps on the outside, and finally at the red dome. Mother's bosom. Their goal for that night.

It was a ridiculous plan. He envisaged them jumping between towers and domes as though they had wings. Hirka laughed nervously. It was a long way down. Dizzyingly far to fall. She pulled the woollen jacket she'd borrowed from the raveners around herself. Rime looked at her, and she nodded. She owed him for the bag. But if he had exaggerated his command of the Might, he was in trouble. She would beat the living daylights out of him, Kolkagga or not.

He embraced her. Hirka locked her arms around his neck and let the Might in. It was stronger than before. It ran through her body and made everything bigger. The distance grew between her heart and her lungs. She had room for more air. She could reach further, see more, hear everything. Details emerged from the darkness. The air became crisp as dried leaves. As though it had fallen apart and was trying to piece itself back together again. Then it grew thick around them, and smelled of scorched earth. Ash and fire.

They jumped.

The Might couldn't stop her from panicking. It just gave her the time and space to recognize the sensation of falling. She could pick the fear apart. Find the various elements of it and put it back together until it was recognizable as panic again, but now in a different way. Rime was a part of her, but also something unfamiliar. A heaviness and a support. He was the earth and the sky, using her to quench its thirst. He got greedier. It started pleasantly enough, like relinquishing all control. But then it was terrifying. She wanted to shout for him to stop, but then she felt the Might make contact with something and they slowed down. They rotated slowly a couple of times. The white dome became a living thing that pushed back against them so that they could land in a controlled manner. Unscathed.

The Might released her, and she clung to Rime to keep from falling off the roof. Her heart was pounding as though she'd run all the way from the city walls. She took a breath. She was alive. And it was glorious!

Rime was poised to jump down onto the bridge that connected

the towers. His eyes sparked. Two circles of light around dark chasms. Wild. Hungry for the Might. He grabbed her hand and they leaped. Rime channeled the Might through her. The air moved around them, pulled at them. Investigated them as they flew, as though it didn't quite know whether they were birds or people.

Then they landed on the bridge. Hirka stumbled and scraped her knee on a broken tile, but it didn't hurt. She was too exhilarated to feel pain. She grabbed Rime. "I thought it was just a story! I thought only the gods could do something like that!" she said as loud as she dared.

"Maybe we *are* gods." He pulled her with him across the bridge, and she heard him laugh. His fingers were locked in hers. He was strong and knew where they were going. He didn't let go of her until they reached the tower with the steps climbing the outside. It had no windows. An old watchtower. Gongs sounded every hour of the day from here. They ran up the steps, all the way to the top. Hirka tried to hide the fact that she was out of breath, but it wasn't necessary. Rime wasn't looking at her anyway. He was standing on the top step, looking at the red dome. They were level with it now. But far away. Really far away.

It wasn't going to work. They'd hemmed themselves in. Hirka wasn't sure they'd be able to go back either. She gave Rime a worried look, hoping for confirmation. They would have to call it off.

Rime stood, sizing up the gap for a moment. His lower jaw moved, as though he was mulling it over. He turned, hopped up, and grabbed the edge of the roof above them. The lowest roof tiles had a recess that directed the rainwater away. It was all he needed to pull himself up. It looked absurdly simple. He reached down for Hirka, and she stared at him.

She knew what he was doing. What he was thinking. He needed more height to reach the red dome. Rime had no intention of turning back. He was really going to do it. He was crazy.

Hirka took his hand anyway. She hopped up and let him pull her onto the roof. All of Mannfalla lay before her. Blindból behind her. Historic places. Mystical places. She had never wanted to come to Eisvaldr. Not the way Sylja and so many others did. All the same, here she stood. Breaking in to see a Seer she no longer believed in. Why?

Her life wouldn't be made more worthwhile by prostrating herself on her knees before the Raven. Yet she was going to throw herself off this roof, possibly to her death, with someone who had been sent to kill her. Kolkagga. A son of the Council that had sentenced her to death. Why?

The wind tugged at her body. The air felt thinner. She suddenly felt like a feather. The wind could blow her off the roof at any moment. She felt dizzy and shut her eyes, but opened them again straightaway, because that just made it worse. A cold spread from inside her and out into her fingertips. She was going nowhere, neither up nor down. She was frozen to the spot. What was she going to do? What was she doing here?

She stared at Rime. She knew. She knew with murderous certainty what she was doing here. How long had she loved him? She pleaded for help, without saying a word. They were so high up. He was so much bigger than her. He was Rime An-Elderin, and she wasn't supposed to be here.

"Sit down," Rime whispered, and helped her down onto the roof. He crouched down in front of her and told her to breathe from her belly. Slower. Slower still. His voice merged with the wind, but she heard what he said.

"We're high up. It's a perfectly normal reaction. Just relax. We're safe. I know what I'm doing, Hirka. We can make it. Nothing can hurt you."

She shook her head feverishly and swallowed. He didn't get it.

"Why can nothing hurt you, Hirka?"

She managed a smile. "Because I'm already dead?"

She took a couple of deep breaths. A couple more. It was just a funny turn. She had started to think about completely different things. Things she should never think about. She was the rot. He was not for her. Could never be for her. She got up. The red dome drew her gaze. It would be suicide. But what did it matter when she would never have what she wanted? She ran her hand over her face.

"You remind me of your father when you do that." Hirka chuckled. Was it possible to look like someone who wasn't your real father? Rime cupped her face in his hands. "I know I can do it, Hirka. I can feel it with every fiber of my being. We can't give up now. If you're going to do it, do it for truth. For justice."

No. I'll do it for you.

But she just nodded. Rime asked her to climb up onto his back and lock her arms around his chest. He was going to carry her like a rucksack. He embraced her with the Might, took full advantage of what little run-up the roof afforded, and then launched them both over the edge.

The terror was twofold. She could crash to the ground and have her body broken. Or she could stay here, close to Rime, and be broken on the inside. Did he have any idea what he was doing?

It all happened so quickly. She could feel the wind and Rime's hair whipping at her face. Yet time also passed so slowly that she could have counted all the lights in the darkness below her if she'd wanted to. His Might swept through her. Cleansed her. Cleared the dust from every part of her body. It was difficult to take. No secret was safe from the Might. It grew stronger than the wind. Cascading through her veins. She could feel every drop of blood in the unstoppable force flowing in and out of her.

Feelings that were not her own welled up inside her. Rime's will and strength. His doubt. *Doubt? What doubt?* Pain sliced through her head. Too much. It was too much! She could open herself to even more, but it was too dangerous. It would lay her bare. Expose everything she was. Everything she felt. They were going to fall.

Rime propelled himself forward with everything he had. His shoulder blades separated under her. His fingers reached for the edge. The Might held its breath as they collided with the base of the dome.

Hirka gasped for air and lost her grip on him. She slid down his body. Her bag was weighing her down. She fell. Her hands groped at thin air for something to grab onto. Rime grabbed her forearm. There was a jolt, and she was hanging. Her shoulder was burning. Her elbow was burning.

She was hanging above Mannfalla. From the red dome. A hemisphere, big as a mountain behind Rime. He looked terrified. She started to slip and he tightened his grip around her wrist. Hirka swallowed.

"One point to you if you pull me up." She smiled to hide the fear in her voice.

A moment passed, and then he remembered. His eyes found their strength again. He pulled her up. She tried to kick herself away from the wall to make it easier. Finally she stood with her stomach pressed against the curved roof, clinging on. She found a foothold and dared to look down. The edge around the dome was narrower than her foot. There was ridiculously little to walk on. Rime smiled at her.

"Still think you can fly?"

They were the same words he'd used at the Alldjup. He started to laugh. She smiled and tried to shush him but she was laughing too, so it wasn't much help. Laughing now of all times was so ridiculous that it took them a few moments to stop.

"Sure I can! You've seen me climb," she managed to get out.

"I've also seen you fall," he replied.

She wiped away the tears and managed to stop herself from bursting out laughing again. She was alive. "Before the summer, I thought the worst thing that could happen to me was being sent home from the Rite with a message to come back next year. Because I wasn't strong enough. Two months ago I was like everyone else."

"You've never been like everyone else."

"At least I was a child of Ym! An ymling. I was people!"

"People are the worst. You're probably better off being menskr." He smiled. A broad smile that reached his eyes. Then he started to inch his way forward along the edge of the dome. It was covered in tiles, each the size of a thumbnail. They were closely set in every shade of red. Deep red, copper, blood-red. In some places there were faint trails in the red, where the rain had weathered them.

Then she spotted a dark cavity above her. She fumbled for it with her fingers. A window ledge. "Rime …"

He stopped. Hirka pulled herself up onto the ledge, and Rime followed. There were tall windows all the way around the dome. The ledge was wide enough to sit on. Rime pulled out his knife and started to pick at one of the hundreds of pieces of glass in the ornate window. It was pitch-black inside.

"Can't you break it?" Hirka whispered, even though it felt like they were an eternity away from the walls of the hall and the unsuspecting guardsmen who patrolled below.

"They'll hear us."

"Who? They're sleeping like babies! And anyway, all of Mannfalla is going to know we're here before the night's over."

Rime kept fiddling. She shifted impatiently. "Can't you use the Might?" Rime stopped what he was doing. He looked at her as though she had suggested wishing away the window. But then he grabbed her hand. This time, the Might was like an old friend. She felt Rime draw it through her and into his fingertips. She became his hand. His hand became the knife. The knife became the wrought iron. They became one. She could transform the world if she wanted to, at this very moment. The heat raced through her body, picked the iron apart, and put it back together again. Rime lifted it with the knife. The iron hung above the blade of the knife like a boiled eel. A couple yellowed pieces of glass popped out, free after a lifetime enframed. Rime cut off the flow of the Might.

Hirka grinned while he picked up a piece of glass and turned it in his hand, like it was something he'd never seen before. "You didn't know that was possible, did you?"

"I thought it might be," he said, but she could tell he was lying.

Hirka had slimmer hands, so she reached in where they had removed the glass. She managed to open the hasp on the inside, so that they could finally climb inside the Council Chamber. Hirka forgot to be afraid of encountering someone. She was just grateful to have her feet back on a floor. To be surrounded by walls again.

The room was impressive. The inside of the dome had an ornate ceiling, but it was impossible to see what was depicted. It was too high up in the darkness. A row of columns ran along the outer wall. In the middle of the room she saw the outline of the table with the twelve chairs surrounding it. She walked over to them. It was impossible to resist. She put her hand on the back of one of the chairs. If only Father could see her now! Or Sylja. How many people outside the Council had seen this room? The thought brought goose bumps to her arms. She saw something gleaming and noticed the golden names engraved in the surface of the table. She ran her fingers over the letters.

An-Elderin.

"This is where you would have ..." Hirka looked at him. He suddenly seemed much bigger than before. His face was obscured by shadows. It was impossible to see whether he was nodding. "Do you think they'd engrave 'Tailless' and add an extra chair?"

Rime didn't laugh at her joke. "Does it look like they're ready for new blood?"

She looked at the names that ran around the table.

Kobb, An-Elderin, An-Sarin, Taid, Saurpassarid, Kleiv, Vanfarinn, Darkdaggar, Jekense, Fell, Jakinnin, Vangard.

They had been there since time immemorial. They were names everyone knew. She could see his point—you don't engrave names in gold unless they're meant to stay there.

It had been so easy to accept before. They were old families. Families who could interpret the Seer. Blue-blooded. Skilled in the Might. It was only natural that few could challenge them.

Now she was no longer certain. If what Rime had said was true, a lot of people might have been able to do just that, had it not been for the Rite.

"Come."

Rime had clearly found the motivation he needed to continue. He carefully opened the only door in the room, and they emerged into a dark corridor with a vaulted ceiling. He led them down a staircase and into a kind of indoor garden. He stopped behind a row of trees and pulled her close. He shushed her before she could ask what they were doing. A moment passed, then a guardsman came walking along the corridor with heavy steps. He reached the end, turned, and went back again.

She was glad Rime had grown up here.

They snuck ahead to a wider corridor with a familiar door at the end. Red. Shiny. She'd been here before. Unease filled her body. She wanted to turn back. This wasn't a good place to be.

She held out her arm to stop Rime, but he was too far ahead of her. She had no choice but to follow him through the door. Into the Rite Hall. She stood on the platform above a baying crowd, but this time there was nobody here. The voices were an echo. The hall was empty and colorless in the dark. She was standing in the exact spot where she had been dragged away like a lamb to the slaughter. *A monster. The rot.* She had to breathe from her belly. The way Rime had taught her.

You should be dead now.

They had dragged her off, and ever since then they had wanted her dead. But here she stood. In their most sacred place. Hirka could feel a smile blossoming on her lips. They had treated her like an animal. Like one of the blind. But they didn't know what children of Odin were capable of. She hadn't known either. Until now.

She turned to Rime, who was standing in front of the double doors that the Council had used during the Rite. There were no handles, but he placed his palms against them and gave a gentle push. Then he took a step back. Hirka heard three mechanical clicks in the wall, and the doors swung outward of their own accord.

The wind came in. Blew past them and into the hall. It blasted along the curved walls behind them. In front of them was a narrow bridge with tall spires along both sides. The bridge that would take them into the Seer's tower. It was just as she remembered it. The floating tower, with no other support than the slender bridge. The tower that demonstrated His unfathomable powers. Some said He held it up with the Might. Others said He didn't even need to. The Might flowed so powerfully around Him that it shaped itself. He *was* the Might.

Rime hesitated by the door. He stared at the floating black rock, which was adorned with golden pillars. Pillars that didn't touch the ground. It was as though a mountain had fallen from the sky but never landed. It had simply remained suspended, and later people had seen fit to adorn it with gold and glass and make it into the Seer's hall. Hirka had never seen another hall like it. The pillars and the yellow glass made it look like an immense lantern. A floating light.

Rime placed a hand on her shoulder, but she didn't think it was to comfort her. More to check that she was still there. This was his world, after all. Not hers. He had grown up here, but even he had never crossed this bridge. Nobody other than the Council had crossed it. Maybe that was why he had become Kolkagga? Because the notion of meeting Him was too terrifying?

I'm not afraid.

And she meant it.

She took the first step, and they crossed the bridge. The entire way she waited for something to happen. For the bridge to start shaking until they fell off. For the tower to start shining. For an omnipresent voice to speak to them. But nothing happened. They got closer and closer. Between the pillars were the tallest windows she had ever seen. Bits of glass shaped like teardrops, the color of fire, pieced together again and again, until they were the height of twenty men. The doors were a textured expanse of gold. This had to be the birthplace of all riches. A house built for the sun. For Him.

Hirka placed her hands on the doors and gave them a shove. Once again she had expected something extraordinary to happen, but the doors simply opened, like any other door. As if He was waiting for them. Hirka turned to look at Rime, smiled, and walked inside.

Hlosnian's tree!

The room they stepped into was enormous, as was to be expected. But nothing could have prepared her for the tree. The Seer's tree. It was a tree like no other. It grew from the center of the room, stretched upward, and branched off in every direction, like tendrils of ink. Black as the night. Gleaming. Was it stone? Or burnt glass? Both? She stared up at it, and it seemed to change character as she walked around. A storm, frozen in midair. Randomly, but always in the same direction.

She remembered the bitter look in the eyes of the stone carver as he spoke of his despair at not being able to create anything close to it. Hirka understood. She stared up at the twisted trunk and at the impossibly thin branches running around the outer edges of the room. Higher and higher. There were thousands of them—each touched by the grace of the Seer. Nobody could carve this from stone. It wasn't possible. What was it Hlosnian had said? This was the Might as it used to be. Ancient forces. What else had he said?

You shouldn't be here.

She'd thought he meant she shouldn't be in his home. That he was busy working. On his sculptures. But maybe he'd meant something else entirely. Had Hlosnian found out that she had traveled here through stone? Hirka walked up to the tree. Out of the corner of her eye she saw Rime raise his arm as if to stop her, but she couldn't stop. She ran her hands over the trunk. The stone was cold and soothing. It whispered to her. Called to her. She remembered the tree back home. Where she had sat counting the leaves in her head, until Father came and chopped it down. She started to climb.

"Hirka!"

She turned and looked down at Rime. He could never have done what she was doing now, she realized. He had made it here, but would go no farther. To his mind, the Seer was too powerful. Too holy to challenge. So it was up to her. Wasn't that why they had come?

"How else are you going to meet Him?" she said, continuing upward. It was like climbing cold glass. She looked down at Rime again. "Besides, I'm already dead, remember?"

She reached the center of the tree. The place where the trunk branched out in every direction. The place where He lived. She pulled herself up over the edge and into the hollow in the middle.

It was empty.

Hirka found that she wasn't surprised. A part of her had never believed she was going to see Him. Had they come all this way for nothing? Had He left the tower? Left His own tree? Rime had said that the Council had convened without Him. Had He gone away? Was He sick? Dead? Had they moved Him? Or …

Hirka leaned over the edge and stared down at Rime, who was on his knees looking up at her.

"He's not here."

Rime got up. She sensed she needed to repeat herself, so she flung her arms out and spoke louder.

"He's not here!"

"Where … Where is He?"

It was a ridiculous question, but there was no need to point that out. She shrugged.

"Of course He's here," Rime said. He started to search the room, even though there was nothing else there. Just a door, directly across from the one they'd come through. Hirka climbed back down. Her unease was back. Stronger. She had to do something, but there was nothing to be done. This unease couldn't be stopped. It wasn't fear. It was certainty, like she'd experienced on the roof of the old watch-tower. The certainty that comes when you realize something you ought to have known all along. It was a feeling of having seen something so hideous that you wished you'd never seen it. Like an open wound on your leg, or a stillborn child. She suddenly wished she could turn back time, so this wouldn't go any further.

"Rime …"

"He's here." Rime grabbed a staff that was propped up between the wall and a polished black table. The Ravenbearer's staff. The table was the only piece of furniture in the entire room. A couple of small bottles and a bowl had been left on it. Hirka recognized the smell. She wished it was something else, but it wasn't.

"Rime …"

"He's in here!" Rime threw the staff aside and pulled open the door. The room inside was like a cave, carved out of the rock. It was full of ravens. Maybe fifty of them. They'd been asleep and started to caw irritably when the door opened. They were perched on beams that crossed the room at various heights. There were the usual shelves of paper and sleeves along the walls. A ravenry. A perfectly ordinary ravenry.

"Where is He? Which one is Him?" Rime looked at her, but she didn't have an answer. Didn't want to answer. He shouted into the room. "Where are you?!"

The ravens' cawing grew louder. Some of them moved uneasily to another beam. Hirka could feel a cold draft from what had to be open hatches in the roof, high above them in the darkness.

"WHERE ARE YOU?!"

Rime screamed. The ravens screamed. Some of them flew around the room before settling down again higher up. None of them answered. None of them came to Rime. They were just ravens. Nothing more. Hirka clenched her teeth, pained by what Rime was incapable of understanding. He walked back to the tree, all the while talking to himself.

"He has to be here. He *is* here. What have they done to Him?" He repeated it over and over again.

Hirka followed him. "Rime …" She picked up the bowl from the table. "Rime, this is dreamwort." He looked at her in confusion. "Dreamwort. A plant. It can knock people out for hours. If you'd taken a sword to the thigh and had to be stitched up, they'd give you dreamwort first. Not in Elveroa, because it's too expensive, but nothing's too expensive here. That's what Urd tried to give me when—"

"What does that have to do with anything?" The despair in his voice made her stomach clench. Outside, atop the red dome, he'd been afraid she wouldn't be able to handle this night. But this night was not for her. It was for him.

"In small doses it makes people lethargic. Sleepy. Makes them sit passively and motionless for a long time. People. Or ravens." She took a cautious step toward him. "Perfectly ordinary ravens, Rime."

He understood. He knew. All she could do was watch the ground disappear from under his feet. She thought he was going to fall, but he didn't. He looked past her. Past her and into himself. His eyes glazed over. Went blank. Suddenly he drew his sword.

He can't handle it!

But then she heard it too. Footsteps on the bridge. Someone stopping at the sight of the open doors, but only for a moment. Judging by the footsteps, it wasn't a guardsman. Just a lone figure. Rime held his sword out in front of him and pushed Hirka behind him. She slipped into the raven room and hid behind the door. She could see Rime through the crack between the hinges. He didn't even attempt to hide. What if it was Urd? She wanted to shout to him, but it was too late. The figure entered from the bridge.

"There was just no way you'd let me keep you, was there?"

Not even Ilume's voice could fill this room. There was no indication of surprise in her voice. She didn't ask how he'd gotten in, or what he was doing there. It was almost as though she'd expected it. Maybe when she'd seen the open doors? Or maybe all her life.

Her pale robe hung straight down from her shoulders, as though she was formless. A pillar of stone. Rime stood with his hands out. His sword was a morbid extension of his arm. His back was hunched and his teeth were bared. A wolf and a pillar of stone. What could an animal do against a mountain?

"What are you doing here?" he demanded.

Only now was Hirka sure that Rime had accepted the truth. What he was actually asking was what she was doing in Eisvaldr, serving on the Council when there was no reason to be here. What was she doing here when there was no Seer? Ilume held out a scroll.

"Sending a letter. That's what a ravenry is for." She lit the torches on either side of the door, and continued into the raven room. Hirka pressed herself up against the wall to remain unseen. Ilume placed the letter calmly in an ivory sleeve, which she then fastened to a clip at the top of a raven's leg. "And if you want to do something without being seen, night is the best time to do it. But apparently you already know that," she said. Then she whispered something in ravenspeak. The black bird took flight and continued up into the darkness toward the hatches.

Ilume watched it for a moment, sighed heavily, and left the raven room. Hirka could see Rime in front of the black tree. The torches made the branches sparkle as though a fire was blazing behind him. His eyes darted around the room. He looked like he had a lot to say, but couldn't get the words out. Hirka understood. Here he was, in the Seer's tower, in front of His throne, and He was simply not here. And Ilume didn't seem worried, or keen to explain. She just stood in front of him in her stone-pillar way.

"And you thought you'd honor me with your presence?" Rime seethed.

Hirka wanted so much to go to him. She could feel his pain. He had so much to say to his grandmother that he didn't know where to start.

"So you accept the fact that I'm here? And you're actually willing to talk to me? That'll be a story for the ages. But then, there are so many to choose from! Let me see … The story about my parents? Now *that* is a story!" Rime was unrecognizable. Fuming. "Pure fiction! They wanted to escape, Ilume And they died. How did they die, Ilume-madra? Are you going to tell me, or should I assume I'm right?"

Ilume shut her eyes for a moment. "Would you accept any answer other than the one you already think you have?"

"Hardly, Grandmother. I can't think of a single reason to believe you."

"Very few can. That's why we need the Seer."

"He doesn't exist!"

"THAT DOESN'T MAKE HIM ANY LESS IMPORTANT!"

It was the first time Hirka had seen Ilume break out of her stone pillar. She was starting to unravel, just like her grandson.

"You're unbelievable! All of you, unbelievable!" Rime clutched his head and started to walk in circles. "You defend a seer who … who never existed. And you act like I'm blasphemous when I point it out. You're lying! Lying to the world. Saying there's salvation when all there is … is this!"

"So you can understand why—"

"Why?! So you can cling to the same rotten power you've always had. Like scavengers! And to keep others from joining the party, you kill their Might before they turn sixteen!"

Even though she was standing some distance away, Hirka could see that Ilume was surprised that Rime knew. This was unobtainable knowledge. Nobody would have told him this, and nobody would have written it down. But then, he never would have known without the help of a condemned child of Odin. A tailless girl who could feel the Might in others.

"You're killing the Might! Even though you know the blind are here, and that the Might could be the only way people can protect themselves! But it must be generations since anyone could put it to any use whatsoever. Why is that, Ilume? Hm? Haven't you been complaining that it's been ages since anyone has shown the slightest indication of affinity for the Might? You've wiped out the Might and now you're complaining that it's gone! You take …" Rime shifted and moved his sword into his other hand. "You take something that doesn't belong to you. Something nobody can own. Because it's the only thing that justifies the twelve families still sitting around the table. Around … Him!"

Rime laughed—a terrifying laugh—while he pointed up at the center of the tree. "That's why Mother left you, wasn't it? She came to you for help. To get justice when Ramoja was raped! And you said no. But Mother wouldn't leave it alone. Isn't that what happened?

She wanted to talk with the Seer Himself. Like I wanted to. So she came here. She knew that it would be the death of her, discovering that He wasn't here, so she fled."

Ilume's entire countenance had changed while Rime spoke. She smiled sadly. "Nothing I can say will make it better," she said. "Nothing will make you understand. Because you've never seen things the way I see them. The world is different in your eyes. It's the Might that the blind crave. Limiting the Might in the world keeps people safe. Giving people a seer is not a lie, but a gift. They need something to follow, and they've followed Him for a thousand years. Do we have the right to take Him from people? I have paid dearly so that people still have a seer. More than you know."

Rime stared at her, wide-eyed. "You're … you're *proud*?"

"Rime …"

"YOU'RE PROUD?!"

"The Seer has taught us that—"

"THE SEER DIES TODAY!"

Hirka could feel the Might rippling out from Rime. It washed over her, and she heard the ravens cooing in delight behind her. She had to stop Rime. He had raised his sword and was running toward the tree, screaming. A wounded wolf.

"RIME!"

Hirka ran through the door, just in time to see sword sing against stone. Everything went quiet. The blade was lodged in the tree. Rime pulled it out and went to take another swing. Then the trunk cracked. The crack continued up into all the branches with a crackle, and they fell to the floor, shattering on the patterned tiles. A black, razor-sharp cloud rained down on them. Hirka crouched down and shielded her head with her arms.

"Rime!"

It was quiet again, except for the screaming of the ravens in the adjoining room. Hirka looked up. The tree was gone. A broken stump was all that remained. The floor was covered in black stone.

Rime stood with his head bowed. His chest rose with every breath. His sword hung loosely at his side.

Ilume stared at Hirka. Her eyes were wider than normal. She had a strange smile on her lips.

Something's wrong.

"Hirka?" Her voice was hoarse. Inquisitive. A drop of blood ran from the corner of her mouth. She was hurt! Hirka took a step toward her, but then Ilume's knees gave out and her body slumped to one side.

Behind her stood Urd.

Ilume was lying in an impossible position, her eyes locked on Hirka. There was a knife sticking out of her back. "Kol ... kagga," she gasped. Then the light disappeared from her eyes.

Urd had a crazed look about him that made Hirka stay where she was. She glanced at Rime, but he hadn't looked up. He had lost the leather strips holding his ponytail in place. His white hair hung down and hid his face. She could see him opening and closing his fingers around the hilt of his sword.

Urd took a careful step back toward the door. And another. Another. He started to laugh. His laughter turned into a gurgling. He coughed and grabbed the collar around his neck. He stared at Rime.

"And they say there's no Seer! You've just made that impossible. Broken into the most sacred of sacred places. Helped me do away with my only opponent in Eisvaldr. Dumped the tailless girl right back in my lap, as if on command. And you've uncovered the one secret that means they'll never let you live. Your parents' blood didn't save them and it won't save you either." Urd had reached the doors. "It's almost too easy. The son of a traitor becomes a traitor himself. In league with the child of Odin, he breaks into the Seer's hall in an attempt to kill Him. He fails, but kills Ilume. I couldn't have asked for more than this. To me, *you* are a seer, Rime An-Elderin!"

Rime looked up. His eyes were narrow slits. "You can't risk us telling them what we know about you, Urd," he said through clenched teeth. "You can't risk us being captured." Rime approached him, very slowly, as if Urd was prey he didn't want to frighten off.

"Ah, it's like looking in a mirror, An-Elderin. I can see it in your eyes. I felt exactly the same. It's like losing all hope, and all obstacles, isn't it? Right now you have no higher power, and no savior." Urd spoke as though he was enjoying himself. He grabbed the doors. Rime raced toward him.

"Fight me! Kill me! You have no other choice!"

"You're Kolkagga. Do you think I'm an idiot?"

Urd went through the doors and they slammed behind him. Rime brought his palm down on them hard, but they didn't budge. He searched the walls feverishly for a mechanism.

"Rime, it's too late!" Hirka heard Urd call for the guardsmen on the other side of the door. Distant shouts were heard. Soon they'd be surrounded. "Rime, listen to me!" She seized hold of him. His eyes were burning with rage. He breathed in gasps, from the top of his chest. He looked at her without seeing her. "It's too late. They're crossing the bridge. We have to get out of here."

"Out? There's no way out of here, Hirka. There are no better swordsmen and archers than the guardsmen of Eisvaldr. We're already dead."

"Not yet!" She held his face in her hands and looked up at him. "Rime, you have to wake up. We're still alive!"

Rime closed his eyes. When he opened them again, he looked half dead. Exhausted, but awake. His eyes alighted on Ilume's motionless body. They could hear footsteps on the bridge outside, far too many of them. Metal shoes striking the stone. Hirka dragged Rime with her into the raven room.

"They'll pick us off with arrows, Hirka ..."

"Not if they can't see us! Come!" Hirka started to climb up toward the ceiling. Rime followed her. The guardsmen stormed into the other room. They heard the crunching of shattered stone. Someone slipped and swore. From somewhere she heard Urd shouting what had happened. About the murder they had committed. He shouted that the Seer was safe, but that the outlaws had to pay.

She climbed higher and higher with Rime at her heels. The ravens cawed around them. She waited for the right moment. It would work. It *had* to work. The guardsmen forced their way into the ravenry, and she knew that a hail of arrows was coming at any second. She filled her lungs and shouted for all she was worth.

"ARKA! ARKA! ARKA!"

She screamed the way Kuro had screamed when they were attacked by the great eagle near Ravnhov. The simplest word had a lifesaving effect. The ravens went berserk. They screamed like mad things and flew in circles around the room to chase an enemy that didn't exist.

Hirka looked down. The guardsmen were barely visible through the flurry of black wings. Two arrows struck the wall below them, but no more were fired. She could hear arguing over the ravens' shrieks. Someone gave an order to stop shooting. You didn't kill ravens unless you wanted to be killed yourself. Not in Eisvaldr. But surely this was an exception? After all, the outlaws were getting away.

The moral dilemma below bought Hirka and Rime enough time to reach the roof hatches. The draft was coming from the other side of the room. The closest hatch was shut. Hirka sent silent thanks to the Seer that she'd always been able to see well in the dark, but then she remembered that He didn't exist. She tried to undo a hasp, but it had been a long time since the hatch had been opened. She had to kick it out before she could crawl out onto the roof. Rime followed.

A volley of arrows hit the ceiling beneath them. The moral dilemma had obviously been solved. One of the arrows continued through the hatch, past them, and into the sky. She felt a blow to her back. For a moment she thought she had been shot, but she felt no pain. She glanced back. The arrow was sticking out of her rucksack. Rime pulled it out and stared at it.

"Ready?" she asked.

Hirka looked at him and waited for the Might. Rime shook his head like a sweaty dog. Not to say no, but to clear his head. He sheathed his sword, put his arm around Hirka, and bound the Might. Then they jumped off the roof and into the darkness.

URD'S CONQUEST

Urd hadn't had long to think, but he had used the time well. The night had presented him with a gift of dimensions he'd never have thought possible. Almost too good to be true. He had to strike while the iron was hot. How he handled the events would determine his fate. It was that simple. Would the Council stand with or against him? Was this the night he would finally get free rein? Become the man who took them to new heights? The conqueror.

Urd had dumped Ilume's lifeless body in the middle of the table in the Council Chamber. She was still warm. The blood had soaked through her robes, staining them red. Ten pale figures sat around him. Silent. Paralyzed.

Ilume's chair was empty. Eir sat in the next chair over, crying onto Jarladin's shoulder. Magnificent. Truly magnificent. She was the Ravenbearer, yet here she was, crying like a child. That was all he needed to win tonight. She had no fight left in her. Her will was broken.

Jarladin An-Sarin stared at Ilume. His gaze had lost the steadiness it usually had, and if anything, the ox's nostrils were flaring even more than usual. Leivlugn Taid did as expected: closed his eyes and shook his head. The eldest man on the Council was useless to him. Noldhe Saurpassarid had dispensed with her foolish grin for once. Her tears fell freely and unashamedly. Sigra Kleiv? Urd wouldn't have believed it possible for her to be any uglier, but the angular and mannish woman clearly didn't take well to being dragged out of bed in the middle of the night. She pressed her forehead against her folded hands. The rest of them stared at the body with a mixture of distaste and grief. Only Garm Darkdaggar's eyes rested on Urd. Keen and curious.

Urd searched for the emotion he wanted to stir in them. He held onto it and got up. He brought his fist crashing down on the table. He had their attention. He raised his fist again, opened it, and let black shards of glass spill out across the tabletop. He squeezed his hand around the final pieces so they cut into his palm. He kept his head bowed and squinted through half-closed eyes until he saw the blood fall from his hand and hit the table. Only then did he drop the final pieces.

"I have failed you. This is … all because of me." He spoke with a tremor in his voice. He had to start unsteadily. So he could show these mightless ymlings how to pick themselves back up again. Something none of them had mastered.

He heard Miane Fell's awkward voice. "Urd, my dear … This isn't your fault." Urd hid a smile. He couldn't have asked for better puppets. He raised his eyes and looked at her. Looked at them all. "This is entirely my fault! I wanted to spare the embling. To postpone her sentencing. If I had acted differently, Ilume might …" He closed his eyes as if in pain before continuing. "Ilume might still be alive. My lack of experience has gotten us into this mess. Plunged us into darkness. I haven't slept a wink since the embling killed three of our own and disappeared. I've been wandering these halls, seeking a solution. When I saw the open doors tonight, I knew something was wrong. And when I heard the tree shatter …"

He opened his eyes again and saw how they were hanging on his every word.

"And there was nothing I could do! Nothing! I'm new in this circle. I looked up to Ilume. Trusted her wisdom. Her doubts about me were plain for all to see, and that cut me deep, but I'd promised myself I'd make her proud of me one day. Only for her to be killed by one of her own blood! The grandson who refused his place and turned his back on all of us, Kolkagga included."

He knew the time was right. The grief was clawing at all of them. Their helplessness was palpable. Blood ran in a rivulet from Ilume's back toward his name in the tabletop. The letters were soon outlined in red.

He straightened up.

"But I'm not the type to run like a dog with its tail between its legs when I am faced with opposition. I'm my father's son! I am to blame for the indescribable injustice that we have suffered. And I promise you: I will fix it. I have informed Kolkagga of what has happened. But I also intend to make use of my family's resources. My guard and I will all go out and find the murderers before they can do more wrong. Before they share the knowledge they now have. This Council will prevail if it costs me everything I have. If it's the last thing I do."

Urd felt warm satisfaction spread through his body as he watched Jarladin well up. He had Jarladin! That meant he had them all. He had to leave. At once, while he still had the upper hand. And before anyone could stop to think or discuss anything. He turned away from them and headed for the door. Then he stopped and looked back at them again.

"I suggest that you continue with the Rite as of tomorrow. I'll be back when our position is secured." He reached for the door.

"Urd ..."

It was Jarladin's voice. Urd smiled before replying. "Yes, fadri?" He added the honorific even though that was unusual among peers. It left a foul taste in his mouth, but it would serve him now. A sign of humility. Respect.

"I was wrong about you. I apologize."

Urd waited a beat before answering. He didn't turn around. "Your mistake is nothing compared to mine." He left the room as the most powerful man in the world. The Council would be preoccupied by the Rite. He was excused from participating. He had complete control of Kolkagga. And most importantly: of Rime and that tailless wretch.

BEYOND SALVATION

Blindból. *Lair of the blind.* It would be hard to find a more appropriate name. They had fumbled their way through it in the darkness until Hirka had asked Rime to stop. She'd said it was because she was exhausted. Said they had to seek shelter before the storm set in. That much was true, but it was actually an excuse to get Rime to calm down. He was shaking. They couldn't continue with him like this.

The night was charged with the Might. Intense. Expectant. Hirka could feel it in every fiber of her being. A tingling under her skin. An ache in her veins. They were sitting high up on the mountainside, on one of the many fingers of the gods. Like castaways hoping to remain unfound. A foolish hope, because they had far to go. There was only one place to go, now that Eisvaldr would chase them to the end of the world. Now that nothing could be like before. They had to get to Ravnhov through Blindból.

There was no alternative, but Rime had taken some convincing. Five days—maybe more—through Kolkagga territory, without being seen? The only hope they could cling to was that it would be the last place Kolkagga would look for them.

Hirka hugged her knees, trying to keep warm. In front of her, Kuro sat on a branch that twisted over the cliff edge. He was always there when she needed him most. A taunting reminder of the Seer who no longer existed.

Suddenly the Might flashed across the sky, and Hirka gave a start. Kuro just shook himself off and took a few steps closer to the tree trunk. The spruce needles looked sharp in the dark. She clung to the idea that they were like tiny spears. That nothing could get past this tree, to reach her and Rime. Foolish thoughts, but she had made peace with the fact that the mind did foolish things to survive. You believed what you had to believe, under the circumstances.

Again she pictured the light going out in Ilume's eyes. Heard her words.

I have paid dearly so that people still have a seer.

The jump from the Seer's tower had cost Hirka a lot. The Might had been more unbridled than ever, a hunger eating away at her. She could still feel traces of it in her body, pulsating in her veins, colored by Rime's incredible anger.

He was sitting with his back against the rock that was sheltering them. Another flash of lightning lit up his face, but it faded quickly, leaving him in the dark again. Then came the thunder. Blindból raged. Soon they would be soaking wet.

The glimpse of his face tore at Hirka's heart. Grief had extinguished the light in his eyes. Emptied them of everything but blackness. Grief over Ilume. Over the Seer. Over the fact that this was how it was going to end for them. Because if they were being honest, even Ravnhov couldn't stand against Mannfalla. It was only a matter of time now. The Council had all the reasons it needed. Urd would paint a picture of the rot and the outlaw, and the whole world would lap it up. The fugitives who had broken in to kill the Seer. Who had killed Ilume. At the behest of Ravnhov. They didn't stand a chance.

Rime had wanted to stay. Wanted to fight in Eisvaldr alongside Ramoja. But he had realized that it was impossible. Whatever their plans were, he would put the raveners in even greater danger. And Hirka wasn't too stupid to understand that he had come along for her sake. She would never make it through Blindból on her own.

He'd lost everything helping her. Maybe she could talk it away, talk away the suffocating blanket weighing them down—like she always did. She could indulge her curiosity, maybe ask him what had been niggling in the back of her mind the whole way here.

"How could the tower float without the Seer? Isn't He the one who shapes the Might that holds it up?"

"It doesn't float. It's never floated." Rime's voice was dark.

"What do you mean? I saw it . . ."

"Mirrors. They make it look like the tower is floating. Especially from inside the Rite Hall, when the doors are opened. Genius, right? I was nine when I figured out how it worked. But I didn't say anything."

Hirka shrugged. "Would it have mattered?"

"Of course! Had people known, then maybe they'd have realized—"

"Realized what? That He doesn't exist? You didn't."

The white fire in his eyes returned. She was nearing the heart of the matter. A raindrop splattered against her hand. Soon there would be more.

"Would *you* have realized? What if you'd seen a lot more, Hirka? Seen the Council manipulate people your whole life so they could appear more powerful and cleverer than they actually are? Yes, I knew how they twisted the law to their own advantage. I knew that mirrors made the tower look like it was floating. I knew that a number of ingeniously placed windows bathed the twelve in light when they sat down in the Rite Hall. I've always known. Their hoods are lined with gold so their faces are always aglow. A mallet is pulled over a brass gong beneath the platform when they enter. You don't hear it, but you feel it in your body. It's like the world is vibrating when you see them. Simple, yet effective." He tugged on the collar of his tunic, as though it was suddenly too tight. "I never believed in *them*. How could I believe in Him?"

Hirka knew why. She had always known why. All her life she had seen it, in the eyes of the sick. Of those who bled. Those who suffered. She knew Rime better than he realized. She looked at him and tried to smile.

"Because there was nothing else to believe in."

The rain came, the heavens weeping over a conversation nobody ever would have thought possible. Rime's eyes wandered. The immensity of what they were talking about was starting to sink in. Hirka feared the fallout. She wanted to tell him she was relieved that there was no definitive answer. It meant nobody could claim to be in the right. Nobody controlled her life. The fate of the child of Odin was not predetermined. She determined her own fate. Orphaned, homeless, and godless. She was free.

But that wouldn't help him now. She had to give him something he could hold onto, now that everything had been taken from him.

"Nobody actually lied to me about the tower, Rime. People assumed that it floated and went on assuming for a thousand years. A thousand years is a long time. And the more people say something, the truer it becomes."

He laughed cheerlessly. Then he clenched his fists, opened them again, and stared at his palm. "I've killed for Him! Fought for His word!"

Hirka bit her lower lip. Rime had always been the strong one. The one who had to pull her up. Now he was unraveling before her eyes. She couldn't let that happen.

"Who are you, Rime?"

"You know that better than anyone, don't you? You've said so yourself. I'm one of the Council's murderers. An assassin for a false seer. I'm already dead."

Hirka moved closer until she was right in front of him. She wrapped her hands around his face. He was so ridiculously beautiful. She had never seen eyes like his. Light gray rings of wildness where his soul fought for control. She ran her thumbs under them, where the skin was bluer. His pupils dilated and contracted with his pulse. Wolf eyes. He blinked as though he'd never seen her before.

"Who are you?" she repeated.

"I'm Rime. Rime An-Elderin." He spat out his family's name.

"What's important to Rime An-Elderin?"

He laughed, almost scornfully. His jaw clenched under her fingers. "His word. The Seer's words were important. The only thing that was important."

"What were the Seer's words, Rime?"

He recited them automatically, as though they bored him for the first time. "Strength. Love. Truth. Justice."

"Are those words still important? Without Him?"

He looked at her as though the question was impossible. "There's no Seer, Hirka. They've—"

She let go of his face. "Do you mean to tell me that you've fought for a raven? A mangy old bird?! Or have you fought for what He meant to you? What He meant to you still exists, even if He doesn't. For a thousand years the Seer has been the answer to everything we don't know, and Ilume was right! Whether He exists or not doesn't matter! Because Rime An-Elderin exists. Does strength matter to him?" Rime stared at her. "Answer me, Rime."

He gave a slight nod. He was so close to her that her chest ached. She could hear Father whispering warnings from Slokna, but it was too late now. His voice couldn't drown out her desire. The weakness in her body. Rime nodded again, a few times. The sky succumbed and the rain hit the mountain with the force of a landslide. It soaked through their clothes in an instant. The ground turned to mud around them.

"It matters," he answered hoarsely. The rain ran down his face. Dripped from his pale lips, almost blue in the dark. Hirka fought to allay her thirst for the Might, but her body wouldn't obey. It readied itself. The blood exploded in her veins, as if in anticipation that he would bind. Something was happening. She could see it in his eyes. She knew it was coming before he grabbed hold of her. His hand plunged into her hair and he pulled her toward him. His lips pressed against hers. Dripping wet. Fierce. Hirka lost all feeling in her arms. She wanted to wrap them around his neck, but they wouldn't move. He grabbed her head with both hands and it felt like that was all that was holding her up. He kissed her like a man starved and she reciprocated. She didn't know where the instinct came from. The fearlessness. The certainty. The need. She didn't even think he'd intended to bind, but now the Might had seized both of them. Her body awoke and demanded it. She pressed against him and heard herself gasp.

Dangerous! This is dangerous!

The Might brought with it the truth of who she was. This was not for her. Rime was not for her. She was the child of Odin. The rot.

This will kill him! He knows that!

She felt the strength return to her arms. Rime was kissing her because he no longer had anything to lose. He didn't care whether he got the rot. Hirka tore herself free and pushed him away.

He gave her a joyless smile. He knew what she was thinking. "Is the rot the only thing you choose to believe in, Hirka?"

Her body screamed at her to give in to him. He had kissed her without rotting. A little more couldn't hurt … But the blood coursing through her veins told her that it was a false hope. If she drank in more of him now, she'd never be able to stop. Never be able to get enough. And then it would be too late. The rot would either show itself to be a lie or to be the truth. The risk was too great. It would always be too great.

Her forehead fell against his chin. He put his arms around her and pulled her close. "I'm Rime An-Elderin," he mumbled into the top of her head. "Strength matters. Love matters. Truth and justice. We'll get them. Not in His name, but in my own."

She closed her eyes against his chest and listened to his heartbeat. The most beautiful sound she'd ever heard. The most beautiful thing she'd ever felt. And yet the worst thing. She'd gotten a taste of what could never be hers. Not without it taking his life. It was unbearable.

BLOOD

Blindból was almost more difficult to navigate in broad daylight than in the dark. The mountains cast overlapping shadows to create a forested labyrinth where people were never supposed to set foot.

The valley had started to turn yellow and orange. It got cooler as they traveled farther north and up to higher ground. That was a sure sign they were approaching Ravnhov, but their progress was intolerably slow. Half a day's toil across mossy rocks seemed completely wasted when they realized how little distance they'd put behind them. It made Hirka think back to the evening Father had revealed the truth about her. She had run to the Alldjup, taken a tumble, and dreamed she was an insect that could disappear in the moss. Now her dream had come true, whether she liked it or not.

The worst thing was that there were easier ways of getting there. They could have followed small streams along the valley floor where the terrain was easier. They could have enjoyed the sun on their faces. Or they could have gotten almost all the way there using Kolkagga's network of rope bridges and paths. But if they used any of those routes, they'd be easy targets for the black shadows.

Up ahead of her, Rime was like a millstone grinding relentlessly onward, strong and lithe. When he paused—sitting down to drink from the one waterskin they had, or to eat a handful of golden cloudberries—she knew he was doing it for her sake.

She might have been faster if it hadn't been for the plants. These mountains were a healer's dream. No matter where she looked, she saw vengethorn and soldrop. There was enough yellowbell to bring down the fevers of everyone in Mannfalla. Opa grew wild at slightly higher altitudes, often on the eastern slopes. If she hadn't seen what opa could do to people, she'd have chewed it the whole way to give her a boost. They'd walked past bloodweed at one point as well. The poison that had taken Father. Enough to send twenty men to Slokna if you didn't know what you were doing. She could probably have bought a house for just that one clump, had it been legal. Had she not been a condemned outlaw, of course ...

Her backpack was so stuffed full of plants that she couldn't carry any more. Leaving behind the plants she passed was unbearable, so she'd started looking at birds instead. Owls with speckled blue plumage, hawks, and colorful songbirds. There were also animals they needed to steer clear of. They'd seen a bear a couple of times, and the night before, they'd heard a wolf howling at the moon. Luckily, there were easier pickings than Hirka and Rime, so they were able to walk in peace.

Hirka could see the Might at work in this place. The timelessness. How everything was interlinked with everything else. How nothing could have been any different, or anywhere else, at any other time. It was a mixture of mortal danger and perfect safety, like being close to Rime when he was binding the Might.

She told him how the Might felt different in different places. Familiar, but not the same. He smiled broadly for the first time in days. It seemed the Might was a good topic of conversation for him. It never stood still. It trickled through the earth, flowed with the water, pulsed with life. The Might was all that was. All that had been. And nothing was the same in any two places in this world. There were stone whisperers in Eisvaldr who believed the Might was also all that *would* happen, but that was a discussion as old as the life force itself. No one could prove it, but fortune tellers still made a living from reading the Might in people.

Hirka felt a pang of guilt. She'd done exactly the same when she'd patched people up, or given them teas or extracts for illnesses. No one liked hearing that she had reasoned her way to what they needed. They wanted to hear that she listened to the Might. That she just knew. Just like that. What would they have said if they knew she couldn't even bind? That the only Might she knew was that which flowed through those with blue blood, like Rime? The certainty that she would never belong anywhere started gnawing at her again.

You shouldn't be here.

Hlosnian's words echoed in her mind as if he were right next to her. She was becoming more and more convinced that he was right. If Urd's madness had even a grain of truth in it, it was the only way of stopping the blind. She would have to go back the same way she'd come.

She wasn't sure how long she'd known. She'd suppressed the thought. She didn't even know whether it was possible. Or whether it would solve the problems. Not to mention what awaited her on the other side. The great unknown …

No! There were other ways. She could live in Ravnhov.

Until Mannfalla's army breaks down the wooden gate.

She could flee farther north! To Ulvheim. Live under the ice. She'd heard people did that.

Until they realize what you are and hunt you like one of the blind.

Anything seemed better than going into the unknown, but vanquishing the blind from Ym had to come first. As long as she was here, on the wrong side. As long as she lived, Urd had opportunity. People would die. And Urd had clearly lost control. What would happen if he made a mistake? Would deadborn swarm into the eleven kingdoms? Would there be another war, like the ones described in legends? And what would they do this time, without the Seer? Hirka felt dizzy. She'd caused so much suffering already, so much death, just by existing. There was so much blood on her hands. And Rime's hungry kiss had made it all too clear that she still had more to lose.

She was still battling that thought when she caught sight of something irresistible. A hot spring. She'd been tired and itchy for days. There had been moments when death seemed a tempting solution to all her problems, so the prospect of a hot bath was a godsend. Steam rose from the surface. A sickle-shaped blessing at the foot of a rock that plunged deep down into the water. It was so deep she couldn't see the bottom. The water was pale green and clear. It whispered to her. *Come. Rest. Cleanse yourself.*

She stopped. She looked up at Rime, who was still walking. It wasn't the first they'd seen, and apparently there were several that Kolkagga used. "Rime ..."

Rime stopped and turned to look at her. It didn't take him long to work out what she wanted. He shook his head. "The hot springs are the first place I'd look."

"Do I look like I care?" Hirka could hardly remember what they were running from anymore. Or why Kolkagga were something to fear. After all, Rime was one of them. "We've been walking for five days, Rime. If they haven't found us by now, they'll never find us."

Rime gave her a stern look. Hirka sat down on the ground with her arms crossed. "The way I see it, either Kolkagga slaughter us or we get eaten by our own fleas. Your choice. I know about these things. I know we'll be killed by a fever if we carry on like this. Tiny critters will gorge themselves on our filth and dig into—"

"Fine. We'll stop here, but be quick." Rime disappeared around the side of the rock to keep a lookout and to give her space. Hirka tore off her clothes and dropped them into the undergrowth. Her skin puckered into goose pimples. There were small black flowers growing around the life-giving water. They reminded her of fairy's kiss, but they were the opposite color. She'd heard that all things had their opposites in the kingdom of the dead. Maybe she was already dead and had actually been wandering around Slokna for days.

She was about to jump into the water when she heard Rime shout from the other side of the rock, "Needless to say, don't forget to check how hot the water is before you jump in."

Hirka blushed. "I'm not stupid, you know!"

She dipped her big toe in. It was hot. Best to take it slow. Little by little, she coaxed her body down into the water, until she was sitting on the rock slope with her feet drifting in the deep and only her head above the surface. No ymling had ever had it so good.

Embling. No embling had ever had it so good.

She grabbed a fistful of moss and scrubbed herself until she was red. She still had the soap she'd been given when she first arrived in Mannfalla. It had been broken into two pieces by the arrow that had pierced her bag. The mark of the Seer was split down the middle and almost washed away. She needed to get clean. To wash away the heavy thoughts and what remained of the girl who had once been afraid of the Seer. Hirka ducked under the water and rinsed the last of the bark dye from her hair. The red was back, brighter than she remembered it. She felt the water tug at her feet. A current far below. Like the Might. The earth lived and breathed beneath her. Where did this water come from? And where did it end up? When she breathed out and let her body sink deeper, the pull felt stronger. Dangerously strong. She could just let go and let it take her ... Drown her. Would she be accepted by the earth? Would they flow as one? Would that solve all the problems? Or would the paths between worlds stay open as long as she was here, dead or alive?

She could hear Kuro cawing somewhere far away. An echo from a dream world above her. She pulled herself back to the surface and sat down in the undergrowth until she was dry enough to get dressed again. Not without some reluctance, because her clothes really needed cleaning as well. Not just cleaning—boiling!

"Have you drowned?" Rime's voice came from the other side of the rock, more irritated than worried.

"Yes."

He met her halfway around the rock. "I won't be long," he said as he took off his shoes.

"I wasn't long either." Hirka picked up her bag and walked around the rock. She sat on a ledge and emptied her bag out next to her. It had rained heavily. She was worried about the condition her things might be in. This was a good time to repack. The air was cooler, the light whiter. It wouldn't rain again now. She started to sort the plants she had gathered.

Rime will be quick. In and out again.

She had bloodweed, vengethorn, and yellowbell.

He'll take off his Kolkagga blacks. The clothes that set him apart from everything else. He'll just be Rime. In a hot spring.

The spiral-shaped stone from Hlosnian. A couple small linen bags containing Father's valuable herbs.

Naked.

Hirka stuffed everything back into her bag. She raised her hand to the wolf tooth around her neck. Her fingertips grazed the lines scratched into it. Eight on one side. Seven on the other. That wasn't right anymore. He'd gotten one for pulling her up out of the Alldjup. Not that she'd had much choice than to concede that one. But he'd also helped her during the Rite. And saved her from Urd. Saved her life. A couple times. Definitely. Still, that could all be factored into the same point.

Hirka pulled out her pocketknife and scratched a neat line into Rime's side. It stood out more than the other marks. The first in more than three years. She had clearly grown since then, because she didn't feel as grumpy now when allowing him points. She smiled, pleased with herself. Grown-up and mature. Wiser. He really ought to have been given an extra point for not rotting yet, but she'd never bet against that.

If Rime found out she still wore the tooth with their points carved into it, he'd laugh at her. Call her a child.

He doesn't know about the current. He might drown!

It was probably best she kept an eye on him. Hirka shouldered her bag again and crawled carefully to the top of the rock. There was a crack up there she could see through. Just to make sure he was safe, of course.

Rime had gotten out of the spring again. He'd put on his black trousers and strapped his sword belt back into position. His white hair clung to his bare back. He had broad shoulders and a narrow waist. His spine formed a valley down his back, disappearing beneath his waistband. His tail hung straight down but curved where it met the ground. He bent down to put on his shoes. A pendant swung away from his chest, hanging from a leather strap around his neck until he straightened up again. She was too far away to see what it was, but she guessed it was a Seer amulet, something he still wasn't ready to part with.

He laced up his shoes. He looked strong. His arms were smaller than Father's, but the ripple of his muscles was more defined. Had the Might done that, consumed all the excess? It was as if he'd been carved from stone. Hirka hid a smile behind her arm.

Right. He's not drowned. Good.

She forced herself to look away from him and out across the landscape. They were near Ravnhov now. If they were lucky, they'd spent their last night in Blindból. The mountains were barer here. Pale and gray. Some of them were already snow-topped. A shadow in the corner of her eye made her duck down even though she was already hidden. What was that? What had she seen?

Two black-clad figures were wending their way down the mountainside. Her blood turned to ice.

Kolkagga!

They were almost impossible to see, even though she knew they were there. Her breathing hitched and her mouth went dry. Her arms tingled and wouldn't cooperate.

Down! Get down!

They'd been found. It had all been for nothing. She coaxed her feet down the side of the rock and ran toward Rime. He met her gaze. "I know," he whispered, but he didn't move.

"Two of them," Hirka swallowed.

"Three." He tightened the belt holding his trousers up.

She looked around for the third, but couldn't see him.

"Hirka, I need you to listen to me. Do you understand?"

She nodded and waited for him to tell her to run. But he didn't. She wondered whether to run anyway. He pulled his wet hair back into a ponytail and secured it. He did everything painfully slowly. Moved slowly. Spoke slowly. It made her want to scream.

"Keep track of where they are at all times and try to be as far away from them as possible. Don't run away, and don't come near us. Stay where I can see you, but move so that I'm always between you and them. Understand?"

Hirka didn't understand, but she nodded anyway. Her heart was in her mouth and the only clear thought in her head was the one telling her she had no idea what to do.

"Turn around and walk. Now!"

Rime gave her a shove and she backed away. She kept going until she reached the rock, where she stopped and looked back. He was still fixing his belt as if he had all the time in the world while three figures appeared behind him. His upper body was still bare. Unprotected from the shadows behind him, who were all in black. Only their eyes gleamed through narrow slits in their hoods.

She jumped when Rime suddenly whirled around. She could barely see what was happening, but he drew his swords, crouched down, and lunged forward, the flashing blades sweeping along the ground. He hit the closest of the black shadows, whose leg broke with a nauseating crack, causing him to topple over onto his back. They'd thought Rime hadn't seen them. Now they were paying the price.

The injured man tried to get up, but to no avail. Half his lower leg was hanging limply, so he stayed down, hissing and lashing out with his sword arm. Rime brought his foot down on his elbow. It shattered. His hand opened and he dropped his sword.

Hirka's stomach twisted. She'd seen pain and suffering her entire life, but always as a healer. People with cuts and broken legs had come to her to find relief. To be put back together again. She'd never seen anyone fight like this. To maim. To crush. To kill.

And it was Rime.

He stood with his swords raised on either side of him. Bared his naked chest like an invitation and started sizing up the two who were left.

"No one needs to die here today." His voice was steady. His eyes fixed on a point between the two shadows, both of whom had drawn their swords.

"You're here because you think I'm a traitor, but we're the ones who've been betrayed. All of us. Nothing I say will stop you, but I'll give you a chance to choose anyway. No one needs to die here today. The Seer is a lie."

Hirka slumped to the ground in despair. His words were meaningless. This wasn't a truth you could convince anyone of in the middle of a fight. No one would stop and say, "Really? Well, I'll be." It was too great a truth, and the way Rime delivered it, it could only be interpreted as one thing.

"Blasphemy!" The shout came from the shorter of the two shadows. He raised his sword over his head and brought it down across

Rime's body. But Rime wasn't in front of him anymore. He was above him, and on the other side. He was dancing. Hirka felt the Might flow toward her. It hadn't been like this those first times in Elveroa. It had grown. Now it was keen as a knife's edge. Balanced. Full of purpose. She could taste steel in her mouth.

"You were always the most devoted of us, Launhug. If you choose to die for Him, you die for the Council's lies."

"As we have sworn to do," Launhug replied.

He lunged at Rime. Hirka's entire body twitched. She wanted to help. She had to do something. Rime was defending himself well, but it was two against one. If he hadn't taken one of them out before it began, he'd be dead now.

Hirka sat as if in a trance and watched them dance around each other. A macabre partnership with moves she would never be able to master. But this was no dance. This wouldn't end before someone died.

The nameless shadow rushed forward and swung his sword straight at Rime's head, but Rime had more than swords to defend himself with. He landed a kick under the shadow's chin. Hirka heard his neck break. His body hit the ground and lay still. One against one.

Launhug had come closer. His boldness made no sense considering the fate of the others. Rime adjusted his grip on the swords. He was the better swordsman, by far. He knew he would win, but Hirka could tell it bothered him. It would be a tragic victory. He prepared to deliver the final blow.

"You were supposed to bring good luck!" Launhug shouted. "You were the An-Elderin child. I believed in you!"

Rime stopped. He lowered his swords. Hirka felt the Might falter under the weight of his despair. What was happening? What was he thinking? He was going to die!

Raise your sword, Rime!

Hirka acted quickly. As Rime half-heartedly parried Launhug's attacks, she ran toward them. Launhug would kill Rime. Kill her. What gave him the right? Hirka drew her knife, threw herself at Launhug, and plunged the knife into his shoulder.

She screamed, holding the knife with both hands. Hot blood seeped forth under her hands. Launhug fell over onto his side and pulled her with him. He stared at her, eyes wide with shock. With recognition. He'd seen her before, she realized. On the roof in Ravnhov. Hirka let go of the knife and pulled away from him. What had happened? That was her knife. Her knife was sticking out of his shoulder.

She looked up at Rime and backed away. She needed to get out of here. Rime stared at her. Launhug was lying on his front behind him, but Rime no longer cared about the shadow. Rime came toward her. He looked like a wild animal. He was bleeding from a wound on his upper arm. He reached out to her with one hand. She didn't want to take it. Couldn't take it. What had he made her into? She backed even farther away.

Hirka stared at the black-clad man with the knife in his shoulder. He sat up, fumbling for his sword. Hirka pointed. She tried to shout, but no sound came out. Rime sensed the danger and turned as the sword made contact with his side. He screamed. The Might left her, leaving an icy cold in her chest. Launhug backed away, but it was too late. Rime aimed a kick at his knees and they were knocked out from under him. Before the shadow had time to fall, Rime pulled the knife out of his shoulder and plunged it into his chest. Launhug opened his mouth as if to shout, but no sound came out. Hirka turned away and closed her eyes. She heard a blow land. She didn't know where. Didn't want to know where. Silence descended. Then she heard Rime fall.

She got to her feet and ran toward him. Rime was on his knees, his back straight. His head drooped forward. This was all wrong.

Horribly wrong. It terrified her to see it, but she didn't have a choice. She had to help. She bent over him.

His left side had been slashed open. Blood poured from the cut like a river, running down into his waistband. It was already saturated. She could see the white of a rib. Her feet gave out and she fell to her knees. She looked around. Along his body. Along the ground. Three dead. All in black. Launhug on his front, lying half in the hot spring. He had turned the water red. The water she had bathed in. The current in the deep was pulling the blood down. It was like it was glad to be leaving the dead body and diving down into the unknown.

Something happened inside her as Rime's body started to slump forward. It was as if a candle had been blown out by the wind. Extinguished. She was no longer Hirka. She was something else. She was somewhere she was of use. She had a role. She was already dead. She started to speak. Calmly.

"Rime, the others are dead. I can't help them. But I can help you."

He didn't reply. She gripped his upper body and lowered him down onto his side so that the wound was facing up and he couldn't see it.

"Don't say anything, Rime, just breathe and listen to me." She tried to laugh and mimicked his voice. "I need you to listen to me. Do you understand?" She thought she could see the shadow of a smile. She tore off her bag and pulled out the plants. "You've got a small cut. It feels worse than it actually is."

He gave her a quizzical look. She smiled as reassuringly as she could. "I'm going to clean and bandage it, and then we can have a proper look at it when we get to Ravnhov in a couple hours."

He smiled and closed his eyes. She couldn't trick him. He was Kolkagga. He knew how serious this was, she could tell. "This is nothing, Rime. Not even close to the worst thing I've seen. Lie still for a moment while I stitch you up. Just for now."

She found a needle and thread, which she dipped in yellowbell. It looked like he might need internal stitches as well, but she couldn't do those here. They didn't have time. The ravens would come. They'd lead more Kolkagga to them. She just had to hold him together until they reached Ravnhov.

There was no point wiping up the blood. There was too much of it. He didn't react when she shoved the needle through his skin. First on one side of the cut, then on the other. She pulled the ends together. The wound started to close. She made another stitch and it closed even farther. More with every stitch. Her eyes started to sting. She blinked to keep her vision clear. He'd see that this was nothing. He wasn't in any danger.

Twelve stitches weren't enough. Nowhere near enough. But they'd have to do. She had spaced them evenly. Rime needed to get back up on his feet again. Quickly. She cut a trouser leg off one of the shadows to use as a bandage. He wouldn't be needing it anymore.

"Rime, I've stitched you up and put some yellowbell on it. I'm going to bandage it now."

Rime still wasn't reacting. She tore up the black fabric and wound it around him. Several times. It would have to do. "It looks good, Rime. You're starting to look like Kolkagga again." She smiled at him. "Sit up, carefully now, so I can tie the ends."

He sat up, his face twisting in pain.

"It feels worse than it is. Take all the time you need. Try not to move your arm. And chew these." She handed him some opa berries. The leaves alone wouldn't be enough. These would keep him going for a while. He did as she asked. His lips were cold against her hand. She tied the ends of the bandage at his back. His pendant was in the way, so she brushed it aside. It ended up hanging in midair, where it spun a couple times. She stared at it.

It was a shell. She reached out and held it in her hand. *R* and *H*. Eight lines under each letter. Something welled up in her chest, threatening to choke her. Filling her throat. She swallowed and swallowed. Her fingers were shaking now. Rime sat with his eyes closed, waiting for her to tell him what to do. The bandage was already wet. A darker stain against the black fabric. She got up. She stood swaying for a moment.

I got up too quickly. That's all.

She found his shirt and together they managed to get it on. "Come on. It gets cold quickly at night and we need to get to Ravnhov before the sun rises again."

Rime got up. His arm hung limply by his side. He walked slowly and stiffly. But he was walking. She hadn't been sure he'd be able to.

We don't have much time.

They stumbled their way through the landscape. They no longer cared where they walked. They followed the valley floor, where the going was easiest. She wanted to run. Wanted to get him to safety. Into a warm bed. To give him something to make him sleep so she could work uninterrupted on his wound. For a moment she wondered whether Rinna or someone else in Ravnhov would be able to offer advice, but she knew it was a false hope. She knew best now. Father was dead. Even the Seer was dead. There was no one else to ask.

Until they got there, all she could do was talk. Talk about anything she could think of. About Ravnhov. About the weather there. The beautiful houses made of stone and wood that looked like they were part of the mountains themselves. About how they huddled together in the narrow streets. About the thatched roofs. About Eirik. About the town gate made of whole logs. She talked about the stone circle, and about how Father had found her. And about Hlosnian, who had known she didn't belong here.

She could hear ravens nearby. Lots of them. Kuro had company. So she talked about the ravens, and about Tein. How he'd seen her in the bathhouse. And she talked about tea. And plants. The medicinal plants she'd used on his wound. It would heal in no time.

She heard him stop behind her. He sat down, smiling like an old man who had found the best place in the world to sit. "Rime, we can't stop now. We'll rest soon." She went over to him. His face was paler. "Rime, I know you're tired. You can be tired later!"

Rime lay down, resting his head on a rock. "I'm … coming. You go on. I'll … follow." His breathing was shallow. Hirka screamed at him.

"On your feet, Kolkagga!"

He didn't move. The wind was cold on her cheeks. They were wet with tears.

I'm just tired. We're both tired.

"I'll help you." She grabbed him under his arms and lifted his upper body. He didn't react. Not so much as a wince. Hirka wiped her nose on her sleeve and lifted again. "Come on!"

Rime's body slumped back onto the ground. She could feel her composure slipping. She couldn't pretend anymore. Rime was fading fast. She was going to lose him. "The Might, Rime! You need to hold onto the Might." She shouted in his ear. Hammered her fists against his chest. "Use the Might, you idiot!"

Her last word was nothing more than a hollow cry. Like a wolf's howl. The small group of ravens shrieked and flew in bigger circles around them. Pain turned her stomach. She felt nauseous. This wasn't real. This wasn't happening.

She felt a prickling heat and realized he was trying to bind. Desperate, she seized onto it. Clung to the Might. Let it flow through her. Life force. He needed life.

In the name of the Seer, Rime …

But there was no Seer. Rime's eyes turned glassy and she heard herself shout that he wasn't allowed to go. She lay down on top of him. Laid her head on his chest and clung to the Might. She had to give him everything she had. But it was gone. What did she have to give him? Intense fatigue seized her, pressing her face down into his chest. She grew dizzier. The Might drained her.

So tired.

Rime …

Someone was coming. Figures in the fog moved across the rocks. Kolkagga. More Kolkagga. It was over. His hand slid down from her arm and flopped into the undergrowth. Small white things were falling onto his face. Snow? It was snowing.

Much too early.

She slipped into the Might. Escaped into it. Became one with the snow. A snowflake. She became cold and white. Danced in the air. She fell down onto Rime's face. Melted and disappeared.

THE CHIEFTAIN AND THE BLIND ONE

Where am I?

Dark beams. A leaded window. Pain? No. Just the recollection of pain. Rime knew straightaway he was going to wish he'd never woken up, but he couldn't work out why. It was just a feeling.

He'd been here before. Or had he just opened his eyes before? There were no glass windows in Blindból. He wasn't back in the camp. Not with Kolkagga. He was floating above the floor. No. A bed. He was lying in a bed. Definitely not with Kolkagga.

Something moved in front of the bed. A dog? Red hair. Hirka. She was sleeping on a blanket on the floor. He felt warmth fill his chest. He'd give anything to know the truth about the rot. There was a rustling in the trees outside. A raven calling. Another one answering. Otherwise quiet.

There is no Seer.

The reality was spelled out to him as though he were reading it in a book. He turned the pages, one at a time, and he remembered. He ought to have been dead. Rime lifted his arm and looked down at what he expected to be a gash in his own body. An opening through to his heart. It was bandaged. Tight across his chest. He sat up, ignored the dizziness, and put his feet on the floor. It was cool. Soothing. It felt like he had been warm for a long time. Since the snow.

Snow. Had it snowed? A dream?

He got up and had to support himself with the bedpost for a moment. Whose bed was this? It was spacious. A simple wooden bed. Above it, a woven banner hung against the wall. Blue with a golden crown. The old kings of the north.

He was in Ravnhov. Rime smiled briefly. If only Eisvaldr could see this. The crown was a banned symbol. A reminder of the hard times before the Seer, it was said. It brought misfortune.

They brought misfortune on themselves.

Grief howled in his stomach like a wolf. A cry to the moon that nobody could hear or reply to. An emptiness the like of which he'd never before felt. He had nothing. He was no one.

Ilume had fallen before him. She had confirmed all his fears. What more could she have done to hurt him? Die. That was the one thing. And she'd done that. What had she died for? A lie. For a false god, and a delusion of sovereignty. His choices had driven her to the edge. But he wasn't the one who had killed her.

Urd …

Rime clenched his fists. Pain shot up his side. So he was alive. He had fought and survived. Not everyone had been so lucky.

Launhug. In the Seer's na …

A small avalanche of consequences came crashing down on him. A false seer. What was going to happen to all the sayings? *In the Seer's name. Go with the ravens.* What about all the holy days? The Seer's halls? The augurs? The books? What about the laws? For a brief moment he understood Ilume. This was what she'd been talking about. Suddenly he understood why the thousand-year-old lie mattered to her. What else could they do? Tear down the cornerstones and build new ones out of sand? Out of nothing?

Better that than the lie.

Rime tiptoed around the sleeping girl and looked for his swords, but of course they weren't there. His clothes were folded on a wooden stool with a sheepskin over it. Both his Kolkagga blacks and his light guardsman clothes. They had emptied his bag. His throwing knives and poison arrows were gone too.

He dressed as the person he now was. Kolkagga. Rime An-Elderin—the protector and heir to the Council—no longer existed.

He glanced out the window. There was a candlestick on the sill. The tallow stuck up like a bone pipe. Outside, spruce trees climbed the mountainside. Houses huddled together on steep slopes. A wild landscape that someone had attempted to tame. He had a vague recollection of someone telling him about this place.

Hirka.

Muffled chatter and shadows on the ground below revealed that the house was guarded. Anything else would have been a shock. Rime left his hood behind and walked toward the door. Every step sent pain shooting up his side. He needed a mirror. He had to see what was left of him. But he also had a more urgent matter to attend to.

He pried open the door silently, so as not to wake Hirka. She was lying on her side like a wrung-out cloth, with her knees tucked up but her head turned in the opposite direction. She had one arm covering her eyes. The other was wrapped around her bag. He closed the door behind him. He was standing at the top of some steps that led to a courtyard. The buildings encircled an enormous spruce tree.

He wasn't alone. Seven men guarded the house. One of them was sitting on the bottom step, leaning against the wall. His eyes were shut. His helmet was pushed so far forward that it almost looked like his nose was broken. A sparrow hopped around him on the ground, pecking at what remained of his meal. His sword was resting on his knees.

Another guard stood leaning against the wall, absentmindedly picking at the clay in the foundations with a pocketknife. A couple more sat on the ground throwing stones around. Some of them were talking quietly about how people frowned upon them for just standing here every day. That didn't surprise Rime. He was in enemy territory. But seven men to guard someone who was half dead? They clearly let superstition get the better of them in Ravnhov too. And clearly it was no secret that he was here. He was everything they despised.

He cleared his throat.

The group stumbled into position with such haste that it cost one of them his footing. But he managed to stay standing. They drew their swords and held them out. Now that they were standing, they actually looked fairly disciplined. Like they could all defend themselves. Not well enough, but still.

"Take me to Eirik Viljarsón, Eirik the Stout. The one who you call chieftain." Rime spoke loudly to make sure that his voice didn't fail him after an unknown amount of time in bed. One of the men nodded and started to go. Another grabbed him and held him back like a dog, without taking his eyes off Rime. "Why do you want to see him?"

Right. Power games it is. Didn't they know where he came from? Rime knew all there was to know about power games. He'd had his fill of them a long time ago, and he was only half the age of the dark-haired warrior in front of him.

Rime didn't answer. He walked down the steps and stopped in front of the bravest of them. His adversary's eyes darted between him and the others, as though he was searching for support that wasn't coming.

Oh, for Seer's sake, I'm unarmed.

But Rime said nothing. He waited for the men to make up their minds.

"I'm not sure he's in!"

Rime would have laughed on a normal day. One of the others took mercy on his fellow guard to prevent an embarrassing situation from developing. "We'll check. Come."

Rime walked in the middle, surrounded by seven nervous men. He noticed a charcoal drawing on the wall. A circle with arrows pointing toward the center. The old symbol to ward off the blind and the undead.

To ward off Kolkagga.

The chieftain's household showed signs of having just woken. So it was morning. He hadn't been sure. All activity came to a stop where they walked past. Girls and boys in blue hesitated with baskets or linen in their arms. Some ended up with their hands hanging in midair, halfway through feeding the hens and collecting eggs, as they followed Rime and the warriors with their eyes. The grindstone stopped. The horses stopped. He was death incarnate, an enemy among them. He was Mannfalla.

"Wait here." The bravest of the guards entered the great hall, a central wooden building he recognized from Hirka's descriptions. Despite Rime's certainty that nothing mattered anymore, he couldn't help but feel excited about meeting Eirik. According to Hirka, he was a good-natured teddy bear who was afraid of medicinal herbs. According to Eisvaldr, a bloodthirsty heathen.

Eirik came out into the yard and looked to be a bit of both. He scrutinized Rime from head to toe without making the least effort to conceal it. He rubbed his shoulder, which hung lower than the other, as though the weight of the world rested there and required his attention. But he didn't seem burdened.

He dismissed the men, telling them he wanted to be alone with "the shadow." Rime smiled crookedly. Eirik didn't know how right he was. He meant shadow as in Kolkagga, a black shadow. But now Rime was a shadow in more ways than one.

One of the men protested, but Eirik raised a bushy eyebrow, and that was the end of it. Eirik turned and started to walk away. "Come. There's something you need to see," he said in a gravelly voice. The guards watched them go. Rime followed Eirik down a path that went behind the buildings and farther up the mountain. Rime recognized the pointed turfed roofs from Hirka's stories. The town right beneath them. The bridge over the ravine where the ravens lived. It was beautiful. Enduring, timeless, like the camps in Blindból. He was about to say so, but he stopped himself.

"My men think I've lost my mind, letting you live. Harboring Mannfalla's assassin. One of the shadows who sent me halfway to Slokna in the most cowardly way possible. A knife in the back. Hidden in the shadows like an animal. Like the blind. Had it been up to them, you'd be raven fodder by now. Have I lost my mind, Rime An-Elderin?"

Rime understood at once why the Council wanted this man dead. He was a man with convictions. A man who made choices, and who was prepared to face the consequences. Eirik walked ahead of him on the path, with his back to him. The same back that one of Rime's own had thrown a knife at, but he didn't look back. True enough, Rime didn't have a weapon, but Eirik had a knife at his hip that would have been ridiculously easy to get hold of. But Eirik had just told him that he had chosen not to kill him. Rime felt the need to make it clear that the deed had already been repaid.

"You must have lost your mind if you think your men can stop me from killing you."

Eirik turned to face him. "They're not there to stop you, Kolkagga. They're there to keep you alive."

Rime studied the bearded face for signs of deception or hidden motives. He found none. Eirik spoke plainly, without expecting anything other than an honest answer in return.

"I don't want anyone dead, chieftain. Not north of Mannfalla. I realize that Ravnhov would like to see me in pieces, but I also realize there's a reason I'm still alive."

They started to walk up the path again. It grew cooler.

"I thought the girl was our best hope," Eirik said. "Blue blood from Ulvheim, right? Old blood. With disdain for the Council. Skilled enough in the Might to rip the ground out from under Mannfalla's army. I was told that she turned stone to dust when someone tried to smash her head in. That she survived things that would have knocked the Might out of full-grown men. The raven came to her, they say. Wild and untrained."

Rime ran his hand over his face and smiled resignedly. Talk about making a mountain out of a molehill. Misunderstandings that could pit kingdoms against each other. But it seemed that Eirik had long since figured out that Hirka wasn't what he'd hoped for.

"We know what she is now. A child of Odin. Unearthed. But she certainly isn't mightless. Hirka promised to help, and she has. She has brought us more than we could dream of. An heir to the Council! Ilume's grandson! Ravnhov is strong, Rime An-Elderin, and the outcome of this war has not yet been decided. But *you* are our insurance. That's why you're still alive."

Rime smiled. Honest words. Not strategic. Eirik said it the way he saw it. Rime decided to do the same. "I'm not insurance. I guarantee an attack. Urd Vanfarinn hungers for Ravnhov, and he needs no other reason to attack than the fact that Hirka and I are here. We're outlaws."

"Do you think we're blind and deaf? We know what you've done. We know what Urd has done. I'm sorry that you've lost Ilume, but you won't find us grieving. Ravnhov will celebrate every single dead chair. I know you've betrayed your own, but that doesn't change who you are."

Rime realized that Hirka hadn't made a secret of anything while he had been fighting to escape the clutches of Slokna. She had told Eirik all there was to tell. Ravens had presumably been flying between Ramoja and Ravnhov every day since that night in Eisvaldr. Had Hirka told them about the Seer? Did Ramoja know? And the raveners? How did you describe that in a scroll? That the tower was empty. That there was no salvation. That they were alone.

Everyone is alone.

They reached a pass in the shadow of two snowy peaks. It was like walking into winter. A wall of ice rose up just ahead of them.

"Doing all right?" Eirik asked without turning or stopping.

Rime could think of countless things that weren't all right, so there was no telling what Eirik was referring to. "With what?"

"Your side was sliced open a few days ago."

"I'm doing better than I should be. Thanks."

Eirik chuckled. "I thought the girl had suffered a blow to the head when she first came here. Her bag full of horsetail and vengethorn and the gods know what. I wouldn't have rubbed that filth on me if I were two steps from Slokna. But there's life in you yet, isn't there? And in me. That speaks in her favor, I guess. You were out for days, so to be fair, you shouldn't be on your feet. People say the Might held you together. One of the more hysterical ones among us says it's because Kolkagga can't die. They're blessed by the Seer. I suppose they'll have to find someone else to blame now."

They know. Ravnhov knows.

Eirik's voice didn't change. He talked about the nonexistent Seer as though talking about the weather.

"Aren't you going to retaliate?" Rime asked.

"For what?"

"For everything! Eisvaldr has committed a thousand years of injustice against you! You've been coerced and oppressed. Lied to. After the war the northlands were stripped of their crowns, robbed of their kingdoms. Weighed down by debt to Mannfalla. You had to subjugate yourself to our great name. My forefathers. And now they're amassing an army under the pretext that you're harboring traitors. Traitors to a Seer who doesn't exist. Why don't you retaliate, Eirik? You could have killed me!"

Eirik stopped and turned once more. "Many mistakes have been made. Lives have been lost. People have suffered needlessly and lost much because of these mistakes."

Rime nodded. He felt his jaw tensing. This was what he had come for. He was going to pay the price. Eirik drew closer until he filled his entire field of vision. "Most of them were committed before you were born, boy."

Rime blinked as though he'd just woken up. He looked at the chieftain. He felt dizzy. He had to answer, but what could he say? He'd grown up in Eisvaldr. He was part of the problem. He'd never confronted it. Just run away. Joined Kolkagga and added insult to injury by being a weapon for a system he despised. He had made mistakes. Many mistakes.

But Eirik kept talking as if none of that mattered. "A wise woman I know once said that collecting other people's mistakes is dangerous. You soon end up with so many. And it's even worse if you take them on as your own."

"You're making a mistake if you think my only crime was being born in Eisvaldr."

"Come," Eirik replied.

He led them toward a wall of ice between the peaks. It was the height of many men and shone bluish white above them. Eirik continued through a crack that barely accommodated his girth, and Rime followed. It was like walking at the bottom of the sea. Muffled creaking could be heard from the glacier. They were at the mercy of the ice's temperament here. If it decided to move, they would both be crushed to death. Rime could see a distorted reflection of himself on its surface. He looked like a ghost. The crack widened into a cave. There was a figure on a platform of ice and snow in the center of the room. Asleep. Dead?

Rime stepped closer. Something was wrong. He could feel it in the pit of his stomach. A growing unease. He knew what he was looking at. He'd never seen them, never heard about anyone seeing them. But he couldn't have been more sure of what he was looking at now than if it had been a dog.

It was one of the blind.

Rime's arm moved involuntarily to his hip, but he had no sword to draw. It wasn't moving. He—for there was absolutely no doubt that it was a he—was lying on his back with his arms by his sides. Skin as white as bone. A purple wound gaping across his stomach. Lurid colors, perhaps intensified by the light from the ice.

Rime walked toward the creature as though in a trance. The body was built like his own. The arms. The chest. The same muscles stretched over the same places, and seemed to be made for the same purpose. He didn't know why he'd expected anything else. But it was the small differences that made his blood run cold.

The fingers ended in claws, but they weren't like claws on any animal he'd seen. They didn't grow out of the fingers. They were *part* of the fingers, as though someone had sharpened them with a knife. Hardened skin that tapered into a curved thorn.

The head was slightly narrower than what would be considered normal. Wild black hair was splayed out on the ice beneath him. The head was tilted. The face twisted into a smile that might have been a scream. The eyes were shut. The mouth half-open. A blue tongue was tucked behind two sharp canines. The tools of a carnivore.

Rime felt like he was standing on the edge of a precipice. He was looking at something he was never meant to see. Something not of this world. He walked right up to the body and lifted the eyelid with his thumb.

White.

Completely white. No iris, no pupil. Not even a vertical slit like a cat. Though he had no idea where he'd gotten that from. The blind were blind. At least there was truth in *some* of what he'd been told. But that was no relief. He let go of the creature. The cold lingered on his thumb. Different from the cold that was freezing his breath in front of him. He turned to Eirik.

Eirik stood with his arms crossed, waiting. Waiting for Rime to digest what he was seeing.

"I … I didn't know … I didn't believe …"

He recognized the truth of his own words. Deep down he hadn't believed. The blind were back. He'd heard it. The Council had openly discussed it, but it wasn't something you believed until you saw it. What had he actually thought? Or hoped? That it would turn out to be something else? Wild animals? Or that the Council would be proven right in their theory that it was lies spread by Ravnhov? That same Council was still reeling, so what was he to do with this discovery?

Rime stared at the blind one. Fear awoke in him. Poisoned him. He slowed his breathing to maintain control. The fear wasn't dangerous. He recognized it. He'd known it as a child. A child who had almost met his maker. The weight of the snow. The feeling of being suffocated.

Nothing can harm someone who is already dead.

Nothing *he* knew of. But he didn't know about them. Who were they? How could they be stopped?

Eirik's voice reminded him that he wasn't alone. "You thought it was a strategic rumor. You thought it was a lie from the north. An excuse to prepare for war. To accuse Mannfalla of not being able to protect anyone."

Rime could feel his anger rising, hot amid all the ice. "The twelve believed it. Mannfalla believed it. Personally, I never saw what you stood to gain from it. The blind would make the whole world flock to the Rite, the same Rite you want to distance yourselves from. Starting such a rumor would make no sense whatsoever."

Eirik studied him, his head bowed in contemplation. His beard lifted up on one side, as though he was smiling. But he didn't comment on Rime's assumptions. He nodded at the blind one. "There were two. Maybe more. Nobody can be sure, I guess. We were hunting them when we found you. They'd found you too. I assume they smelled the Might when you killed your own."

That hit Rime right where it hurt. *His own.* Brothers in arms who had fought and sacrificed their lives for a lie. Maybe he could have saved them. If he had just found the right words, before the first blow. Rime swallowed.

"I would have seen them. There was nobody there. Nobody but us."

"Nobody sees them, boy. The name is apt. They make others equally blind. But they kept their distance, and you can thank the ravens for that."

Rime suddenly remembered seeing the sky through the fog of pain. Ravens. Lots of them. Black blotches shrieking amid white snow. Hirka dragging him.

"That's why they haven't attacked Ravnhov?"

Eirik nodded. "They've done plenty of damage in the surrounding area. Trust me, you don't want to see a man sucked dry of the Might. He looks like them. Hardly distinguishable. Pale. Bloodless. With eyes rolled back in his head. They draw the life force out of you. Old women say they feed on your soul. And they do it regardless of whether you're a man, woman, child, or bear. They go after life, regardless of its form. If you're going to kill them, you have to be prepared to sacrifice men. They die like ordinary people, but ..."

Rime continued for him. "But it comes at a cost?"

Eirik ran a big hand over his face. "You think you have them, then they disappear. Melt into the mountain."

Rime felt a shudder tear through his body. The only way he knew how to stop them was to send Hirka ... where? Home? Where was home for a child of Odin? Certainly not here. She didn't belong here.

"The doors ... They come from the stone circles."

"Yes, we know," Eirik said. "We have the same stories here. We wanted to tear down the circle at Bromfjell, right near here, but then that daft old stone carver showed up."

What was he talking about?

"Who?"

"A couple of days before we found you two, a crazy stone carver arrived here from Elveroa."

"Hlosnian!"

Eirik raised a bushy eyebrow. "You know him?"

Rime shook his head. Not in response to Eirik's question. He simply couldn't believe it. Hirka had been right. If anyone knew how the old circles worked, it was Hlosnian.

"He carved the Seer icon in Elveroa. What did he say?"

"I'm afraid he's not the man you remember. Unless he's always talked nonsense. He said the tree was gone. The old codger babbled like a three-year-old when we wanted to tear down the circle at Bromfjell. He said if we did that, we'd never be able to keep them out. *A broken door can't be locked.* Those were his words. We had a vote and the majority chose to listen to him."

"Vote? What do you mean?"

"All of Ravnhov. A show of hands. After all, lives might have to be sacrificed today to save lives tomorrow."

Rime couldn't believe what he was hearing. They'd done what? Assembled every single soul in the town and just *asked*?

Eirik didn't seem to notice his amazement. He just continued. "The stone carver believes there's only one way to put a stop to them. The girl has to return home. To where she came from."

"No!" Rime didn't want to hear it. It was the wrong solution. It was the weak solution. The solution that punished an innocent. "There's another way, Eirik. Urd Vanfarinn's death. This is his blindcraft. He's the one who brought them here. Without him, they won't find the way."

"Are you certain?"

Rime closed his eyes. "No. No, I'm not certain. But we have to act as though I am. We can't ask Hirka to leave Ym. Even if Hlosnian knew how, it's not an option. Nobody knows where she comes from, or what she'd be going to. It's beyond reason. You might as well burn her alive."

Eirik rubbed his shoulder again. "It's not our decision to make. It's hers."

Rime looked at the blind one again. A freak of nature. Not because it was so unlike him, but because it was so frighteningly similar. Nobody knew where they came from, or how many of them there were.

"How do they kill?"

"We don't know."

"How often?"

"We don't know that either. We think they come in groups and disappear again after a couple of hours. In two places we've found nothing but ashes remaining, but that's because people have burned the houses and the bodies when they've found the dead. Nobody who has seen the dead can blame them. We've heard the same stories from other places. So we think these two were left by … the pack."

"Rejected?"

"Either that or someone got too eager. Ran too far to catch their ride home." Eirik laughed, but it was a nervous laugh. An unpleasant sound from such a big man.

"Come, Rime. You haven't had breakfast yet, and you've been surviving on nothing but drops of the girl's blind brew for days."

Rime could hear the warmth in his voice, even though he was insulting the brew that had kept him alive when he didn't have the sense to watch his back. And for the first time, the gnawing feeling in his stomach was definitely hunger and nothing to do with sleep or illness.

They left the crack in the ice and headed back down toward the chieftain's household. It felt wrong to leave the body unattended. Sick. And not without danger. "Are you just going to leave him here?" Rime asked.

"What else should we do? Burn the blindling?"

The word sent a chill down Rime's spine. *The blindling.* It was as if he were talking about an everyday pest. Rats. Or insects. Rime stopped.

"They could spread disease. Or even worse, what if someone from the town wanders up here and chances upon him? Panic would break out!"

"You've spent too much time in Mannfalla, shadow. Hide him from the people, is that what you mean?"

"I'd have thought …"

Eirik turned to Rime. "You'd be hard-pressed to find an ymling in Ravnhov who hasn't been here yet. They've seen him, all of them."

TWO LEADERS IN RAVNHOV

Hirka opened the door a crack and snuck into the great hall. She looked around. It was smaller than she remembered, probably because Mannfalla and everything she'd seen there had skewed her perspective. But it was still impressive. The two rows of logs holding up the roof, each of them wide enough to hide behind. The fireplaces in the end walls she could stand upright in. The gallery above, running all the way around the hall like an indoor balcony.

But there was something new in the room. White stone sculptures filled the entire corner under the stairs and had started spreading out into the room. Someone had taken pity on the smallest among them and stood them on the long tables, where they looked very out of place. Hirka smiled at the thought of Unngonna, who, despite all the keys attached to her waistband, couldn't find room for Hlosnian's ceaseless output.

Where was he?

The sudden sound of a chisel revealed the stone carver behind a pale stone block: an unborn sculpture. It was so tall that he was standing halfway up the stairs, chipping away at the top of it. He had his back to her. His red tunic had faded even more. Hirka guessed it had been wrestled away from him to be washed after he came here. She moved closer to see what he was doing. He had cut grooves into the stone all the way up, as if it were a huge measuring stick. She smiled.

"Have you given up on trees, Hlosnian?"

Hlosnian chuckled, but he didn't turn around. She moved closer. Then he turned and laid a wrinkled hand on her shoulder, but he didn't reply. Didn't do anything. His hand sat there for a moment before he collected himself and asked her to sit. Hirka cleared away a wooden bowl, a cup, and an empty wine bottle from the steps and sat down just above him. He pointed at one of the stone trees on the long tables.

"That is now the most beautiful tree in the world," he said, completely without pride. He was just stating a fact.

"So you knew when the tree in Eisvaldr shattered?"

"Knew? No, I'm an old man. All I know is that I know less and less. But it wasn't difficult to tell. I woke up one night and suddenly this tree was the most beautiful tree in the world."

Hirka shook her head. He seemed more lucid than before. His eyes were focused and he was speaking clearly. But it was still difficult to make sense of what he was saying. "So why did you come here?" she asked.

"Because you shouldn't—"

"I know. I shouldn't be here. What can we do about it?"

"As long as the stones are standing, anything is possible. Did you know that the wild men here wanted to pull them down?!"

"You can't blame them, Hlosnian. People are scared of the blind. They've killed one here and promised we'll go up to see it when—"

"I don't see why it's so difficult for people to understand. A door can only be locked as long as it exists. I've been telling them since I arrived, but they just stare at me like sheep. It's like we don't speak the same language." Hlosnian continued to chip away at one of the grooves. "Few know where the doors are, and even fewer can use them. And what's the solution? Tear them down! Where would we be if we let ourselves be ruled by fear alone? Hmm? In the past, people were killed and wars fought for those stones alone."

"I think wars are still being fought for them."

Hlosnian stopped what he was doing and looked at her with one eye half-closed. "Wised up now, have we?"

"It comes with being an outlaw," Hirka said, smiling.

Hlosnian snorted. "An outlaw. There's no such thing. Being an outlaw implies lawlessness, lawlessness implies a law, and the law comes from men and women like you and me. Do you feel lawless, Hirka? Do you have no laws to live by?"

"I have plenty, but they're mine alone."

"Well, then. There you go."

Hirka was becoming increasingly fond of the old stone carver. It was like he built his sentences differently than other people. A separate language you had to learn, but as soon as you mastered it, everything made sense. There was no point exchanging only a few words with him. That just led to confusion. But after a while, the words flowed like milk. Good and satisfying.

Hlosnian told her it wasn't as simple as she'd thought. It wasn't that the blind were there as long as she was, it was that they could be brought to Ym as long as she was there. He scared her, saying that no one knew what other creatures might come through as well. People knew of the blind and Odin's kin from the myths, but who was to say that's where it ended? What about the stories from the north about the kingdom of ice? The songs about pixies and dragons? For all they knew, the stones could be used to visit Slokna.

Longing for Father gripped her for a moment. *Visit Slokna.* If only it were possible … but she didn't have to think about it long to realize that there were some places people weren't supposed to be able to visit.

The old man expertly dodged all her questions that he couldn't answer as if she'd never even asked. For example, who built the first circles and how old they were. Or about what the place she came from looked like. Or whether it was true that she could spread the rot.

"How fares the heir to the chair?" he suddenly asked.

She blushed. That description had never been more wrong. "He turned his back on the Council a long time ago, Hlosnian. He became Kolkagga. And now that he's an outlaw, they'll never give him the chair, not even if he decides he wants it. He's going to lose everything. He doesn't think his uncle is strong enough to hold onto the house and their wealth. The rest of the Council will seize the lot."

Hlosnian didn't seem to care about any of that. "So he's up and about?"

"Yes. He's up and he's seen the blind one, and now he's sitting with Eirik and—"

The doors to the hall crashed open. Eirik stormed in. Others would have found it difficult to make the doors budge at all. The sun streamed in behind him, casting his shadow across the floor. A small army of warriors followed him. The doors stayed open.

"Where?" he boomed.

A young man took off his helmet and dragged a hand through his muddy brown hair. Hirka recognized him. He had collected her from Maja's inn when she first came to Ravnhov, the night Villir had been stabbed in the thigh. That felt like a hundred years ago. He wasn't nearly as scary as she remembered him.

"Near Dvergli. Only half a day from the lake where Aljar found all those fish that had gone belly up the other day."

The others shifted restlessly. Eirik rubbed his shoulder. "Foggtarn?! Aren't they pretty well defended? We've sent ravens and messengers to every house in Foggard! What are they doing out on their own?"

"They've got kids and carts with them. Fully loaded. They're heading our way, chief."

"I know what they're doing, Ynge! Don't they realize we're on the brink of war?! And that the blind have been sighted in the forests? Those kids are as good as bait!" Eirik flung his hands out in exasperation and stared at his men, who looked sheepish. He sighed. "How many?"

"About fifty."

"Choose eight men, Ynge. We leave at once. And make sure they're men who won't wet themselves every time a twig snaps."

A familiar silhouette appeared in the doorway and Hirka's blood ran cold. She got up. She knew straightaway what was coming.

Rime took a step into the room. Chainmail clinked as the men backed away from him. "Do you need men, Eirik?"

After a few seconds, Eirik nodded. Rime cast his eyes over all the men in the room. "Where are my swords?"

"I'd rather arm one of the blind!" It was Tein. Hirka hadn't noticed him among the others. He looked to the men for support, and they didn't disappoint. They pointed at Rime and grumbled. Arming an enemy was insane. A onetime heir to the Council. Kolkagga. One of them asked Eirik whether his wound had healed so quickly that he'd forgotten. Eirik cut them all off. "Enough! Give him his swords."

Everyone was silent. Eirik stared at Rime as the men left the room, one by one. His gaze was a wordless curse. A promise of a one-way trip to Slokna if Rime betrayed his trust.

"Then I'm coming too. Someone needs to watch your back," Tein hissed at his father.

"Someone needs to look after Ravnhov if we're going up against the blind, lad."

"I need one more thing that can help us," Rime said, looking up at Hirka. She closed her eyes and swallowed.

"I'll come," she answered.

"Ah, it's like that, is it?" she heard from Hlosnian, who had started carving again.

Everyone was quiet as they rode through the forest. All they could hear was the muted sound of hooves on the ground. The men sat upright on their horses' backs, trying to move as little as possible. They'd swapped their clinking chainmail for leather. Hirka wasn't used to riding, so she ran alongside them, making sure not to run ahead or fall behind. Eirik thought that would make her too easy a target.

Hirka felt naked next to the armored men sitting high up on their horses, swords at the ready. They left dark tracks in the thin layer of snow on the path. The rest of the forest was still colored by the autumn, protected by tall trees. The occasional stray snowflake danced between them. More would come before the moon was full again. She stole glances at Rime. Had she really pushed him away when he had kissed her? She couldn't believe she'd been able to resist.

Hirka tugged at her jacket. She had borrowed it from Ramoja the night they broke into Eisvaldr. She might never have the chance to return it. Unngonna had scrubbed the wool until it was almost falling apart, but the sleeves were still stained a rusty red from Rime's blood. She'd said it needed throwing out. A bloodstained jacket was unlucky. But to Hirka it was a reminder that she was still alive, against all odds.

Kuro stayed closer than usual, curious about the ravens in cages hanging above the horses' backs. They hadn't been able to bring that many of them. There was a fine line between having ravens for protection and having so many that they attracted attention. The same applied to men. They'd have preferred to bring more men, but too many would attract danger rather than keep it away. No one was sure of anything, though. It was like planning a battle against ghosts. So, they were eleven men. And Hirka.

She said a silent prayer to no one in particular. A prayer that they would make it home safe. Particularly Eirik. If anything happened to him, it was over for Ravnhov. For them all. Tein was in no way ready to take over—whether he wanted to or not.

The sun was low in the sky by the time they found anyone. Sounds from the north made the men straighten up and hold their breath. The ravens cawed in agitation. They could hear people. Ordinary people. Eirik closed his eyes, but it was hard to tell whether it was because he was relieved or because the villagers were being so reckless. Hirka could hear them more clearly now. A baby crying. A mother calling out to playing children. And pigs?

The people came into view between the trees. A ragtag group on a slope, fighting their way through the ferns with carts and animals. Eirik called out and started moving toward them. He waved Hirka and the others with him.

A man came to meet them. He was thin and dressed in gray. His gloves had holes in both thumbs. Three of him could have fit within Eirik's bulk.

"I'm Eirik, chieftain of Ravnhov. These are my men."

"And Hirka," Hirka said.

"Haven't you heard there are blind in the area?" Eirik continued.

The man nodded and threw a nervous look back at the others. "Yes, that's why we're not using the roa—"

"Who are you, boy?"

Hirka smiled at how the man took no notice of Eirik calling him boy, even though he was old enough to be her father. "Gilnar. Son of Elert. We've come all the way from Vidlokka, and—"

"Where's Beila? Didn't she read the letter the raven brought? You can't move half a village when Mannfalla has seventy thousand men surrounding Ravnhov!"

"Seventy thousand?!"

The number spread among the group like wildfire. The Council had seventy thousand men here. War was a fact. Hirka called out to them. "It's true! There's not a man left in Mannfalla!"

Gilnar looked at her like she was from another world. Little did he know. The men behind them started to laugh. Then the strangers did too. Eirik looked down at her and winked. "Where's Beila?" he asked again.

"She died. Seer knows how old she was. She wouldn't leave. We left only after she died."

"She was right not to leave. You were safer at home. Ravnhov is full to bursting, so we're sending everyone on to Skimse. Didn't you get the raven?"

"Only Beila received the ravens. We didn't know …"

Eirik sighed. "We'll accompany you to Skimse."

Their relief was touching. Fifty men, women, and children felt safer with eleven men—and Hirka—from Ravnhov.

"May the See—" Gilnar glanced up at Eirik's bearded countenance and decided to express his gratitude in a way that smacked less of Mannfalla. "May the ravens bless you!"

Eirik reorganized the group so that everyone was walking in a long line, two by two, with the children in the middle. Then they moved slowly onward, with the men from Ravnhov at the front and rear. Hirka joined the party at the rear, walking alongside Rime, Eirik, Ynge, and an older man whose name she couldn't remember.

It quickly became apparent that the villagers had been walking for a long time and needed rest. Eirik forced them on, away from Foggtarn and a little way along the river. By that point, their pleas were too heart-wrenching.

Eirik stopped at the foot of Stellsfall, a waterfall four men high. The roar piqued the children's curiosity and their crying stopped as they forgot their hunger and fatigue. Hirka crouched down and washed her hands in the ice-cold pool. Spray from the waterfall misted across her face. She never felt clean anymore, not even when she'd just taken a bath.

Hirka looked back over her shoulder. Rime was helping a girl his age repack. The bag was digging into her shoulders. The girl blushed when Rime helped her put it back on again. Hirka felt an unfamiliar emotion blacken her heart. That girl didn't have the rot. She could do whatever she wanted.

Rime met Hirka's gaze and she turned away. Sometimes it felt like her life had only been about him. Particularly since their trek through Blindból. Since the kiss. She had lived at his bedside. Eaten there. Slept there. He had slept so deeply that he couldn't be woken. Absent. Right in front of her, but still too far away. That was how it had always been. Like when she'd climbed up to see him on Vargtind. Or seen his house in Mannfalla. And when she'd realized he was Kolkagga.

Who was he now that he was no longer sleeping? Now that everything he'd fought for was gone? Who was he now that he no longer had the Seer? Or Kolkagga? Or a seat on the Council?

But Hirka knew who he was. Maybe he didn't, but she did. She saw him every day. She knew what he was capable of. She heard someone coming and wiped her hands on her jacket.

"Are you hurt?" It was a girl of around eight. Her mouth and fingers were stained with blueberry juice.

"No," Hirka said. "I was born this way. Without a tail."

"I mean your arm." Hirka looked down at her red jacket sleeves. The girl had been talking about the blood. She wasn't even interested in Hirka's lack of tail. Hirka beamed at her. "It's not mine. I killed a giant. Boo!"

The girl squealed in delight and ran away.

"Why aren't you telling anyone?" Rime had snuck up on her.

"What's to tell?" Hirka pulled her sleeves down past her fingers to coax the warmth back into her hands.

"That it's my blood. That you patched me up."

She hadn't spoken to him since he'd woken up. Hearing him say such things made it all come back. The wound in his side. His eyes when he fell to his knees. Hirka swallowed.

He crouched down next to her and washed his hands like she had done. "The Council wash their hands after every meeting. There are silver basins outside the doors. Spotless. Unbreakable. So shiny they can see themselves in them. Did you know that?" he asked.

"No."

A sound drew Hirka's attention. Or rather, lack of a sound. Something was different. The waterfall. Rime leaped to his feet. She did the same. The ceaseless roar from the waterfall had turned into something else. The water was gone. Sand poured from the precipice instead. Endless quantities of black sand, which fell down into the pool and sank to the bottom. Hirka felt her breath catch in her chest. Her mouth went dry.

"They're here," she whispered.

"They're here!" Rime shouted to the others, drawing his sword. He ran toward Eirik, pulling wide-eyed villagers along with him so they were all huddled together. No one knew what was going on. A child started to wail. Then another. The warriors shouted to each other. Hirka stared at the dry waterfall. The flow lessened and dust blew over an edge worn smooth by time and water. She could hear the others screeching at each other. They wanted answers, to know what was happening. Whether it was the blind. Whether they were going to die. All this fear. *Because of me.*

A man screamed. She turned to look, but Rime and Eirik were in the way. She couldn't see what had happened. The little girl she'd spoken to before fought her way out of the huddle, which was threatening to crush her. She ran toward Hirka. Hirka grabbed her arm, and together they moved away from what had been the waterfall.

Fifty men, women, and children thronged together, all trying to get into the middle of the huddle. The eleven men from Ravnhov stood around them with their swords raised. Eleven men and Hirka.

Hirka passed the girl to her mother. She spotted Rime and Eirik arguing about something. Someone was missing. Who? Who was missing? She heard someone mention Gilnar. The first villager they'd spoken to. He'd been standing next to the carts, but now no one could see him. Rime wanted to go and look for him, but Eirik didn't want him to leave the villagers, who were in a panic. They were like a dragon with multiple heads. A wounded monster. The sound traveled until almost all of them had joined the morbid chorus.

Hirka saw something move at the top of the cliff. She ran over to Rime and pointed.

"I know. Come on," he said. He grabbed her hand and pulled her along with him up the slope to the top of the waterfall. It was covered in ferns. She couldn't see where she was putting her feet, but she managed to stay upright. Rime shouted over his shoulder at Eirik. The chieftain swore and followed them with two men.

Then came the Might. It flowed through her from Rime, once again enabling her to isolate her fear. To pick it like an apple. To study it, taste it, and be content in the knowledge of what it was made of. By feeling it. A fear that was intense and demanding. Like Rime.

He let go of her hand and spun around in front of her with his sword outstretched. He thrust and stabbed. As if dancing with someone she couldn't see. Then he channeled even more of the Might through her and she saw. A pale figure. Naked. Unarmed. White teeth gleaming from behind lips pulled into a sneer. He moved like an insect. A fly. One moment he was right in front of Rime, and the next he was ten paces away. The only thing that belied his movement was a shadow across the trees in the background. It was unreal. Like a dream.

Hirka was dangerously close to Rime, but she had to be. He needed her. And if anything happened to him, it would have to happen to her as well. She couldn't imagine it any other way. The Might tore at her body like the wind at the roofs in Eisvaldr the night everything fell apart.

They were here. The blind were here. She hadn't believed ... not really. Had anyone?

Rime was fast too. Too fast. He moved too close and a cut opened on his arm. She could feel his fear of the impossible movements. Of not knowing what he was up against. She felt his anger take over. And she could feel it when he decided to survive.

The Might was an extension of him. It came before and after. A sword in front of his sword. He threw himself around the blind one and attacked from the side. But his blow met no resistance. It died in the air. Intention without completion.

Eirik and his two men came from the other side and Hirka saw the blind one hesitate. He turned his head to look at the new enemies on their way up the slope. Was he listening? Scenting them?

Rime seized the opportunity. He danced around the figure in one movement and swung his sword at his back. The blind one howled like an ymling. He fell forward into the ferns. Rime swung again. Hirka didn't see where the blow landed, and for that she was glad.

Then Ynge shouted. He was crouched down on the slope. His hand was gripping the chin of a lifeless body. Gilnar. The man who'd gone missing. Ynge stared down at the corpse-pale face. His eyes were white. His cheeks hollow. Wrong. Everything was wrong. This wasn't supposed to happen. That's why they'd come. So this wouldn't happen.

Rime waved his hand in a gesture signaling that Ynge should let go of the dead body, but it was too late. The others had seen him. Seen the dead man. One of the elder villagers screamed and came running. Hirka felt the scream in her spine. It went right through her. Her fault. It was her fault. The certainty grew until it completely filled her. Owned her. This was happening because of her. They were here because of her. And she could feel them. Smell them. Not just the dead one. There was another one. And he was here. Close to her.

Hirka slowly turned around.

He was standing on the edge of the cliff, at the point where water turned to sand, the water becoming black and heavy around his feet until it was swept out over the edge by the wind. He stared at her with blind eyes.

She moved closer. She was sure he was looking at her. Should she say something? That she was the problem? The reason they were here? That they could stop now, that no one had to die?

Hirka suddenly realized her legs were wet. She was standing in the water. Had she walked out here? So much water … but still she was thirsty. She dragged her feet onward until she was standing in front of the blind one. He moved one shoulder back, as if preparing to attack. But he didn't. Why wasn't he doing anything? After all, she was right in front of him.

He was taller than her and spectacularly naked. He stooped as if to get closer. His eyes were a colorless membrane, but he was definitely looking at her. He was curious. He reached out to her with a muscular arm. Slowly, so that she could see it coming. She knew she would end up like Gilnar. Pale and bloodless among the ferns. But the urge to touch the creature was stronger than the urge to run. She reached out to touch his hand with hers.

Somewhere behind her, someone screamed her name, but she couldn't help anyone now. Couldn't tear her eyes away from the blind one. His lips pulled back, baring his teeth. Then he cocked his head, like Kuro did sometimes. And blinked. He was marveling at her. It was like he'd smelled something he'd never smelled before. Like she made no sense to him, and he didn't know what he was about to kill. His claws moved as if to grip her hand. The screech of ravens made him stop.

The ravens. Someone had remembered them and set them loose. They came closer, flying in circles around the blind one. He pulled his hand back and brought two fingers to his throat. He looked at her. It was a scarily deliberate action. It meant nothing to her, but it was *supposed* to mean something. A sign. Then the ravens came too close and he crouched down.

A shadow flew over her head. At first she thought it was the blind one. But it was Rime. He hurled his sword before disappearing over the edge of the falls. The blade quivered, lodged in the blind one's back. He dropped like an empty sack before tipping over so that his upper body was hanging over the edge of the cliff. Then the water started to flow again. Cautiously at first, like rain. Washing away red blood.

Hirka got up, gripped the hilt, and pulled. The sword left the body with a nauseating squelch. She was suddenly having trouble moving her legs. The water. The water was rising. She needed to get out! It had reached her thighs and wasn't stopping there. She was soaked. A strong undertow seized her. She fought to keep her head above the water, to no avail. Her body was washed over the edge. She was in free fall. Panic gripped her and her arms flailed. There was nothing to grab hold of. The waterfall raged around her. With her. Then she was one with the water again.

Swim.

That was the only thought in her mind. Swim. Now, at once.

So she swam. Her clothes were heavy, weighing her down. The sword was stopping her from taking proper strokes, but she couldn't let it go. Then she would drown. As long as she had Rime's sword, she had to survive. If she let it go, there would be nothing for her above the surface. The sword was part of him. It would pull her up.

Her lungs were burning. Had she swum the wrong way? Which way was up? Surely the light had to be up? She reached the surface, but she still couldn't breathe. Someone grabbed her. Dragged her ashore. She threw up water. Gasped for breath. Precious air. Rime rolled her onto her side. More water came up. He loomed over her. Water dripped from his hair down into her face. She spluttered the words out.

"If ... if you think I'm giving you a point for that, think again."

His chiseled features softened and he collapsed onto his back. They lay there for a moment, just breathing. Then he got up, pulling her with him. When she was on her feet, he grabbed her and tipped her backward, scooping her up into his arms. Then he threw her. Hirka's shriek was smothered by the spray as she landed. She staggered to her feet, ready to take her revenge. But Rime was already shielded by a wall of children wearing manic grins. Eirik stood like a mountain off to the side, looking between Hirka and Rime. He shook his head and turned to leave.

"Mannfallers," he muttered. Then he shouted to the others.

"Load up the dead. We need to keep moving."

The ravens didn't settle down again until after the people of Vidlokka arrived in Skimse, along with Gilnar's body. Kuro had stayed closer to Hirka than he usually did, all the way back to Ravnhov. Now and then he crossed the path ahead of them, as if to let them know he was still there if they needed him. Proud as only a raven can be.

The fresh snow had melted on the paths. The journey back was cold, but Hirka knew it could be so much worse. She could be dead. Now she had dry clothes and a bellyful of hot stew from Skimse.

She looked up at Rime. He was still wearing his Kolkagga blacks.

They had dried off a bit, but he still had to be freezing. Eirik had kept him out of sight. He didn't want to make anyone in Skimse uneasy, and he didn't have time to explain what Kolkagga was doing in Ravnhov either.

Hirka thought that said a lot about how people perceived Kolkagga and Mannfalla here. You could carry the bodies of two blind through the town on horseback, no problem, but Kolkagga would make people uneasy. When they rode through Ravnhov, people came out of their houses. No one said anything. No one asked what had happened. But Hirka could feel the hope in their silence. These were the last of them. They *had* to be the last. Now they were safe. Now they only needed to worry about the army of seventy thousand men from Mannfalla.

Eirik didn't stop until they were outside the great hall. People flocked together to see. Rime jumped off his horse and jogged up the steps to the room he'd been given. She suspected it was as much to avoid attention as to get changed.

Everyone clustered around them. The children were the most eager and the ones who dared stand closest to the blindlings, as they called them. Eirik had to ask them to keep their distance. He gestured to Tein, who was standing a short distance away with his arms folded across his chest, and asked him to help the men carry the blind up to the ice.

That was when the silence ended and the questions started. What had happened? Were there more? Who killed them?

"You have him to thank," Eirik replied, nodding at Rime, who was coming back down the steps. Rime tightened his belt, unaware of what was happening. He'd changed his clothes. He was wearing his guardsman clothes, which complemented his white hair. He looked just like he had the first time Hirka had seen him again. At the Alldjup. Back when he'd been like a stranger after three years away.

She knew him now. He'd gone in as Kolkagga and reemerged as

Rime An-Elderin. He looked up and stopped in his tracks as if frozen. Everyone was looking at him.

"What?"

No one answered. Hirka bit her lower lip to conceal a smile. So much for not drawing attention to himself. Rime carried on down the steps. The crowd parted before him, letting him cross the courtyard. Hirka looked at the faces around her. They were relieved, but most of them also communicated something else. These were the expressions of people who were glad of the help, but who had never asked for it. She could see herself in these faces. She must have looked like that when Rime pulled her up out of the Alldjup. Happy to be alive, but with wounded pride. Ravnhov had been helped by Kolkagga, and the chieftain was acknowledging it.

"Your swords." Tein's voice. It was unsteady, even though he was shouting. He reached out expectantly. "You have no right to bear arms here, An-Elderin."

Rime stopped and turned to face Tein. Hirka's breath hitched. Something was going to happen. She could hear the wind in the trees behind Rime and Tein. They stood only a couple paces from each other.

The two were a study in contrasts, much like Ravnhov and Mannfalla. Tein the complete opposite of Rime with his dark hair, fur-lined jacket, and ruddy complexion. His eyes were narrow slits, his lips taut and colorless. Tein was full of hate—a hate that threatened to consume him.

She could tell that Rime was trying to read him. To work out how far he was willing to go. An eternity passed. Then Rime's hands moved to undo his belt. Tein gave a lopsided smile and drew his sword. Hirka's eyes widened when she realized what was happening. Tein didn't want Rime's swords at all. He had deliberately misread his actions. He was acting like he thought Rime was drawing his swords instead of surrendering them. Tein wanted to kill Rime.

Eirik took a step forward, but Hirka stopped him. "The more people get involved, the more people die," she said, her voice barely recognizable. "Give Rime a chance and no blood will be shed." Eirik eyed her doubtfully. But he stayed where he was.

Rime closed his eyes and took a deep breath. He opened them again and drew one of his swords. Hirka couldn't believe what was happening. She'd had her hand around the hilt of that sword. She'd pulled it out of one of the blind. She'd dragged that narrow blade out of the water. But not for this.

She glanced behind her. People stood as if mesmerized, every single one of them. More came running. No one would do anything. They'd been waiting for this for generations. This wasn't two young men having an argument. This was Ravnhov against Mannfalla. The Council against the crownless kings.

"Don't make me hurt you." Rime spoke quietly, so only Tein could hear him, but Hirka heard every word. It wasn't arrogance. It wasn't a display of power. She knew Rime. This was a plea.

But Tein didn't listen. "You've been hurting us for a thousand years, Kolkagga!" Tein's voice shook with disgust and fear. "You're nothing here. The Council has no power here. This is Ravnhov!"

Tein leaped forward and swung his sword at Rime. A gasp rippled through the crowd. Rime dodged effortlessly. Hirka put a hand over her mouth. The chieftain's son was condemning himself to humiliation, and he was too young to realize it.

Tein swung again. This time from the side. His movements were much slower and heavier than Rime's. His sword was broad. It sang against Rime's narrow blades. It sang again as he pulled it back. Tein panted. They circled each other. Hirka could see that he was starting to understand what he'd gotten himself into. Somewhere deep inside, Tein knew he was going to lose. All the same, he screamed at Rime, "You have no right! You can't play king here!"

"Which of us is playing king?" Rime replied. His patience was wearing thin. Tein shrieked and ran at him with his sword raised as if it were a battering ram.

"I HAVE ROYAL BLOOD!"

Hirka could tell that Rime had had enough. This would end here and now. He danced around Tein. Swung at his arm. Tein yelped and dropped his sword. Rime kicked him in the back of the knee and the chieftain's son fell to the ground. In an instant, Rime was in front of him with his sword to his throat.

"So tell me, Tein, son of Eirik, what would you do if you were king? How would you stop the blind? How would you overthrow a corrupt council who swear by a lie? And how would you explain to the world what you've not even managed to explain to yourself? That you're supposed to lead them?"

Hirka wanted to cry. It couldn't have gone any differently, but this wasn't the outcome people needed. "Rime …" It was just a whisper, but he heard it.

Remember who you are.

Rime looked at her. Looked at the people holding their collective breath. At Eirik, who was opening and closing clammy fists. Then he took a step closer to Tein. Hirka knew what he was doing. All she could do was hope it worked.

Tein grabbed Rime's leg and pulled. Rime fell to the ground and let go of his sword. He didn't drop it. He let it go. Tein put a foot on his chest. Rime started to laugh. "You're good, Tein, son of kings."

His laughter was infectious. The onlookers started to laugh. Someone clapped and more joined in. Tein looked around. Then he smiled and helped Rime back to his feet. Tein's friends came over and slapped him on the back. Together they took the horses carrying the dead blind ones and started up toward the ice. The crowd thinned around them.

Only Eirik and Rime were left, together with Hirka, but neither of them were looking at her. They were looking at each other.

The chieftain tugged his beard. His eyes twinkled blue. He knew as well as Hirka that Rime had let Tein win, preventing any blood from being shed. He'd given Ravnhov what they needed.

The chieftain went over to Rime, his footsteps heavy. He put his hand behind Rime's head and pulled it toward his own until they were standing forehead to forehead. They stood like that, the chieftain of Ravnhov and the onetime heir to the Council.

Eirik patted Rime's head a couple times. "If *you* were Mannfalla, Rime An-Elderin, I'd follow you. I'd follow *you*. You hear me?" Eirik's voice wobbled. Rime nodded.

"I'll come back, I promise. You have my word, Eirik."

"That's all I need." Eirik let him go and walked away.

DIVERGING PATHS

Father used to say that he could live without feet as long as his heart was strong enough to carry him. And it had been. At times it had been strong enough to carry both of them, right up until Hirka's life was in danger. Only then had it faltered. Only then had Father given up, for her sake. Father's heart had borne hunger, pain, gossip, and illness, but it hadn't been strong enough to bear Kolkagga. Hirka didn't think hers could bear it either.

She was in the raven ravine looking out over Blindból. She had stood here with Tein once, listening to him rage against past injustices. Now she was sitting here because it was the only place in Ravnhov where she could escape the sounds of preparation. Chainmail and swords. Shields being stacked in carts and transported to the battlefield. She only had a few days left, and she didn't want to fill them with the sounds of imminent death. All she wanted was to hear the ravens chattering—the rest merely spoke to people's folly.

The raven ravine cut through the plateau where the chieftain's household was situated, and it ended in an open scar in the mountainside, high above the forest. Here she sat, hidden at the bottom of the ravine, but still high above the world. Blindból looked deceptively easy to travel through from here, but she knew better. The valleys were deep and the forests dense. It took hours to reach each of the towering stone pillars. And from the forest floor they all looked the same, which meant you thought you either were walking in circles or had lost your wits.

Hirka looked up at the top of Bromfjell. There was a raven ring up there. A stone circle. The way out of this world. Hlosnian had given her the verdict earlier that day. Seven days. That was all she could have. Then they had to go up and look. Maybe he could help her get home. The earth had a pulse, he'd said. Sometimes the Might was powerful, other times faint, like a vague memory. Hlosnian said that he wasn't a skilled binder. His gift was his sensitivity. That was why he'd been a stone whisperer for the Council. He'd been able to listen to the pulse. Feel the Might ebb and flow with the seasons and the weather. Stone had memory of the Might. Stone remembered everything that had been and everything that was. Hlosnian needed a powerful flow to help her get home. That would come in seven days.

Everything inside her resisted, but it was like fighting against the waterfall when she had been swept over the edge. It didn't matter what she wanted. Her path had been chosen a long time ago. Ravnhov could never be her home, no matter how at ease she felt here. And Rime could never be hers, no matter how much of her heart he possessed. The unfairness of it all was so overwhelming that she could have drowned in it. She had to leave. And all that she loved had to stay.

Someone was approaching. She knew without looking that it was Rime. He had his own way of walking. Her thirst for the Might awoke, and it annoyed her. What was she? A cat in front of an empty dish? She would have to learn to live with that feeling, because she was never going to see him again.

He crouched down next to her. He was ready to leave. Dressed in black, with his bag on his back. Kolkagga. Hirka dangled her feet over the edge because she knew that he wouldn't do the same.

"Thinking about the war?" he asked.

She shook her head. "I'm thinking about salvation."

"That might have been possible once, but the Seer doesn't exist." It was the first time she'd heard him say it without pain.

"He exists if you let him exist."

"You sound like Ilume," he said.

"You should have listened to her. She knew. There is a seer. *You* decide whether He exists. *You're* the Seer, Rime."

He laughed abruptly. "I don't have any power to change people's minds."

"Then what's the point in leaving?"

He didn't answer at first. That confirmed her suspicions. He was in the process of making a decision. The wrong decision. "I don't belong here. I'm Kolkagga."

"Kolkagga?" Hirka snorted. "That's probably the worst place to be if you don't have any power."

"Time will tell. I have to answer for what I've done."

Hirka clenched her teeth. He was talking like a fool. As though he didn't understand how the world worked. Him, the boy who used to laugh at her because *she* didn't understand. Because *she* was naive. He was going to return to Kolkagga. Roll over like a dog. Offer his life in exchange for the men he had killed. What good was that going to do? What good had it done Father?

"So what are you, Rime? A child? Are you Tein? Is that what you are? You can't run anymore. There's nowhere left to go. You think you're being responsible by letting Kolkagga kill you for what you've done, but that's not responsibility. Dying is also running, Rime. You're taking the easiest way out of all."

He looked surprised. What had he expected? For her to say, "Thanks for everything and good luck"? For her to understand? *He* was the one who didn't understand. Hirka got up. "You once asked me who I was. But you're the one who doesn't know who you are, Rime. I'm Hirka. I'm the tailless girl. The child of Odin. I'm the one who doesn't belong here. All you had was the Seer. Who are you without Him? Already dead? What a load of crock." Her heart grew heavier with every word. She saw a look of pain cross his face and it made her ache so sweetly that she couldn't stop. "Do you think I'm just running away, Rime? Do you think I want to leave this world? Obviously I don't want to, but I'm doing it anyway. Because I have to. And because nobody can do it for me."

He didn't reply. His eyes followed her while she paced back and forth along a ledge that dropped farther down into the ravine. The ravens stirred anxiously in the bushes.

"You're heir to a seat on the Council. Something you never wanted and never asked for. But you know what, Rime? You might not want it, but nobody else can do anything with that position. Nobody else can topple the Council that you love to hate. Nobody else can prevent a hundred thousand men from clashing out there on the battlefield. Nobody!"

She pointed at the forest. "In a few days, the sky will be black with shrieking ravens, and they'll be able to eat their fill. Because you're blinded by hate. Don't you see that the Council is the only place the world can be changed from? Are you that blind?!"

He didn't get up, and he didn't look at her either. He'd made his choice.

She laughed in despair. "Blind, well … Nobody else can stop the blind, either! Nobody can stop Urd from destroying the world in the most despicable way imaginable. Nobody else can make him pay for Ilume. And nobody else can stop Ramoja. Do you really think a group of raveners can do the job you're meant to do? They're going to die, all of them. A senseless bloodbath while you're hiding in Blindból!"

As soon as she was finished, she realized how long she had been wanting to shout that. She'd thought it would help, but it didn't. Talking like she despised him didn't make her despise him. It just made her feel bad.

He stood up.

"What difference does it make what I do? You're leaving anyway." His voice was sharper than normal. Hirka's arms fell to her sides. The weight of what he had said struck her. Shattered what she thought she knew.

He needed her.

She had thought it was the other way around. That it had always been the other way around. Now she saw everything they had been through in a new light. He hadn't helped her during the Rite because she needed it. He had needed to defy the Council. He hadn't dragged her through Blindból for her sake, but for his own.

He didn't look at her while he spoke. "I thought I was part of a struggle that meant something. I was Kolkagga. I was the Seer's servant. But you're right. Without Him there's nothing. No purpose. Everything I was slipped through my fingers and disappeared. And the blind are back, so you're going to leave here, no matter what I do. I've already lost this fight."

"No! No, Rime. Aren't you listening? You kept me alive *because* I was going to leave. We've already won this fight!"

He drew closer. "We've only won when Kolkagga hear what I have to say. When they realize they're fighting for the enemy. The world isn't controlled by Eisvaldr, Hirka. The world is controlled by those who control Kolkagga. When they hear me … And when we topple Urd Vanfarinn so that you can stay. *That's* when we've won."

Hirka heard an echo of Ilume's words. Kolkagga. That was the last word that had passed her lips before she died. Hirka looked at Rime and felt a glimmer of hope. She would have given anything for him to be right. He was Kolkagga, he could stop Urd. And she could stay. She could stay here in Ravnhov. Nobody cared about the rot here.

Her hope was extinguished the moment the thought crossed her mind. It was hopeless. It would always be hopeless. Even if Rime succeeded in toppling Urd, even if he took his place on the Council and prevented a war, even if she could stay here, she would never be a part of his world. What was she thinking? Why was she pushing him back to a world where she could never have him? She was never going to see him again. She stared up at him. Tried to burn his image into her mind so she'd never forget. White hair and wolf eyes.

"Give me a few days, Hirka." He stepped closer. So close that she could feel the heat from his breath.

"To do what?" She pressed her arms against her sides so she wouldn't automatically lift them to touch him.

"Eight days, maybe nine. If I'm not back to tell you that Urd is dead before that time, then you can leave. But not before."

She laughed. There was nothing else to be done. "Rime, I can't choose when I have to leave. Hlosnian has given me seven days. In seven days the Might will surge and he can help me get out. And you're asking for eight."

He closed his eyes. Seven was too few. She knew it. Four days through Blindból to Mannfalla, and four days back. And it would be difficult, even for a black shadow without a child of Odin in tow. Rime opened his eyes again.

"Seven days. I'll send a raven when Urd is dead. Promise you won't leave before then." He grabbed her and pulled her toward him. "Promise!"

His lips were cool against her cheek. Her body screamed for the Might, but she said nothing. They were in Ravnhov. The Might was strong here, and she would never be able to resist it. It would pick her apart. Lay her bare. He'd see her every thought. Her fear of the unknown. The poisonous need to ask him to stay with her. To say to Slokna with his world and that he should follow her to hers. And if he realized how deeply she wanted that, maybe that's how it would be. Maybe he'd follow her and let the world burn. That would be almost as horrible as never seeing him again.

"I'm the rot, Rime. No matter what you do, it doesn't change what I am."

He held her face in his hands and smiled. His eyes darted around as though he was trying to figure out how she was put together.

"You're not the rot, Hirka. You never have been and never will be. You're all that is good in this world. *We* are the rot. Not you."

Hirka felt her resistance weakening with his every word. She melted into him. Reached up and kissed him cautiously. A gentle puff against his lips. She could feel the edges of his pendant through his black clothes. An assassin with a childhood keepsake around his neck. He started to bind. She swallowed and backed away from him a little, before the Might could take hold.

"One point to you if you make it back within seven days," she said. His eyes burned white at her. He was a living plea, fists clenched at his sides.

Then he pulled up his black hood and jumped over the ledge.

BROMFJELL

The world ended here in Ravnhov.

Hirka crossed a deserted courtyard and over the bridge. She followed the narrow stone steps down into the ravine and continued between the trees toward the ravenry. The grass was white with frost. No one else had walked there today. No one else would either. Every man over the age of fifteen had left to stand against Mannfalla for the last time. A war she would never know the outcome of.

Many women had left as well. The women in Ravnhov weren't like the women in Mannfalla. Maja had left the inn to lead hundreds into battle.

Hirka reached the ravenry and stopped in the doorway. The room smelled of blood. Two old men were preparing fresh game for the ravens. There was no one else here. The young raveners were able-bodied and on their way to fight. One of the old men spotted her. He shook his head. Nothing from Rime on the seventh day either.

A raven had come from their allies in Mannfalla with news of the Rite Feast, the spectacular celebration that marked the final day of the Rite. Today was a festive occasion. Ravens had also come from the battlegrounds with reports that groups of men had clashed in the forests: soldiers from Mannfalla, from Ravnhov, and a couple from Ulvheim. There had been sporadic attempts to break through the outpost line around Hrafnfell. A small group had succeeded, but they were caught before they reached the chiefdom.

So it had begun. The war was a fact. But in Mannfalla they were dancing. Hirka didn't ask how many had died. She didn't want to know. There was nothing she could do.

She went back to the great hall. Hlosnian was waiting for her inside. The old stone whisperer was standing with his eyes closed and his hands against the stone column he'd been working on for so long. He called it a gossipmonger. A feeler. He nodded at her. Much too quickly, the time had come.

She looked around. She had nothing apart from her bag. What more would she need where she was going? No one knew, not even Hlosnian. Hirka shouldered her bag and they headed out. There were no horses to carry them. They'd all been given far more important jobs. Instead, they walked, along the paths behind the town and up toward Bromfjell. The wind picked up when they reached higher ground, and it started to snow.

Neither of them said anything. The sky was gray when they began their final ascent. They reached a peak and rested for a few minutes. According to Hlosnian, Bromfjell had three peaks. Three caves leading in to the dragon that people had once thought resided within the mountain. Hlosnian's breathing was labored. She felt sorry for him. He would have to walk back in the dark. Alone. Without her.

But he wouldn't be completely alone. Several ravens accompanied them, dancing in the wind like animated scraps of cloth. Maybe they sensed something was going to happen. Or maybe they were monitoring the ebb and flow of the Might, just like she and Hlosnian were.

Kuro sat on her shoulder for the last leg. Now and then he took off and flew around them, communing with the other ravens, but he always came back. What would happen to him? Would he cross the divide with her? Into an unknown world?

They reached the final peak and Kuro once again took flight and disappeared. Hlosnian stopped to catch his breath. Hirka looked around. The world looked boundless. She couldn't see Ravnhov anymore, but she could see the mountains in Blindból. She could see the open countryside where the war would be fought, though it was too far away for her to see any people. And before her stood a stone circle, in a crater at the summit.

It was bigger than she had expected. She counted sixteen stones in the outer circle and eight smaller stones in the inner circle. She and Hlosnian walked along the edge until they found a good place to approach it from. The bottom of the crater was covered in yellow moss. No snow had settled here, even though it was still coming down. It felt warmer in the crater. The air was thicker, almost thrumming. Or was it just her? A flight of white butterflies danced among the stones. She'd never seen the like.

"Winter whites," Hlosnian said. "Apparently this is the only place they can be found."

It was like walking through living snow. On any other day she'd have happily danced among them. But now she was too weighed down by the knowledge that she was leaving forever. And that Rime was probably dead.

He's alive.

The stones were silent gray giants that paid them no heed. They'd always stood here and always would. Ymling or embling, it was all the same to them.

"Should we wait?" Hlosnian looked at her.

"No. There's no reason to wait. Do what you have to do."

Hirka swallowed a feeling of helplessness. How would she survive all alone in the unknown when she didn't even know what Hlosnian had to do to send her there? Which of the stones was hers? Where was she supposed to go? She had to trust that Hlosnian knew. Or that he would figure it out.

They walked in toward the middle, and Hlosnian found the Might. At first it was like a whisper. A trickle. A lot weaker than when she was with Rime. It gradually intensified, as if drawing strength from each of the stones around them, but it was still only a shadow of what she had felt with Rime, and her longing for him threatened to take over. She was leaving him for good. And she didn't know what she was walking into. Fear gripped her, and it was too much for the Might. It couldn't be stopped.

"Wait!" She put a hand on Hlosnian's arm. He looked at her mournfully, the furrows in his forehead deepening. He thought she was backing out, but that wasn't why she'd stopped him. Hirka could see shadows along the top of the crater. She squinted to see better. Had the blind found them? Had Hlosnian done something wrong?

No. It was horses. Men on horses.

Hirka pointed. Men! She felt her fear loosen its grip. Rime! It had to be Rime. Or someone with a message from him. She was saved! Everyone was saved! Hirka ran to meet them.

When she saw who it actually was, her body stiffened. Dozens of men had spread out and surrounded them. Urd jumped off his horse and stormed toward her, his cloak flapping behind him. The Council mark on his forehead made him look like he had three eyes. Three narrow slits. Hirka stumbled back. Urd. It had all been for nothing. Memories flashed before her eyes. The guardsmen in the vaults. The stew she'd hidden in his chair. The way he'd tied her up and stuffed her into a crate. He wouldn't think twice about killing her.

Urd pulled off his glove and raised his fist long before he reached her. She turned to run, but it smashed into her jaw. Her face went numb. She fell backward onto the moss. Hlosnian shouted. She looked up at the sky. Dark clouds edged with gold. Urd's face appeared above her. She turned away, but he wrenched her face back toward his own. Hirka could see a distorted reflection of herself in the gold collar around his neck. He shook her head and smiled.

"Shall we call it even?"

THE BLIND

Hirka was on her back, lying on cold stone. Her arms had been forced beneath her, tied behind her. Every time she tried to flip onto her side, pain shot through her shoulder. Had they broken something? She wasn't sure. Her feet were bound, too, with a leather belt around her ankles. She'd tried to feel for the edge of the stone with her feet, but it was too wide. Instead, she wriggled backward, bracing herself for a fall.

I'm not afraid.

But that was a lie. Hirka *was* afraid. She'd never been more afraid. Not for her own life—she'd feared for that so many times now that practically every moment she lived was a gift. She was afraid of other things altogether. Afraid of all the answers she was never going to get. Afraid that Ravnhov would fall. That the Council would yield to a madman who would destroy everything she'd ever known. Everything anyone had ever known.

Hirka lifted her hips and kicked with her heels so she could inch back a little farther.

Most of all, she was afraid of the certainty that nobody would be able to prevent it. The Council's holy men and women had always been the truth. The law. They'd had all the answers, and the will to look ahead.

But they weren't holy. They weren't even strong. They were just men and women. None of them could do anything to help her.

None of them had stopped Urd. People feared the blind, but who was more blind?

Rime had been right. The world was too big to change. She'd seen that for herself, during the Rite. How pointless it was to try to talk sense into so many people at one time. It couldn't be done. Rime had known that. But he'd set out for certain death anyway, and she'd let him. She fought back tears. They wouldn't help her here.

Hirka felt the edge of the stone against the back of her head. She wriggled a little farther, and then bent her head back. Finally she could see more than just clouds. The downside was that everything was upside down, lying as she was. The stone pillars were still there. They looked like they were suspended in midair. With men between them, hanging like bats. She smiled, until she felt a stab of pain in her jaw.

Maybe she'd already been transported to another world? Was that what it was like to pass through the stones? Looking at a mirror image of reality? Distorted, but still recognizable? Upside down?

She spotted Urd. He was talking to the man who had sacrificed his leather belt to keep her feet together. A heavyset warrior fiddling with the blade of a straight sword. He already had a short sword hanging by his hip, so presumably he had taken the one he was playing with now from one of Ravnhov's soldiers. One of the many on the battlegrounds. One of those they had killed to reach Bromfjell unseen. Maybe someone she knew. She tugged at her hands, and the ropes chafed against her skin. It was no use. She wasn't going anywhere.

"Hirka?"

She gave a start, but then she recognized Hlosnian's voice. "Hlosnian? Where are you? Are you okay?" She looked around but couldn't see him.

"I'm here. On the ground. I'm all right. Are you?"

"Never been better."

"Hirka, you have my word. I'm never going to help him. I'll die before I help him!"

Hirka smiled out of hopelessness, despite the pain in her jaw. "He doesn't need help, Hlosnian. He can open the doors on his own."

Hlosnian snorted. "Urd Vanfarinn? Never in Slokna. He wouldn't recognize a stone whisperer if he sat on one. He wouldn't know where to start."

Hirka didn't have the strength to argue with him. She let Hlosnian feel safe for a little while longer. Soon he'd realize that everything was lost, regardless of what he did or didn't do.

Urd approached her. She braced herself for more blows. He grabbed her by the jacket and dragged her off the stone. She fell to the ground, ending up with her feet drawn up in front of her and her back against the stone. Urd crouched down in front of her. He studied her and picked a bit of dust off her jacket. A gesture Hirka neither understood nor appreciated.

She stared at him. It hurt to open her mouth, but she refused to give him the pleasure of seeing that. "I've never done anything to you, Urd."

"Fadri. Urd-fadri. Didn't anyone teach you any manners?" His eyes roamed around her body. "No, that's right. You're not people, are you?"

She swallowed. "I've never done anything to you. You've no reason to kill me."

"Oh, no. *I'm* not going to kill you. That pleasure is reserved for someone else. That said, I'm sure I'll get some pleasure out of it too."

"Why? How in Slokna can you find pleasure in other people dying? Don't you understand how sick that is? How ruined you are?!"

He grabbed her by the neck and pulled her closer. His pupils were black pinpricks on a pale background. "You like to underestimate me, girl, that's your biggest mistake. What do you think I am? An angry drunk killing someone outside a tavern? Some base scoundrel stabbing people for coin? Do you even know where we are? The kind of power that lies here?"

"So you're killing me for power? I don't see the difference."

He growled like an animal and tightened his grip on her neck. His face was right in front of hers. "I wanted to keep you alive for power. But I'm going to kill you for something far more important."

His breath smelled of death. Hirka pulled back in disgust. She stared at his gold collar. The truth behind Urd's madness hit her, and it was more terrifying than anything she'd imagined. The truth behind his desperation. The reason for the unreal risk he was willing to take, with no regard for anything or anyone else.

"You're dying," she whispered.

A shadow of pain crossed his face, like it was a feeling he no longer owned, but remembered from when he was a child. His hand tightened slightly around Hirka's neck. He caressed her skin with his thumb. "Not anymore, girl. The scar will be a useful reminder to never trust in the rot. I'd rather put my faith in the blind than in your father."

"My father is dead. You've never met him, and he's never done anything to you."

Urd laughed. The sound ended in a gurgling splutter. "So the myths are true, then. Children of Odin have the brains of sheep." A drop of blood ran from the corner of his mouth. He grabbed his neck. "Your father let me rot on the inside when I ceased to be useful to him. That's doing something to me, wouldn't you say? It's true that I've never met him, but I've heard his voice. And you know what, I'd rather swallow my own sword than hear him again."

Hirka felt her fear give way to a need to know more. Of course. Father wasn't the father he was referring to. She was a child of Odin. Her real father was somewhere in another world. And she would never meet him. Or find out anything about him. Unless she survived. Unless Urd survived. This couldn't end here. Not now.

"I can help," she said. Cautiously at first, then she grew bolder. "I can help! Give me my bag. I have yellowbell and vengethorn! I have a salve of soldrop and—"

"A salve?" Urd looked at her as though she were witless. "You have a salve?" He laughed again. The blood at the corners of his mouth ran along his lower lip and between his teeth. He loosened the collar and bared his neck to reveal an open wound. Hirka recoiled from the stench, but she couldn't bring herself to look away.

A raven's beak. Half-open. Embedded in his throat, surrounded by rotting tissue. Discolored skin. The rot.

It was unspeakably horrible. Her father had given Urd the rot. It was no myth. She swallowed. Sadness and disgust welled up inside her.

Urd closed the collar again, and the smell dissipated. "Only the blind can heal blindcraft, child of Odin. And they're going to do just that, as soon as they get the tailless girl. It's as simple as that."

He stood up and looked down at her. "You're a stone sacrifice. You should have been theirs the day you were born, girl. You've just taken a detour."

Behind him, the ravens danced in the wind.

Hlosnian sat on the ground, rocking like a child. He'd tried to move away from the stones, but two of Urd's men had kicked him and dragged him back. Hirka had whispered to him about the Might, and how it saw everything and everyone. About how they would get their punishment, but Hlosnian wasn't listening. He'd disappeared into himself. He was muttering about blindcraft and blood.

Seeing Urd kill the raven had tipped him over the edge. It had been hanging from one of the horses, tied up like a chicken. Urd had slit its throat and collected its blood in a bowl. It had shrieked the entire time. Dead, but not dead. Like Hirka.

"He's going to force stone. Force stone," Hlosnian repeated.

His voice reminded Hirka of the whispering pleas of Mannfalla's most wretched inhabitants, the ones who stood with their hands against the walls of the hall every night. "It's all right, Hlosnian. Everyone dies sooner or later." Hirka no longer felt any fear. The intensity of it had been unbearable, so it had simply disappeared. The space it left had now been filled with sorrow and anger. There was nothing else.

"You can't force stone. Broken doors can't be locked. The dragon ... He's going to wake the dragon. The tree is no more."

A peal of thunder gave Hlosnian a start. He was fragile as glass. The only consolation was that he wasn't the only one. Urd's men had pulled back from the stone circle. They were whispering together in the shadows, while Urd walked around smearing one stone after the other with raven blood. There were seventeen men left. One had already fled, and he certainly wouldn't be the last. Their fear wasn't hard to understand. As terrifying as Urd must have seemed, the deadborn had to be worse. Hirka guessed that none of the leather-clad men would have come had they known the blind were also invited.

"He can't pay the price for forcing it. No one can pay the price ..."

Hirka was close enough to Hlosnian that he could rest his head on her shoulder. It didn't make the stone carver any calmer, but it made her feel better. Supporting him gave meaning to the meaninglessness.

The sky had blackened. The stones jutted out like the pale teeth of a toppled giant. Hirka hoped one of them would fall and break every bone in the body of the figure walking around and making them bleed. Had she not been tied up, she would have toppled them herself. She tried to move her fingers, but there was no feeling left in them.

We are already dead.

Would she meet Rime in Slokna? Father? Was there a Slokna for everyone, no matter where you came from?

Three men approached Urd. She couldn't hear what they were saying, but she could guess. They'd witnessed the killing of the raven. Urd had brought bad luck on them all. Superstition or not, the men were agitated. They were only guardsmen, after all. Men with a job to do. Some of them had probably been in the service of the Vanfarinn family for generations. Their families were clothed and fed because they were accompanying a lunatic to Ravnhov. How much did they really know? One of them took off his helmet and pointed at those who had been too afraid to join them. Urd raised his voice, and the men shuffled back outside the stone circle with their tails between their legs. The horses neighed nervously from the shadows, but nobody went to calm them.

Urd came and stood a couple of steps away from Hirka, his back to her. He looked half dead. His fingers were stained red with sacred blood. She caught his smell again. She was amazed that the others could talk to him without showing disgust. They were talking to a dead man. Surely they had to know? She'd saved enough lives and seen enough death to smell the difference.

Then came the Might. It wasn't like Rime's. This was an unwanted presence in her body. Like the heat of a stranger trying to force himself upon her. Like the prisoner who had died in the pits. Then it grew stronger. Harsher. Hirka fought against it. Shut off her body. Urd couldn't possibly know that she was a tool that could amplify his Might. That was a secret she intended to take with her to Slokna.

The winter whites were gone. She thought she saw them, but it was just snow falling outside the stone circle. For some reason it wasn't falling inside—maybe it, too, feared the blind? The ground beneath her felt like it was breathing. The air grew thinner and had a foul taste to it. Hirka suddenly had a sense of infinite space. An emptiness she could fall into. Between the stones, the landscape grew hazy, as though she was looking at it through a fire. So imperceptible that she almost doubted it. Thin blades of grass inexplicably flattened against the ground.

And then pale shadows emerged. Out of nothing, they came. Out of the darkness. From somewhere no one could see. They grew sharper. Became real. Living. And they were coming toward them.

Hirka pressed up against the stone. She couldn't panic. Couldn't cry. She'd encountered the blind before. Stood face-to-face with one of them. And survived. She sat there, alive enough to hear her own heart beating. Alive enough to feel pain.

There was a rumbling beneath her. Like thunder in the mountain. Hirka glanced at Hlosnian. He was staring at the ground. His sweaty hair hung limply over his face. Hlosnian couldn't help anyone anymore.

Men were screaming. So this wasn't a dream. They'd seen the blind too. Urd snarled that he'd personally skewer the first person to take off, but that was a chance several of the men were apparently willing to take. They rode off on their horses as though they had the blind at their heels. Ravens screeched, circling the outer edge of the crater. Chasing one another. They darted in and out of the stones, in groups, like black flames.

What would Rime do if he were here now?

Hirka straightened her back and looked up. Three of the blind were coming toward them. They were pure muscle. They moved with pride, completely unbothered by the fact that they were naked as animals. They could have been ymlings. Well-built ymlings, mind. With white eyes. And clawed fingertips.

Urd took a couple of steps back. She wished she could take pleasure in his fear, in everything he'd thought he could control. But she only felt sorrow. Black sorrow. It poisoned his Might.

Bromfjell roared its disgust, protesting the presence of the pale ones. The first. Nábyrn. The deadborn. Urd suddenly seemed less sure of himself—had he even seen them before?

Hirka felt a change in Urd's Might. He was hesitant, uncertain. These creatures weren't going to save him. Nobody could save him.

The Might was snuffed out in a silent shriek. Then it grew stronger again. Hotter. Better. Familiar.

Hirka jumped up onto her knees and looked around.

Rime?

It had to be Rime! She knew this Might! It was the Might the way he used it. Only him. She wasn't dreaming. She felt his warmth tear through her body like wildfire.

"Hlosnian!" He didn't hear her. The ravens were shrieking too loudly, and Bromfjell was thundering. "Hlosnian!" She tried to crawl toward the old man. He had to know that Rime was here. That salvation was at hand. Hirka could see several of Urd's men running. Where were the others? She could hear someone shouting on the outside of the crater. The sound of steel on steel. Fighting. Urd moved to the side so the blind had a clear path to her. There was nothing between them and her. Nothing. Just the Might. Yet they hesitated. Was it because of the ravens still circling above them like a living cloud? The air was charged. Ready for a storm. Something smelled like it was burning.

A shadow flew over her. For a moment she thought it was Kuro, but he wasn't the only one who made a habit of flying over people. She shouted his name when she realized it was him. He was alive. He was here. Rime was standing between her and the nábyrn.

She jumped at the touch of cold steel on her hands. Suddenly they were free. Black shadows ran between the stones, swarming in the dark. Men were screaming. She could hear them dying. Urd shouted at them to stop running, but none did. Nobody came to help him. Or her.

Hirka fumbled desperately with the leather belt around her feet. She kicked it off at last and grabbed hold of Hlosnian. "Hlosnian! Rime is here! Kolkagga are here!" She pulled on his bindings.

Hlosnian didn't help. He just sat there, rocking back and forth. "He forced the stone. Forced it with blood. The dragon. The dragon is waking up."

Hirka wanted to slap him back to his senses, but it was more important to get him free. Finally she pulled him to his feet. The ground buckled beneath them, making it difficult to stay standing. The bravest among Urd's men waved their swords around in the dark as though fighting figments of their imagination.

Kolkagga.

Black shadows, almost impossible to see. Something flashed on the ground. Someone had dropped a sword. Hirka flung her body toward it. The Might made it frighteningly easy. She could reach farther than her own height. Pain tore through her body, but this Might was Rime's, so she could handle it. She could pick it apart and put it aside. It was so strong. And it played tricks on her, because for a moment, she was sure that she heard Tein shouting. Maybe you went crazy if the Might was strong enough? A new terror filled her. This stream would not be stopped. The Might would rip her apart. Destroy her. Rend her body into tiny pieces.

Urd backed toward her. She squeezed the sword, in case he came closer. The ravens were starting to get aggressive. They were shrieking like crazy, circling, diving.

"The tailless one! Take the tailless one!" But Urd's voice didn't carry. He grabbed his neck and fell to his knees.

Rime swung his sword at the boldest of the blind, but they were too quick, disappearing before the blade could do any damage. He drew on more of the Might. Hirka wanted him to stop. She couldn't take any more. Didn't have the capacity.

Tein and Ynge came running over the edge of the crater, dwarfed by the enormous stones in the foreground. Where had they come from? They were supposed to be on the battlefield, fighting the war against Mannfalla. Did that mean she was seeing things? The world had been turned on its head again. She had died. None of this was real.

Rime drew upon the Might, danced around the blind and sliced one of them in two. The figure fell apart and toppled into the moss before the blood started to flow. The other two backed up against the stones, wraithlike, teeth bared. They, too, feared death, like everyone else—ymlings and emblings alike.

Hirka clutched the sword in her hand. Urd was on his knees in front of her, tugging at the gold collar. It came loose and blood poured from his throat. It looked black in the darkness. Urd retched. The beak in his throat moved. It crawled out from the open wound, as though it was trying to get away from him. The stench of rotten flesh filled the air.

Hirka stood as though bewitched. She didn't want to stare, but the sight was too unbelievable for her to look away. The beak lay motionless on the ground. Urd turned toward her. "Take her!" He screamed as though drowning, as though he were fighting to keep his head above water. Hirka raised the sword and walked toward him. He crawled away from her like a wounded animal. Wild-eyed, on all fours. Hirka heard her own words in her head.

You can't just kill people!

He managed to clamber to his feet, and she swung the sword. His tail was left on the ground, twitching. Urd screamed in pain.

"You've forgotten something," she seethed, and the Might carried her voice above the surrounding chaos. "They're here to collect the tailless one." As she backed away from Urd, she met the milky-white gaze of one of the blind. She raised two fingers to her throat, like the one at the waterfall had done.

"Hirka?" Rime's voice. But she couldn't look at him now. She stared into the blindling's eyes and threw the sword on the ground. Urd reached for it, but the blind got hold of him first. Dug their claws into his shoulders, dragged him backward between the stones, and disappeared. She heard his shouts long after they were gone from this world. Screams from nothingness. From nowhere.

Hlosnian clambered to his feet. "Run! Run, you fools!"

Bromfjell roared beneath them. Thunder from stone. Then the ground ruptured and a column of fire exploded toward the heavens.

THE DRAGON AWAKES

The Might carried her like she wasn't even touching the ground, though she could feel her feet moving. Around her, the mountain spewed fire. It threw up blood, just like Urd had done. Burning red. Leaping skyward. Cracks opened in the ground in several places.

In the name of the Seer, what have we done?

She felt someone tugging at her. Why were they trying to stop her from looking? Somewhere deep down she knew she couldn't stay where she was. Not here, in the circle, in the middle of the crater. But that realization wasn't getting through. It belonged to another time, another place. Right now, she had to look. The fire was like a waterfall flowing in the wrong direction. An unbelievable force pushing up into the black sky, where it dispersed like glowing rain.

So this was what the end of the world looked like. And the beginning of the world.

The Might burned within her, ripping through her veins, through her muscles and her legs. The fire in the mountain was the fire in her. Perhaps they were one. This was home. She was the mountain. She was the dragon in Bromfjell. She saw the fire that had birthed them all, that would end them all.

People shouted around her, through the fog of the Might, but the only one she could hear was Rime. He shouted without words. There was no distance between them that required words anymore.

The Might had burned all obstacles and she could read him without needing to see him. Knew where he was, knew what he wanted.

The stones stood bathed in red light, through autumn, winter, and spring. An immovable circle around the fire. Silent witnesses to the mountain's incomprehensible rage. The ravens screeched around them. Kolkagga gathered around the stones, which offered the only protection from the embers. One of them was supporting Hlosnian. The blind were gone. Urd was gone.

"Here! Here!" Hlosnian shouted, puffing like bellows. "Between the stones!"

He's right. That's the only way out, Rime said from within her.

Red rain fell over the stones. The embers gathered and started flowing in streams between them. The ground was going to fall out from under them. Bromfjell was going to explode. Someone screamed. Rime grabbed her, and she saw him. He'd torn off his black hood. His face was shiny with sweat. She smiled at him. He looked at her like she'd lost her mind.

They were all in such a tearing hurry. Hirka wasn't. She spotted her bag and smiled. The last time she'd insisted on having it with her, it had stopped an arrow that otherwise would have hit her. She grabbed it and ran toward the edge of the crater with everyone else. It felt like she was barely moving—everything was so slow. Hlosnian pointed at two of the stones. Rime had a good grip on her hand, so she had no other choice but to follow him. Everyone else was following him too: Hlosnian, the ravens, Kolkagga. Even Tein and two others from Ravnhov. Now that the dragon had awoken and the mountain was after them.

Rime was holding Hirka in one hand and Urd's tail in the other. All that remained of Urd Vanfarinn. Together they ran between the stones.

Everything ceased to exist. Everything fell silent. Hirka's stomach lurched.

Hirka and Rime ran into an empty space where everything ceased to exist. A space that moved around them at an incredible speed. Bare. Without color. Without light. *Without the Might*, she realized in a panic. This had to be Slokna. A place where everything slept. No. There wasn't even anything that could sleep here.

Wait, there! Flashes of light. Openings in the endless darkness. Stone.

Hirka reached out for them so they wouldn't disappear, so the darkness wouldn't extinguish them. They were pulled toward the stones. The smell of fire lingered in their nostrils. They walked between the tall stones and suddenly all sound came flooding back.

The first thing she heard was people shouting. Again. Stone shattering. Something collapsing. The all-consuming Might was there long before she realized where she was. Long before the walls of the Rite Hall appeared around the panic-stricken crowd within. Rime stepped into the room. She followed him, so full of the Might that her feet were hypersensitive, like distended cushions against the ground. Her entire body pulsated. Was that why they were running? Could they see that she was about to rupture?

But she wasn't what ruptured. It was the room. Hirka looked back at the gaping hole they'd just come from. An open wound in the wall. What had they done? In the name of the Seer …

Rime walked around the curved wall. His feet weren't touching the floor. He was walking on air. Walking on the Might. The wall started to crack. Tumbling down where he walked. The Might raged around him. Small mother-of-pearl tiles came loose and flew across the room. People screamed around them. Ducked and protected their heads with their arms.

It was raining tiles and stone. They came loose from the walls around Rime. From the ceiling above him, drifting past him as if on an oil slick. Slowly. Until he'd passed and they could fall normally. It was as if time stood still around him and no one else. The air crackled. It rained white and gold.

Images on the wall became indistinct. Fell apart. Old sculptures started to crumble. Colors ran. Only the solid stone pillars remained standing. They emerged where limestone and tiles were torn away by an energy Hirka almost couldn't bear.

They were huge. They were many. Hidden in the walls for a thousand years. They had found the stone circle of Blindból. The lost gateways. They had never been hidden in the mountains behind Eisvaldr. They were here. In the Rite Hall. Beneath the red dome.

Rime walked up the steps to the platform at the back of the hall, up toward the Council. Hirka followed him as if in a trance. Unable to do anything else. Paralyzed by the Might. The men and women of the Council had gotten up. Some of them shouted for the guardsmen, who were trying to ensure people got out without trampling each other. Hirka could see every drop of sweat on their foreheads. Every glance they threw at the ceiling, praying it wouldn't collapse.

Hirka spotted Vetle. Ramoja and the other raveners. The Might read them like an open book. They were ripe with purpose and clearly not here for the same reason as everyone else. The people in Mannfalla were here for the final day of the Rite, all starched skirts and fine shawls, here to celebrate and to dance. The raveners were dotted among the crowd. The raveners were here to put an end to an era. They just hadn't begun, and now they never would.

Hirka thought back on her own Rite with a weary smile. People had scattered in every direction then as well. Some tried to get to the north exits, others the east. Some wanted to stay put and see what was happening. Some cried out for the Seer.

Rime approached the Council. There were only ten of them. Ilume was dead. Urd was dead. And the Rite Hall was falling apart. Eir stood with her hand over her mouth, staring up at the stones looming over them. The world's most powerful men and women had never known what the hall was hiding. They stared at Rime.

Rime had lost control. Hirka had to get through to him, stop him. The Might was going to destroy her. He was giving her everything he had. He'd forgotten her. Forgotten everything. Everything apart from the ten people standing in front of him. Beneath him. The air around him was so saturated that his feet weren't touching the ground.

His eyes burned white. He was everything that had ever lived, everything that did live, and everything that would ever live. He was the Might. And he flowed through Hirka. Her skin thrummed, pulsated. Her mind crackled like it was full of sparks. Her veins wanted to press their way out of her arms. She clung to reality.

Rime threw Urd's tail on the floor. It uncoiled and blood seeped from the end before it lay still. Eir and the bearded councillor, Jarladin, were standing closest. They both backed away. The others came closer to see what it was. When they realized, they looked away in disgust. None of them said anything. They stared at Rime, waiting for an explanation as to why he had desecrated the hall.

Tell them who you are!

"I am Rime An-Elderin!" Rime's voice carried through the hall. It came as if from an immense empty space contained within him. Echoing inside. People stopped what they were doing. Some eyed the cracks in what remained of the walls warily, but their fear gave way to curiosity. "I am son of Gesa, daughter of Ilume of House An-Elderin. I am here to claim my seat on the Council."

Eir took a step toward him. "What have you done, Rime ..." Her voice was a whisper. It was drowned out by his voice, which was carried by the Might. But she tried. Cautiously. As if standing before a madman. "In the name of the Seer—"

"Stop the lies, Eir. You've failed. Urd is dead. Devoured by the deadborn he brought here. The enemy was among you every single day, but you didn't see it. You did nothing. I'm here to lay claim to my seat."

Hirka clenched her teeth. The Might flowed with his words. Every *S* tore at her muscles. Every *T* struck her bones and reverberated through her entire body. He was drowning everything out. She didn't have room to breathe. She could see everything. Hear everything with an intense clarity that forced itself on her. She wanted to scream. But it was Rime who screamed.

"Give me the seat, or give me the Seer!"

Hirka could hear hundreds of whispering voices in the hall. Just like when she'd stood before them herself. As a child of Odin. Some of them had shields. She'd seen two of the men standing closest to them in Ravnhov. They looked at each other and tried to suppress smiles. As if Rime hadn't just mocked the Raven, and as if Hirka wasn't dying.

But she was dying for Rime. It was worth it. He needed her now. He'd lost touch with the world. He'd become something else. The councillors were mere shadows compared to him. He hung there, every feature accentuated as if he were carved from stone. More defined than reality itself. She feared him now. Feared what he was doing. What he was capable of doing.

She'd dreamed that the Council would fall. That they would pay. For Father. For the days she spent in the vaults. For the lies and for the wounds on her back. Now that they only had moments left, she was terrified of the consequences.

"Where is the Seer?" Rime asked.

A thousand eyes in the hall stared at the Council and at the Seer, who remained silent on the Ravenbearer's staff. No one was shouting anymore. Everyone had quieted in anticipation. Anticipation that turned to fear from one moment to the next. Fear that the Council would fail in this one task. Giving Rime An-Elderin a seer to bow down to. One of the councillors shouted for the guardsmen.

Asked them to seize the blasphemer. But none of the guardsmen moved. None of them were listening.

The hall was waiting. Waiting to see whether the Seer would reveal Himself. Whether He would punish the blasphemer. The Might revealed to Hirka that people were starting to understand. She could feel them flailing like the ground had disappeared from under them, and she would have cried for them, had she been able to. It was a pain too intense to bear, because it emanated from so many.

She took a step closer to Rime. Her feet were heavy, as if encased in iron. Her arms were lead weights that wouldn't be budged. She couldn't reach him where he hung in the air, only one step in front of her.

Then she felt them arrive. Hlosnian and Tein. Kolkagga. People shouted and pressed together in the middle of the room, away from the stones. Kolkagga came out between them. Black as night, they stepped out from the space between worlds. From walls that were no longer there. Hlosnian was holding onto one of them. Tein and Ynge were holding onto each other. Guardsmen threw frantic looks at each other. Someone made the sign of the Seer, as if warding off blindcraft.

Hirka wanted to tell them to move. But she couldn't shout. Couldn't tell them that the ravens were on their way. And then they came. Thousands of them. They came screaming out from the nothingness between the stones and immediately filled the hall. She had never seen anything like it—a storm of wings and talons with only one thing in mind.

Rime. Rime and the Might around him.

They flew around him in circles. A black, living pillar. The raven sitting on the Ravenbearer's staff took flight and joined the fray. Rime hung in their midst. Wolf eyes in a whirlwind of birds. The Might swelled until the floor creaked and the ceiling groaned. Hirka had to fight to stay standing. Three windows shattered and the glass fell down toward them, but it stopped when it encountered the Might. The shards hung in midair, glittering like colored rain around the ravens.

Hirka saw Tein come toward her. She looked at him. Said a silent prayer through the Might, imploring him to act.

He gave you your victory in Ravnhov. Now you need to give him his.

Tein smiled as if seeing her for the first time. He nodded at her, walked up the steps and kneeled before Rime. The Council he'd spent his young life despising stared at him, at the golden crown on his chest. A warrior from Ravnhov. And he was bowing to Rime.

The hall fell to its knees. First those standing closest, then the rest, like a wave. They dropped to the ground and pressed their foreheads to the floor. Covered it with their acknowledgment, like small mounds in a landscape. Black-clad mounds showed who among them was Kolkagga.

Hirka shouted to Rime, but there was no sound. She shouted again, but the sound was lost inside her. Everything was lost inside her. She was an abyss for the Might. She was going to fall into herself and disappear.

Eir was the first of the Council to bow. The Ravenbearer kneeled before Rime, and the rest of the Council did the same. Some more willingly than others, but they couldn't let the Ravenbearer bow alone. Hirka felt Rime's disgust wash through her. He despised them, no matter standing or kneeling.

The last thing she saw was Hlosnian groping his way along the wall. He wasn't looking at the Council or Rime. He had traveled the stone way, and found the biggest and first raven ring. Nothing else mattered. His fingers tore at the tiles to bare the gateways that had been hidden from the world.

Then she felt her knees hit the floor. She fell. First to the ground. Then into Rime. Everything turned to light.

BACK IN BLINDBÓL

Hirka was floating above the ground. In a dream where she was dead. Or had just been born. Green conifers and white fairy's kiss slid past. She'd had this dream before. Rime carrying her through the woods from the Alldjup. He'd saved her, stopped her from falling.

She smiled. He didn't get it. She'd fallen a lot farther than the depth of the Alldjup this time. He couldn't pull her up from here. No one could. She'd fallen inward. Seen the world for what it was. Seen herself for what she was.

She missed the ravens. Where was she? She thought for a moment that she was stuck in the space between worlds. The emptiness between the stones. But then she felt wind on her face. The warmth of the hands that were carrying her. Breath against her ear. There was something here. Between the stones there was nothing, but there was something here. Maybe she was asleep in Slokna.

But she'd had this dream before. She'd been here before.

Her body was no longer hers. It was empty. A fragile shell that could be crushed by a puff of wind. A strange void under the watchful gaze of wolf eyes. She was being guarded. Guarded by something eternal. Something strong.

She'd had this dream before.

Shadows talking. She couldn't hear what they were saying. Couldn't see them. Just sensed them. Then she was lowered into the cold.

Alone again.

This was more familiar to her. Being alone wasn't a dream. Being alone was reality. The way it had always been. The way everyone was.

Light flashed through the grass. She was surrounded by green. She'd become an insect. Shrunk and disappeared into the undergrowth. And now that it had finally happened, it brought her no joy. Nor sorrow. It just was what it was. Peace.

Hirka blinked and her surroundings grew sharper. She hadn't shrunk. She was lying on a mat, on a wooden floor, looking out at the grass. A gray woollen blanket covered her up to the waist. Grass and a floor? She was inside and outside at the same time. She recognized Rime's smell. Where was he? What had happened? Her jacket was folded neatly beside her, but she was still wearing her clothes. Hirka pulled herself up onto her arm. Her entire body felt bruised, but she couldn't see any damage. No marks. No wounds.

The room was bare. The folding doors in front of her were pulled aside, opening onto a green mountain. Two ravens danced in the wind. They dove down into the depths in front of her and disappeared. She was high up. She was in Blindból.

"Everything will be different now."

Hirka gave a start and turned toward the voice. A man was sitting in the middle of the room. His skin was the color of burnt almonds. He was bald and dressed in black. Kolkagga.

There was a hole in the floor between them. A simple open hearth, with a cast-iron pot steaming with ylir root. The man poured the extract into a bowl and held it out for Hirka. She took it and drank. The smell awakened her senses, sharpening them beyond recognition. The tea tasted of a hundred different things, and she could track each and every one from fire to stone, through earth and seasons. She closed her eyes. The bowl was rough against her fingers. Everything was exactly as it seemed.

"You know what I mean," he said.

Hirka opened her eyes again. She knew what he meant, but she didn't know how he could know. He looked at her, but without looking her directly in the eyes. He was looking somewhere behind her. As if he were just imagining her in the room. He spoke with great solemnity. His words were commonplace, but weighted by fate. Hirka suddenly felt like she'd been waiting for him all her life. She opened her mouth to ask about Rime, and what she was doing here, but he interrupted her before she could. "I have something for you."

"What?"

"You can have it when you've finished asking all your questions."

Hirka closed her mouth. It was tempting to pretend she didn't have any questions. But not tempting enough. She finished the bowl of tea and was about to start asking, but he spoke before she could. Hirka smiled. He was like Tein, but at least Tein waited until she had started talking before he interrupted.

Tein. He bent the knee to Rime.

She remembered.

"You're on the top of Aldaudi, in one of the Kolkagga training camps. You're in Blindból." Finally he looked directly at her, as if he was expecting a reaction. She resisted the urge to say she'd been in Blindból before, and that it didn't frighten her. Instead she laughed.

"Is that funny?"

"No. But it's beautiful."

He smiled the smile of a young boy. How old was he? Forty? A hundred? Impossible to say.

"I'm Svarteld. Master of Kolkagga." He picked up the pot and Hirka held out her bowl for a refill. The surrealness of the situation dawned on her. What would she have said if someone had told her that she would end up sitting in Blindból drinking tea with the head of Kolkagga? But that wasn't the only thing she wouldn't have believed only a few months ago. What if she had been told that before the onset of winter, the Council would fall, and an attempt would be made to sacrifice her to the blind? Maybe not knowing was a blessing.

She took the bowl again. Hot with fresh tea.

"I'm Hirka. The tailless girl. I'm menskr. A child of Odin." It was her turn to look at him, expecting a reaction.

"So I hear," he said, unmoved.

Hirka sat up carefully. She stretched her legs, then pulled her feet toward her and let her knees fall apart so that she mirrored his posture. He removed the lid from the pot and added some fresh soldrop petals.

"You needed rest," he said. "That's why you're here. The Might took you to the brink. That sort of thing can chase your nerves outside your body, but in a good way. You hear everything, see everything, and—"

"Feel everything."

He smiled briefly. "The world's been turned upside down out there. Being in Eisvaldr would drive you mad right now. If you lived long enough."

"If I haven't gone mad yet, I doubt I will anytime soon."

"No one knows which way the wind will blow. Don't forget who you are. You were there when the Seer fell. You're the embling who arrived with the deadborn. Don't get me wrong, there are people who think you're the Seer, but there are more who think you brought about His downfall. You weren't safe in Mannfalla. So he brought you here."

She knew who he meant.

"Where is he? I have to see him."

"Rime is busy in Eisvaldr. The world can't be righted overnight." Svarteld looked at her. "Not normally," he added. So Rime had taken Ilume's chair, and now he was going to try to reform the eleven kingdoms.

"Is it good or bad?" Hirka asked.

"The world being turned upside down? That all depends on who—"

"No, I mean what you've got for me."

"I don't know."

"Am I going to be happy or sad when I get it?"

"I don't know that either. Have you asked all your questions now?"

She hadn't. "The war? What's going to happen to Ravnhov?"

"Nobody knows for certain. The fighting stopped when Bromfjell belched out its glowing innards. They say the battlefield split open like a scab. Who knows, that might have killed more people than the fighting, but in any case we now have a fragile truce. Rime is in a tug-of-war with the Council for the third day running. They're clinging to their chairs. Nobody wants to accept the blame for Urd Vanfarinn's election to the Council. Some still want to destroy Ravnhov. It will always be that way. Rime has hard times ahead of him. It's impossible to say what he'll choose to do. Maybe he'll do away with the entire Council. Maybe he'll build a new one. Maybe he'll disband Kolkagga."

"Maybe he'll just get rid of the silver basins from the halls," she said.

They smiled at each other like old friends. "Maybe. Whatever he decides, I'm at his service."

Hirka remembered that she owed him a thank-you. "You followed him! You came with him to Ravnhov, and you helped us when …" She remembered what she had done at the stone circle and stared down at her hand. She could feel the weight of the sword that had taken Urd's tail. The sword that had made him a sacrifice for the blind. Dragged away by the scruff of the neck, screaming into nothingness. She swallowed before she continued. "When the blind came. You followed Rime, even though he had killed three of his own, and even though he was an outlaw. Like me. Was it on your orders?"

"Kolkagga don't give orders. We follow them. I followed Ilume's."

Hirka was taken aback for a moment. "Ilume's dead."

"Yes, who other than Ilume can give orders from Slokna?" He laughed, making it sound like he'd almost forgotten how. He continued. "A raven arrived with a letter from Ilume the night she died."

Hirka remembered. They'd been standing by the tree, before it shattered. Ilume had entered. She had sent a raven. Before the argument with Rime. "She asked you to follow Rime?" Hirka could hear the doubt in her own voice.

"Ilume knew that the Council's days were numbered. She knew she had reason to fear for her life. She wrote as though she was already dead."

The wind chased a pine cone into the room. It rolled toward the hearth. Svarteld got up and threw it back outside. His movements were strangely controlled. As though everything he did was ripe with purpose. He closed the folding doors before sitting back down. His eyes alighted on the fire. It was reflected in his eyes, but Hirka was certain that it was the other way around. He was the fire. The flames were trying to reflect *him*.

"Almost thirteen years ago, I received an order. That order wasn't sent by raven. I was asked to come to Eisvaldr, to the An-Elderin family home. The snow was knee-high in Blindból, so it was dusk before I made it there. Ilume was sitting on a bench in the garden, as though it was summer. She had her back to me. Snow had settled on her robes."

Svarteld's voice was gravelly, and he spoke with long pauses between his sentences, as though he didn't know the story himself. As though it was happening as he told it. "Her daughter, Gesa, had left Mannfalla. Together with her husband and her six-year-old son, she had set out for Ravnhov. She carried with her knowledge that could never be allowed to reach them. Kolkagga's orders were to stop them."

Hirka suddenly felt ill. "She ordered their death?"

"That was the will of the Council, to start with. But Ilume had bargained with them. Rime, Gesa's son, was only six. He didn't know what his mother knew, and even if he did know, he was too young to understand. Of course, An-Elderin's opponents were keen to kill the boy too. To put an end to the family line. A family that had had a seat at the table since the first twelve. But that didn't happen. An-Elderin has more friends than enemies in Insringin. Ilume had to sacrifice her daughter, but she was able to keep her grandchild."

Hirka stared at the dark figure in front of her. A man who was to all intents and purposes a stranger. "How could you obey an order like that? Kill innocents because they knew the truth about everything?!"

He gave a crooked smile. Emptied his tea bowl and set it on the floor. "As fate would have it, we didn't have to kill them. The snow did the job for us, but that doesn't mean their blood isn't on our hands. It was the Might that woke the snow. The Might we used to move past them quickly and unseen. But even if I'd used my sword, I do not decide who is guilty and who is innocent. That is up to the Council. We are the Council's sword. We don't ask why. The Seer has His reasons. Or He would, if He existed. And maybe He does exist, in another form. Rime has made good use of these past few days. He's had to. There needs to be order. Had he not acted as he has done, the power vacuum left by the Seer would have led to war. Chaos. Nobody other than Rime could have seized the opportunity. Nobody else could have done what he's done. Torn down and rebuilt on the same day. He wants to give Urd's chair to Ravnhov. Can you imagine ..."

Hirka suddenly felt restless. She was sitting in no-man's-land while Rime was hard at work in Eisvaldr, surrounded by Council families and power-crazed guilds. Svarteld seemed to think for a moment before he continued. "But regardless of what he chooses, our job will be the same. We carry out his and the Council's will. That is the price we pay for order."

Hirka shook her head. "What is it with you? What is wrong with Kolkagga? You talk about death and about killing as though it were the most natural thing in the world."

"Isn't it?"

"Nobody has the right to take another person's life."

"That's true. No one has the right to take a life. But all of us are already dead."

Hirka rolled her eyes. "Yes, so I've heard."

Why hadn't Ilume said anything? Why hadn't she explained to Rime what she was thinking, what she was doing? Hirka pictured Rime's clenched jaw. Wolf eyes. Presumably he wouldn't have listened, regardless of what Ilume had said.

"Svarteld, have you told Rime about Gesa?"

"Rime knows. He put the pieces together a long time ago. His head and his heart are in the right place."

"You're fond of him." It wasn't a question on Hirka's part. It was a realization.

"I dug him out of the snow. Dug him out to hand him over to Ilume. So that he would grow up as one of them. As an An-Elderin. I carried him in my arms through Blindból, and the whole time I thought he would have been better off dead. Then came the Rite, and he shocked Eisvaldr when he chose us. He wanted to be Kolkagga. A weapon. A servant. I couldn't let that happen. If anything happened to him, we would all be punished for it. So I was hard on him. I took him to be a frightened pup who would run off with his tail between his legs at the first sign of opposition. But Rime didn't give in. I pushed him harder. Maybe because I started to believe in him. He's strong. Fast. He listens. He makes it worth it. So, yes, I'm fond of him too."

Svarteld looked her in the eyes. She blushed.

"But you know, Hirka, nothing he's been through here can measure up to what he has to go through now. Politics aren't for just anyone."

"And he hates politics!"

They laughed. Hirka felt a warm sense of fellowship. She was almost ashamed, because of what this man was.

"So what do you have for me?"

"Are you finished asking questions?"

"For now, yes."

From his shirt pocket he pulled out a pendant that she recognized immediately. Rime's. The shell with their points on the back. He dropped it into her lap.

"Rime says he gives up. You win, girl."

Hirka felt her cheeks give way to an unstoppable smile. It almost hurt. She laughed and buried her face in her hands. Her eyes grew moist, and she had to blink a few times. Svarteld got up.

"We need to get some food in you. Then we have to go out and train, now that you're on your feet."

"Train? What for?"

"Fighting. That's what we do here. And as long as you're here, that's what you'll do too."

"I haven't even managed to stand up yet!"

"Then it's just as well you came here."

Hirka had a sinking feeling he was serious. But food sounded divine. "Do you have honey bread?" She gave him a hopeful look. Svarteld stared at her like she'd just asked for bloodweed and turned to leave.

"Let me guess," she muttered. "That's not what we eat here ..."

THE DEAL

"Was that supposed to be *vargnott*? More like *tied-in-knots*." Svarteld didn't laugh at his own joke. He contented himself with looking skyward, as if to spare her blushes. Hirka glared at him. Her entire body ached, and she wasn't making any effort to hide that fact. The dark-skinned man had nodded, indicating her discomfort was noted, but all the same, he asked her to try again. And again. And again. As if he wasn't paying her any heed. Hirka would have damned him to Blindból if they hadn't already been there.

"It wasn't *vargnott*. It was *I'd-rather-not*."

"Ah! I see," he said. There was a brief pause before he continued. "Try *vargnott*."

Hirka shook her head despairingly, but Svarteld wasn't someone you said no to. The man had high expectations, and she was amazed to discover she wanted to live up to them. After all, it was easier than being asked to bind. This was at least theoretically possible. She would always be able to move quicker or kick higher. She would always be able to do more and more, until she woke up one day the person Svarteld thought she should be. Imagining that made her feel like she could stay in Blindból forever. Of course, that was wishful thinking. She didn't belong here, and she knew what she had to do.

Hirka took two steps forward, lifted her thigh parallel with the ground, spun, and kicked. This time, she leaned her upper body to get higher, and she balanced with her arms. She put her foot down again without falling and turned to face Svarteld with what she knew was a smug smile. He didn't look impressed. "I see we'll need to work on your balance since you don't have a tail," he said.

Hirka was contemplating throwing a rock at him when another Kolkagga approached from the path. The newcomer bowed with his hands together in front of his chest in the sign of the Seer. Hirka realized that a lot of things would stay the same even though everything had changed.

"Master Svarteld, a party is coming from Eisvaldr. Three palanquins, eighteen bearers, and eight guardsmen."

Svarteld raised an eyebrow. "Councillors? Here?"

"We think so, master."

"When will they get here?"

"They'll be here before nightfall, but it'll take them a while to get up here. The bearers look fatigued. They might need help."

Svarteld looked at Hirka. "Sounds like a matter of great importance."

Hirka scooped up a couple yellowed leaves that the wind had swept into the room. There was nothing else to tidy. There was another building for meetings in the camp. It was as beautiful in its simplicity as everything else here, but there were benches with cushions for people who weren't used to sitting on the floor. Hirka had decided she didn't want to use it. If the Council was here to talk to her, they would have to come to her. On her terms.

Only six months ago she'd have been terrified of such a meeting. She'd have bitten her nails to the quick. Now she only felt mild unease. And that wasn't for fear of what they would say, but rather what she would say and how she would react when she saw them again. The same people who had made her an outlaw, thrown her in a pit, and sliced into her back with a sword.

No good can come from collecting wrongs.

She had wanted to change into her own clothes before they arrived, but Svarteld had said she should wear the clothes they wore while training here. He wanted to show the Council that they were looking after her. That she belonged here. Hirka had laughed and asked whose side he was really on. He'd said Rime's.

His name had gone through her like a stone through water, sending ripples of longing through her body. She so wanted to help Rime, to talk to him about everything that had happened. To see him. To check that he was still the same. Just one last time before she left this world for good. But Rime wasn't with the approaching party, she was sure of that. He'd never let anyone carry him as long as he had legs.

She sat down on the floor with the glowing hearth in front of her. She let her knees fall to each side, imitating the position Svarteld had been in when she'd first woken up here. It felt right. The traces of the Might were able to flow freely through her body. She blew on the coals and put a pot of water on to make tea. The door was open and she could see a line of guardsmen rounding the pine tree outside. All of them were peering nervously into the abyss. Hirka suppressed a smile. She'd only been in the camp for a couple days, but she was already used to living on the flat mountaintop. She couldn't think of anywhere she'd rather be than here, two steps from the precipice.

The guardsmen didn't come in. They split into two groups and positioned themselves on either side of the door. Erect and looking across at each other. Not even out here in Blindból could the Council move without making a performance out of it. But then again, they had traveled through the wilderness to see her. That was something.

Eir Kobb climbed out of the first palanquin. The Ravenbearer.

Hirka swallowed. This was serious. Behind her came a man she thought was Jarladin from the An-Sarin family, and a slim man she didn't recognize. He could have been anyone. None of them really looked like their pictures on coins and amulets. The councillors came in without taking their shoes off. They looked around in bewilderment. There were no benches or chairs to sit on. Hirka gestured to three sheepskins on the floor. They would be sitting closer to her than she liked, but at least the hearth would be between them. The coals created distance, but she knew she didn't need it. Not anymore. She had been one with the Might. The fire would always be between them.

They kneeled on the sheepskins. Eir put her hands flat on the floor to support herself on the way down. She sat with her knees pulled up in front of her. Jarladin mirrored Hirka's posture. He was visibly strong. He sat with his back straight like there was no other way, even though he had seen sixty winters, maybe more. The third councillor hesitated, but sat down once the others had done so.

Eir had a lined yet childlike face. Roots from Blossa in the east. Large, deep-set eyes. A small, almost flat nose. She seemed fragile, but Hirka knew that was an illusion. The Ravenbearer rearranged her robe so it lay better on the floor before finally turning to Hirka.

"You know who we are?"

The question was unnecessary and they all knew it. The three people sitting before her wore identical robes and all had the same black mark on their foreheads. Hirka opened a wooden box and added a pinch of tea leaves to the pot.

"You're my executioners. Tea?"

They exchanged glances. If they thought that was all she had, they were in for a shock. Hirka smiled coolly. "I don't share your desire for blood. You're safe to drink."

She felt stronger than ever, likely emboldened by the certainty that she was leaving for good. There was no reason not to say things as they were. No one could hurt her anymore. She was already dead, as Rime would have said.

The third councillor, the one who had hesitated the longest, forced a laugh. Hirka handed him a bowl of tea and he took a sip. It seemed they really did need her for something. Something they were willing to risk a lot for.

"I don't recognize you," Hirka said.

He regarded her with sharp eyes. His hair was cut so short that his head looked bumpy. He was thin, with deep lines framing his mouth.

"I'm Garm-fadri. I represent the Darkdaggar family on the Council."

Hirka nodded at him. "Garm. I'm Hirka. The tailless girl."

The other two looked at each other. They clearly hadn't had to introduce themselves in years. Maybe they'd never had to.

"I'm Jarladin-fadri. I represent the An-Sarin family on the Council," said the strong ox with the shining white beard.

"I'm Eir-madra, of the Kobb family. I bear the Raven." The last word had a telling weight.

"Still?" Hirka asked.

Garm suddenly leaned over the hearth. "Who raised you, girl? Wolves? Do you have any idea who you're talking to?"

Hirka took pleasure in how easy it was to get under his skin. Jarladin gave an almost imperceptible wave of his hand, and Garm leaned back again, his jaw clenched. Hirka poured tea into the other two cups and handed them to Jarladin and Eir. They exchanged brief glances as they drank. Hirka could almost hear Rime laughing behind her.

Look at them, he'd say. *Look at how they're calculating their moves.*

Hirka would have replied that they weren't being calculating this time. That they wanted to ask for something and simply didn't know how. She decided to help them out. "What brings you here?

I'd have thought Eisvaldr needed the Ravenbearer more than ever."

Eir met her gaze, her eyelids heavy. "Tomorrow is my final day as Ravenbearer. I'm passing the staff to Rime. It's his. He's earned it."

Hirka had feared and hoped for this. There would be a handover ceremony tomorrow. For Rime. Ravenbearer Rime … An unreal thought. But the reason she'd given was as false as could be. "You mean it's the only thing you can do. Because people are demanding it."

Eir scrutinized her, put her cup down, and tried again. "The demands of the people are fickle. We focus on the demands we make of ourselves. But you're right, Hirka. People saw him in the Rite Hall. Mannfalla saw him. Men, women, children, guardsmen, Kolkagga … They saw him, and it was like he had stepped straight out of the old stories. Borne by the Might, surrounded by ravens. And he has Ilume's blood. He's the lucky child. Loved and feared. But he took their Seer from them. That kind of damage can only be repaired by giving them a new one. So tomorrow, on the steps in front of what's left of the Rite Hall, I'm giving the staff to Rime."

Hirka shrugged. "He'd have taken it anyway if he wanted to." She threw a look at Garm, who suppressed a twitch of his top lip, dangerously close to baring his teeth at her.

Jarladin intervened. He knew his colleagues well. "You have a lot to answer for, Hirka. You've torn down something that's been standing since the start of our era. The damage is irreparable. When you haven't seen twenty winters, you don't understand the consequences. None of us doubt you had good intentions. Your hands were forced by Urd—"

"Who was one of you," Hirka interjected.

He nodded. "One of us. But we—this Council—are all that is keeping the world from falling apart at the seams."

"The world was here before you, and it will be here long after you've been given to the ravens. The only threat to the world came from you. One of you. Rime was right. You failed us." Hirka felt a tingling sensation. A familiar warmth crept up through the floor and into her thighs. "Let the Might lie, Eir. It won't help you here. It won't make you seem stronger or wiser. It won't make me easier to convince. I know it too well."

The tingling stopped momentarily and the three councillors looked at each other with unconcealed astonishment. She could read the question in their eyes: was she bluffing, or could she feel the Might in them? She regretted saying anything for a moment. Rime clearly hadn't told them everything. She couldn't risk giving too much away, but she had put her fear behind her. Fear was an old friend, but it no longer had any place in her life.

The wind tore at the trees outside. A couple of rust-colored leaves danced across the floor before settling and fluttering at the edge of the straw mat. A portent of autumn. A sign that there were still things left to lose. Hirka continued before they had time to think about what she'd said. "What time does the ceremony start?"

Eir gripped the bridge of her nose between her thumb and index finger. She had bags under her eyes. They were all exhausted. Garm was quick to anger, and Jarladin had started to slouch. Hirka felt a surprising stab of compassion. The Council had cost her more than she could say. But now they were balanced on a knife's edge. They'd lost a lot as well. And if Rime wanted, they could lose everything. "You've built your own funeral pyres." Hirka had meant it to sound comforting, but quickly realized it hadn't.

"You're right," Eir said. "We've failed in many things. We're not too proud to admit that Urd was a mistake. Our mistake. The Council's mistake. But the world hasn't ended yet. We're still here, and we need to create new order in the chaos. With Rime's help. And yours."

Hirka wanted to laugh at the empty words, but she didn't. She just waited, forcing Eir to continue. "Rime is being hailed—and rightly so—for stopping the blind. He is the new hope. But as long as you're here, Hirka, they'll be able to come back."

Hirka sampled her disappointment and concluded it wasn't that bad. She'd expected something like this. They hadn't come to ask for help. Or forgiveness. They would never accept her as an ymling. They wouldn't even accept her as an outsider. They were here to ask her to leave Ym. If only they knew how unnecessary their journey was. Hirka had no intention of staying.

"If they come back, we'll stop them again. We know how," Hirka said.

"But you're not safe here," Jarladin said. "You're a child of Odin. The rot. People will demand your blood!"

"I thought you didn't concern yourself with the fickle demands of the people."

Jarladin only hesitated for a moment. "They don't need to demand it. They'll take it if they want. Living in Mannfalla will cost you your life. A lot of people want to see you burn, Hirka."

"I've heard that a lot of people claim I'm the Seer too." Hirka sipped her tea. It was lukewarm. She was tired of this charade. "Say it like it is. You have your hands full with Rime. You fear what we're capable of together, and the idea of having a child of Odin in Eisvaldr sickens you."

"We don't think—"

"Particularly one with ties to Ravnhov. An embling you've made an outlaw, and who makes you look worse every day she continues to live."

Garm sprang to his feet. "This is pointless! She has no desire to help!"

Eir tried to stop him with a look, but he left the room with his robe flapping after him. Eir looked at Jarladin. "Would you excuse us?" she asked him. She wanted to speak to Hirka alone. Hirka interjected before Jarladin got up. "No. I want to talk to him," she said, nodding at Jarladin. The two councillors exchanged looks again before Eir got up and left. Hirka put the pot back over the fire and picked up his cup.

"Is it from here?" he asked.

Hirka smiled. This time it reached her eyes. "Yes, it grows wild in the mountains. In tall tea bushes that have been here since before the red dome was built. Before Eisvaldr."

"If only everything else were seen in the same light," he said. It sounded like he meant it. Hirka gave him a fresh cup.

"Listen, Jarladin-fadri ..." He tried to suppress a smile at the sudden use of his title. It was charming and made him look younger. He had narrow yet piercing eyes. His white beard was the same color as Rime's hair. Maybe that's why she'd chosen him. He drank as she spoke.

"I know what I am. And I know what you're thinking. You didn't have any bad intentions either. We have to assume that all twelve—well, eleven excluding Urd—had the kingdoms' best interests at heart. You acted out of fear and ignorance, but you want to repair the damage. I'm not part of that plan. I'm a rogue element. As long as I'm here, people will doubt you. Doubt your motives. Some people might want to elevate me to the Seer's right hand. The girl who stood behind Rime. Other people want to kill me. Maybe you all still think that everything can be salvaged. That the truth about the Seer hasn't spread or that you can spread another lie to pick up the pieces. Either way, I'm not a child anymore. I know you don't want me here."

"We must seem like monsters to you."

"No. Not anymore. You want me out of this world, and Hlosnian knows how. But you don't have the power to force me. You see ... I like it here. Peace is assured. It's a nice place to be. Tea grows wild and the mightiest man in the world is my friend. I'm safer here than anywhere else. Who knows what's on the other side of the stones?"

Hirka believed what she was saying, so it wasn't difficult to lie. Jarladin closed his eyes. Moments passed before he opened them and answered her.

"You have to understand, we'd never let you leave empty-handed. You'd leave a wealthy young woman. Perhaps with guardsmen at your side. You'd—"

"I have everything I need and I can take care of myself. There's very little I want in the world."

His eyes lit up. "But you do want something? Name it!"

"Jarladin-fadri, I could make it easy for you. I could leave Ym and you could once again stand tall as the Council you've always been. You wouldn't have any outlaws hanging around in Eisvaldr as living proof of the Council's mistakes. Of how little the stones, the most powerful weapon this world has ever seen, are understood. No one knows where Urd got that knowledge from, but at least he understood the value of it. Yes, I could leave so everyone else could forget."

"But you won't?"

She met his gaze. "Would *you*?"

He lowered his gaze, stroking his beard with his thumb. He didn't need to reply. Of everyone on the Council, Jarladin was the one she trusted most. This educated ox was a man of his word. He just needed to give it to her. The time had come.

"I could leave," she said. "If it were worth it."

"We'll pay the price, Hirka. Tell us how much."

"I don't want riches. I want your word. Rime is an An-Elderin, and Kolkagga. He's strong, I've seen him take out his own. But that doesn't make him immortal. He's going to question the way things have always been, and you don't do that without making enemies. Many of them in Eisvaldr, in his own house. I want your word that he'll be safe in that chair. Promise me that you'll watch his back. That you'll fight for him like the stories say you fought for Ilume. She wanted nothing more than to see him do what he's doing now.

You need to come down hard on those who wish him ill. You need to keep an eye on the Council and be his friend. If you can promise me that, I'll go."

Jarladin made the sign of the Seer across his chest. "I promise. I swear to the Seer."

"Swear on your life."

"On my life. I swear."

Hirka breathed out, and it was like expelling poison that had been tormenting her for days. "Good. One more thing. There's a man in the vaults. A performer, with puppets. He's harmless. His only crime was telling you he'd seen the blind. For that, you locked him up. He is to be a free man tomorrow."

"If he isn't already, it shall be so."

Hirka nodded. Jarladin didn't even say he'd have to discuss it with the others. They'd already discussed this, and clearly no price was too high for a world without Hirka. But she could tell he was restless. His bottom lip was moving up and down like he was chewing it inside. Hirka was pretty sure she knew why.

"In return, I'll spare you Rime's wrath by leaving of my own free will. You never asked me to leave." She got up. He did the same.

"If they have a seer on the other side, may He bless you, child of Odin."

She gave him a lopsided smile. Jarladin left the room. Hirka watched the councillors and their entourage until the final guardsman disappeared between the mountains.

Hirka was awoken by a presence in the room. At first she thought it was an animal, then realized it was a black-clad Kolkagga pouring water into the pot from a wooden bucket. He had his hood down. His face was broad and his eyes dark, like Ramoja's. She sat up.

"Svarteld's on his way," he said. He looked at her like they knew each other, but she didn't recognize him. He held out his hand. She took it.

"I'm Jeme. I was on Bromfjell with you." He let go of her hand. "If I weren't Kolkagga, I could have told my grandchildren." He started blowing on the fire he'd lit.

She rubbed the sleep out of her eyes. She was cold. The pain the Might had caused her was gone, replaced by a stiffness for which Svarteld alone was responsible. "Thanks, Jeme."

"For what?"

"For Ravnhov. For coming."

He smiled, but with a wonder in his eyes that told her he didn't understand why she was thanking him. The autumn cold plucked at the skin on her arms. She'd slept in the tight, sleeveless shirt that was no longer as white as it had once been in Elveroa. She pulled her woollen tunic on. Unngonna had gotten someone to repair it in Ravnhov so that Hirka looked almost presentable.

"Do you always get up this early?"

"I was one of the last ones up."

"One of the last ones up? I can hear an owl out there!"

"It's confused. Up you get." It was Svarteld, suddenly in the room without warning. A shadow one moment, right in front of you the next. "We need to get going if we're going to make the ceremony. Jeme, can you alert the others?"

Jeme bowed. "Right away, Master Svarteld." He left the room. Hirka shook her head. "Does anyone ever refuse you, Svarteld?"

"What does that mean?"

"Refuse. You know. When you ask someone to do something and they say no. Or tell you they have a better idea."

"Interesting theory. You'll have to tell me more about it sometime. Right now, we're leaving for Eisvaldr."

"Let me tell you more about it now. This is how refusal works. No.

I don't need to get up because I'm not going to Mannfalla. It's a bad idea."

"It's not an idea. It just is."

"Listen, Svarteld, it was bad enough that the rot was there when the lie about the Seer came out. It'll only be worse if I'm there when Rime becomes the Ravenbearer too. Me being there will only spread fear and panic. And even if I were like everyone else, I've nothing to wear. Simple as that." Hirka lay back down again, smiling, and pulled her blanket up to her chin.

A heap of black clothes landed on her stomach. She cracked open one eye to peer at them. Svarteld was holding out a sword.

"Two birds, one stone. You're going as Kolkagga."

HEIR TO THE CHAIR

The Rite Hall was no more. It was from here that the Council had extended its reach throughout the eleven kingdoms, but now there was little to indicate it had ever been there at all. The red dome was gone. Jagged segments of its ruins rose up beyond the walls of the complex like painted mountains. Only the stones were left, along with fragments of the wall that had concealed them for a thousand years. Now they towered up toward the gray sky. Half ruin, half monument.

The floor was still there. Red leaves danced across the motifs, getting snagged in the scars where the benches had been. The ground crunched beneath Hirka's feet. Brooms and pickaxes from the restoration work had been cleared away for the ceremony. It was about to start on the steps behind her, so that the floor could be spared. For generations people had walked across this floor without understanding its importance. Now the learned claimed to know all about it, and the eldest to have always known.

Hirka walked down toward the steps and stood next to Svarteld. He'd been right, of course. She was able to walk around undisturbed as Kolkagga. Nobody looked at her. Only little children dared to stare at the black shadows. Before she would have loved the feeling of being invisible, being a shadow. Today she didn't need it. She knew what she was capable of. Today she wanted to stand in front of Rime as herself.

But she couldn't. She'd made a deal with the Council to ensure his safety. He was never going to see her again.

She stood with the other Kolkagga, at the top of the steps, some distance behind Rime. She'd hoped it wouldn't hurt to see him. After all, it would be from a distance—but she realized now that no distance in the world would ever be enough. She would have given her life for him. The memory of his Might still wreaked havoc within her. A stinging pain that afflicted her every time she thought of him. Every time she heard his name. There was an empty space inside her that no one else could fill.

He stood tall, as he always did. His white hair was tied back. His waist was nipped in by his sword belt. It had to be the first time in history that someone in the Council had carried a weapon. At least since the first twelve, who had all been warriors.

The Council formed a semicircle in front of Rime. The guardsmen were lined up on the steps like stakes in a fence of black and gold. All of Mannfalla was gathered below, a teeming crowd spread across the market square, all the way to the wall, where more were arriving and squeezing in through the archways. The boldest among them had squeezed onto the bottom steps, which were otherwise reserved for the Council's friends and families. Hirka wasn't surprised to see Sylja and her mother there. She also spotted Ramoja and Vetle. That boded well, because it meant that nobody knew what the raveners had been up to. Not even Rime could have saved Ramoja's life if their treachery became known.

Drums began to play from one of the nearby rooftops. Different rhythms interwove to form a captivating whole that reverberated throughout Hirka's body. Seven dancers snaked their way up the stairs. Their dresses were so thin that they might as well have been naked. The one at the front was called Damayanti, and was apparently known throughout Ym, though Hirka had never heard of her. Small stones glittered on her skin, curving over her chest until they disappeared behind shimmering fabric. Long veils hung from wrists and encircled the supple bodies dancing for Rime. For the new Ravenbearer.

Hirka suddenly felt empty. She was leaving. For good. She was going to leave the colors, the music, the nature. Ramoja, Eirik, Vetle, Tein. And Rime. She was going to leave Rime. He would never find out that she was here now. And soon he would forget her entirely. When the snow came, he would have the world's most beautiful dancers to keep him warm. They would line up for him.

But they would do that whether Hirka was there or not. Maybe she would have been able to keep them at a distance, as the rot by his side. The child of Odin. The malformed blight of Eisvaldr. She was left with a bitter taste in her mouth. That would never happen now. She would never be the reviled witness to Rime's life and rule.

Eir closed the Book of the Seer. She had clearly been reading from it, but Hirka hadn't heard a single word. The old Ravenbearer stepped forward and handed the staff to the new one. Just the staff. Without what had been the most important part of it for generations. Without the Raven.

The difference was more to be felt than seen. In truth, Eir hadn't carried the Raven, the Raven had carried her. Her place had been secure. Her responsibility had ended at the top of the staff. Handed to the black bird that had borne the world with a natural inviolability.

Rime, however ... He carried an empty staff. He had no one above him. He stood alone. Everything rested on his shoulders.

Maybe the loss of a seer would, paradoxically, make the Council stronger? At least as long as Rime was there. Sure, he had the Council around him, but he would never be able to trust any of them. He had to be as strong in front of them as in front of the people. Hirka yearned to go to him. To tear off her black hood and shout that she was here. But she probably wouldn't have even if she could.

Rime raised the staff, and Mannfalla erupted in a roar of celebration. Unanimous adulation for the only thing they had left to bestow it on. The augurs celebrated too, their hands raised against the dancers' flurry of flower petals. They celebrated as though everything they'd based their lives on wasn't a lie. Hirka stared at them and realized that the Seer was never going to die. Real or not, they would always find Him, somewhere.

Rime turned and came up the steps. His forehead was still bare and Hirka swallowed a lump in her throat. Not only was he the first on the Council to bear arms, he was also the first not to bear the mark.

The Council followed him. Coordinated and directed like a puppet show. She checked that she was in line with the other Kolkagga. Nobody coming up the steps would see that she was tailless. Tight bandages flattened her chest. Her red hair was hidden under a hood. Only her eyes were visible in the clothes she wore. An assassin's garb. She was one with her surroundings.

Rime walked past. He smiled faintly at them. He was more beautiful than ever. Hirka bowed her head. For a moment his gaze rested on her. She thought she caught a hint of recognition, but then he kept walking. The crowd dispersed, but the celebrations carried on. Groups walked home, to various stalls, to work, and to parties. Hirka had just one thing to do. She adjusted the straps on the black Kolkagga bag that concealed her own.

"Interesting," she heard behind her.

Hlosnian!

Hirka turned and gave him a hug. "How did you find me?"

"You had to be here somewhere. It was just a matter of looking."

"For someone without a tail?"

"For someone with traces of the Might in their eyes. Svarteld says you need me. Where are you going, Hirka?"

"First I have to get out of these clothes. Then I have to say goodbye to the teahouse owner on the Catgut. And then I'll need your help."

"Oh, I doubt that, but I'll be there all the same. So they asked you to leave, did they?"

Hirka hesitated for a moment. "You could put it like that."

"You don't need me. You probably never have."

"Crones' talk, Hlosnian," Hirka said, and smiled at the thought of Father.

"Oh, now. Don't speak too loudly of things you know nothing about, child of Odin. I didn't raise a finger to help you when you ran between the stones on Bromfjell. The others had to be whispered in, but all you needed was the Might. You weren't born here. The same rules don't apply to you, and we should be glad nobody knew that. Especially Urd Vanfarinn."

Hirka shuddered. The distance between worlds had suddenly shrunk, and she wasn't sure she liked it.

"So I just need the Might to leave?"

"There's no *just* with the Might. Have you spoken to Rime about it?" Hlosnian led them after a stream of people heading toward one of the feast halls in Eisvaldr.

"Svarteld's going to talk to him. Afterward. After ..." She couldn't complete the sentence. Hlosnian didn't reply, and she was grateful. He put a hand on her back and led her into the hall. This was a party for the Council's nearest and dearest. Their nearest and dearest three hundred, it looked like. Long tables covered with gold and glass platters stretched from wall to wall. An abundance of food was carried in on decorated trays. People sat shoulder to shoulder, chatting away. Hirka saw Sylja leaning over the table to get Rime's attention. Her heart suddenly felt like it was being crushed. Wrung out like a washcloth.

It doesn't concern you. Get out of here.

"I can't be here, Hlosnian. They can't see me here."

Hlosnian's eyes drifted across the fully laid table. While people were busy sitting down, he filled the pockets of his red tunic with syrup cakes and nut slices. He licked his fingers and led her back out. "Then let's go and look at the stones."

They walked up toward the naked hill. A scar in Eisvaldr, the crater where the Rite Hall had stood. The mountains of Blindból were visible between the stones. Hirka placed her hands on the rough surface of one of them. Stone had memory. Was there anything these stones hadn't seen in a thousand years? Or perhaps longer. Regardless of how old they were, they were impressive.

"If you'd have told me in the summer that I was going to stone-travel before the winter set in, I'd have sent you packing." Hlosnian stared at the stones with reverence.

"Stone-travel?" Hirka smiled at the notion. It seemed like she was learning something new every day now.

"They're also called stone ways. Someone in our guild calls them 'Bifrost,' the trembling bridge. The bridge between worlds. 'The stone doors' I've heard since I was a child. 'The blind ways.' 'The raven rings.' This was the biggest and the very first of them. The one thought to have been torn down, or lost in Blindból somewhere. People forget too quickly. Or maybe we live too long ..."

Hirka smiled. Only Hlosnian could be so confusing. "Why raven rings?"

Hlosnian jumped as though he'd just realized she was there. "It was believed ravens could fly freely between them. They don't need the Might. It lives within them."

So Kuro could come with me.

"I like the stones better than the hall," she said.

"Yes. People like us will always prefer this to the fancy packaging," Hlosnian replied, and she was pleased to be counted as "us."

The circular floor was almost completely intact. An anomaly in nature, encircled by towering stones. A place the gods wanted to keep hidden, but which was now there for all to see. The motifs were faded, worn away by a thousand Rites. There were tiles missing in some places. Maybe that had happened when she and Rime passed through, when the walls had caved in.

Hirka remembered standing on the platform during the Rite, looking at the floor from above and seeing the whole motif. A multi-pointed star. Now she could see that each tip ended at a stone. The spaces were filled by the strangest things. In a couple of places, the motifs were so worn that it was impossible to see what they were meant to depict. In other places, they were full of creatures and fictional beasts.

"The floor is a map, isn't it? It's almost unbelievable. Surely someone must have known?"

"Most things seem clearer in hindsight," Hlosnian replied. He picked remnants of the walls away from the stone. "We think it depicts what was expected to be found between the stones. How right that is, nobody knows. But we know that the inner circle was torn down. You can see the scars here."

He pointed at one of several places where the tiles gave way to flat stones. An inner ring of smaller stones had been removed.

Insringin.

The Council was often called Insringin, the inner circle. Hirka had always thought it meant the Seer's inner circle. Maybe it did, but the name could have come from something much older than the Rite. Older than the notion of the Seer. Hlosnian pinched the bridge of his nose and shook his head. "They didn't know what they had! Maybe they were shortcuts to each of the kingdoms. Gone!" He flung out his arms in dismay. "Destroyed. Forever."

Hirka tried to console him. "But the outer circle still stands. That's the most important part. Imagine we'd never found it." He nodded, but didn't seem encouraged. A familiar croaking came from above them. Kuro landed on the top of a stone and stared at Hlosnian's pockets. That raven could smell cake from the end of the world.

Suddenly she realized what she was about to do. A wave of anxiety washed over her. "Hlosnian, do they have cake where I come from? Or honey bread?"

"Definitely."

Hirka swallowed. The little things she didn't know grew bigger. They became a hole that threatened to swallow her. "Do they even have food? Animals? Forests? Weather?" The air got stuck in her chest and she clutched at the stone.

Hlosnian grabbed her with both hands. "Child, they have everything you need."

"How can you know that? Nobody's been there. Nobody's met anyone from there. Nobody's—"

"Because you wouldn't have existed if it was different. Your ancestors wouldn't have existed and couldn't have given birth to you if they hadn't lived in a world that gave them everything they needed to survive. It's logical, child. Logical."

There was a touching tenderness in his eyes. He was right. She breathed easier. She had ancestors. She wasn't alone. Urd had also said she had a father, but she'd heard more than enough about him.

Urd lied. He lied about everything.

"Come," Hlosnian said and pulled her forward a couple of steps. "This is where you come from." She stared at the motif. It was simple. Two pale men, one of them on a horse.

"How do you know it's this one?"

"Well ... It's a combination of things, really. The lettering. The age of the motif. The feel of the Might when—"

"Hlosnian ..."

"Neither of them has a tail."

"So you want to send me to a completely unknown world based on the fact that you can't see tails in a picture of two men whose backs we can't see?"

Hlosnian smiled and nodded a little too eagerly. She pretended it was comforting anyway. The fact she was leaving everything behind was hard enough to process on its own, but no one knowing for sure what way she should go? That was too much.

She searched for details in the picture. The men were dressed the same. Chainmail with white tabards over the top. On their chests she could see traces of a red cross that narrowed in the middle. Maybe a family crest.

So they have warriors there too.

But there was a tree behind them. That gave her a sense of ease. So this was her new home? And these were the stones she had to pass between. She looked up, but couldn't see anything but mountain. No shimmering in the air. Nothing to indicate that you would cease to exist if you walked between the stones using the Might.

That was the most terrifying part. You couldn't travel through them without the Might. Hlosnian could help her, or someone else. But menskr were unearthed, like her. They couldn't bind.

She could leave this world, but she would never be able to return.

THE GATEWAYS

The gong struck nine before Hirka left Eisvaldr and walked down the Catgut. It was dark. That made it easier to remain unseen even though she'd finally put on her own clothes. They were worn but wonderfully familiar.

The celebrations still weren't over. Scantily clad women clung to swaggering men outside the inns. Some of them had celebrated the Ravenbearer in moderation and were in a fit state to walk home again. Others dozed on benches and would wake up feeling wretched in the morning. Hirka could have helped them. She could have offered onion soup and herbal tea when they needed it most, but she wouldn't be here tomorrow.

Hirka pulled her woollen cloak more tightly around her. It was heavy and as green as a spruce tree. A gift from Jarladin. At first, the councillor had presented her with a cloak worthy of a ravenbearer. Shiny silk decorated with silver thread and blue stones that would have attracted attention no matter what world she arrived in. She'd politely declined, and in a rare moment of insight, the councillor had brought her this simpler one. It was wonderfully ordinary, and had no other purpose than to keep her warm and unnoticed. Just what she needed. No one could see that she was tailless, and the hood covered her red hair.

Hirka turned off the Catgut, passing the darkened upholsterer's workshop. The tidy network of streets became a labyrinth of alleyways that sloped down toward the riverbank. Hirka hadn't lived here long, but she knew them like the back of her hand. The teahouse was half on the river, like a raft. The light outside was out, but there was a glow from the fireplace inside. There wasn't anyone sitting around the low tables, but the cups and saucers hadn't been cleared yet. Unsurprisingly, Lindri had been open late as well. It wasn't every day a new ravenbearer was sworn in. Particularly not one who hadn't spent a single day on the Council.

Hirka opened the door, and hollow tones from the wind chime inside announced her presence. Lindri glanced up from his boxes of tea to say he was closed, but words failed him when he saw her. His wrinkles made it look like he was smiling even though he wasn't.

She walked toward him, weaving between the tables. He leaned on a stack of tea chests with one hand and put the other on his hip. His attempt to look stern was unsuccessful. Hirka bit her bottom lip to quell the anguish she felt. The anguish of having left him without a word, and of having to do the same again. He nodded several times, the way old men often did when contemplating the inevitability of everything. Then he pulled her toward him in a trembling motion. He patted her gently on the back. His voice was rough when he finally spoke.

"Why didn't you say anything, Red?"

Hirka didn't reply. She rested her chin on his shoulder and closed her eyes.

"You should have told me, Red. You should have told me." He took a step back and looked at her. Hirka smiled. They both knew that she never could have said anything. He put the kettle over the fire and blew more life into the embers. She pulled a linen pouch out of her bag and gave it to him.

"Use this. It grows wild in Blindból. There's nothing else like it."

He weighed the pouch in his hand, but his eyes rested on her.

"They say you're a child of Odin. That you killed guardsmen and fled to Ravnhov. Some people say you started the war there. Others say you stopped it. You woke the dragon in Bromfjell and clove the land in two. Then you came here and tore down the Rite Hall and rebelled against the Seer. Some say you killed Him. Others say Rime An-Elderin did. Many say He never existed at all. If you wanted to remain unseen, you've well and truly failed, Red."

"I've failed in many respects, Lindri."

He brewed a pot of tea that they took out into the back garden. Not that it had ever actually been a garden. It was a platform on the river that was overgrown with climbing plants. The Ora was black in the darkness. A couple lanterns swayed from the boats in the distance. The stars were so clearly reflected that it was impossible to tell where the river ended and the sky began. Did they have stars where she was going? Were they the same stars or different stars?

Hirka held nothing back. She told him what had happened, and she told him she had to leave again. It was both terrifying and relieving to get it all off her chest. She and Lindri had never had much time to talk, but they hadn't needed to. They had been brought together by what they both knew best.

Lindri listened. He comforted her with questions she had never thought to consider. Was she sure she'd be going somewhere different? Maybe all places were the same place. And maybe she wouldn't need the Might to come back if she ever wanted to. Maybe they had other ways where she was going. You never knew. As long as they had tea there, she would be fine. And Lindri was absolutely sure they would have tea.

They had the entire evening to themselves. Hirka didn't get up until the gong struck eleven. She needed to get back to the stone circle before midnight. Hlosnian wasn't going to wait any longer than that. He'd mumbled something about the ebb and flow of the Might, but she was pretty sure he just wanted to go to bed early. They went back into the teahouse.

Hirka was about to shoulder her bag when the door crashed open. The wind chime clattered. The embers from the fire flared up in the draft, casting a red glow across Rime's face. Hirka could feel heat lashing around him, like tongues of fire no one could see. He'd used the Might to get here.

Lindri put the teacups down on the counter, made the sign of the Seer, and bowed. "Rime-fadri, you honor me. What can I do for you?"

Rime didn't reply. Didn't notice him. He stared at Hirka and took three long strides toward her. "You were going to leave. You were going to leave and you weren't going to tell me."

His eyes were cold amid all the heat. Full of accusation. Hirka chewed her bottom lip and said a silent prayer for strength. This was going to make everything much more difficult. She tried to smile. "Don't you have any guardsmen with you? I didn't think they'd let the Ravenbearer out without—"

"You were going to leave. Tonight. Without saying anything."

Hirka put a hand on Lindri's arm. He was still bent forward, not daring to make eye contact with the Ravenbearer. Right now, she couldn't blame him. "Up you come, Lindri. We're going to need something to drink."

Grateful, he disappeared behind the counter to do what he did best. Hirka pointed at one of the low wooden tables surrounded by stools with sheepskins draped over them. "Sit down, Rime."

He landed on the stool like someone had dropped him. He bowed his head so that his hair fell forward, hiding his face. She had to sit directly opposite him to see it. His breathing evened out. She could hear every breath. His chest expanded rhythmically under a blue shirt she'd never seen before. He needed to wear more layers. Winter was coming.

He sat there with his eyes closed. His swords stuck out to the sides, reaching down to the floor. His hands had a firm grip on the tabletop, as if he were forcing himself to sit there.

Lindri came over to them. He gave Hirka a questioning look and she nodded at the table. He put the tray down. His deep, measured breathing told her that he was concentrating. He supplied wares to Eisvaldr, but clearly he'd never made anything for a raven-bearer before. His leathery hands poured hot water over the cups and the pot to warm them. He rinsed the tea leaves in cold water. Then he poured the hot water over them and let it stand. As he worked, he threw stolen glances at Rime, who sat as if carved from stone.

When Lindri felt that the tea had steeped for long enough, he poured the tea into two cups, which he set down in front of Hirka and Rime. Then he picked up the tray again and left them. Steam rose from the cups and caressed Rime's face. He looked up and met her gaze. Wolf eyes. White through the steam. This time wild with hurt. Ready for a fight. Betrayed.

His body language was enough to tell her that he was waiting for an explanation. And that no explanation would be good enough. Hirka dragged a hand across her face, letting it rest on her chin for a moment while she collected herself. She met his pained gaze again. When she thought she knew what she was going to say, she opened her mouth. She closed it again. There was nothing to say. She sipped her tea. Rime didn't touch his.

"You're leaving. Tonight. Aren't you?" His hoarse voice belied a twisted pleasure in knowing he was right.

"I'm leaving."

"And you weren't going to tell anyone."

"No. I wasn't going to tell anyone."

Rime got up so suddenly that he upended the table. The cups crashed to the floor. He pointed at her. His eyes were those of a stranger, as if Rime was gone and someone else was occupying his body. She hadn't been close to him since the Rite Hall fell. Since the Might had torn her apart. Maybe it had done the same to him.

Maybe so much so that he wanted to kill her. That would be the best way to go. Anything was better than this.

"What are you going to do, Hirka? Burn the cabin and run through the forests to Ravnhov? After everything we've been through?!" He started pacing back and forth like a man possessed. "You asked me to rise up! You made me do this! We've turned the world on its head. And now that it's done, you're leaving. What am I supposed to do?" He stopped and looked at her again. "What am I supposed to do?!"

The weight of the simple question pressed down on Hirka's chest. This wasn't about her. This was about the weight of the world. Rime was carrying it on his shoulders, and he didn't know what to do with it.

She got up. His gaze softened. Faltered. "They asked you to leave. They've forced you. That's how it is." There were traces of hope in his voice. She shook her head. She walked over to him and was pleased when he didn't back away. The Might recognized her and caressed her in calm waves. Sorrowful, but with a certainty that smoothed the sharp edges. It laid bare the anxiety and made it easier to handle.

"What am I supposed to do?" he repeated. More hollowly now. Exhausted. Behind him, the wind chime sounded, moved by the flow of the Might. She put a hand on his cheek and studied him. Burned him into her memory so she could take him with her.

"Who are you, Rime?" she asked.

He took hold of her head like a starving man. Pressed his nose to her temple. "I'm Rime. Rime An-Elderin." As he whispered, his lips drew the words on her cheek. He needn't have made a sound. Her skin would have known what he was saying regardless.

Speak. Say anything.

"You'd have been safe here, Hirka. No one and nothing would have hurt you. I'd have destroyed anything that sought to destroy you. You'd have lived a good life in Eisvaldr."

"As a curiosity? An abomination the wealthiest would pay to see? Or as a source of fear and chaos? I don't belong here, Rime."

He hugged her harder. "I'm the Ravenbearer. I could forbid you from leaving."

"But you couldn't stop people from giving me a wide berth or drawing a sign of protection on their chests when they see me. Or hating me because the blind can find their way here as long as I'm here." Her heart longed for him to say he could. An impossible promise, but if he was willing to make it, maybe she could stay. Hirka realized that her will was about to crumble. That couldn't happen. It was now or never.

She pulled away and put on her bag. Something inside her screamed *no*, demanding she take her bag off again and ask him to make good on his promises, ask him to give her a good life here. But she knew that no one had the power to do that.

"You can do a lot, Rime. But you can't stop people from being people. Just look at the Seer. You can tell them He's not there, but a lot of them will never stop worshipping Him. Just like they'll never stop fearing the rot."

"There's no such thing as the rot, Hirka! How deeply do I have to kiss you before you believe me? Are you going to let old superstitions get the better of you? You of all people? I'm not scared of it! Stay here and give me the chance to prove it's a lie." He came toward her again. Took her chin, as if to kiss her.

She lowered her head. "I've seen it, Rime …"

"What? You've seen what?" He stopped.

"I've seen the rot. Urd had it. The beginnings of it. His throat was being eaten away from the inside. And he said he'd gotten it from my father."

Rime let his arms drop to his sides. He closed his eyes and cocked his head, as if to push her words away. Hirka went over to Lindri, who was standing poorly concealed behind the sliding door into the back room. He embraced her. Pulled away again and shook his head. He looked at her like she had taken leave of her senses. As perhaps anyone would have. Anyone who hadn't grown up like her.

"Will you walk with me?" she asked Rime.

He came. Calmer now. Absorbed by a problem he wasn't going to solve. They left the teahouse. She didn't look back. The sounds from the Catgut were muted now. It was midnight. The inns were ushering out the final few revelers. A bedraggled cat slunk between the walls of the houses with its tail in the air. The wind had picked up. They walked in silence through the wall and across the square. None of the guardsmen looked their way. Flower petals from the ceremony were strewn across the pale stone steps like blood on bone. The stone circle emerged from the darkness. She could see the outline of a windswept raven on top of one of the stones. Kuro, with his head pulled down between his wings. She hadn't dared hope, but maybe he would come along.

She put her bag down on the floor and looked at Rime.

"Hlosnian will be here any minute."

"Hlosnian's not coming. He told me you were leaving. So I locked him up."

She took a step back from him. "You locked him up?!"

"I couldn't let him help you. Don't look so shocked. He wouldn't have come anyway. He was so full of cake and wine that he was asleep before I even locked the door."

Hirka laughed, but it felt so wrong that she stopped.

"He begged me to give you this." Rime took a leather bag from his belt. She opened it. It was difficult to see the contents in the dark, but there was definitely a book. Smaller than the palm of her hand, but thick. She crouched down and tucked it into her own bag. "Who other than Hlosnian would think to give me reading material for the journey?" She got up again and looked at Rime. "So you're going to help me?"

She turned to walk away, but Rime put an arm around her and pulled her close. She leaned her head back against his chest, grateful that she had her back to him. That she couldn't see him in that moment. Or be seen. The wind ripped the final leaves from the trees. The stones remained silent. Waiting. Giants that would take her away from this place.

Then came the Might. Abrupt and all-consuming. Leaves dragged across the floor and disappeared between the stones. Rime's white hair blew into her face like it had the night they flew over Eisvaldr. Eternity washed through her. Earth. Stone. Dormant power. He pressed her body into small pieces. She came apart and mixed with the pieces that were Rime.

The dome rose up above them. The dome disappeared again. Shadows went by. Shadows of people who had once lived. Then they disappeared as well. The landscape grew desolate through winters and summers. Only the stones remained. She was all that had lived. All that did live. All that would ever live. The Might burrowed its way closer to her heart, hungry for everything she'd hidden away, and she let him have it. Everything apart from the one thing he could never see: how much of her was his.

He gripped the pendant on her chest. The pendant he had left with her in Blindból. His hand burned feverishly against her skin and she felt her body come alive. It was violent. Dangerous. She shut herself off from the Might and was glad she managed it without screaming. Rime put his lips to her ear. His voice was rough like stone.

"Urd found a way. I'll find a way too. I'll find you. And I'll bring you the truth about the rot."

Hirka could tell he believed it. She didn't. But still she let the thought warm her.

She called to Kuro. "Kuro! Hreidr!" The word came so naturally that it was as if she'd never used another word for "home." The raven circled them a couple of times. Then he flew between two of the stones and disappeared.

Reluctantly, Hirka pried herself from Rime's embrace. "Follow the ravens," she said with a shrug. Rime didn't reply. She put her bag on and passed between the stones.

The space between worlds enveloped her.

ACKNOWLEDGMENTS

It's all or nothing, they say, so I hereby stomp all over that by only mentioning *some* of the people who deserve thanks for making the Raven Rings trilogy a reality. I'll skip right past Kim and Mom because obviously I couldn't have done it without them.

Consultants

Alexander K. Lykke: language consultant, Old Norse guru, fantasy enthusiast, and font of ideas.

Maja S. Megård: my dear friend and the only one who was allowed to read and comment as I wrote.

Karen Forberg: brilliant editor and the first person to tell me it's a good book.

Terje Røstum: colleague and kick-ass web developer at Kantega.

Emma Josefin Johansson and Stian Andreassen: developers at the amazing Gnist Design.

Knut Ellingsen: geologist with knowledge of all things stone.

Tom Haller: probably the only professional ravener in Norway.

Lars Myhren Holand: the photographer who made me look clever.

Øyvind Skogmo: merciless final-round proofreader.

Writing a book is often difficult when you have a full-time job, unless you're lucky enough to have the best job in the world. I happen to be that lucky. Thank you to all my wonderful colleagues at

Kantega, and in particular Marit Collin, the best boss in the world. I want to be like her when I grow up.

Gyldendal is a warm and wonderful publisher that welcomed me with open arms. My most heartfelt thanks to everyone there, especially my amazing editors, Marianne Koch Knudsen and Bente Lothe Orheim. They've made both me and the book better.

To Fuglen, Supreme Roastworks, and Java, the best coffee shops in Oslo, and their absurdly lovely staff. To Outland, the store where I found myself. To Michael Parchment, who taught me what I'm capable of. To the lovely people at Fabelprosaikerne, and everyone who gushed about the advance copy. You're the best. To everyone who reads, writes, blogs, and tweets about books. To everyone I follow, and everyone who follows me. To fellow author Tonje Tornes, because two heads are better than one! To all the friends and acquaintances that encouraged me, particularly my old comic and role-playing buddies (Look, Endre! Hirka's come to life!).

Finally: a very special thank-you to the man who opened the gateways to other worlds for me, and who will probably never understand how much that means. Thank you, my dear Ketil Holden.

CHARACTERS

Damayanti	a dancer
Eirik Viljarsón	chieftain of Ravnhov
Hirka	the tailless girl
Hlosnian	a stone carver and stone whisperer
Gesa An-Elderin	Rime's mother
Kaisa of Glimmeråsen	Sylja's mother
Kolgrim	Elveroa's village bully
Kuro	a raven
Launhug	a Kolkagga
Lindri	a teahouse owner
Ramoja	a ravener; Vetle's mother
Rime An-Elderin	heir to the An-Elderin seat on the Council
the Seer	a god
Slabba	a merchant; Urd's lackey
Svarteld	Rime's master
Sylja of Glimmeråsen	the wealthiest girl in Elveroa
Tein	a son of Ravnhov
Thorrald	Hirka's father
Tyrinn	a prisoner in Eisvaldr
Urd Vanfarinn	an aspiring councillor
Vetle	a simple boy in Elveroa

COUNCILLORS

Eir Kobb	**Miane Fell**
Freid Vangard	**Noldhe Saurpassarid**
Garm Darkdaggar	**Saulhe Jakinnin**
Ilume An-Elderin	**Sigra Kleiv**
Jarladin An-Sarin	**Spurn Vanfarinn**
Leivlugn Taid	**Tyrme Jekense**

PLACES

the Alldjup a gorge with the River Stryfe running through it

Blindból a forbidden mountain range

Bromfjell a mountain near Ravnhov

the Catgut a main street in Mannfalla

Eisvaldr a walled city within Mannfalla; the home of the Council and the Seer

Elveroa a small village

Foggard the region where Elveroa is located

Gardfjella a mountain range

Glimmeråsen the largest and most prosperous farm in Elveroa

Hrafnfell a mountain range

Mannfalla the biggest city in Ym, where the Rite occurs every year

mother's bosom the dome in Eisvaldr that houses the Council Chamber

the Ora a river running through Mannfalla

Ravnhov an independent settlement in the region of Foggard

the Rite Hall a large ceremonial hall, located directly beneath the Council Chamber

Sigdskau a forest near Ulvheim in which there is a stone circle

the Stryfe a river in Foggard

Ulvheim a town in the north

Vargtind a mountain in Elveroa, with ruins at its peak

Ym a land in the known world

CONCEPTS

binding the act of using or drawing upon the Might

the blind an ancient people feared throughout Ym and believed by many to be mythical. Synonymous with deadborn, nábyrn, the nameless, the first, and the songless.

blindcraft the feared and forbidden way in which the blind use the Might

blue blood someone, usually from a powerful, well-established family, who is a skilled binder

child of Odin someone from another world, born without a tail, who cannot bind the Might. Synonymous with Embla's kin, child of Embla, Odin's kin, embling, and menskr.

the Council the twelve individuals who interpret the word of the Seer and govern all of Ym, also known as Insringin

jarl leader of a town or community

Kolkagga the Council's assassins

the Might a powerful current of energy that flows through the world, which ymlings can draw upon for strength

the Rite a coming-of-age ceremony during which young people are given the Seer's blessing and protection

the rot a disease believed to be carried by children of Odin. Also a derogatory term used to refer to them.

Slokna where the dead go to rest

unearthed unable to use or draw upon the Might; mightless

ymlings people from the land of Ym; those born with tails and the ability to bind the Might. Synonymous with Ym's kin.

Siri Pettersen made her sensational debut in 2013 with the Norwegian publication of *Odin's Child*, the first book in The Raven Rings trilogy, which has earned numerous awards and nominations at home and abroad. Siri has a background as a designer and comics creator. Her roots are in Finnsnes and Trondheim, but she now lives in Oslo, where you're likely to find her in a coffee shop. According to fellow writers, her superpower is "mega motivation"—the ability to inspire other creative souls. Visit her at SiriPettersen.com, or follow her on Twitter or Instagram @SiriPettersen.

Siân Mackie is a translator of Scandinavian literature into English. She was born in Scotland and has an MA in Scandinavian Studies and an MSc in Literary Translation as a Creative Practice from the University of Edinburgh. She has translated a wide range of works, from young adult and children's literature—including Bjarne Reuter's *Elise and the Second-hand Dog*, which was nominated for the 2019 Carnegie Medal—to thrillers and nonfiction. She lives in Southampton on the south coast of England.

Paul Russell Garrett translates from Norwegian and Danish, with drama holding a particular interest for him. He has translated a dozen plays and has a further ten published translations to his name, including Lars Mytting's *The Sixteen Trees of the Somme*, long-listed for the International Dublin Literary Award, and a pair of novels by Christina Hesselholdt, *Companions* and *Vivian*. Originally from Vancouver, Paul is based in east London.

Siân and Paul have previously collaborated on a translation of *A Doll's House* by Henrik Ibsen, which was commissioned by Foreign Affairs theater company and performed in 2015 in east London. They hope their shared passion for bringing Norwegian literature to English-speaking audiences will continue in future collaborations, and they are currently translating the next two books in the Raven Rings series.

THE EPIC ADVENTURE CONTINUES ...

Siri Pettersen
The Rot (The Raven Rings Book 2)
On sale now
ISBN 978-1-64690-001-5

Siri Pettersen
The Might (The Raven Rings Book 3)
On sale now
ISBN 978-1-64690-002-2

A NEW SERIES BASED IN THE WORLD OF THE RAVEN RINGS SAGA

Siri Pettersen
Iron Wolf (Vardari Book 1)
On sale February 2023
ISBN 978-1-64690-015-2